OUT OF FIRE

ALSO BY EMILY K. BRAY

In the Cards

Out of Fire

Out of Fire

The Kabrum Chronicles Book II

Emily K. Bray

Torchflame Books

Vista, CA

ISBN: 978-1-61153-601-0 (hardcover)

ISBN: 978-1-61153-599-0 (paperback)

ISBN: 978-1-61153-600-3 (ebook)

ISBN: 978-1-61153-660-7 (large print)

Library of Congress Control Number: 2025906460

Out of Fire is published by: Torchflame Books, an imprint of Top Reads Publishing, LLC, USA

For information about special discounts for bulk purchases, please direct emails to: publisher@torchflamebooks.com

Cover design and interior layout: Jori Hanna

To the people who do the next right thing.
Even when it's hard.

CHAPTER ONE
MERIN

Merin stumbled over the remnants of a table. Her heart dropped. How many of these torture devices was she going to find? How many rooms of this building had been used to torture Magics? The leather straps still held on to the edges of the wooden planks. She took a hammer and snapped them off. The leather was smooth from use. She could feel the hatred from the Magics who had been held down on this table for years of abuse. She threw the leather into the scrap bucket meant for Tiernan to burn. Budget or no, none of these tables would be used again.

It had taken a full year for the Council to completely close the Refuge after Aer's sacrifice. Six months to declare it would turn into the school, and six more for them to actually get around to doing it. Merin figured they did it more out of fear of citizen approval than a genuine sense of remorse for what they had done. But whatever the reason, they had finally turned the keys over to Korvo. When they had finally got into the building, they realized the kids had destroyed almost everything on their way out, and while Merin didn't blame them, it gave them a lot more to do before they could open the school.

The floors were strewn with shattered glass and broken shelves. She swept up some of the shards that were scattered over files. Formal, official files, no indication something was horribly amiss. She stared at the thick brown files. There were names along the tops of

Magics she had never heard of. She wondered how many of them were not around anymore. Where was Bryce's file?

Wood scraped against the floor as Bryce kicked it out of the doorway. Merin tried to hide the files. There was no need for him to be reminded of what had happened here. He was still waking up screaming.

"What are you trying to hide?" Bryce knelt next to her.

"Nothing." Merin tried to use the dustpan in her hand to block the angle that had the little named tags from Bryce's view. She may not know the names, but that didn't mean Bryce didn't.

"Files? I've seen them before. I saw them take mine out every time I was here."

"I wasn't trying to hide them." The look on his face told her that he didn't believe that for a moment. She hoped he would tease her, but instead, he just shrugged.

"Just give them to Tiernan to burn."

There was something cold about his eyes when they were in the middle of the Refuge. Something distant that she longed to understand. It was the cold wall she felt between them. The hot nightmares that drove Bryce to wake screaming. But mostly, it was an emptiness she felt compelled to fill. His eyes glanced over the rest of the junk in the room, and he let out a sigh. She couldn't tell if it was for the amount of work that still lay ahead of them or something much more sinister crossing his mind.

She nodded. He got up, grabbed a few pieces of wood under his arms, and headed back out the door. He was quiet while they worked, and Merin was sure this was one of the longer conversations they had had while under this roof. It didn't keep her from hoping to hear his normal humor. She stepped out into the corridor and watched him haul the pieces down to the staircase. His tanned skin glittered with sweat, and his muscles pushed against the edges of his shirt. He looked healthy and strong, but she couldn't ignore the haunted look that said this place terrified him.

And, of course, she heard it in his sleep.

Kor called it dealing with his demons, but Merin thought it sounded more like the demons were still dealing with him.

Tiernan ran up the staircase, bumping into the wood that Bryce was trying to toss over the side.

"Tiernan, I swear to the Twelve Gods," Bryce snapped, but the little boy was already past him and near Merin. He came skidding to a stop in front of her. Bryce turned and took a few steps toward him, and Tiernan stuck out his tongue. Bryce started to smile before something caught his eye and he turned back to the pile of wood he was throwing down to the first floor. The smile was gone.

"Merin?" Tiernan asked. Merin looked down at the little boy.

"Let him be, Tiernan. Imagine if I asked you to go back to the Hadran prison where they held you."

"I set it on fire."

"I know. So let Bryce throw the tables down the stairs. Let him destroy as much of this place as he can."

Tiernan looked at her and then over at Bryce. Tiernan's common tongue wasn't great yet, but he had finally begun to laugh and smile.

"Could you start the main hearth with these?" She handed Tiernan the large pile of files Bryce had told her to burn.

He took the files and ran back through the hallway past Bryce. She could hear the crackling of the paper and knew he had already set fire to them before he had even made it to the stairs. A little laugh drifted up from the staircase as Tiernan moved along.

"I like his laugh," Merin said, walking over to Bryce. She rested her forehead against his back. She knew better than to put her hands on him. He was refusing any sort of magic healing, and nothing good had happened to him here when people put their hands on him without permission.

"He still won't play with the other kids," Bryce said. She could tell he was watching Tiernan. Even though the Hadranian General had disappeared, Bryce still struggled to let Tiernan out of his sight for too long. No one blamed him for what had happened, but Bryce blamed himself.

"Give him time. It's only been a year. It's not easy for him to communicate. And he's been alone most of his life," Merin said, nuzzling into the space between his shoulder blade and spine. She felt him relax slightly against her forehead.

"You sound like Kor," Bryce said. His voice was full of a tricky melody like the noise a river makes along a rocky bed. Entrancing like his smile. It sucked her in every time.

3

"Probably because he told me the same things when I asked earlier," she said.

He turned then, and her face was now resting on his sternum. He lightly brushed a piece of hair behind her ear. He stared at her. He said nothing, and he didn't need to. He had never been good with words, so she didn't force him.

"Hey, you two," Korvo called from the other side of the hallway. "This place isn't going to clean itself."

Merin felt a blush spread across her face. Bryce's cheeks smoldered a little, but he just averted his gaze. He brushed past her and went back to load another round of wood scraps over the edge of the stairs.

"He's in a worse mood than normal," Kor said once Bryce was out of earshot.

"You think?" She hadn't thought that. For a moment, she had her normal brash Bryce back.

"No arguments. No back talk, no swagger. What room are you cleaning out?"

"Hard to tell. The kids destroyed a lot on their way out, but I found another one of those tables, the ones with the straps, in there."

"I wish I had known how bad it truly was in here."

"The Council wouldn't have changed their mind any sooner. For all we know, they might have been the ones to agree to torture. You have done everything you can," Merin said.

The smile Kor once wore as a testament to his rebellion drooped. More and more, he looked tired. For the first time, Merin realized that he was only an inch or two taller than Bryce now and not even as tall as her father. She hadn't grown much in the last year of their lives, maybe half an inch if her hemline was to be believed, but Kor just didn't seem as big as life as before. He was somehow deflated.

"We should get back to cleaning. It may have taken them a year to give us the keys, but they only gave us a month to clean it all up."

His smile snapped back into place—the one that screamed about hope, honesty, and better times ahead. But she knew him better than that. His yellow-green eyes were screaming about how tired he felt, and his olive skin was shining from sweat.

"All right," she said, crossing in front of him to go back to the room with the files. When she got closer to him, she whispered, "You don't have to use that fake smile with me."

"It's not fake," Kor said, but already the corners of his mouth drooped again.

"Fake enough. You need to give yourself time. Aer—"

"Time is not a luxury I have."

"Kor . . ."

"You wanted me to be honest. That's the honest truth. We need to finish cleaning, and just the three—well, four, if you count Tiernan—of us aren't going to cut it." His voice wasn't angry. She had heard him angry. This was desperate. The voice of a teacher the last time they would answer your question. The sound of a dog right before it decides to flop on its back or bite. This was something she hadn't heard before. This was Kor near breaking.

"Then ask for help. The people are still listening. They hang on every word you say in the Wall District. The boy who saved the children. The one who made them listen. You are a hero with an army he could command."

Kor flinched slightly, and she knew she had picked the wrong words. She skipped ahead to the crux of the issue.

"But every time someone comes here to help, you send them off to some other part of the city."

"I see the pain in their faces. I feel the subtle memories left here. I can't make them stay. There are some wounds that only time can heal."

"You're letting Bryce stay," Merin said. She heard her voice run sharp.

"Bryce needs to deal with his demons," Kor said. She heard the dismissal of the conversation. She knew he was done. But she pushed anyway. Demons be damned, they weren't going to keep pushing her away like this.

"You keep saying that. But if we don't show people the changes we are making, we're never going to get them to come to school here. To trust us here. We can't let them stay afraid."

"When we finish cleaning out these rooms," Kor said, turning away from her, "I'll ask people to stay."

Merin shifted uneasily. Conversations like this just made her feel like an outsider. The soot Raven's head she had drawn on her chest had long ago washed away. And somehow, she was back to being the Magic who had never suffered. The one that could never understand.

She grabbed a broom and walked down the staircase. If Kor and Bryce weren't going to let people come work, she could at least make the entrance look nicer for the few brave kids she had seen daring each other to go further and further inside the building.

Thoughts thrummed through her mind as she pushed remnants of glass, cobwebs, wooden splinters, rat feces, and anything else she didn't want to identify into a pile. She'd ask Tiernan to get her the dustpan the next time he ran by.

In the midst of her thoughts, Merin heard footsteps behind her.

"Tiernan," she said without looking up from her sweeping, "run and get me the dustpan from the hearth." The footsteps moved away quickly, and Merin circled her pile with the rough bristles of the old broom, getting it ready for when Tiernan got back.

"Is this it?" A man's voice.

"Who are you?"

"Dustpan deliverer, at your service." He held the metal pan out to her, and she reached out and grabbed it slowly.

She looked the stranger up and down. His pants were fashionably cropped like he was going out for a ride on a horse, and his jacket was finely made. His hair was combed neatly to one side, and his eyes were blue like her own. Merin didn't recognize him, and his clothes were nicer than anything anyone in the Wall District had. He looked like he was about Kor's age, but at times, Kor looked much older than his eighteen years, so it was hard to tell.

"I was hoping I could be of some help," the man said.

"You want to help clean out the Refuge?"

"I . . . I think it's the right thing to do. I've read all the reports from Councilman Jaqui."

"Who are you?" Merin asked.

"Hayden Nagely. I just got back into the city."

"As in the Nagelys who run three-quarters of the shops in the market square?"

"That's the one. I've been exploring some of the northern cities for better trade partners, and I came back to something even better."

"Are you a Magic?" Merin asked. She squinted a little to make sure the clothes weren't a trick. Sure, occasionally a Magic did well for themselves and rose up in society, and maybe things were different outside of the city, but even though the Refuge had been disbanded and the school had been formed, public opinion about it had been mixed. Some people thought the rat-infested torture chamber was exactly where children with magic should be, and the fancy clothes Hayden wore didn't leave any room to see a black Raven tattoo.

"No," he said, hesitating, "although I think it would be great."

Merin frowned.

"I mean, clearly, there is systemized inequality, but to be able to connect to the universe, the elements, in that way. Don't you think it would be great?" His voice drifted around like a bunch of cherry blossoms falling to the ground. Romantic, but not necessary.

"It is." Merin kept her voice flat.

"Oh, you're a—"

"A Magic. Yes." It felt good saying it out in the open. She had spent the last year with the people who had already known about her powers, so she hadn't gotten used to saying it out loud yet.

"How can I help Ms. . . .?" Hayden looked around him. Merin recognized his tight lips and furrowed brow from the first time she had seen the Refuge in the light. She saw it again for the first time. Dirty, corroding, and now filled with broken furniture.

"Merin. Just Merin," she said, sticking her hand out. There was no reason to get her family involved here. She wasn't even really sure where she stood with them right now. Half of the time they seemed relieved that she was fine, but Merin couldn't shake that her father had been helping the Council try to turn the people against Magics. And her mother refused to even discuss Bryce or Kor. Merin hadn't slept many nights there. Kor had given her the key to Aer's apartment.

"How can I help, Merin?"

Merin hesitated. Kor was the one who gave the assignments. But Kor wasn't here, and there was no reason to turn away extra hands that had never been in the Refuge before. Unless the cards were telling him something he wasn't sharing, she couldn't see why he wouldn't let someone help.

"We're cleaning it and getting it ready to be a school—a boarding school if needed—for the younger Magics in Kaybrum."

Hayden's eyes floated over the pile of trash she had swept to the large pile of broken tables and beds that Bryce had been piling up near the stairs. While Hayden looked, another pile came tumbling down. Dust flew to every inch of the place, and Merin felt the hole Aer had left. She and her winds would have corralled that dust in a matter of moments. Merin pictured her hair swirling among the winds as it ate up all the dirt within minutes.

"Where should I start?" Hayden asked. Suddenly, the image of Aer was gone, replaced by the yellowish reflection of dust in the small streams of light the dirty windows let in.

"We're taking all of the useless things down to the first floor to be burned." She pointed at Bryce's heap of snapped wood. "Cleaning everything so that the smell—" She paused. She couldn't spend too long on what the smell was. It was easier to just pretend that it was mold or human waste, not fear and desperation.

"On it," Hayden said. He rolled up his sleeves. His skin was smooth and clean. The rustle of his shirt left a light scent in the air, like when Rachael did laundry. It felt foreign in the dank room. "Is there anything we should be saving?"

"Any furniture that could be useful. Bed frames, but throw away the mattresses. Desks. Chairs. That sort of thing. If it's not broken beyond repair, just put it with useful things," she nodded to the other side where a small group of furniture was waiting.

"Why? If it's broken?"

"We're on a tight budget," Merin said. The confusion on Hayden's face would have told her he was from money, even if his last name hadn't. She had the same reaction when she started hanging out with Bryce. Now she was embarrassed she had ever thought like that. "Korvo knows how to work with wood. He can fix most things. And if he can't fix it the regular way, we can try magic." Her mind thought back to the broken bed that Bryce had spent the last of his protective plants fixing so a little boy wouldn't have to sleep among the rats. If only he had used them to get away from the Watchers instead, then they wouldn't have brought him to that room. The one he woke up screaming about.

She let out a deep breath. It would have just been someone else. Bryce would feel worse about that.

"Are you all right?" Hayden asked. His eyes darted over her quickly.

"Just a lot of work to do," she lied. She wasn't sure she could trust an outsider yet. Aer had trusted one, and look how that had turned out. Aer was in her grave, and the rest of them bore the weight of her death.

Tiernan ran by. His hands were full of more files that were crackling on the edges. They almost looked happy to burn. When he saw Hayden, he stopped. His eyes grew big, and his little arms dropped the mess of files. The flames that nibbled at the pages now consumed them. A tiny piece drifted and landed on Merin's arm.

She yelped as the coal ran out of fuel. It was a momentary hurt—more surprise than actual pain. Tiernan's bottom lip began to waver. She reached for him, but he began to run before she could get to him.

"He's just worried that he hurt me," she said, stomping on the edges of the files, putting them out as best she could.

Hayden reached down to grab the files.

"Just leave them to me," she said. She felt herself forcing a smile like Korvo had been doing. She had no idea what the files contained. What sort of information she would find within the pages, and there was no reason a non-Magic should see the personal information of someone without their permission. The files shifted in her arms. They were lopsided now that parts had been consumed by the flames. A file slid into view: BRYCE SEGAL. The corners were burnt, but it was one of the thicker files. She hugged it closer to her so that Hayden couldn't see. Bryce was not a criminal, but she couldn't trust a non-Magic to see that heavy of a file and not make snap judgments.

As if on cue, Bryce came thundering down the stairs.

"Merin!" Bryce called, running into the room. His face looked gaunt, terrified, and sharp.

"I'm fine, Bryce,"

"Tiernan said you were hurt."

"A little bit of paper he was burning landed on me," she said, squeezing the files closer to her. This was the first time she wished she hadn't taught Bryce how to read. Seeing the file would just bring back everything that had happened to him in the Refuge. He'd go back to not speaking. "It's nothing to worry about. Tiernan is just sensitive."

"Hello," Hayden said, sticking out his hand.

Bryce looked at his outstretched palm and stared. "Who the hell are you?" he asked.

"He's helping, Bryce."

"I'm Hayden—"

Bryce had already walked away. She could see in the way he walked that his shoulders were tense, and she was sure Hayden saw it too when Bryce kicked some of the debris out of the way and didn't slow down.

"You'll have to forgive him. This place . . ." she trailed off and gestured around.

"It's fine. Just tell me where I should start."

"Over there," she said, halfheartedly gesturing to a vague place in the middle of the Refuge. Hayden gave her a short salute and then headed over into the mess. Flustered—the last five minutes had gone about as badly as they possibly could have—Merin tried to find Tiernan to get him to burn the files, but the little boy was nowhere to be found.

She heaved the majority of the pile into the great furnace that heated the whole building, but something made her hold on to Bryce's. She didn't want him to see it if he came back before Tiernan did, so she slid it into her bag. She'd keep it hidden until the fire got started.

CHAPTER TWO

BRYCE

BRYCE REGRETTED KICKING THE BROKEN LEGS FROM THE table as soon as he did it. First of all, it was probably salvageable until he had sent another leg spinning down the hallway. And second, because he was going to have to spend a long time trying to make Merin not worry.

She had finally relaxed with him earlier. He could almost still feel her forehead resting on his back. It was warm and soft and felt like summer. Even without using her healing skills, just the touch of her skin was enough to explode through the darkness in him.

Well, most of it.

But that man, with the nice clothes and the shining blue eyes. Bryce spat on the ground. It had felt too much like before. Too much like when the Hadranian General had looked him in the eyes before he lit the match. He couldn't let Merin see the terror.

He raised his arms and tried to loosen his shoulders by rotating his arms around, but nothing seemed to loosen up the giant knot that had formed beneath his right shoulder blade.

Maybe the worst part of all was that he was jealous. Jealous of Hayden's clothes, his confidence, his smell, his hair. It was the world that Merin belonged with. Even though she had been living mostly in Aer's old apartment, and he had spent more and more time with her, there was something that was always going to make them different.

11

The fact that he had lived in the Refuge, and she was here only to save it.

He hoped she never ran across his file. He'd been sending them to Tiernan to burn, but there were so many, and he hadn't found his yet. She didn't know. And if he could help it, she never would.

"Bryce, you look terrible," Kor said, coming around the corner.

"Some rich guy is here talking to Merin. She says he wants to help."

"And what part bothers you? His money, talking to Merin, or wanting to help?" Kor asked. He raised his eyebrow, and Bryce snarled.

"All of it."

Kor laid his gnarled hand on his shoulder, gave it a couple of friendly taps, and then went the way Bryce had just come.

Alone again, Bryce looked for something to do. Teaching kids in the gardens had given him a focus for the last six months, but he still felt restless. He felt the loss of Aer in everything that he did. His limbs felt heavy. And at times it seemed he was taking her loss harder than Kor. But he knew that wasn't true.

He took a deep breath and counted to seven. He held it burning in his lungs for another count of seven before he finally released it. He tried once more to try to get the muscles in his back to release, but it was futile. If it wasn't going to get better, he might as well clean out the room.

This was one of the only rooms the kids hadn't destroyed. Maybe some of them didn't know it was here. Bryce hoped that was the reason and not because it had scared them the most.

This might have been the worst room of all, but mostly because it only lived on the verge of his consciousness. A horror that he could never quite remember whether he had dreamt it. One where he woke up not knowing where reality and fantasy had commingled, leaving him confused and wondering. It might have been worse than waking up screaming. At least he knew that had been real.

He had been relieved when Kor had agreed to let him clear it out himself. It was a lot of work, moving all of the furniture by himself, but he figured Kor was going to be busy with whoever this Hayden guy was, so he had some time.

He moved the chairs and long table into one of the rooms for a classroom. They were plain and nondescript. Nothing that, out of context, would remind the kids of the pain of this room. When he came back, the room was mostly empty. He took in the room looking for something that would tell him what was reality and what was nightmare.

The rooms where they tortured him had been bad enough, but this room. This room was silent. No Watchers were present. No one mocked you when you came in. At least in some way, the mocking had meant they saw him. They recognized him as a person. But in this room, he had been nothing.

The first time he had been in the Refuge, he had been sent back to the beds after they had strapped him to a table and almost drowned him. There, the other kids attempted to console him. He remembered their nods, and one of the older kids had given him half his dinner and taken the dirty water in front of him away. He had been thankful for them. Kindness in what he thought was the worst thing.

But the second time, with his feet swollen from the whipping they had received, he was sent to this room. A sterile place. A man had held his arm down on the long table and stuck his forearm with a needle. He had felt it. Like the tip of a rose thorn squeezing through his skin. Not once did the man speak to him other than to give him commands. And when it happened the second time, Bryce attempted to fight back. He refused to expose his arm. Then, the gas had appeared.

Bryce shuddered. He had almost forgotten about this room. The blurry faces that had worked above him. The times they referred to him by number instead of by name: 3571. His consciousness going in and out.

But as soon as he had seen the white walls and the floor with a drain in the bottom for no reason, the missing restraints, the holes in the walls for the gasses to come in, the masks the men wore as they talked around him like he wasn't there, like he wasn't alive, like he wasn't human, 3571—it all had come back to him.

"What is this place?" Kor had asked when they got the heavy metal door open. It was like a safe, thick and dull.

"I'm not sure," Bryce had said. Then the light showed it to him. Immediately his throat began to close. He grabbed for his neck and reached out a hand to warn Kor. To tell him to run, that soon the gas would make him unable to fight back, but Kor stood there looking terrified.

"Bryce? Bryce! What's wrong?"

Bryce's hands scratched at his throat as if he couldn't find any air.

"Bryce?" Kor's voice had gone in and out, and Bryce wasn't sure if he was dreaming. He collapsed onto his knees. "Focus on me, Bryce. MERIN!"

"No. No Merin." Bryce croaked out. He couldn't have her see him like this again. Dying in the Refuge.

"Bryce, what's wrong?" Kor asked, kneeling next to him. His voice was higher than normal, and there was no trace of his familiar smile and calculating brow. He reached one hand out for Bryce's shoulder and another one to the cards at his side.

He pulled one. Bryce couldn't see its face. But Kor's brow began to relax.

"Bryce, listen to me. You are going to be okay. You are going to be fine. Take a deep breath."

Bryce shook his head at him. He could feel he was running out of air. He took a small, shallow breath. Then another.

"Deeper," Kor said.

Bryce did as he was told.

"Count to seven."

He counted. The air filled his lungs. His throat was scratched but fine.

"What is this place?" Kor asked when Bryce was finally taking small breaths again.

"Hell."

"This whole place is hell," Kor said, leaning his back against the cold metal door and pulling his knees to his chest. They sat in silence for a few minutes. The two of them looking off in different directions, seeing their own hells.

"I have no better answer than that."

"Do you want me to get Merin now?"

"No. Please don't tell her. She still looks at me like I might break at any moment."

"You almost died less than six months ago. Can you blame her?"

"No, but I can't make you all worry again. I already failed once. I need to do this—"

"Deal with your demons. I know. But this place has got more demons than I thought, and eventually, that's gonna run thin with Merin. She just wants to help."

"She doesn't understand."

"Have you tried to explain?" Kor asked.

"I don't want her to know."

"Then you can't fault her for not understanding. You two might come from different worlds, but you care about each other. You have to let each other in eventually."

"Eventually. But not now."

"Take it from me," Kor said. He rose and looked down the long hallway back to the rest of the Refuge. "Sometimes now is all you have."

Bryce didn't know what to say. He opened his mouth to speak, but the guilt of Aer's death strangled him in a different sort of way. The words felt slippery and heavy, and they just kept dropping off the side of his tongue before he could make them work.

Kor took a deep breath—Bryce wondered if he counted to seven like he had so often told Bryce to do—and started walking back down the hallway.

"I'll let you handle this, Bryce. But eventually, someone has got to help us with the rest of this place."

Now there were only locked metal boxes with large locks left in the room. Bryce pulled on the handles that jutted out from the sides, but he couldn't make them move. He tried sinking down a little and using his center of gravity to get better leverage, but still, they didn't budge.

"What do we even need this room for?" Bryce asked the empty room. It didn't answer. He tried one last time to get the three boxes to move. Nothing. He picked at the locks. There were people in the Wall District who could teach him how to pick locks. Aer had always been deft with her winds, feeling the spaces between the tines, but this was his demon.

And right now, this was as far as it could go. He closed the door and slid the large metal bar, locking it from the outside. He added a chain and a padlock around the handle just in case kids came exploring.

He shuddered on his way out. His back was tighter than before, and he felt like it was driving his right shoulder or a rib out of place. Maybe he should talk to Merin.

They had made a lot of progress in his absence. The fire was blazing, and for just a moment, part of his back relaxed, but it wouldn't be enough.

The Refuge had taken on the orange glow of the fire mixed with the amber glow of the setting sun coming through the filthy windows.

But there were neat piles of useful furniture and trash, and the first floor almost looked good enough to have people enter. If it weren't for the streaked windows and the lingering smell, the place would have been transformed.

"Bryce!" Merin said from the other side of the hearth. Her face was dirty like she had wiped her hand across her forehead a few times in the last hour, sweat trapping the dirt in finger-length strips.

"Hey, Merin," he said, walking quickly over to her. His chest felt like a surging whirlpool. He wanted to let her magic flow through him as he lay his head in her lap and let her play with his hair and sing under her breath as she worked. But she had sensed Tiernan's trauma when she had worked on his head; what if she could feel his? He hesitated.

"I have to say we've gotten a lot done today," Hayden said, his perfect hair coming from behind the counter where they had once checked in forlorn Magics. He, too, had sweat forming at the edges of his hair, and his clothes were covered with a fine layer of dust.

Bryce could feel the sweat dripping down his back, and he knew his palms were equally sweaty.

"Sorry for earlier," Bryce said. He forced his hands into his pockets and looked around.

"Nothing to fret about," Hayden said. His smile spread across his face like he was giving Bryce a present. It took a lot of self-control not to spit on the ground.

Kor had told him that fighting couldn't be allowed even now that the Refuge was gone.

"We have to show them we're something better than they think we are," he had said, and Bryce had already failed him once. He wasn't going to do it again.

"It's looking great down here," Kor called from the second floor. The fake diplomat smile was plastered on his face. Merin was right;

he wore it almost exclusively now, but maybe it was for Hayden's sake.

"How far are you from opening?" Hayden asked Kor as he came down the steps, Tiernan hovering behind him.

"We can open the school now." Kor looked around. "We'll put everyone in the cafeteria to start until we get more of the school cleaned up. Thanks for the help."

Bryce felt his eyebrow inadvertently go up. Kor hardly sounded like himself. He always sounded a little different when he was talking to the larger groups in the middle of Bethlem's or when he was practicing his speeches and didn't think Bryce was listening. But now he just sounded distracted.

"Well, I don't know about you boys," Merin said, "but I'm going to go home and bathe."

"I'll walk with you," Hayden offered.

"It's all right. I'll be fine." Merin said, going for her bag at the corner of the room.

"You shouldn't be walking around at night," Hayden said.

"Is that so?" Bryce asked. He felt the words come out like venom. "Too many Magics out?"

"I . . . uhh . . . That's not—I mean, that's not . . ."

"It's all right. Bryce will walk me home. Won't you, Bryce?"

Bryce nodded. He put his arm around her waist.

"Thanks again, Hayden, " Merin said, and she headed for the door. Bryce followed behind her. He hadn't noticed how dark it had gotten. Tiernan's fire had lit the Refuge's first floor as bright as the midday sun. The warm summer night refreshed Bryce the moment he stepped outside.

"At least you didn't try to fight him," Merin said. "He did help. Maybe not all non-Magics are bad."

Bryce ignored the thought. "Are we walking to Aer's or . . . ?"

"Aer's. I haven't talked to my parents in the last few days, and if I show up covered in dirt, I'm not even sure my mother would let me in the door."

Bryce nodded, but he felt a fire burning in his belly.

Merin grabbed his hand, and part of the fire went down. If she went back to her parents, they wouldn't get to spend as much time together.

They walked and listened to the light summer breeze bring them sounds from the Wall District. Since the closure of the Refuge, the Wall District had become even more crowded and hectic as children ran around in the streets unsupervised. But it sounded like hope to Bryce.

"We could walk the long way," Merin said.

"Through the garden?"

She nodded. The garden took them through a very different part of town, but Bryce was not one to complain. The only time he felt like the world might be better was when Merin was next to him.

"Kor's stressed," Bryce said, eventually having to say something.

"I know. I think he's trying to shoulder everyone's burdens on himself. Do you know he plans on formally applying for guardianship of every single child who lives at the school?"

"Guardianship?"

"He'd be legally responsible for them. Like an adoptive parent."

"He's eighteen."

"That's the legal age of adulthood. He can do it. He already applied for Tiernan."

"So he's Tiernan's dad?"

"*Guardian.*"

"Is there a difference?"

"There is to Korvo. He corrected me three times when I helped him fill out the paperwork."

"I don't think Kor values fathers."

"But why? He wouldn't tell me."

"You've never been kicked out for what you are—"

Merin opened her mouth. Bryce could see the beginnings of denial.

"Your family will still let you come home. They know you have magic. It's Kor and I that they don't like."

"I know that we had different childhoods, Bryce."

There was the ever-present wall that felt insurmountable. How could he explain his father's disgust? How had Kor's father sold him to the Hadranian General? These were things that were incomprehensible.

"Does Tiernan know?" Bryce said after a minute.

"I doubt it."

They were in the gardens now, and Bryce let his hands run over all of the plants. In the summer, they exploded with energy, and even now, in the middle of the night, they moved toward his hands, the leaves wrapping around his fingers. He detangled himself gently from each plant and kept going so he didn't fall too far behind Merin.

"The plants love you." Merin smiled. "Should I be jealous?"

"It never used to be this much," Bryce said looking at where one of the roses had accidentally scratched him as it tried to be closer to him. "Ever since—"

Ever since the General had opened the link between him and the plants, it felt like too much of his magic was being released every time he touched something green. He hated to admit he didn't trust himself to spend nights sleeping in the garden anymore.

He looked up at Merin. "Do you think Tiernan struggles with control now? He did hurt you."

"He didn't mean to," Merin said, self-consciously rubbing at her hand where there was a small welt.

"Still," Bryce said more to himself than her. The fear plagued him: Somehow, he would end up hurting her without meaning to. But worse, he would lose control and be exactly what non-Magics had thought he was his whole life.

CHAPTER THREE

TIERNAN

HE LET THE FLAMES RUN OVER HIS FINGERS: OVER, UNDER, over, under. Round and round. It calmed him. Gave him focus. The flames moved with the whim of his subconscious. It gave him time to think about everything else.

He hadn't meant to hurt Merin. He'd never hurt anyone until the General had put that collar around his neck. He scratched at where a small scar was hidden underneath his growing hair—where Aer's lightning had freed him from the collar.

The little balls of fire licked at the edges of his fingernails, and Tiernan waved them away. He had control.

"Tiernan," Kor called from upstairs. Tiernan dutifully ran up to him. He had created a little bedroom for the both of them. Three beds sat nestled up against the walls. Everything else had been cleared away. Even the windows had been painstakingly freed from the heavy grime.

"Is it better than the roof?" Kor asked after Tiernan flopped on the bed and smiled.

"Is Bryce still up there? Tiernan asked, looking over at the third bed, and then glancing up at the ceiling. Bryce would have been multiple floors above them.

"Probably," Kor said, sitting down on the edge of his bed. He rubbed his hand. Tiernan watched him out of the corner of his eye.

"He hates this place," Tiernan said somewhere in between a question and a statement.

"We have to give him time."

"Does he hate me?" Tiernan asked. His memories jolted over the last six months when Bryce had first taught him the word love. He had placed his hand on his chest and repeated it to him. It had felt like something new entered his life, something that he was missing but didn't know.

"Why would he hate you?"

"I burned Merin today," Tiernan said.

Kor pulled his knees into his chest. There was silence for a minute.

"That explains why he was so out of sorts today," Korvo said, but Tiernan could see it in the smile he gave that he didn't mean it. He had heard Merin and Bryce talk about how forced Kor's smiles had been, and now he saw what they meant. His eyes were somewhere far away, like when he looked at the cards he was reading, but now nothing was in front of him. It was like he was hiding the truth. "You didn't mean to hurt her. She wasn't hurt badly."

"But she can't heal herself," Tiernan said, scooting toward Kor. The beds felt far apart even though there was probably only a few feet in between them. Kor's empty eyes made him feel too far away.

"People hurt themselves all the time. We're all covered in knicks and bruises. Being Magic doesn't protect us from life's little inconveniences. We get sick. We bleed. It's part of being human."

"But . . ."

"Bryce doesn't hate you. He could never hate you or Merin. He's trying so hard to keep you all safe because he loves you."

Love. There was that word again. Even when Bryce had taught him the word, he had been talking about Merin. It was the first time Tiernan had felt something like that. A feeling of warmth like the light licks of a flame or the heat of the sun on his face, but in his heart. He felt it for Merin and Bryce and, of course, Kor. They were as close to a family as he had ever had. The *only* family he had ever had.

"Kor, who do you love?" Tiernan asked. He wanted to take it back as soon as he said it. He took a deep breath as if he could suck the words back into his mouth. But they were out there in the world.

"There's a lot of different kinds of love," Kor said. Tiernan could hear the little quiver in his voice, and he noticed that he switched back to Hadranian. "There is love like the kind between Merin and Bryce. Where, somehow, the other becomes half of your soul. You feel lost without them but also need to make sure that you are still your own person." He paused for a minute. Tiernan wondered if he would mention Aer. "There is the kind of love I have for Bryce. He's like my brother. I'm proud of him when he wins, and I am behind him when he loses. I love my people. The Magics in this city. Everyone who resists being treated like a second-class citizen."

Tiernan produced a flame on his palm. He looked at it with the intensity of someone trying not to seem disappointed by the answer.

"What about Aer?" Tiernan asked.

"Let me finish," Kor said.

"I loved Aer. She was my right hand, my calming wind, but she was something I could never control. Control is the wrong word. I would never have wanted to control her. She was the wind. Reckless and strong. She didn't need me like I needed her."

"Do you regret letting her use her last strength to save me?"

"Do I regret it? No. I miss her. I feel her absence when I turn to tell her something and she's not there. But if you would ever let me finish . . . I swear you are getting more like Bryce every day. If you would let me finish, I would say this. Tiernan, I love you. You are strong and complex. You are forgiving, confident, and you will do amazing things with this world. I will never hate you. I will never abandon you. I might get annoyed at you. I might not even like you every second of the day, but you are family here. I made sure of it."

"What if someone took me back to Hadran?"

"I'd find them. And if Bryce didn't beat them dead before I got there, I would make sure they never hurt you again."

"Why?"

"You're family."

"No, why? Why would you love me?"

"Do you love Merin? Bryce?" Kor asked.

"Yes."

"Why?"

"I just feel it."

"Then there is your answer." Kor took a few steps from his bed and laid his palm flat on Tiernan's chest. "Forget everything else."

Tiernan's thoughts drifted to the brand on his chest that had marked him for execution. Before, it had felt heavy, a daily reminder that the world was not something he could trust, but now, he hardly felt it at all. Instead he felt the steady beat of his own heart against Kor's hand.

"Now," Kor said, switching back to common, "I am tired, sore, and not any closer to being done. We only have a few more days to get this place up and running. I'm going to sleep."

Tiernan reached for the light, but Kor shook his head. "You can leave it on. I can sleep anywhere."

Tiernan gave one last look over to the empty third bed and turned out the light.

His dreams were filled with flashes of lightning.

CHAPTER FOUR
KORVO

Whatever sleep he was going to find, it eluded him. There was nothing that could bring his eyes to stay closed. There was just the feeling of a clock ticking down. He got up, slowly so as to not wake Tiernan, and he headed to his makeshift office. There was just enough light so that he could read the cards.

He laid them out one by one. He felt the intrinsic ticking of the clock around him, so he laid them out like a clock face. The first card at one, the last at twelve. He set the rest aside. He had avoided them for a while after Aer's death. Everything had been clouded by it. The cards showed him answers to things in fits and starts. Especially since his hand was no better after he had stuck it in the middle of Tiernan's flames. But he already couldn't sleep.

There was no longer the impending end he had seen with Aer. But it wasn't like all the hurt had gone away. Bryce's face when they went into that room with the heavy door. What had that place been? When they first started taking the place apart, Kor had asked Bryce to tell him everything that had happened.

He had, making Kor promise he wouldn't tell Merin. Kor had followed him around to every room and listened to every story. Every piece of torture he had gone through. But he had never mentioned that room. Not until they opened it.

Kor shook his head. He didn't think that Bryce had been keeping it from him. It was just a place he had tried to hide even from himself. His mind had pushed it deep to protect him.

The cards spoke of hope. The cards spoke of grief. And sacrifice. Of people coming together. Normal life. Then why couldn't he sleep?

A cold breeze blew through the window of the office, sending a shiver down Kor's back. He went back for the quilt he had bought for his bed and wrapped it around himself. The fire had died down a bit, and it was darker in the office. Too dark to read the card for more answers. He stared into the night.

It felt like nothing was over. He squeezed his eyes tight, trying to force himself to fall asleep.

Sometimes, Aer came to him in his dreams. The first few times, he thought maybe he was just wishing too hard, but eventually, he figured it only happened when he fell asleep at the large table Bryce had brought him from Aer's old apartment. The one he had carved with Aer's winds.

More and more, he found it was the only place he could fall asleep. Bryce and Merin chalked it up to him working too hard now that the school was finally opening. And it was true that sometimes he fell asleep looking over numbers, lessons, or any number of the things they still needed to accomplish before the school could open fully, but some nights, he just wanted to see Aer.

The dreams started the same. A flash of lightning, so similar to the one that had taken Aer from the world. From him.

"Sleeping on the desk again," Aer's voice would slowly form in the winds in his dream. Instead of physically blowing, they seemed to swirl in iridescent clouds. Kor wondered if this was how they always looked to Aer.

"I wanted to talk," Kor said, still searching for Aer's face in the clouds. Sometimes he never found it. Sometimes, all of her was there, clear and solid, like he could reach out and touch her. Sometimes only her eyes drifted through the winds. Most often, it was just the sound of her voice.

"About?" A laugh echoed through the winds. Bouncing off of different places, sounding in a thousand different memories of her laugh.

"Everything," Kor mumbled. He used to tell Aer everything. Shared the hardships and the setbacks. Shared the triumphs and joys.

Until Tiernan had come into the picture, she was the only one who had seen the execution mark on his chest. He had to tiptoe around what he could say to Bryce and Merin. They were still kids, and he still felt the need to protect them from the worst of the world that he and Aer had seen. They deserved to be kids in love. As uncomplicated as their lives could be. They didn't have to shoulder being soldiers. He let his thoughts drift as he watched the clouds.

"I'm waiting."

Kor knew he was just talking to himself, to his subconscious, which so desperately wanted Aer to still be alive, but it felt real—more real than when the cards showed him images of the future. Even though his mangled hands had severed the connection a little, this felt more real than when he had full use of his hands.

"Bryce is still sleeping outside," Kor said.

"That kid is more plant than person."

"He's still afraid."

"Good."

"Aer—"

"The work isn't done. They should all still be afraid."

"The school is helping." His voice shakier than he intended.

"Is it?"

"It is." He hesitated.

"You know, he's still out there. The General escaped."

"I know. This is bigger than him. It's always been bigger than him." Kor sighed.

"He's still a threat. Along with the technology they created."

"I know. We don't know if there are long-term effects." Kor shuddered. What if Tiernan wasn't out of danger yet?

"Best to ask the madman himself."

"Aer—"

"Korvo?" Her voice sounded far away, almost pleading. It didn't fit with her snarky attitude moments before.

The dream started to get fuzzy. The swirls of lights shifted and grew darker until everything was black. Kor realized he was looking at the back of his eyelids.

He raised his face off the table. Marks from the carvings were pressed into his cheek. He rubbed at them.

The General was still out there. The conversation had come back to the General again. Aer had been right before. Handling things his way was never going to be enough. But her rash actions had cost her life and almost Tiernan's and Bryce's as well.

It was still dark outside the freshly cleaned window of his office. He could probably still get a few more hours of sleep if he went back into the bedroom. But somehow it didn't seem like he would find any rest. He quickly tiptoed in, dropped off the quilt, changed his clothes so no one would realize he hadn't really gone to bed, and set out to clean the rest of the windows.

It was grunt work. Hauling buckets of water around the spiral staircase that made up the interior of the building. But windows were repetitive; they could be easily cleaned in the dark, and he needed some time to think.

He pressed the rag into the water. In the dark, he put his hand a little too far in, and the water soaked into his sleeve. Kor sighed. He rung the extra water from the rag back into the bucket and methodically dragged it across the windows. Wiping years of grime and hatred away with each stroke.

But he couldn't wipe away his conversation with Aer. The conversation with the part of him that hadn't forgiven himself for letting the man responsible for torturing Bryce and Tiernan, for killing Aer, for years of torture against all Magics, escape into the night with not so much as a word.

The General was probably somewhere celebrating in style. Sipping some strong whiskey in his crystal cup that he had received in recognition of his work. Kor couldn't even bear to think about what was happening to the Magics in Hadran. How many of them were having magic pour through their veins so quickly that they were being burned alive by it? How many of them had already died? How many of the people he knew were left in Hadran? Probably none.

If only he had the power that had come from the General. The power to extend his magic. Let the magic flow through his hands again. Then things could be as real as they were in his dreams with Aer, and maybe he would be able to know what was happening in Hadran. The cards could tell him where his friends were. Maybe he could still save them where he had failed Aer. Maybe he could find the bastard that was responsible for all of this.

He shook his head. Nothing good could come from messing with magic. It was natural, and changing anything about what was natural could only end in more tragedy.

He let the rag drop into the bucket with a splash. The window was clean, and moonlight trickled into the corridor. He was on the second floor. This was where he had spoken to Bryce while he had been trapped inside. He put his hand on the glass. If only he had known then what would happen. If the cards had been clearer. If he still could read the future like he used to. If he had done more.

He left the rag and bucket there and went off to find something. Something he had hidden from Merin and Bryce. Something he had locked away even from himself.

He didn't need to light the lights that hung in this back room. There were lots of rooms that had lost their use once they had taken over the Refuge. This closet would not be missed. It would not be seen. With deft hands, he slid them over the desk that he had cramped against the back wall. His fingers reached the brass knob that had once been a lock for the drawer. He had forced it open. It hung uselessly except to give Kor a landmark in the dark.

He pulled at the drawer. It stuck slightly but eventually gave in and opened slowly. Kor's hand hesitated. His fingers hung in the darkness, debating. Doubting. But eventually, guilt lowered his fingers into the drawer. He felt the jolt immediately as soon as he touched the cold metal, smooth against his bumpy hand.

His inner light brightened, spreading like a thin stream to fill his torso with warmth and light.

He pulled it out of the drawer, but he didn't look at his hand. He had no plan. He had no reasoning. This was not part of the overall process. He was a man of twelve-step plans and five-year strategies, but here he was, holding the very metal collar that had killed Aer. That had pushed her to the limit until she could hardly control herself. That had given her the power to call down lightning despite being exhausted after fighting for hours.

He felt its heft in his hand. Part of him wanted to chuck it into the fireplace that heated the entire school. Watch it burn and melt and wither into the flames. But the other part wondered if Aer would have let it go. If she had survived, would she have been able to give up the power that she had? Would she have been able to give up a weapon in the fight?

"Kor?" Bryce asked. "Why are you wandering around in the dark?"

"Bryce, I didn't expect to see you inside here at night," Kor said. He slipped the metal into his pocket. The moment his skin left contact with its smooth surface, he felt a sudden emptiness. A sudden reminder that his magic was limited and that the General was still out there. That he had failed.

"I heard noises, and I had to check them out."

Kor could tell Bryce was nervous. He wasn't more than a step away from the window, and Kor doubted he would come any further into the building.

"Just me washing windows and puttering. Getting an early start to the day," Kor said. He knew his smile would not have convinced Bryce in the daytime, but it was probably too dark for him to notice. At least he hoped.

"You need sleep," Bryce said, leaning against the central column.

"I could say the same about you," Kor deflected. "You can't get any kind of proper sleep up there."

"Better than in here. At least up there when I wake up screaming, I don't worry Tiernan."

"Still having nightmares?" The metal in his pocket felt heavy against his leg.

"I'm not sure they'll ever stop."

"Are they about the General?" Kor didn't need to say any more. He didn't need to remind Bryce of the feeling of being burned alive.

"Sometimes. Sometimes this place. Spending this much time here, it's like bits and pieces keep flooding back, and when I'm asleep, I have no idea if they are memories or just nightmares."

"Maybe you should be sleeping at Aer's with Merin."

"You're telling me I can go sleep with Merin?"

Kor could barely see the grin cross Bryce's face. Then it dropped.

"I don't want to wake her. Besides, if I'm there, who's going to call you out for working at all hours of the night? You need a break."

Kor again felt the heaviness of metal in his pocket. Maybe he did need a break. It wasn't like him to act without a plan. But what plans did he have left? He had spent years on the school. Years trying to establish where they stood at this very moment. And besides cleaning out a few more rooms on a few more floors, there wasn't much else to do. He hadn't realized he hadn't thought about what came next. He had always assumed he and Aer would figure it out like they had all those years before. Step by step. But Aer was gone. And all that was left was the piece of metal in his pocket.

He hadn't let her be buried with it. It had felt cruel to leave her literally chained by the General. It had taken a lot of convincing to get the mortuary to cut it off her neck. Kor had supervised. He had insisted he be there to make sure they didn't do anything like cover her Raven's head tattoo. As much as she hated the jagged ink, it was part of her. Part of her story. It stood out against her pale neck as she lay there on the table.

"Kor?" Bryce said, snapping Korvo from his memory.

"Huh?"

"You sorta spaced out there for a minute. You really need to get more sleep."

"Right." He glanced outside. He still had an hour or so before the light began to trickle in through the windows. "You're already inside," Kor said. "Why don't you just stay with Tiernan and me?"

"You know that's not going to work," Bryce said. He had already opened the window and let out his spindly legs. He had grown at least three inches in the last six months.

It was hard to imagine the angry kid Kor had found on the street. *Peace looks good on him,* Kor thought, trying to convince himself that he had chosen the right thing. But the metal in his pocket pressed against him, reminding him that peace was a long way away.

"I'll be back in the morning," Bryce said, already out the window.

"Yeah, you know tomorrow . . ." Kor hesitated. Bryce still felt like losing Aer was his fault. It had taken him months to go to her grave.

"I know, you're visiting Aer. We'll get the day started without you."

"Thanks."

CHAPTER FIVE
BRYCE

Bryce heaved his way back up to the top of the Refuge. *The school,* he corrected himself. The Refuge had died with Aer. But even though they had put a new sign on the front and cleaned out the bottom floor for classes, it still carried the wisps of nightmares he couldn't undo.

And maybe it was because Kor reminded him of Aer. Maybe because he had stepped foot into the Refuge—school—at night, but Bryce knew he wasn't going to find any solace on the top of the roof, no matter how close he slept to the heat coming out of the main chimney. Instead, he grabbed his jacket and climbed down the rickety ladder.

He was used to the ladder now. It had rusted spots in places, and when he could focus, it didn't faze him at all. Three steps on the left-most side of the ladder rungs, then two on the right. Skip a rung by the window with the crack in the sill. But his mind was elsewhere, and his foot slipped on the rung, jolting him to a stop. As he caught himself, he felt his heart leap into his chest, but more than that, he felt the tug of the plants from far below him. Tiny weeds growing out of the road. Even packed hard by carts and feet and sleepy with the night, they pulled to him. Reached for him.

Bryce hugged the ladder. His cheek resting on the cold metal rung. He breathed deeply. Once. Twice. The plants began to relax. They eased back into their sleep, dreaming of the sun that would come in an hour or so.

He waited until he couldn't feel them at all. He tried to focus only on the cold metal he held on to. The plants had always come to him when he called. He just wasn't sure if he had called to them or if they had started responding on their own. Ever since the General had messed with his abilities of control, things like this were happening. At first, he didn't mind, but now he wasn't sure who or what was in control anymore.

Once he had calmed down, he made his way down the ladder with little effort. Now that there was absolutely no chance to sleep, and a walk through the garden would only tempt the plants to come to him more, there was only one option that gave any sort of peace to Bryce. Merin.

He started the short walk to Aer's old apartment. Merin had started living there after she stopped letting her parents keep her magic a secret.

He stood in front of the door. Half expecting to be met with a burst from Aer's winds. Bryce missed her. Missed the fire she had. Missed her songs and even her silly winds. But there was no wind to greet him at the door. He sighed. Maybe he should go with Kor in the morning to her grave.

He raised his hand to knock. His knuckles were scratched from the edge of the rung he had slipped from. There was a little bead of blood. He dropped his hand to his side and rubbed the blood on his pant leg. If he knocked, would Merin think he had been fighting? She wouldn't say anything. But she would watch him for a few days. He had seen her out of the corner of his eyes, watching him as he worked with the children. When they were in the Refuge—school, he reminded himself again—she was always watching. He didn't need her attention focused on him. He was trying to put on a brave face for her, and he didn't need anything getting in the way of that.

He sighed, staring at the door. If he had stood this long outside when Aer was there, her winds would have told her someone was there. She would have thrown open the door and looked him up and down, calculating what he wanted. But Merin was asleep, and she would stay that way until the sun crested the walls and trickled into this low-level apartment. She wasn't used to being up in the middle of the night. Merin was used to sleeping through the night on a comfortable bed.

He wouldn't wake her. Bryce sat down and leaned his head back against the door. He hugged his knees up to his chest.

"I should tell her," he whispered out into the darkness. He listened for a sign. A cart rumbled by. He was hidden from the street, but he could still hear the man driving the cart.

"Take all them Magics and ship them out to sea, I say," the man said to whoever was in the cart. "Then, when they lose control, they'll just take themselves down and not the whole city. You said you haven't been back in a while. Well, they made a school for Magics. Can ya believe that?"

The cart rolled down the avenue, and the man's words were lost to the nighttime.

"I'll take that as my sign to wait," Bryce mumbled to the universe. He hadn't told Kor or Merin about how the plants called to him. That the light inside of him had gone from a bubbling brook to a raging river, and he was barely keeping his head above water.

He was glad that they needed him at the school. Even if it was running errands or cleaning, it gave him something to do. And it gave him a reason to avoid doing what he had done before. Wander the garden or help Vycky and her wife in the flower shop, but then someone might notice. And while things were good with Magics and the rest of the city, that didn't mean they wouldn't turn on someone as soon as they knew that they didn't have total control. And he wasn't sure he had control anymore. Of anything.

His magic, his feelings for Merin, his nightmares, his life. Bryce felt them slipping through his fingers like he was grasping at the sand Vycky used in the bottom of her vases of dried flowers. His magic was out of control. He did know he could feel this way about someone, but still, he was keeping her at bay. How could he explain the horror? He didn't have the words. He had thought the nightmares would go away. That when the Refuge was taken down, they would fade, but they hadn't. They had only gotten worse.

His consciousness teetered on the edge of sleep. Familiar faces came and went. Aware, Bryce had the ability to tell himself he was dreaming. Knowing that the things in front of him weren't real.

Dream versions of his friends were running toward him. First, little Tiernan, a wide smile, a hand reaching out to him, until right before Bryce could grab his hand, Tiernan caught on fire. The fire sputtered between images until it consumed him in one great flower of heat and flame. Kor ran after him but couldn't reach him in time. Bryce stared at his hands where Tiernan should have been. He looked up at Dream Kor. He glared. His yellow-green eyes stared through him like it was his fault. Because it was. It was his fault.

"You're dreaming," a voice called to him somewhere outside the flames and glares. "Bryce?"

Bryce lifted his head from where it lay on his knee and opened his eyes. The sky was rosy, but he was still in the darkness. A different dream. No, he was outside. He looked behind him. Merin. Beautiful, wonderful, smart, kind Merin. Not the dream version that never captured how truly wonderful she was in real life, but the real-life Merin.

"I . . ." it took him a second to fully register that he was no longer in his nightmare.

"Have you been sleeping out here all night?" Merin asked. He was thankful she didn't ask what his dream was about. Sometimes she hesitated like she wanted to ask, but she didn't. Not anymore.

"Just an hour or two," Bryce said. The dream had made him feel like it was a lifetime, but the sun hadn't even fully risen above the wall. The apartment was still shaded.

"Are you feeling okay?" she asked. Her hand reached down and touched his shoulder. He felt the instant relief of her magic flowing through him. It always felt like a cool drink of water on a hot day. Just releasing tension wherever it touched. He felt the ache in his back from sleeping against the door lift.

"I am now," he said. He rolled his shoulders a few times and stepped away from her hand. He loved the feeling of her magic and the feeling of her skin, but he was too afraid to let her do anything but the surface. Too afraid that she might find the deep, dark parts of him that were scarred and bruised. He didn't want her to see those parts, but more, he didn't know who he was without them.

"Come on, we best go get to work. Kor will expect us to get through another room or two by the time he gets back. Unless, of course—"

Bryce knew what was coming next. She would ask about Aer. He had thought about going during the night. Maybe he should give in. "I'm ready to work," he said before he even consciously realized it.

"Let's go then."

They walked slowly. The steps between the apartment to the doors of the school were few, but they still strolled. There was little space between them, and their shoulders rubbed on occasion. Bryce felt a twist in his stomach when he thought about grabbing her hand. In the safety of the school, in the dark apartment, those places it was fine. But out here. Everyone knew who he was. What he was. They judged him. And even though his clothes were not as dirty, and he hadn't been in a street fight in a while, he wasn't sure he should be allowed to touch Merin.

Merin looked at him. Her eyes narrowed, and her head tilted ever so slightly to the side like she was asking a question. Bryce shrugged. Her fingers brushed his. His heart jumped from the sheer joy of it.

"Which rooms do you want to tackle today?" Bryce said switching gears, trying to make his fingers listen when he told them not to latch onto hers. The school would have no students today, but that didn't mean they didn't have plenty of work to do.

"I want to tackle the rooms we left on the second floor," Merin said. Bryce could feel her watching his reaction. On the second floor were the "reeducation rooms." Rooms he had been tortured in for being a Magic. Rooms that made his mouth go dry and his heart shiver. He tried not to show the stress on his face.

"Sure. I'll haul the rest of the furniture out."

"You could start with the far rooms." There was a hesitation in her voice. It made him cringe thinking about how she had to tiptoe around him so much that she had to think about what room he cleaned.

He shrugged. How could he explain everything to her?

"Bryce! Merin!" Tiernan called from the door. "Kor left a whole list of things for Bryce to do."

"Just me? Show me the list." He started to run after Tiernan but felt his feet grow heavy as he entered the building. He still followed Tiernan up to where Kor had made the three of them a bedroom. His bed had yet to be slept in.

Bryce wrestled the list from Tiernan.

"See, right there." He pointed. "Merin's going to be really disappointed if you can't read her name."

Tiernan stuck out his tongue. "I can read it. But her jobs are boring. Let's go break some more of the furniture."

"We're supposed to be cleaning," Merin said from the doorway.

"Fine."

Bryce handed her the list. He had to admit the jobs listed did seem boring. He wasn't sure what the word curriculum guides meant, but he knew it was no job for him. He let his hand brush Merin's as he passed through the doorway.

While she was out, he would get the furniture out of the reeducation rooms. He would show her she didn't need to be afraid.

CHAPTER SIX

MERIN

AFTER PICKING UP SOME ITEMS FROM SCHOOLS AROUND the city, Merin wandered into the market. The main marketplace was not a place Merin went often. It was even more crowded now that Magics had been able to set up shop within the confines of the square. Historically, they had been allowed to operate in the Wall District but nowhere else.

Aer's sacrifice had opened many doors for Magics beyond just the Refuge being shut down.

Merin waded through the crowds, looking less at the wares people were selling and more at the people around them. She could see quite a few black tattoos sticking out under people's collars, sleeves, or pant legs. More than she had ever seen in this part of town together at one time. It made her happy, and in the same breath, it made her nervous. She couldn't quite put her finger on why. She wasn't afraid of the Magics, but maybe she was afraid for them. What if someone caused a problem? She tried to shake the fear from her head and just be happy that they were being a little more accepted within Kaybrum.

She scanned the crowd for Hayden. She hadn't really known she had come to see him until she had arrived at the marketplace. He had been a big help with cleaning, and having someone with that many connections and that much money wouldn't be a bad thing for them. She knew his family operated most of the marketplace in one way or another, so it was a safe bet that he might be around somewhere.

"Merin?" Hayden said, coming up from behind her. It made Merin jump a little. How had she missed him?

"Hayden, I didn't see you there."

"I figured. You looked pretty focused on something. Need help finding anything?"

"No, I uhh . . . I was looking for you."

"For me?"

Merin took a moment to look at him. He was in plain clothes, and the only thing that gave away his wealth was the ironed quality of his pants and shirt.

"I guess I just didn't see you. I wanted to thank you for your help the other day."

"Oh, that was nothing. I'm trying to get a shipment of lumber sent over to the school."

"You are?"

"Yeah, it's not a problem. We actually have a little too much in the warehouses anyway. With all of the Magic stalls moving into the marketplace, we have to make sure we are diversifying our products enough to keep up."

"Right," Merin trailed off. She wanted to believe he just wanted to help out of the kindness of his heart, but maybe there was some other sort of motive behind him. Her mother had always taught her that people were a game of politics and power.

"I was just about to head over to Gesepi's if you wanted to tag along. You might know what you need a little better than me. And don't I know having too much of the wrong thing is even worse than having too little of the right thing."

"Gesepi's? That's where Korvo works," Merin said. Kor had still been picking up shifts at the carpenters to be able to make sure there was food on the table for Tiernan while they spent most of what he had saved on the school. It was clearly exhausting him, but Kor never complained.

"Great. That's even better. I'll lead the way," Hayden said. Merin had to almost run to catch up with him. His long legs took quick, confident strides through the busy marketplace. He weaved in and out of groups of people so easily that she would lose him for seconds at a time. He never seemed rushed or in a hurry, just efficient and elegant as he walked. She stumbled through the mess of people behind him.

Gesepi's was at the far corner of the marketplace in a permanent building, much like all of the craftsmen. They had been here since the beginning, and most of the furniture in Merin's parent's house had come from Gesepi's when it was his father's place before his. Merin had never actually met Gesepi.

When they reached the door to the building, a wooden sign hung over it. It was newer than the rest of the wood, and the intricate woodwork screamed Kor's name.

"Hayden, you've returned from the North, have ya?" An older man said, rising from a chair ten feet to the right of where they were standing. Merin hadn't noticed him. His skin was like soft leather, and he seemed at home in the chair he had moved from. He was wiry, and you could still see the muscles made from his years as a carpenter.

"Gesepi, have you moved since I left? You were sitting there when I said goodbye."

"Don't need to move so much anymore. Got me a good crew."

"And too much lumber on your hands," Hayden said, leaning on the edge of the building.

Gesepi laughed. "I wondered when you were gonna get down here and tell me I'd taken up too much of the warehouses with wood. Doesn't it feel better in there feeling the potential? Feeling what it could be?"

"I care what it *will* be. Profit." Hayden was still smiling his flashy grin, and Gesepi laughed, but there was an edge to Hayden's voice that made Merin sure if he was really joking at all. "I've come to take it off your hands."

"And what do you need with all that wood?" Gesepi asked.

"Not me. The school for Magics," Hayden said like it wasn't a big deal for someone who wasn't a Magic to be giving them something for free. Gesepi raised his eyebrow a smidge but said nothing.

"I was wondering if I could steal Korvo for a minute to talk about what they'll need the most of."

"He's in the back. You'll find him somewhere amongst all the orders that have been flooding us."

Hayden let himself into the building and took a steep left turn to head back toward what Merin assumed was the workshop.

"Thanks," Merin said as Hayden moved out of sight.

"Best be careful with that one, little lady," Gesepi said.

"Oh, I'm not—We're not—" She stumbled as she crossed over the floorboards following him. Merin leaned her head back out the door, making eye contact with Gesepi. "Why?"

"The Nagelys are all the same. He's a nice enough boy. Really does take care of the people here, but profit is king, and everything is business. Best run along and find him."

"Right," Merin said. She gave the old man one last look and hurried toward the workroom.

It was almost like dusk in the back of the shop. There were plenty of lights, but stacks of chairs, tables, and other projects blocked the light and sent shadows at all different angles around the room. She stepped quickly, trying not to let her dress snag on any of the tools or splinters that jutted out trying to grab her.

The room opened up with one window in the background. Finally, it felt like mid-morning again, and the space felt expansive around her. Nearest the window, Korvo was bent over a table. He was so focused, Merin wasn't sure he even saw Hayden standing over him.

Merin went to open her mouth to say hello, but Hayden put his finger to his lips to stop her. She watched Korvo instead. He ran his fingers over the table with his eyes closed. He was reading the stories encased in the wood. She knew he could do it. She had seen the table he had made for Aer and some others, but she had never seen him actually do it. It was the same kind of magic that ran through him when he read the cards. A connection to the Earth. To the cycles that made the Earth what it was.

Carefully, he took a chisel to the edge of where he had been touching and carefully tapped out a few pieces of wood. He did it slowly, eyes still closed, and the pattern became clear to Merin as she watched him work. It was an ocean. Or what she had been shown of oceans from books. Korvo had seen the ocean. Lived on it, according to Bryce. Maybe that was why he didn't need to open his eyes, or it was all magic. After a few minutes, he set the tools down and looked up.

"Do the others get jealous you're hogging all the good light when you don't even need to see to work?" Hayden asked. Merin looked at him, surprised. She had been thinking something similar, but she hadn't thought to say it out loud.

"Not when my work is so much better," Kor said, standing up and reaching out his hand. Merin noticed he hadn't been switching to his left anymore. He was no longer trying to appease everyone and keep them from what had happened to him. Aer had changed his mind on a lot of things. "What brings you both by?"

"Gesepi's been filling up our warehouse, so I figured I'd kill two birds with one stone and free up the space in the warehouse and help you guys out at the school."

"How so?" Kor asked. He wiped his tools off with a towel, much like Bethlem did to the bar glasses when he was trying to seem aloof and disinterested.

"Giving you some of the wood."

"Giving?"

"Giving. What do you need? Probably not tables like this, but solid wood will replace a lot of those broken pieces you're trying to stitch together."

"It certainly would help."

"Well, anything you want is yours. We're going to be paying Gesepi, so he'll have no problems with it. But if anyone does, just tell them to come talk to me."

"Thanks, Hayden. We really appreciate it." A smile swept across Kor's face. The first real one she had seen in a while. Maybe she was judging Hayden too much. The old man had thought she was trying to date him, not work with him on a project. If Kor trusted him enough to let his political smile drop away to a real one, she could suspend her disbelief too.

"Well, I've got to be on my way. Merin, are you coming?"

"Go ahead, Merin. I'll be busy here for a few more hours. I'll see you back at the school."

Merin nodded. Had she said anything while she was there? She couldn't remember anything. Why was she still letting herself fall into the background? Was that something she had learned from her parents? Or from hiding her magic her whole childhood? Or, she thought, did she just lack something that they all seemed to have? Yes, she had spoken to the people the night Aer died, but people have been known to survive bear attacks. Survival and adrenaline were powerful drugs, and without them, was she doomed to stay quiet and reserved her whole life?

"When did you know you were a Magic?" Hayden asked suddenly.

Merin shifted her thoughts back to the man in front of her.

"Always, I guess. Most feel it always. It's like, well—Kor calls it our inner light—it's always there. That connection to the world, our magic, is just inside of us." She could feel hers even now rippling slowly through her like a creek bubbling over rocks as it made its way to the ocean—the ocean she had never seen.

"Right. What does it feel like?"

"Magic?"

He nodded.

How to explain magic?

"It feels different to everyone, I think. Mine feels like that refreshing first sip of water that coats your throat on a summer day. Or the first time you sink into a bath after a hard day. Where you can feel the dirt and grime and worry float away from you."

"That's quite specific."

For some reason, Merin blushed. "Well, it's something like that anyway."

They walked back through the marketplace, but this time, Hayden kept pace with her. He let groups pass by them instead of weaving through them. It was a lot easier for Merin to concentrate on him.

"So you were in the North for a while?" Merin asked.

Hayden nodded. "It's nice to be home. Much too cold during the winter. But it has such a nice summer. Have you ever been?"

"I've never left Kaybrum."

"Really? Never? Not even beyond the walls into the countryside?"

The countryside made her think of Bryce. Bryce had come from the country, Kor and Tiernan from the South. It was only she who had never seen the other side of the big metal walls that surrounded the city.

"Well, we should go."

"Someday," Merin said with a small smile. She hoped he got the hint that she was done talking about her leaving Kaybrum. "What were you there for? Business?"

"Always. A few new partners and a few old ones that needed to be checked up on."

"And it took years? It feels like everything in Kaybrum takes you five minutes to do or decide to do."

"Kaybrum is a city that my fathers created. Everything here has a shortcut. But outside of the walls, you have to force a shortcut to the things you want, and sometimes that means you have to take the long way around once before you get there."

"Sure," Merin said, but she really wasn't sure at all about what he was talking about. There were no shortcuts for Kor in Kaybrum, but maybe that had more to do with magic and less to do with the city itself.

"I've got some meetings I have to attend," Hayden said, stopping short of the exit for the marketplace. "But, I'd love to talk more tomorrow when I stop by the school."

So he was coming back. She nodded, and he took off back through the crowd at breakneck speed. She lost sight of him after only a moment.

Kor would still be at work for a few more hours, so she decided to go and get some more cleaning done in the school. She had a feeling she'd find Bryce there anyway. She just had to stop by Aer's—her apartment before.

Although she had taken down all of the window coverings Aer had plastered up on the windows so she could sleep during the day, the apartment was still dark. There was very little Merin had done to make it feel more like a home. Was that because she didn't want to disturb Aer's things or because she wasn't ready to admit her parents weren't as fond of her now that she was going around telling people she was a Magic? Why couldn't she even understand her own thoughts?

She could have spent the better part of the morning getting so lost in her thoughts she wouldn't be able to find her way back, but Bryce would be at the school. She grabbed her bag full of cleaning supplies, and a folder came toppling out of it. She picked it up. Bryce's file. It was crammed full of paper. She flipped through them.

3571 continues to show increased activity while under the gas.

She continued, reading bits and pieces here and there.

3571 needed fifteen more strokes of the rod before it hit the threshold. Must send it for further investigation. Note: More gas may be needed as 3571 has grown since last entry.

Merin shuddered but couldn't bring herself to stop looking through the pages. There were pages of these documents. Not one of them mentioned Bryce's name other than the first page. There it was in bold letters. Bryce Segal #3571 Earth/Plant Age when first admitted: 13.

It had been almost four years since that first page had been placed in his folder. Why had the Refuge kept such records and for so long?

She had meant to burn the file, but now she couldn't. Not with her thoughts spinning like this. This was her chance to understand what Bryce had been through. She stepped over to a dresser that was still filled with Aer's clothes and opened a drawer. She buried the file under enough things that it didn't look strange. Not that the boys would go around opening drawers. It had been long enough that if they were going to move the contents, they would have done it by now.

With the file hidden, she picked her bag back up and headed toward the school.

CHAPTER SEVEN
BRYCE

KOR HAD ALREADY LEFT FOR WORK BEFORE BRYCE HAD dragged himself into the building. He wasn't sure why it was still so hard to come inside. It looked nothing like it had a few days prior. The windows were letting in light, and the air smelled like something other than dirty kid bodies. He tried to shake how he had seen it when he was thirteen. The whole building had seemed bigger, more menacing. Probably because he had grown half a foot since he was thirteen. He'd always been strong—years of farm work can do that to a person—but he'd gained most of his height since he had come to the city.

Still, the building made his skin crawl. And finding the room where they had gassed him had really just been the worst part. How he could have forgotten a place like that was beyond him.

He felt it around his neck. Nothing was there, but just being in the building made his throat feel like it was closing. After finding that room, things had gotten worse. What else might he find in the back corners and shadows of this place? He thought he had dealt with all of the demons, but they kept becoming new ones.

"Bryce?" Merin called from the doorway.

"Up here," Bryce said, stepping away from the window he had climbed in through. She was beautiful. Even when he saw her every day, he couldn't believe that she would want anything to do with him. Sure, he wore clean clothes now, but she was perfect.

"What are we cleaning today?" she asked, walking up the stairs to stand next to him.

"Do we have to clean right away?" He asked, putting his arms around her. He tried his best to forget the building around him. He let his hands find the small of her back and buried his face into her neck. Her hair tickled his ears, but he just nuzzled in deeper.

"Merin!" Tiernan yelled from a story above them. Bryce heard his little feet flying down the stairs. He waited until the little boy was next to them to disengage from Merin's embrace. He wanted to hold on to it for just a second longer.

"Tiernan, can you help Bryce move the broken wood today?" Merin asked.

"We aren't going to use it?" Bryce asked.

"Kor secured us a free shipment of new wood."

"Kor secured or our new friend Hayden?" Bryce asked.

Merin just gave him a little smile. Bryce rolled his eyes.

Tiernan ran off to gather little pieces to burn in the fire. Bryce went for the larger pieces that might be of help later.

Bryce hoisted the broken joists of a bed onto his shoulders and dragged them. He was going to put them in the back alley behind the school. He had never felt the need to spend time out there. It was usually coated in garbage, and while it was a break from the air inside the building, nothing seemed to grow there.

When they took over, Kor had suggested that Bryce make a little garden in the back to feel more at home. At first, it felt like a good idea, but after the first few plants died, Bryce refused to try anymore. Each little seedling had felt like a cut across his body. It was like the scars from when the plants burned through his magic were visible.

Bryce still had the vision, though, of what could be back here. On the building, they could grow beans and other things that would climb and climb and cover the outside. He could grow sunflowers in the eastern corner that would follow the pattern of the sun, and everyone who stayed in the school would be able to see them from the windows. A low patch of soft moss for the corner, for naps or studying. And bramble bushes. The kind that grew berries along the exterior. If Kor ever asked, he would say it was to get people to interact with them, eat the berries, and maybe start talking. That would have been an answer Kor would have liked. But truthfully, it was so Bryce could ask the thorns to grow, to protect them, and to keep people out. That was an answer that Aer would have liked. But maybe that thinking had gotten her to this spot. Maybe it had to be both at the same time and actually mean both. Merin could mean both. He could try.

But it didn't matter anyway. Nothing would grow in this place. Bryce didn't blame the plants, but it did make him curious. He set the broken bits of bed down on the ground and then sat down. He crossed his legs and let his hands fall to his sides. He closed his eyes and tried to concentrate on a message.

"What's down there?" he asked. He sent the message through the dirt. He could feel the plants rushing to him.

"Don't rush. Dangerous ground. Just tell me." The plants slowed. He could feel them coming up around him, careful not to be underneath the cobblestones.

Slowly, little sprouts began to pop up on the edges of the cobblestone patio. Bryce admired them. They were strong sprouts, and their vivid green color almost matched his inner light. Then, one by one, they died. They curled and turned brown, and their leaves turned papery and brittle. After only a second, it looked like months of decay. Bryce shook his head, trying to make sure he had seen it correctly.

Death. That message was clear. There was death under the cobblestones, but what kind? He thanked the plants, but it hadn't been enough. His curiosity had turned into a morbid need to know. What kind of death waited outside the school?

He placed his palm on the cobblestones. With an edge of the bed, he pried one of them up. Then another. Then another. He cleared out a three-foot circle around him. Once he had the cobblestones removed, it just looked like dirt. Regular city dirt. He wasn't sure what he expected to find, but nothing wasn't it.

They had to have a shovel somewhere.

Bryce didn't have to look long. In the closet where the Watchers had put their coats, there was a shovel in the back. It was old, and the handle was splintered and rough, but it looked like it would hold.

Bryce brought it back out to the patch of dirt he had uncovered. *It's probably nothing,* he told himself. Just years of hatred and fear seeping into the soil. Plants needed peace and care too. They could grow in the harshest of conditions, they could push their way through streets and buildings, but they needed the basics to survive, just like humans.

He dug. The handle chafed at his hands, and he thought about quitting twice. Just how long was he going to dig before he gave up? Maybe until Kor said something or Merin saw him. He could lie and say he was re-attempting the garden, but neither of them was ignorant enough to think a garden needed a three-foot diameter hole that was going down multiple feet. But how many feet?

The answer quickly became clear. Three feet down, the shovel struck something that wasn't dirt, and when Bryce pulled it out, it wasn't rocks either. It was bone. Human bone.

He stood staring at the white piece in disbelief. The plants weren't wrong. There was death here.

Bryce walked over to the fence and grabbed the metal railing. The edges cut at his fingers, but he didn't care. He threw up. His body heaved again and again. There were worse things about the Refuge than he even knew.

Empty, his body constricted a final time, leaving the acidic taste of defeat in his mouth.

It was time to get Korvo. He stepped out of the hole, new anger and reverence for the patch of ground filling him as he walked toward the stairs that would take him up to where he hoped Kor was planning for the next week of lessons.

"Kor," Bryce said, standing at the door. For a moment, Kor looked so distracted that Bryce almost walked away.

"You're getting dirt everywhere," Kor said, shaking himself out of the daze. "Merin won't be happy if she sees that."

"She'll be even more unhappy if she sees what I just found," Bryce said. The coldness in his tone was palpable, and Kor stood rigged. Without a word, he followed Bryce back to the hole in the ground. Bryce showed him the bone still sitting on the spade of the shovel.

"How many?" Kor asked.

"How many bones? I don't know. That sounds like a question for Merin."

"How many bodies, Bryce."

"How many? You think there's more than one?"

"I would bet my life on it. How many?"

"I don't know. I only found one bone. The plants won't go near this area. They keep dying." He gestured over to the papery remnants of the young sprigs that had been growing so quickly just a few moments ago.

"We need to purify this place."

"Kor, you're getting way ahead of me. Slow down. My mind doesn't work as fast as yours. What are you saying?"

"There have always been stories about Magics that never came out of the Refuge, right?"

"Yeah, but those were just stories to scare each other with. They must have been sent to labor camps or back home, or . . ." Bryce looked down at his feet.

"Or they never left."

"They died in the Refuge?"

"It happened in Hadran. Those were prisons, but it was the same. Dead kids bring people outrage even if they hate what they are. My guess is that this is not the only bone you would find. It is not the only body you would find. And I forbid you from digging anymore."

"But shouldn't we give them a proper burial?"

"They would only use it as an excuse to close down the school." Kor's face was harder than Bryce had ever seen it. There was no glimmer of hope, no thrill of justice, just survival.

The two boys said nothing for a long moment. Kor stared down at the ground as if communicating with the dead. Bryce watched him, waiting for something to do.

"We need to purify this place," Kor said finally.

"Purify?"

"Things grow in cemeteries?" Kor asked. Bryce was hardly following, but he nodded his head. He even had a little patch of flowers growing right over Aer's grave. "But nothing will grow here. Why?"

"Because it's not about the bodies?" Bryce asked. He knew growing up that death had meant fertilizer. They had thrown plants and debris into piles to cultivate the soil. Dead things nourished the earth. So why wouldn't the plants grow?

A story about the Twelve Gods flashed into his mind. When

Dimian, the god of order, had decided to try to wipe out the Magics, he smote a group in a field. The other gods had been upset, so Dimian had hidden the Magics by burying them. And nothing ever grew there—a horrible blemish out in a field. A Magic's Hand, the people in the village called it. Now and then, there would be a part of a field where nothing would take, and they called it a Magic's Hand.

"Dimian—" Bryce started, but Kor cut him off.

"How did the gods restore the land?"

"Fire. They burned it." It was an old practice to control burn part of the crops to prevent a Magic's Hand from happening, but Bryce figured that had more to do with the actual soil contents and less because the gods had created some ritual.

"Fire burns everything," Kor said. He was still staring straight down. "Even hatred. Even fear. Even Magics."

"I don't want to tell Tiernan."

"Agreed. You'll have to do it yourself."

Bryce nodded, but he wished the older boy would look at him. Place a hand on his shoulder or something. For the first time, Bryce wondered where Kor sought comfort from the harsh world around them. He remembered Vycky teasing him because he had never noticed that Aer and Kor were together, but now he could see that with her being gone, it was what had taken the spirit from him. Not the work, not the school, but the inability to share it with someone.

Bryce reached out his hand, but Kor had already turned to go. Bryce watched him walk away. What would he say? Nothing could make this all right.

He piled the broken pieces of wood on top of each other and used the dirt from the hole to form a circular barrier around where he would light the fire.

Bryce closed his eyes.

"Twelve Gods take them. Let them rest easy. And let the people who did this meet sweet and painful justice." There were twelve; at least one of them had to be hungry for some justice.

He felt the hot sting of his tears as they ran down his face. He didn't wipe them away. There was no reputation to protect alone with the flames. There was no one he needed to pretend to be strong for. He wept openly and honestly for the first time. He let the anger he had felt melt into despair and fear. And then, within a few more sobs, it changed again into a pounding in his heart that wasn't anger, but its kin, something more like passion. Something like justice.

He stayed until the tears were dry on his face from the flames, and he knew everything would burn. Then he walked inside, put his best Korvo political smile on, and attempted to find Merin.

CHAPTER EIGHT

KORVO

Was it his fault? He had jinxed the entire day, maybe the entire world, because he had felt happy for a total of three hours in one day. He had felt hope. Not like a frail and fluttering dove but hope that felt like sunshine. Warm and bright. So solid he felt he could grab hold and it wouldn't break.

And then there were the bodies. Nightmares that not even Bryce knew.

The air around him felt sharp, shrill, and cold. Hope was not a bird in a cage today. Hope had dissolved and left a large hollow in his chest.

He almost turned around and went back out to the garden. They should be buried properly. They should be treated like people, even if it was only in death, but he couldn't force his feet to turn and go back.

The school would not be enough. He had known that somewhere in his mind—that the school wasn't enough, but he was tired. For so long, that had been the goal. End the Refuge; start the school. Protect them. He slammed his right fist into the metal of the fireplace. It sent a shock up through his elbow. How had he thought he could protect them when he clearly didn't even know what he was protecting them from?

It was people like the General who let kids die like that. People who kept getting away. People who had to be stopped.

"Bad timing?" Hayden said.

"Just some bad news," Korvo said, straightening himself to his full frame. Hayden looked to be the same age as him, but somehow, he felt like he needed to prove himself.

"Ahh, speaking of news," Hayden said, leaning against the railing of the stairs. "I rushed over when I heard something from my contacts in the East."

"The East? Why do you know anyone in the East?"

"I have contacts everywhere. It would be bad business to just let a whole market disappear because they have some strong religious zealots and a bad reputation for making people miserable about it."

"What about the East, Hayden?"

"The General that caused all the hullabaloo around here. The one I heard you knew. He's in the East now."

"Good. Let him run back to where he came from. The whole push against Magics started because of the East pushing on Hadran."

"Among other things. The people of Hadran sure did take to it, though. You can't blame the East for that."

Kor forced himself to swallow the words that were sitting on his tongue. How had he been smiling at this man mere hours ago, and now he wanted to punch him in his perfect face? "I can blame the East for letting people like the General govern them."

"Now we can agree on that. Anyway, I heard he's headed toward the capital."

"Running home with his tail between his legs," Kor said, feeling a little more elated than he probably should have, given the last hour. But it felt good that they had forced the General out. Out of Kaybrum and Hadran. He was back in the East, where he could stay.

"I don't know if I would say that. Things in the East are brewing. I can hardly get tea leaves shipped out of there on time. I'm really going to have some issues keeping the marketplace running if I can't make tea. That will be a huge blow to my profits this month—"

"Hayden," Kor lashed out, "I swear on the Twelve Gods, I do not care about your profits. What do you know about the East?"

"Roads are being blocked off. Government searches. Pulling high-ranking generals and priests back from abroad. Sounds to me like they are about to try something big. Something with all of their forces."

"And why are you telling me?" Kor asked. He looked again at the man in front of him. His hair was slightly damp at the edges, and his boots were covered with dirt. It really did look like he had rushed here.

"Just figured you would want to know. Information is a priceless commodity."

"Is there anything else you've heard?" Kor asked. He felt heavy. The smile Merin and Bryce were saying he was forcing felt like a weight pulling him under.

"No, but I'll let you know if I hear anything else."

Kor nodded, "You've been doing me favors all day long. Could you do me one more?"

"Sure. What?"

"Don't tell Merin or Bryce."

"Bryce is the guy who looks like he wants to snap me in half?"

"That would be correct."

"You got it."

"Thank you again for the work the other day, and the wood. And this information."

"I'll come by tomorrow to help with some more cleaning," Hayden said. He gave a brief little salute and turned back down the stairs.

When Hayden was fully out of sight, Kor sat down. He was too tired to keep standing, so in the middle of the staircase, he tucked his head into his knees and tried to will himself to go and help the others. He stayed like that for a long time. Someone had even draped a quilt over him.

When Bryce walked by, he put his hand on Kor's back but said nothing. Kor was sore enough when he looked up he realized he had been there for at least an hour. He let out a long, hard sigh. Was he ever going to do anything to actually help?

He felt for the cards he kept at his side. The old, tattered edges comforted a little. He pulled them out and began to slowly shuffle. Hand over hand, the cards mixed. When they felt right, Kor laid them out on the stair below him. One for each of them until . . . . Until he found an answer.

Kor traced the carvings he had made in the table lazily with his fingers. He drew a deep breath. Visiting Aer's grave was comforting him less and less. He didn't feel like she was there anymore. That she had been sucked up by the earth and came back to life in his dreams.

He placed the cards next to him on the table. The metal collar sat on his leg. He couldn't bring himself to look at the cards while he was holding it. What if his hand was too damaged to read things even with its help? Or maybe what if he didn't know what they were saying?

He laid his head down for a moment placing his hands in his lap. His eyelids, heavy with worry, closed.

"Giving up?" Aer's voice reached him the moment his eyes closed.

"No," Kor said, but he wasn't sure he meant it. He was spending so much time trying to convince everyone else that things were fine and under control, but the awfulness just seemed to surround him. That room, the bodies that Bryce had found, these were horrors that he wasn't expecting.

"What's next?" he said into the ether of his dream world.

"What do you think?" Aer appeared then. All of her at once. She looked like he remembered her. Her long, thin hair, wild and loose. Her sharp eyes looking at him demanded the best version of himself. The eyes that believed in him.

"I have to stop the General."

"Because of me?"

"Because of you, Tiernan, Bryce, me, my friends in Hadran. All the Magics that will come after us."

"Do you really think killing one man will do that much?"

"I didn't say anything about killing, Aer."

"Right. Do you really think that 'stopping' one man will matter in the long run?"

"Probably not, but it's got to be the next step."

"School's not enough?"

"That's not fair. It was never supposed to fix everything. Just start a trickle of things going our way. It was never going to get us—"

"Justice. I think that's the word you are looking for."

Justice? Was that what he had been hungering for? Was that what was missing? The school had brought some sympathy to their cause.

People had wanted to help, but no one wanted to atone for their actions or beliefs. They wanted to sweep it under the rug, to be on the right side of history without facing what that history really meant.

"You're thinking maybe it was a victory for non-Magics as well," Aer said. She had always been able to read his moods, but in these moments between real dreams and real life, she seemed to be able to read every thought. See it on his face or hear it in his voice.

"How could it be a victory?"

"You know how. Now they solved the problem. They solved Magics' suffering. They can pat themselves on the back for a job well done. Those who felt even a smidge bad about how we were treated can sleep more easily at night. Turn their attention to the other issues of the world."

"Is there a way for us to win without them winning?"

"I'm not the idea guy. I was, what did you call me, a good soldier. But what did that get me? In all honesty, Kor, a win is a win." Her voice dropped some of the acid it had when they talked about the issues in their lives. It was softer, like a gentle breeze. "I was wrong."

"I was wrong," Kor said.

"I didn't say you were right," she laughed. Kor smiled. Her laugh could always make him smile. When he was at work and couldn't remember the sound of her voice, he always imagined her laugh, and from there, he constructed her voice. Just like he was doing now. Creating a version of Aer that was going to tell him what he already knew he had to do.

"I have to leave Kaybrum. I have to go east."

"We can agree on that. But my way and your way aren't going to make it work. You have to find something new. Maybe take Bryce and Merin with you."

"Someone needs to run the school. If it fails, it just proves them right. We are uneducated swine who need someone to hold our hands and look after us."

"Fine, take Bryce. Merin will be able to handle it."

"Bryce needs to see this thing through. He needs to be here, see the Refuge disappear room by room until he can stand to be in it a moment without snapping at someone or—"

"Okay, okay. Bryce can stay. The winds agree with you, and it's very hard to argue with them in this place. Will you take Tiernan?"

"I can't force him back through Hadran."

"You don't need to go through Hadran to get to the East."

"I am not a mountain person. I am not a snow person. I'll take the sea."

"I wish I had gotten to see the sea. The winds always brought good things from the sea." Her voice seemed lost in the memories of something he couldn't place. Kor shook his head; maybe even his subconscious had trouble pinning down Aer. "You have to go now," Aer said. Her eyes looked at Kor. And they mirrored his own. Memorizing everything about the other so there was no possible way to forget. Dreading the end of the dream. Her body started blurring into an opaque mist; her eyes were last to disappear, but then there was nothing—just the black of the back of his eyelids. Alone again, Kor lifted his head. It had only been a few minutes, but it had felt like a lifetime.

He had to go east. He had to go now.

He packed while mentally constructing the lists and things that Merin and Bryce would need. There was the school schedule and the vendor schedule. He would have to quit work and hope there would be a job when he got back.

He packed his bag. When he had left Hadran, he had only managed to grab the cards and the clothes on his back before he made a run for it. He tried to think back to what he would have needed: a canteen, changes in clothes, a jacket to keep the harsh sea winds from freezing him to the bone at night. The essentials were easy. There was still room in his bag for items of comfort. Comfort he would desperately need in the days to come. He picked up the cards but put them back on the table to do a reading. He put a picture of Merin, Bryce, Tiernan, and himself from the day he got the keys to the school into the bag instead. He looked around the room. Books were too heavy. He wouldn't need any woodworking tools or ledgers from the school. He stood. The silver collar tumbled to the floor.

It couldn't hurt to bring it. He could leave it in the bag, and it would just be a reminder of Aer. And a reminder of why he was leaving. Of why he had to go. He picked it up; the smooth metal felt cold against his skin. In his left hand, the heft of the metal was light. It seemed so strange that this small thing had done so much damage. Could do so much damage. Maybe it would be a betrayal to use it, but it would also be a loss to not see if it helped see the right path forward. See that this really was the right thing to do.

No one needed to know.

No one knew he had it.

One reading. His fingers shook as he reached for the cards. There wasn't much else to do but lay the cards out. But still, he shook. The clasp on the pouch came apart easily, and he could feel the cards calling to him. He felt the stories they held yelling into his mind. They swirled with a vividness he had never experienced. Not now, not before acid dulled his connections, not ever. He let his mangled hand grab the cards. He shuffled them, almost making him nauseous with how fast visions flew by his eyes. Finally, he felt the feeling of completeness that told him it was time to draw the cards.

His fingers rested on the top of the deck, almost afraid of what he might see. If the cards told him not to go, would he still do it? If they told him to go, what would they show him going toward?

The first card. Change. It screamed of change. Flashing between visions of the dusky floors of the school with its half-washed windows and layers of dust to the sea. Waves crashing against wood. There was the sea breeze. The spray of the water as you glided through the water. The wind.

"Kor?" came a voice in that wind. A voice he knew. The cards didn't normally give him voices. They gave images and feelings but never voices. Nothing so concrete as voices. The voice sounded far away and close all at the same time, like it was being swirled around in the breezes like a tumbleweed.

"Aer?" He said. He couldn't help himself. He knew this wasn't a dream. There was no way her voice had come to him.

"Kor?" The visions were still on the ship. He was high in the mast. When he looked down, he could see the deck far below. Around him, storm clouds burst with rain, and the wind whipped around him ferociously.

"I'm here. I'm here!" He cried. He felt the water on his cheeks. Too real. It was too real. He drew his hand away from the card and placed it on his face. Tears had fallen on his cheeks. Not the ocean, but tears. He was still in the school. Aer was gone.

Maybe the cards were showing him the past, but Aer had never been to the ocean.

He took a series of deep breaths to try and calm his nerves. Held each one while he visualized the inner light inside him. Calmed it to be just the faint glowing light that guided him every day. When he felt like he had done enough, he put his hand down to the next card.

Towers loomed. They were the color of sand. Everything was the color of sand. The walls surrounding the tower looked like they had just risen up from the beach itself. On the beach, a dark brown horse ran by. It was a war horse that was clear even if it didn't wear any regalia. Its muscles rippled as it ran. Its mane was tufted out of the way. It ran like it had seen battle, steadfast without wavering from what was in front of it. It kept running faster and faster down the beach. The beach seemed to stretch endlessly. The only hint that there was anything beyond the beach was a dark spot that seemed to grow.

The dark did not give Kor any feeling. It was not death or destruction. Not grief, but not happiness. Just dark. He wanted to know more. He turned his head, and the vision changed. A Phoenix and crow perched on the tower's roof. The Phoenix lifted its wings to spare the crow from the sand that had kicked up and was closing in on them. It pelted through the Phoenix wings, revealing behind the red feathers was another crow. He heard them shriek. Kor pulled his hand away. Everything had been real. He expected sand to come out from his hair and his clothes when he stood.

To no one in particular, he said, "They could have explained themselves better." He tried to shake off the feeling he was still somewhere far away—shake the sand and the waves and the sound of Aer's voice. But in a way, the cards had told him something. Whatever his destiny was at this point. The path he was going to choose. It wasn't here. He had to leave Kaybrum.

He stuffed a few more things into his bag and slipped the metal in last before he closed the bag tight. Travel light. Move fast.

Now, the hard part. He sat down with a pen. He would need to explain where he went, but not in too much detail that would make them follow. The school had to survive.

Bryce, he started. *Don't be mad.* The words flowed. He covered the page. There was so much more to say, but there was no more room, and Kor decided it was good enough.

He grabbed papers from the drawers by his bed. Put them in a box to take to Bethlem. He hid the note under his pillow. There was no use in anyone finding it before he left. He'd leave tomorrow night. The full moon would help him.

CHAPTER NINE
HAYDEN

HAYDEN SMELLED LIKE SWEAT. THERE WAS DIRT UNDER HIS fingernails. He could feel it there without even looking. He stretched out his fingers as if that would help with the situation, but of course it wouldn't. He decided to clasp his hands behind his back.

"Hayden," Father Christi summoned from behind the office door.

Hayden took a deep breath. It had been a while since he had seen his fathers. They had been the ones that sent him to the North for the last three years. He had spent his time traveling around Ravos and The United North, finding new deals but mostly staying out of his fathers' way. When he got back to Kaybrum, there had been a note waiting for him in the office—a command to take advantage of the magic situation.

His fathers were not in their office in Kaybrum. They had gone off to the islands to try to establish the first main trade routes to the West with the help of his grandfather. They were always thinking bigger.

It wasn't like Hayden had hated his time in the North. Even his clothes reflected his time there. They were still cream to white as his fathers demanded, but there were hints of embroidery around the edges and under the collar. Things that spoke to those years alone in the North. The hard-won victories he had and the nights he spent all alone with no one to talk to.

Only Father Christi ever responded to his letters. Father Marco never responded, although Father Christi sometimes forged his signature at the bottom. It never looked like his handwriting, but Hayden appreciated the gesture.

"Hello, Fathers," Hayden said. He did a mental checklist. His posture was correct, his hair was in place, a pleasant, not-too-eager smile on his face. Everything was in order, but he could feel their eyes roll over him for faults.

"You've done relatively well," Father Marco said. "Almost enough to prove you deserve the Nagely name."

That was something he had been almost living up to his whole life. He wondered if he had been their natural-born son, would they put him through all of these trials and tribulations, but he wasn't, and it didn't matter. He would deserve the name someday; he was their only heir after all.

"The market has improved quite a bit since you've been here," Christi said, looking down at the papers in front of them. Hayden tried to hide his wince. He had gotten that from Hayden's desk. While their desks were neat, files and papers stacked next to each other in calm, collected ways, Hayden was chaos incarnate. His desk looked as if a whirlpool had spit out pages and notebooks somewhere far from where they came. He had meant to clean it. Twelve Gods, he had meant to keep it clean. It was one of those things that was always on the list of to-dos but didn't get done.

He had helped clean the new school for Magics but didn't even get his office cleaned for his fathers' return—not that he had known they were coming.

"I see that the Magics are really pulling the numbers, and the Eastern Exchange has been doing well. You need to support them more. The East is acting funny, and we need to keep the supply lines alive as long as possible. You never know what they will want to start importing."

"The Eastern Exchange just sells trinkets and other things."

"In different times, people adapt to survive," Marco said flatly. Hayden opened his mouth to speak but decided against it. Father Marco didn't appreciate his thoughts when they weren't asked for.

His fingers picked at the dirt beneath his fingernails behind his back. He knew they would notice, but he couldn't stop himself.

"Hayden," Father Christi started, "how many times do we have to tell you not to fidget?"

Hayden knew better than to answer that he couldn't help it. His entire body felt the need to move. Standing here talking without something to write with, something to tap, something to move, he felt trapped.

There was silence.

"We are going to be going to the North."

"The North?" Hayden asked. The idea of his fathers poking around in what he had accomplished for the last three years felt like a slap in the face. They still didn't trust him.

"Mainly in Wayfarth," Christi said. Hayden wondered if he saw the tension in his face. "We still have little contact in that area, and they have a great supply of fish from the cold sea and all of the black wicker that we can use in the West. We won't be gone for too long, six months to a year at most. We trust you here, Hayden."

The words felt like a dream. Trust. They trusted him with Kaybrum? The place where the Nagelys had started their trading empire. The place where they had met and married. Of course, that was more of a business deal as well, but it still had to mean something.

"That doesn't mean we don't expect more from you. Things could be better. They can always be better."

"Yes, Father."

"And clean up that office."

Hayden understood he had been dismissed. He walked slowly to his office and used the edge of a stiff paper to try and get some of the dirt out from underneath his fingernails. The mess was too big to tackle right now. Besides, they would be gone in a few days, and he could go right back to the way it always was.

He closed the door to his office and sat for a moment.

His fathers would never care that he had done something good for people today. That he had helped people who needed help. Profit was always king to them. But Korvo and that girl Merin had friends. People who cared how they were feeling and knew them inside and out. People who weren't transactions but real friends.

Hayden wondered what that was like. He wasn't sure he had ever had someone just care about him. He had two leading theories of where he had come from.

1. He was not supposed to be born. A child of scandal that his fathers took advantage of. This made sense with his blue eyes that seemed to only exist in the upper class, but it seemed less likely that no one would know about it.
2. The Nagely family was wealthy enough to pay someone to have been his surrogate mother. That he was always a transaction, even before conception. That one hurt the most but seemed the most logical.

His fathers had sealed the records tightly—if there were any at all. He was a Nagely now, and Nagelys made the next generation better for Nagelys.

As he sat there thinking, the faces of the people at the school, even that angry kid, Bryce, kept flashing in his mind. He had gone there to help, to see how it could be helpful to him in getting the Magics more ingrained in Nagely trade versus their own marketplace in the Wall District, but he knew he was going to go back even if they couldn't help him.

His nails finally clean, he went about finding his idea notebook. Well, the current version of his notebook. This was volume five since he had come back from the North a few months ago. He opened it to the next blank page and wrote *Korvo, Merin, Tiernan, and Bryce* at the top. Then drew lines beside each name, making columns all the way down. He listed everything he knew about them. It wasn't much, but that could change.

CHAPTER TEN

TIERNAN

TIERNAN INSTANTLY RECOGNIZED THE SMELL ON BRYCE'S clothing. He had been near a fire; that much was obvious, but there was more. He knew what had been burning even if he couldn't smell it. He could see it on Bryce's face. The blank stare. He had seen that look before when he was in Hadran.

"Bryce?" Tiernan said as they sat down together. It took him calling the older boy's name a few times before he responded.

"What?" Bryce asked. His eyes were elsewhere. Tiernan understood.

"That fancy guy that helped Merin the other day was here again today."

"Hayden?" Bryce grimaced.

"Why don't you like him?"

"He's not a Magic. He's just trying to make himself feel good by helping us. Either he'll get bored or wait until someone congratulates him on a job well done."

"He seems nice."

"Yeah, to Merin."

"Merin is nice."

"Merin is the nicest, but there's a reason why people smile at her on the street and not us. You may have noticed that she looks a little more like Hayden than she does me. Merin comes from Kaybrum's elite. I would bet he's only coming back because of her."

"But he didn't even talk to Merin today. Just Kor. Whatever it was, it didn't sit well with him. Kor's been sad all day."

"He didn't talk to Merin?" The slight levity at knowing Hayden wasn't blatantly trying to steal his girlfriend was almost immediately disbanded by knowing exactly why Kor had been upset today.

"Shouldn't we be happy that he's trying to help?" Tiernan asked, taking the last bite of his dinner.

"We should. Just don't start liking him more than me," Bryce said, scooping up both of their plates.

Tiernan watched him from the table. Bryce had grown taller since he had met him, but there was more. He seemed more comfortable in his own skin. He hadn't gotten less angry or any calmer, but comfortable was something.

Of course not comfortable enough to stay in the school overnight. Tiernan already saw that he had grabbed a few blankets to take out to the roof that night. Even though it was warm out, Merin always made sure he had something to take with him. She didn't want him to feel like he was sleeping out on the street again.

"You're not going to stay with us again?" Tiernan asked.

"Not tonight, I got too much on my mind to be stuck in here."

"The beds are pretty soft."

"I know, Tiernan. I just . . . I . . . Well, would you go back to Hadran?"

"Maybe." They were always asking him that. Tiernan couldn't help but wonder what Hadran was like when he wasn't stuck in a cage. Kor talked about it with so much wonder that it had to be something to see. But he had not spent any time in those parts of Hadran. He had seen the inside of a cage and the road that brought him to Kaybrum. He had no reason to want to go back.

"Would you go back with the General?"

"No!" Tiernan said. "I burned that place."

"Right. This is that place for me, and since I can't burn it to the ground. I just have to spend some time in the fresh air. Maybe tomorrow."

"Yeah, right," Tiernan said, but his thoughts were on what Bryce had burned that day. It would be a cold day in hell before Bryce made his way down to the bed that Kor had made for him.

When the dishes were cleaned, Bryce gave one last apologetic smile and then disappeared with the blankets out the window and up to the rooftop. Tiernan thought about joining him. He had to admit it was nice up there. There was a cool breeze that seemed to always be there. He felt close to Aer, and since no one ever really talked much about the person who had saved him, he felt that was the easiest place to get to know her, through the breezes that still seemed to look for her there.

But Bryce's face had not indicated that he wanted company, so Tiernan settled for sitting next to the window where the breeze fluttered in from time to time and thought about Aer.

It's not that he hadn't asked about her, but he knew it was still a painful subject for them. They had all known her for years; he had known her for days, weeks maybe, and during that time, his little family had been split, which didn't leave him much time to get to know her. He had barely spoken any common tongue when she was here. But she sacrificed herself to save him.

Tiernan let a single tendril of fire leap into his hand. He molded it, letting it take a lightning shape and then revert to its regular flame.

Ever since the General had put the collar on him, it had been a little harder to control the flame. It rushed to his fingers like a dam breaking instead of the gentle warmth it used to feel. It was like the natural connection he had to his magic had been changed.

He wanted to ask Bryce if he felt it too, but what if he didn't? What if he hadn't noticed anything changing, and it was just him? What if they started to worry about him? That he didn't have control. He had seen the faces in the crowd as the fire had consumed his life force. As he burned Kor's hand. They had been terrified. He couldn't let his family, Bryce, Merin, or Twelve Gods forbid, Korvo, look at him like that. That would be worse than anything he had experienced so far in his short life.

He took a deep breath and held it like Kor had taught him to do. It always seemed to help Bryce calm down, but oxygen only fanned Tiernan's flames. He let out the air in a big whoosh. He closed the window. Not all the way, just in case Bryce decided to come in, but enough that bugs or bats couldn't get in.

He climbed up to the bedroom expecting to find three empty beds, but Korvo's was already full. He looked over to see Kor tucked in with the covers up to his chin. It wasn't cold in the room, but still Kor seemed to shiver. Kor always seemed to be cold, and tonight, he must have just gotten a chill. Tiernan thought little of it, and he brought the blanket from Bryce's bed over and placed it on top of Korvo. The shivering stopped, but the pained look on Kor's face didn't go away.

Tiernan turned out the lights and fell asleep. Things always seemed to be better when the sun was out.

***

When he woke up, the sun was already high in the sky. Korvo was gone, but that wasn't much of a surprise. To make the school work and get enough money for them to live on, he was often at Gesepi's before the sun rose. It gave him time to work with silence around him, he said. But Tiernan could tell things were tight.

What was out of the ordinary was Bryce's blanket was covering him instead of back on Bryce's bed. Attached was a note. That wasn't so strange either.

Kor often left them notes of things he needed to get done. Checklists for Bryce and Merin or things he needed them to pick up from Bethlem. He picked up the note and headed out to where Merin had already set up breakfast. She looked nice. Her hair was braided over one of her ears, and the blue dress she had on matched her eyes perfectly. Tiernan had to admit that her blue eyes scared him when they first met. The blue eyes of the elite in Kaybrum scared him still when he wasn't expecting them or saw them out of the corner of his eye. But right now, with that dress, he couldn't remember why. They looked nothing like the harsh, icy eyes the General had, and nothing Merin could ever do would scare him.

"Korvo left a note," Tiernan said, sitting down at the table. Merin was not a good cook. He guessed she had never cooked before, so when it was her turn to make breakfast, they often just had granola and fruit.

"What does it say?" Merin asked. She was always asking him to try to read things to work on his skills. She was a good teacher. Without her, he would still be bumbling through sentence-long conversations with Bryce.

"It starts with Bryce's name. Shouldn't we wait for him?" Tiernan asked. For the first time, he saw how long this note was. It looked more like a letter than a brief checklist of things to do.

"Are you just trying to get out of reading?"

Tiernan breathed in. "'Don't be mad.'"

"Tiernan, I'm not mad at you. I just want to help."

"No, that's what Kor wrote."

"He wrote what?"

Tiernan handed her the paper. He watched her eyes scan it quickly.

"Get Bryce."

"Is something wrong?" Tiernan asked. His heart skipped a beat. Yesterday, Bryce had that awful look, and Kor had gone to bed so early. He should have known this wasn't going to go away in the morning.

"Just get him," Merin said. Her eyes never left the paper, but she sat herself down in a chair. He could see her eyes reading it over and over again.

He opened the window and popped out into the morning light. It was already getting warm, but the breezes kept him company as he climbed to the top of the tower. The sides were tattered and still in terrible shape. Kor had told them not to worry about the outside. It was going to be a diamond in the rough, he had said. "Let people remember that we made something great out of the ashes of something terrible." It had sounded meaningful and powerful, but Tiernan assumed they didn't have the money. Whenever funds got short, Korvo gave rousing speeches and put on his best smile. Whatever had happened now, he was sure Kor would make him feel okay about it with a speech. And even though Bryce pretended that he wasn't moved by the speeches, he always seemed relaxed after too.

When he reached the last rung of the ladder that led to the top, Bryce was still asleep. The blanket Merin had given him was twisted around his body like he had thrashed around in his sleep.

"Bryce? Merin needs you." Tiernan tapped him on the shoulder. Bryce's eyes fluttered open.

"Hey, Tiernan."

"Merin needs you."

"Did she burn something for breakfast again?"

"No, something Kor left in his note."

"He's working today? I thought he was taking the next two days off to get all the wood Hayden was giving us."

"He probably decided he could work a few hours while you were still sleeping."

Bryce slipped a shirt over his head and tousled his hair back and forth.

"You gotta convince Kor he's doing too much," Bryce said, staring out over the city. "He's done so much, you know. For us. For everyone out there. And if I'm tired, I know he has to have his feet dragging. It doesn't do any good if I tell him. He just fake smiles at me. You know the one."

Tiernan nodded.

"But you. You might be able to convince him to slow down. I hear him, you know, at night sometimes. He gets up and works while we're sleeping. He can't keep that up."

"I know he gets up," Tiernan said. Kor always tried to be quiet as he moved around the room, but Tiernan hadn't slept well since Aer died. He had just figured that Kor hadn't either.

"Well, I guess we all need some more sleep," Bryce said, putting his hand on Tiernan's shoulder. "Let's go see Merin before she burns this whole place down."

Bryce started down the ladder. Tiernan took a second to feel the wind on his face for a moment.

"Thank you. Thank you for letting me have this family," he said to the winds. Whether he was talking to the gods or to Aer, he wasn't really sure, but the winds lifted his hair, and he took that as enough of an answer.

When he got through the window, he found Bryce standing facing away from Merin. His hands were clenched onto the back of a chair. His face had drained of color, and a single tear had rolled down Merin's face.

"What's wrong?" Tiernan asked, but he was met only with fake smiles.

"Merin and I need to talk. Will you clear the second floor of any files?" Bryce said.

"Sure," Tiernan said. He moved to the edge of the room and hid behind the door frame.

"Read it again," Bryce said.

"'Bryce, don't be mad. Actually, you can be mad. I'm letting you down again. I've been wrong this whole time. I was wrong about Aer, and I was wrong about the school, and I was wrong that I was doing enough." Merin stopped reading. "What is he talking about, Bryce?"

Bryce just shook his head. "Keep reading."

"I know that I need to do something beyond the school. You and Merin will be able to handle it. And I'm sure she is reading this now. You will do fine. Stick to the plan, and you'll be okay until you get your feet under you enough to run it on your own. Hayden might help. Bethlem will always be there. Just remember to actually pay for your drinks from time to time.

"I need to do more for you, for Aer and Tiernan. So I'm leaving for the Eastern Capital."

Tiernan gasped, but they didn't hear him.

"The General will be there. Something big is happening, and I'm going to stop it. I've walked too long along the lines non-Magics have set out for us. I've behaved, and I've failed. I tried to keep you from the horrors of this world, and I keep leading you all right into them. Things I never even knew could happen. I will not fail this time. I will get you justice."

"This is how he's getting justice?" Bryce sneered. "Walking into a suicide mission."

"You don't know that. Kor is—"

"You read it. He's going to the Eastern Capital—where they are gathering people like the General. How could it not be?"

"Kor's going?" Tiernan asked from the doorway. He thought he understood most of it, but they were talking fast, and there were some words he just didn't know. *Suicide mission. Justice.* But he understood enough. He knew *the General.* He knew *failed.*

"Kor's gone," Bryce said, sitting down for the first time. He rubbed at his hair, causing it to frizz. "Kor's gone, and I can't run a school."

"I can," Merin said. Tiernan looked up at her. The tear from earlier had dried on her cheek, but there was a focus in her eyes.

"And what about the kids?" Bryce asked. "He had taken guardianship of all of them. What happens now for them?"

"There's a second page," Merin said, turning the letter over. She started reading, "'Bryce, I have left all of the guardianship papers with

Bethlem. They are in your name. Fight for them, Bryce. Let Merin help. Don't push her away. Take care of Tiernan. I'm trusting you. I'll be back.'"

"See, he's coming back," Tiernan said. Neither of the older two looked at him. He swallowed hard. They didn't believe he was coming back. Merin's shoulders drooped, and Bryce pounded his fist into the table.

Merin finished the letter, "'May the Twelve Gods watch over you. I'll be back. Korvo.'"

He had said it twice: He would be back. It had to be true. Tiernan smiled. The others just didn't believe it. Kor had traveled alone through Hadran, a place that wanted to kill him. There was no reason he couldn't get to the Eastern Capital. It had to be a long way from Hadran. Tiernan had never even heard of such a place.

"How do you get to the Eastern Capital?" Tiernan asked after the silence had stretched a moment too long.

"Through the mountains," Bryce said. His gestures were wild. "Straight into the snow where he'll freeze himself to death in a single night."

"I don't think he'll go that way," Merin said. She rubbed Tiernan's head.

"There's no other way to go," Bryce said. He pointed at a map Kor had salvaged from someone that he had put on the wall to teach Tiernan about the country outside of Kaybrum.

"Sure there is," Merin said, walking over to the map. Tiernan followed her fingers as she drew them down outside the walls of Kaybrum, down the familiar landscape he had fled through. Her slender, pale finger then arched through the edges of the jungle to a large dot.

"You think he'll go back to Hadran?" Bryce asked.

"No, he wouldn't," Tiernan said. "Right, Bryce? You wouldn't go back there if it were you, right."

"I told you this school, what used to be the Refuge, that was my Hadran. And here I am, standing right in the middle of it."

"Merin, isn't there some other way?"

She shook her head. "He'll go to Porttown, and he'll cross the sea."

"Great, the ocean. We'll never find him," Bryce said. He rubbed his temples, but his face didn't seem to relax.

"He isn't that far ahead of us," Tiernan suggested, but Merin's soft smile made him realize that it was a stupid thing to say. They weren't going after him.

"I better get the stuff from Bethlem," Bryce said. His voice was devoid of any hint of emotion.

"Right," Merin said, "we have a school to run."

Tiernan tried to see what was going on in their eyes, but neither of them would make eye contact. Not with him, not with each other.

"I'll go tell that fancy guy, Hayden," Tiernan suggested.

Bryce just waved at him.

"Great idea," Merin said, but he wasn't sure she had even really heard him.

Bryce got up from the table and slowly made his way down the staircase. Tiernan followed closely behind.

When Bryce turned left to go toward the Wall District, Tiernan froze. If Bryce saw him now, there would be no way he would catch up to Korvo. He breathed in the count of seven. It filled his lungs with just enough bravery to turn right and run for the front gates of the city.

He didn't have a school to run. He had to help Kor.

CHAPTER ELEVEN

BRYCE

"Good morning, Bryce," Bethlem called as soon as he opened the door. His warm, dark features looked friendly as ever. The softness of his face just made Bryce want to open up about everything that was going wrong. No wonder his bar was almost always filled, even in the early mornings.

"Not so sure about that," Bryce said.

"Wake up on the wrong side of the roof this morning?" He was busy cleaning glasses and hadn't stopped to really look Bryce in the face.

"More like the wrong side of the world."

Bethlem leaned down on his elbows so he was face to face with him. "What's wrong?"

"You talked to Kor this morning?"

"Yeah, he stopped by real early. I hadn't even changed the sign over to open. Said he had pressing business."

"Did he tell you what that business was?"

"This and that. He dropped some papers off for you and Merin, but you don't usually hate paperwork that much."

"Did he tell you where he was going so early in the morning?"

"Work, I figured. We didn't chat long."

"Bethlem, Kor left. He left Kaybrum. He went after the General."

"He did what?" Bethlem's voice carried across the bar. People

74

looked up at him, and Bryce scowled. "Go to the back. I'll be there in a minute."

Bryce let himself into the back room. The same room where he had introduced Kor to Tiernan. That seemed like it had been years ago now. He felt like he had lived a decade in the last twenty-four hours.

"Here's everything he brought." Bethlem set a box down in front of Bryce. Bryce sighed. He couldn't even read the letter Kor had left them. How was he ever going to get through all of this stuff? He let his forehead hit the edge of the box.

"Tell me again where Kor is." Bethlem set a glass of cool water in front of Bryce. He lifted it, took a sip, and then the story came out. About the garden, the letter, all of it spilled out of his mouth. Bethlem was silent the entire time. His face was set in the careful and clear concern that didn't give away what was happening inside his mind.

"He says he was wrong, but what could be worse than leaving me in charge of the school?"

"Let Merin handle the school. She's smarter than the rest of us combined. You focus on the contents of this box. The kids he trusted you to protect."

"Talk about wrong. He trusted me to protect Tiernan, and he got himself tortured under my watch. I don't know why he would leave me with these charges." Bryce thumped his head against the box a few more times.

"Kor was wrong," Bethlem said.

"Yeah, I know."

"Kor was wrong about being wrong. No one else has done more for Magics in this city than him. He's just one person. But," Bethlem took a deep breath, "he was not wrong about you or Merin. He knows what you are capable of. He's seen your strength firsthand."

A voice called for Bethlem at the front of the bar.

"I'm back here," he answered. He gave Bryce a small smile. Bryce tried to smile back, but it was a strained effort. He felt tired. He had asked the gods for justice, and somehow Kor had decided it was his divine mission to get it for him. *Serves me right*, Bryce thought, slowly sorting through the piles of papers in the box. *I should know not to ask the gods for anything. If they cared enough to do something right, there would never have been nameless kids buried by the Refuge.*

"Morning, Bethlem," a much too familiar voice said. Bryce glanced up. Hayden.

"Good morning, Mr. Nagely. How can I help you?"

"I was still wondering if you had considered my offer to open another bar right outside the marketplace."

"I've been thinking, but who would run this one if I was off on the other side of town?"

"More business over there," Hayden said. Bryce wasn't even sure if he had noticed him sitting there. Probably for the best. Kor had said to get him to help, and anything that was going to come out Bryce's mouth at this point weren't going to be pleasantries.

"Plenty of business right here, or did you not see I have patrons this early?"

"I did. And I also saw that it seemed to be working just fine while you were back here talking to . . . Bryce, wasn't it?"

Bryce raised his eyebrows in acknowledgment.

"Bethlem?" a voice called from the bar again.

"You see, though, they still need me," Bethlem said. "If you'll just excuse me for a moment."

Bethlem ducked out of the doorway and disappeared into the bar.

"Did Tiernan find you? The little boy that lives with us at the school?"

"No, I haven't seen him since I was at the school. Why?"

"Never mind." *Great*, Bryce thought. Now he was going to have to go find Tiernan after this.

"If I see him, I'll let you know. I'm stopping by the school later today."

"What's your angle? You're trying to get Bethlem to move, helping the school. You're awfully friendly with Magics. I've been told you just came back into Kaybrum, but I don't remember you helping out before you left." Bryce could hear the words pouring out of his mouth, but he didn't care enough to try and stop them. A small voice in the back of his mind reminded him that Kor had specifically mentioned Hayden in his letter, but the rest of his mind just wanted to punch someone, and Hayden seemed as good a candidate as any.

"See the world a little bit, and it changes minds," Hayden laughed to himself. "Besides, Magics are an untapped market. Plenty of profit to be—"

Bryce didn't blink. His fist rose without his brain even knowing it was happening. It connected with Hayden's jaw in a second. The older boy stumbled back. His hand went immediately to what was already forming into a bruise. Bryce charged forward and grabbed him by the collar. Being so close to him, Bryce could smell him now. He smelled clean and fresh like Merin, but he also had a scent he couldn't place.

"If you could let go," Hayden said calmly. "I have some meetings I have to attend before I stop by the school, and I'd rather not look too rumpled. The face—" he winced as he brushed it with his fingers again—"well, there's nothing to do about the face now."

"I don't get you," Bryce said. Letting the fabric slip out of his hand. It was wrinkled now, but not so much that someone might notice right away.

"What is there to get? It's not like I haven't been punched before."

"And you aren't mad?"

"Being mad is bad for business. Don't punch me again, of course, and I still don't really know what that was all about."

"Magics have survived years of torment. Tortured. Branded. We are not an untapped market. We are people who are finally getting the first taste of freedom. People who are on the edge of something good, and you want to take advantage of that."

"If it makes you feel better, I want to take advantage of everyone," Hayden said. Bryce felt his hand ball into a fist again. He stepped back so as not to punch him again.

"Don't you have any self-respect?" Bryce asked. He looked Hayden over. He was everything the upper class should be. He had the look and the clothes. He had bright eyes and a dashing smile. But there was nothing that told you about who he was. It was like Hayden had just appeared out of a storybook.

"What do you mean?"

"What do you believe in besides money?"

"Same as you. People. Freedom."

"You are not the same as me. You will never understand what I have gone through, what it means to want freedom and not have it. You travel the world, and yet you know nothing. I may have learned to read months ago. I may not be able to write much more than my name. But at least I know where I stand and what I believe in. Freedom is just a start. And people? I don't believe in people. I believe in my fellow Magics. I'll take your help. So will Kor and Merin and maybe even Bethlem, although he doesn't need it. But you will *never* understand."

"Maybe someday, I hope," Hayden said. He nodded toward Bethlem, who had come in behind Bryce.

"If you understood us at all, you wouldn't say that," Bryce said.

"You might be right," Hayden said. Then he stepped by Bethlem back into the main bar.

Bethlem said nothing for a second.

"Kor wasn't wrong, you know."

"Huh?" Bryce said. His hands were finally starting to relax from the fists they had formed at his sides.

"I don't think you needed to punch the guy, but Kor wasn't wrong to trust you with the young Magics of this city. You know them. You understand them. And you'll never stop fighting for them. Everything will be okay."

"Sure it will," Bryce said in a huff. He started past Bethlem, but the man stopped him with a hand on his shoulder.

"And Kor will come back."

"He better," Bryce said.

CHAPTER TWELVE
MERIN

MERIN HAD TO PULL HERSELF TOGETHER. IF KOR WAS gone, she would have to run the school until he returned. She looked around. They were supposed to open next week.

There were desks for about fifteen children. They could seat a few smaller children together at the larger desks if needed. They may not even have that many to start. The wood was going to be delivered from Gesepi's later that day. She could put Bryce to hammering together beds. That would give him something to take his anger out on.

As much as she felt overwhelmed by everything suddenly being thrust into her lap, she couldn't help feeling like she was finally going to really help. That she was going to do enough. She had felt it when she had told Bryce she could run the school, but that confidence waxed and waned over the course of the day.

"Here to help as promised," Hayden said from the doorway.

"I'm glad you're here," Merin said.

"What are we cleaning today?" Hayden said as he looked around.

"We're not cleaning. I'm sure you heard," Merin said and then spotted the giant bruise on his chin. "What happened?"

"Just some creative differences. Nothing that can't be worked out." He had the same wide grin that Bryce had. One that drew her in immediately, but there was something about Hayden's smile that told her he was hiding the truth. *Maybe,* she thought, *he's just trying to save himself from some embarrassment.*

"If we're not cleaning, how can I assist you today?"

"Honestly, I need some opinions."

"I have those in spades," Hayden said with a chuckle. Merin tried to force herself to smile. Was she already giving up too much of her job to someone else? She shook the thought from her head. She loved Bryce and Tiernan, but they had never been to school. Someone like Hayden had.

"I'm trying to think about the curriculum. You know, everything we're going to need to teach them."

"Well, start at the beginning."

"That's just the thing. There is no beginning."

"Sure there is. Knowing nothing is a beginning."

"They don't know *nothing.* Some of these kids may have gotten a year or two of school before it became obvious they were Magics. Some of them may have been taught some at home, and some of them have no home or school to speak of. And all of them have lived their lives surviving in the city. They know more than you think."

"Nothing may have been a tad harsh," Hayden said, rubbing at his bruised chin.

"I can help make that feel better," Merin said.

Hayden waved her away, "Maybe once I've been helpful."

"If I can't teach them all the same things at the same time, I'm going to need more than just one teacher. Bethlem's got a few people coming in, but trying to make one schoolhouse is going to be difficult."

"Then don't. You can do rounds. Maybe older kids at night with Bethlem's people. Littles in the mornings with you. Having the kids live here means the school can be open whenever. And it means the older kids can go get jobs during the day. The marketplace—"

"Remember, you're trying to help me," Merin said.

Hayden laughed and raised his hands in mock defeat. "I yield. We talk about the school first."

Merin stared down at the desk they were sitting at. It was a smaller one that Bryce had brought down from the top floor. She ran her finger along the edge of the wood.

"Would you pay them full rate?" Merin asked.

"Huh?"

"Would you pay them full rate? What everyone else makes? Bryce makes so little in the flower shops, and Aer always had to work odd hours. People don't pay Magics well."

"Ahh, I see. I don't run the individual businesses, but I can put in a strong word to the people who stalls we oversee. They'll fight it. It will mean less profit for them."

"But it means people won't starve."

"People don't often think past their own front doors. Not like you guys who invite everyone in."

"Is that why you are here? Kor's open doors?"

"I must say, unfortunately, I am a much more complicated man than that."

"Still, I guess I am glad you are here, and you came back. Even when—"

"Enough about me. Let's get back to your problem. You need more teachers."

"Right, but most people who would set foot in here are Magics, and few of them want to come back to this place."

"I don't even remember what this place was," Hayden said, looking around. "Not that I think it was some sort of grand holiday to be here, but this wasn't the place that haunted my dreams, you know," Hayden said.

"I know exactly what you mean. My parents never spoke of it, and if they did, it was framed as a good thing. It wasn't until I met Bryce and Kor that I really understood it for what it was, and even then, I didn't believe it until I saw it with my own eyes."

"What was it like?"

"Horrible. Nightmares upon nightmares. Did you know they used to torture the kids here? Strapped them to tables with their arms and legs bound and did who knows what to them."

Hayden grimaced. He let his eyes drift over the room one more time. Merin followed his eyes. The place looked unassuming, with mismatched desks and chairs ordered into little rows. Books were piled in one corner for Tiernan to put on the shelves when he got back.

"Against their will?" Hayden asked.

"Does anyone agree to be tortured on their own?" Merin snapped.

"Right, of course." He rubbed the bruise on his chin again. It had turned a dark purple now, and the edges had begun to solidify.

"Let me fix that," Merin said. She stood and walked to the other side of the desk. She hesitated, but when Hayden nodded, she cupped her hand around his jawline. She could feel him swallow, but soon, all of that went away when she closed her eyes. She connected to her power, let it run through her hands like water and go toward the aching bruise. She could feel it now, the swelling and the broken capillaries. Her magic moved around them, finding places to soothe and heal.

"What is he doing here?" Bryce asked from the door.

"Bryce!" Merin said. Her hand dropped from Hayden's cheek. The bruise was yellowing now, its edges softly blending in with the rest of his face.

"What is he doing here?"

"He's helping, Bryce. And you know right now we need all the help we can get."

"Doesn't look like he's helping anyone but himself."

"She's just helping to take the edge off of this nasty bruise I got from a dust-up in the marketplace today," Hayden said.

Merin saw Bryce's eye twitch but decided not to ask.

"I was just telling Hayden about how the Refuge was before Kor got control over it."

"Yeah, well, you'll never understand." Bryce was looking at Hayden, but she couldn't help but feel like the comment was directed at her. She thought about the thick file hidden in Aer's dresser that bore Bryce's name.

"Well, I must be off," Hayden said, standing. He reached out his hand, and Merin took it, expecting a handshake. When he raised her hand to his lips and brushed it with a kiss, she was mortified. She could almost feel the heat radiating off of Bryce. "I have to go recruit some new teachers for the school. I'll see you both tomorrow."

Hayden walked out of the school, his shoulders back and confident. If he really could get more teachers for the school, they might be okay.

"I don't like him."

"You don't like any non-Magic."

"That's not true. I like Vycky and her wife."

"That's not a very long list."

"I never said it was."

"He is helping," Merin said, coming closer to Bryce and lying her forehead against his chest.

"But why?"

"As long as he's helping right now, I'm not sure it matters."

Bryce let his fingers push a little bit of her hair from her face. He let it slide through his fingers.

"We could take a midday break," he said, still looking at the lock of hair in his hand, "and go back to Aer's apartment."

Merin blushed. "But Tiernan will be back soon. We can't just leave him here alone."

"Tiernan's not back yet?"

"No, he must still be out looking for Hayden. We probably shouldn't have let him go this morning."

"I ran into Hayden this morning. He must have come straight here after, and no one in the marketplace or the Wall District has seen Tiernan. I went looking for him."

"So where is he?" Merin asked.

"My bet," Bryce said, sitting down on the edge of the desk, "he went after Kor."

"What do we do? We can't let him be out there."

"He'll be okay, Merin. He survived out there once and with a lot less skills than he has now."

"But what if he was always meant to reach Kaybrum? What if the General had someone watching over him, and now he's just out there on his own?"

"Do you want me to go after him? You could run the school for a few days, and I could go."

"Does it make me a bad person that I want to say no? I don't want to do this alone, Bryce. I need you."

"We need each other. Tiernan will find Kor. They'll be safe together."

Bryce stood and put his arms around her. She nuzzled back into his chest.

"We'll be okay."

"Sure. We won't let Kor be wrong about that."

CHAPTER THIRTEEN
KORVO

PORTTOWN WAS NOT NEARLY AS BIG AS KOR HAD THOUGHT it was going to be. In the village where he had grown up, the men had talked about it like it stretched on for days, and fishermen were known for their tall tales, but this was a bit underwhelming.

The docks had a few ships. Mostly small vessels meant for running up and down the coast for quick fishing trips. Nothing more than a day or two. Not the kind of ship he needed. It wasn't an easy trip to get all the way to the Eastern Capital from Hadran, but at least he knew ships.

He lingered around the larger ships, listening to the men talk about what they had in their holds and where they were going next. It would be easiest to trade some work for passage to someone going directly where he wanted to go, but he had no luck.

Maybe he had misinterpreted whatever the cards were telling him. It wouldn't be the first time he had read the fuzzy future a little askew. His readings hadn't gotten better after he had stuck his hand into Tiernan's flames a few months before. The scars weren't as bad and the hand had healed quickly thanks to Merin, but she couldn't fix the connection he had with the cards.

He sighed. With the sea air in his lungs, he thought he would feel better about this plan, but instead, he felt worse. He rested on a barrel someone had left sitting out. He closed his eyes, trying to picture what Bryce and Merin were doing right then. Merin was probably rearranging the books on the shelf for the tenth time, preparing for the students. Bryce was probably smashing the hammer much too hard on the nails as he made the beds from the wood that should have been delivered by now.

Kor had left three days ago. It had been hot even in the wee morning hours when he started out. It had taken him an hour or so to get far enough down the road that he was sure no one would recognize him. With his hand being as mangled as it was, the Raven tattoo was hardly noticeable. A leather merchant had picked him up a few hours outside of the city walls. The man was content to ride in silence, so Kor hadn't had to make up a story to tell the man. Although there wasn't much to tell. He had to head back to Hadran for some unfinished business.

He tapped at the cards. "Some justice," he said to himself as he watched the dock workers go by.

The day stretched out in front of him. With no other choice, he began to set up shop. He laid the cards out in front of him a little at a time and studied each one. He didn't bother reading them. This was only for show. Sailors always wanted to know their fortunes. It didn't matter if he was a real Magic or not.

Within ten minutes, he had his first bite.

"Read the cards for me," a man said. He was about as tall as Kor but much wider. His muscles blocked the setting sun from view. His skin was much darker than Kor's own, but he had similar yellow-green eyes. Kor was back in Hadran, all right.

"I don't read for free," Kor said. The man nodded and pulled out a few coins and laid them down next to the stack of cards. Kor nodded and shuffled the cards.

"What is it you want to know?" Kor asked. The cards didn't really need to know, but sometimes it helped him figure out the future when it was shrouded with fog.

"I've got this feeling in my bones," the sailor said. "Something that comes and goes with bad storms, but it doesn't look like it's going to storm, but my knee, it's been aching all day."

"Let's see what the cards say." It had been quite some time since he had looked at the cards for what was going out on the water, but that's how his family had used his powers for years. Korvo tried to push everything out of his mind and closed his eyes while he breathed in and out. It wouldn't help this man if he got the General's ice-cold eyes mixed up with the sea again.

Slowly, Kor pulled cards from the deck. As he laid them down, the images were clear and sharp. His eyes flung open to stare at the cards in front of him.

"Something wrong?" the sailor asked. He leaned in to look at the cards.

"Just vivid. Let me continue." With each card, another flash. They were pieces to a puzzle that he still had to concentrate to put together. He saw the man on a ship in a different harbor. He saw large nets being loaded onto the ship. He saw the man crying in his bunk on the ship, holding tight to his stomach.

"It's not a storm," Kor said. The future was always hard to explain to someone. Sometimes things could change, but most of the time, it was destiny. "Maybe a sickness." He went on to explain the images he saw. The sailor nodded his head along with him. He put another coin down and walked back to his ship.

That was why futures rarely changed. If the man had stayed away from the docks, he might have been spared whatever would cause him harm, but people were people, and they had to live their lives despite what the future might bring.

With the sailor stowed away on his ship, Kor sat in the darkening night, waiting for the next customer. A few eyed him wearily, and he wondered if he was being stupid to display magic out in the middle of Hadran like this. Telling the future had once gotten him sentenced to death, but he couldn't forget how alive the cards had felt. How clear their images were. Was it just because he was back in his home country, because he was near the sea, or was it something else? Had Merin been able to fix some of the connections that had been frayed? Or maybe he was just on the right path now.

"Are you desperate or stupid?" a woman's voice asked from the shadows.

"Both seem good," Kor said, squinting to make out a face.

"What about crazy?" she asked, moving into the limited light coming from the dock's lanterns.

"I don't know if I would go that far," Kor said. The woman was beautiful. Her skin was dark as the midnight sea, and her hair was piled in large braids around her head. The gold jewelry on her nose and ears caught the light. "Do you prefer one of the three?" Kor asked. He slid the cards from the barrel in front of him back into his pack. This woman was not coming to have her fortune read. He didn't need the cards to tell him that.

"You're from here," she said, looking him over without acknowledging his question. "But I think it's been a while."

Kor felt her eyes judging him where he sat. He let her look as he looked back. She was taller than Merin was. Maybe as tall as Aer had been. She looked stronger than Aer's wispy frame. Aer had always seemed wild and untamed. This woman looked powerful, like a panther in the jungle.

"Perhaps."

"A Magic I've never seen telling fortunes on my dock," she said. "What should I do?"

"Your dock?"

While every inch of her seemed to be filled with prowess, she didn't look like she was dressed wealthy enough to have a government position. He looked closer for a clue as to who she might be.

"That's what I said."

"How do you know I'm not just making quick cash pretending to read fortunes?"

"Because you reacted before you saw what was on the card. I have eyes."

"Must be why it's your dock." Kor wasn't sure what to do here. She didn't seem to have any intention to turn him in or send him away. But there was always an angle when people threw their power into play. Best to go along until he knew more.

"You don't seem crazy. You any good with those cards?"

"You want a reading?"

"I want to know where that ship is going."

"Shouldn't you know where things are going on your dock?"

"Shouldn't you know magic is illegal?"

"Foreign port. Didn't really come with a name tag," Kor said, still trying to weave his way through this encounter. How had he gotten so used to the directness of the people in Kaybrum? He was out of practice for a conversation like this. For the millionth time, he wondered if he had made the wrong choice.

But the cards had been so alive.

"Describe it." Her voice was deadpan, but Kor could sense the edge to it. She had stepped closer and further into the light. What he had thought were decent clothes were much more threadbare than he had originally thought.

"Big port. Multiple docks. Much nicer than your little one here. White stone buildings near the water. Rocky beaches further down the line. A tall tower sticking out."

"Sepsrym."

"Oh, yes, Sepsrym. Clearly," Kor said sarcastically.

"The Eastern Capital," she explained in a huff. Kor flinched.

"But when I asked the dock hands, they said they were going south through Prong's Pass."

"Looking to go somewhere?"

Get it together, Kor thought. *You just gave away more information than you meant to.* But so had she. He finally knew a ship going toward the Eastern Capital. He could sneak onto the ship before they left with the high tide in the morning.

"I've traveled a bit," Kor said, trying to regain his footing in the conversation.

"How would you feel about traveling with me?"

"Depends on where you're going."

"Looks like we're going to Sepsrym."

"Then, unless you are trying to kill me, torture me, or turn me in to the authorities, I'm in." After years of careful planning, daily lists, and nightly agonizing over the right thing to do, Kor was surprised by his own answer.

"I can guarantee that last thing," she said, sticking out her hand. First the glint from her golden rings caught his eyes, but then something much more interesting. A pink scar had risen on her skin, right in the webbing between her pointer finger and her thumb. An X.

"A pirate?"

"And you're a Magic. Both illegal. Looks like we'll have to trust each other."

"Fair enough." Kor stuck out his right hand. Her eyes didn't even seem to register the mangled nature of his hand. Maybe it was the light, but she didn't seem to care.

"We leave tonight."

"Tonight? But it's low tide, and the wind won't pick up till morning."

"The Black Phoenix isn't the fastest ship. If we want to beat something like the Angel Chaser over there, we're going to need as much of a head start as one night can give us."

"I've been around these docks all day, and I have not seen a ship called the Black Phoenix."

"Wouldn't moor her here in the daylight. It's like you've never had to hide from the authorities," she said with a laugh. "Midnight, that last dock over there. Don't be late."

"Wouldn't miss it."

The woman walked away. She had almost disappeared back into the shadows when she turned back around.

"Dacia."

"Korvo."

She nodded once, and then she was gone.

Midnight. He had a few hours to kill. He could find a few more sailors who wanted to flirt with destiny. Or, he jingled the money in his pocket, he could find some warm food and fill his belly.

CHAPTER FOURTEEN

MERIN

"What do you mean Korvo left?" Hayden yelled. Merin shushed him. He sat back down on the chair.

"I thought you knew," Bryce said. "It's not like we lied."

"We open tomorrow," Hayden said.

"We?" Bryce snapped.

"Bryce," Merin attempted to placate him. "Now is not the time—"

"No. There is no 'we.' Not with him. He's helped, sure. I'll give him that. But this is a school for Magics."

"I'm just trying to say that things aren't going to look good for you, and since I've thrown in my hat with you all as a benefactor and teacher, you have to keep this a secret."

"Don't you think they're going to find out? Councilman Jaqui is coming by in the morning."

"Then you lie. You lie until people believe it's working."

"You were just upset at us because you thought we were lying, and lying is your brilliant plan?" Bryce walked away. He rested his hand against the wall and hit it hard a few times. Then he took a deep breath.

"Let me do the lying. You just do your best not to punch someone," Hayden said.

"Merin, I hate him."

"Both of you stop," Merin said. She was tired of listening to them bicker all day long. As grateful as she was for their help, it would do nothing if they couldn't be in the same room as each other without a fight breaking out.

"Councilman Jaqui is doing a ribbon cutting. It's publicity. Smiles and pats on the back. Then, you guys know, they will lose interest in this place. We'll just tell him Korvo is feeling very ill and didn't want to potentially get any of the new students sick."

"And when do you lose interest?" Bryce whispered under his breath.

"Enough," Merin said. "We'll go with Hayden's plan for now. If it doesn't work, I'll figure it out. Both of you go home. We have a big day tomorrow."

"I'll walk you out," Bryce said with a sigh when she didn't budge.

"I'm staying here. I have a few more changes I'd like to make."

"You are not staying in this building overnight."

"She'll be fine. There's a nice big lock on the door," Hayden said, getting up from his chair and adjusting his hair.

"You don't get a say," Bryce said. His eyebrows knit together. Merin could tell it wasn't anger that was going through his mind; it was fear. She placed her hand on Bryce's arm.

"I won't stay the night. Just a few more minutes without you both fighting to get the last few things done before the opening." She leaned in close so only he could hear. "I promise."

"Fine."

Hayden started to open his mouth.

"Goodnight, Hayden," Merin said. He closed his mouth and headed out the door. Bryce gave her one last look and headed out behind him.

She walked around the main school room. It had come together over the last few days. She rearranged the books on the shelf for the umpteenth time. She had gotten more donated from some of her parent's rich friends, and Hayden had brought even more. Of course, they still had all of the ones Bethlem had found for Korvo when he wanted them to teach Tiernan and Bryce how to read.

Tiernan and Kor. Merin took the copy of *The Fire Prince* off the shelf. She ran her finger lovingly over the little boy on the cover. Where were they right now? Were they safe? Had Tiernan found Kor? Were they coming back?

She took a deep breath and put the book back on the shelf and headed back to Aer's apartment.

She should start thinking of it as her space, she told herself, but she knew it wouldn't be that easy.

Merin tried to lay down on the bed, but her eyes wouldn't seem to close. Anytime they did, she just kept hearing Bryce talking about "we" and the comment he made about Hayden not understanding the Refuge. They replayed in her mind over and over, and each time she rewatched it in her mind, she grew more and more convinced he was talking to her.

"Then let me understand," she said to the darkness. She threw her pillow in frustration when the darkness refused to answer back. The pillow hit the dresser.

Bryce's file. She got up from the bed. A single breeze pulled at her nightgown, but she shrugged it off. Winds were always still coming and going in Aer's apartment like they were looking for her, or like they forgot she was gone. Aer always said the wind had a memory that wasn't tied to time like they were.

She rummaged through the clothes in the drawer. They looked mostly like they had been Kor's. A few work shirts, a pair of pants, and Bryce's file. In the feeble lamp light, it looked more imposing than before.

She brought it to the bed and carefully opened it. She laid the cover page down first, and then she began to read in earnest.

It was morning when she had finished. Her eyes were red-rimmed and achy from the salty tears dripping down her face. The first rays of sunlight trickled in through the window, and she knew it was time to get up. She had to face the day, but no amount of book rearranging could make her forget what she had read. Not for a moment. Not ever.

She put the file back into the drawer and covered it up again. Her movements were labored, but she didn't have time to shake the wasted sleep from her face.

It was time to open the school.

Bryce was already there. He was dressed in some of Merin's father's clothes she had taken from her house. They only fit in places, but he looked nice. She wondered if he had come in early just to make sure she hadn't spent the night there.

Last night, she had chalked his fear up to something silly—superstition—but now she knew why the Refuge had haunted him so, and she was surprised he could even make it through the door on his own.

"Worried?" Bryce asked, leaning down to put his forehead against hers.

"Why?" Merin asked.

"It looks like you didn't sleep last night," he said.

"Well, it's a big day," she said noncommittally. "You know I can't fix it myself," she said, trying to distract him.

"You look beautiful," he said.

She blushed.

"The councilman gets here in just a few minutes." She pushed him away. It was like she saw everything through fresh eyes. She had never understood. She realized that more than ever now. No one had.

People started arriving. Most were kids or people involved in making it happen. Bethlem waved from his spot on the other side of the crowd, and Merin waved back.

"Good luck today," Vycky said, coming up to the doorway. She was holding several big bouquets of flowers that Merin didn't recognize. She was sure Bryce knew them.

"Thank you, Vycky," Merin said. "You can put them on that front desk if you want."

"Where would you like Sylvia to put the rest?" Vycky asked. Merin looked up. Vycky's wife was pulling a small wagon behind her with six smaller bouquets. She and Bryce were laughing about something.

"Umm," Merin said, looking around. "Around the hearth. We can move them later to rooms to spruce them up a little bit."

Vycky nodded. "Sylvia, Bryce, be dears and go put those on the hearth for Merin."

They moved quickly, and Merin couldn't help smiling as all of the plants pulled toward Bryce. They may have been cut flowers, but there was still enough connection in the Earth for them to reach for him. Bryce, on the other hand, scowled and pushed the flowers further from him.

Maybe he just doesn't want to get pollen on his clothes, Merin thought. There were too many things to think about today to linger on Bryce's reaction to flowers.

"Let's open this school," Bryce said. His hand lingered on her lower back as he walked by her toward the crowd. Councilman Jaqui was here now. His council robes swayed slightly in the breeze. He was waving enthusiastically to the crowd, but the crowd had very mixed emotions about his presence. While the Council had started helping out Magics, most people weren't ready to let go of what they had tried to do.

Merin didn't blame them. If Kor hadn't invited Jaqui himself, she would have just let them open without any fanfare, but she couldn't go about changing Kor's plans when Korvo was supposedly upstairs too sick to attend.

"Kor is so sorry that he couldn't attend this morning," Merin heard the half-truth come from her lips.

"I'm sure he can watch from a window up there and know that he has helped this city."

"I'm sure he's thinking about it now," Merin said with a hollow smile.

"Let's cut this ribbon and get these kids into school," Jaqui said. Merin smiled for real that time. So much work and sacrifice had led up to this moment, and with another grand wave to the crowd and a ceremonial ribbon cut in half, the school was open.

The crowd thinned out slowly. The first to leave were people like Vycky and Bethlem. People who had seen the transformation a few times through the last few weeks. Next went all of the adult Magics, who glanced around inside for a minute and then headed off to work. They couldn't afford to miss too much work with the amounts they were getting paid. When the crowd was mostly just kids, Merin decided it was time to start. She invited them all to come in.

They followed her but stood awkwardly on the edges of the desks.

"Please come and sit down," Merin said. But the group hesitated. They eyed the room like it could all disappear in front of them. "Would a tour help?" Merin asked. A few kids mumbled affirmatives, so she split them into groups. The older kids were going to walk around with Bryce, the middle group with her, and the youngest group assigned to Hayden, who had been uncommonly quiet that morning.

"I don't often deal with little ones," Hayden whispered into her ear as she got them sorted.

"You know the least about what happened in the Refuge. They won't know much either. It's a perfect fit. Besides, most of those older kids know Bryce. They'd feel safer with him around."

"Okay, but I can't guarantee this will be a top-quality tour."

"Just make sure they aren't afraid."

Hayden nodded and called for his group. "All right there, little humans, let's go see what we can find."

Merin called for her group, and she headed up the stairs. Out of the corner of her eye, she saw Bryce's group, which had been speaking in hushed tones in the corner, spread out across the bottom floor.

When she returned with her group, she found Hayden sitting on top of one of the desks, reading a story to the littlest kids. They were all gathered around one of the larger tables. The kids were smiling, and walking into the scene made her little group lose the last remainder of tension they had been holding on to. She got them seated in a small group.

Hayden's story wrapped up, and she could see there was tension all over his smiling face.

"You seem to do great with them," Merin said.

"It's all an act. I've been stressed since I got here this morning."

"Well, we can switch now," she offered. He graciously nodded. She watched for a second as he strolled over to the group sitting behind desks.

"Ms. Merin? What are we going to learn today?" a small boy with brown hair asked.

"Let's start by figuring out what you all know," Merin replied.

"But I don't know anything," a little girl said.

"Of course you do. You know lots of things. You know your names. You know you're safe here now. You know how to move around the city. And you know how to use your magic."

"But that's not stuff you learn in school? At least I don't think it is," another child said.

"Sure it is. You need all those things in school."

"You need to know magic? But that's why we weren't allowed in school before," the brown-haired boy asked.

"But that's what makes us special. So let's start there for today. Everyone take a deep breath." She walked them through Kor's breathing techniques for the next few minutes. She described how the inner light that they felt within them was their connection to the elements. She had them go around the table and describe what their lights looked like.

They ranged from a glowing purple to a dark brown that shone like molasses. She tried to imagine each one of them as clearly as she could see her own light.

"What does it feel like when you are in control of your magic?" Merin asked them.

"I know. My inner light thingy, it feels smooth," one of the little girls said. Her light had been the color of grains drying in the sun.

"Good. Anyone else?"

The little boy with magic the colors of pink tulips shouted out, "Mine feels warm like when you touch the side of a lantern. But when I do too much, it feels like when you walk with socks over a rug. It stings."

"It feels electric?" Merin asked. The little boy nodded. "Good. Anyone else? What does it feel like when you don't feel like you're in control?"

"It feels spiky, like when you sing too loud and your throat is scratchy but like on the inside."

"It feels like a dam about to burst," Bryce said from behind her shoulder.

"Oh, you're back!" Merin said. She hadn't noticed that Bryce's group was hovering around the outside of the desks again.

"I think they'll all stay for today," Bryce said, leaning in to whisper.

"You take over here, and I'll get them settled into something," Merin said.

Bryce nodded. The kids clamored to be near him, and he smiled when they moved toward him.

By the time they had the last few kids tucked away in their beds for the night, Merin could hardly keep her eyes open.

"I'll walk her home."

Merin lifted her head enough to see Hayden talking to Bryce. Bryce nodded.

She hadn't realized until now that with Kor gone, that meant

Bryce would have to be here overnight to watch over the kids. He was going to have to stay in the Refuge.

"I'll stay," she said.

"You're worthless here tonight," Bryce said, pushing the hair out of her face. "Get some sleep. The gods know one more night in this place won't kill me."

She tried to say something, to find the words to tell him he didn't have to do this, but they were lost in a mix of confusion that had no way of coming out of her mouth in time before Hayden pushed her out into the nighttime air.

"Bryce said your place is close."

She nodded. "It used to be Aer's place."

"If it's so close, there's no need for you to be staying at the school. There has to be some separation between personal and business. Otherwise, you'll never get away from it all."

"It's not that," she said, trying to get the words to come out right.

"I get it. You want to stay with Bryce. Trust me, I got the memo that you two are together. And, even if I didn't, Bryce would kill me where I stand if I did anything other than take you directly home."

"No. It's not about that." The words were right there. She opened her mouth to let them come out, but the only sound that she made was a sob. The feelings she had been holding back all day couldn't contain themselves anymore. She sobbed so hard she had to stand still for a moment just to stay on her feet. There were tears of relief and tears of joy, but mostly, there were tears for Bryce and all of those kids who had ever spent a night in the Refuge. She wondered if any of them would sleep tonight.

"I'll make you some tea," Hayden said when they finally got to her door.

Merin did not respond.

"This is the only tea you have on hand," Hayden commented as he rustled around in the small kitchen. "I'll have to get you to come down and sample some of the tea from the merchant who just started in the corner stall on the eastern side. Quality stuff from the East."

Merin let him prattle on without any response. He continued babbling about the marketplace as the tea steeped. Merin didn't speak until after she had her first sip. The tea scorched her tongue but somehow stopped the whirlpool in her mind long enough to get out a few words.

"You don't understand," she said.

"You all keep saying that. I know I'm not a Magic, but I think I deserve a little benefit of the doubt. I am not out to get you," Hayden said letting his teacup hit a little too fiercely onto the table. A single drop spilled out onto the wood. Merin swiped it up with a finger.

"Just look," she pulled the file out of the drawer. She pulled all but the first cover page from the file and plopped them down in front of Hayden.

"This is what they have been through."

She let her head drop to the table as Hayden skimmed through the documents. She didn't want to see his face. She was too worried that even as a complete outsider, his face would be a mirror of her own.

Their tea had grown cold by the time Hayden set them down. His forehead was creased in a way that showed both confusion and horror.

"Who was this?" Hayden asked.

"Does it matter? There were thousands of files like this in the Refuge."

"Did you keep them all?"

"No, we burned them. This one just somehow ended up getting saved. I read it last night." She gathered up all the paper and slipped it back into the folder in the drawer.

"I need some time to process all of this," Hayden said. "I'll see you in the morning for the first round of students."

With Hayden gone, she was alone with her thoughts again, but one thought was louder than all of the rest. She needed to understand more than just words.

CHAPTER FIFTEEN
TIERNAN

A cart had taken Tiernan to the border, but it had taken him another hour to convince himself to cross.

Finally, he took one more step across the border. He cringed like something would fly out and attack him, but nothing did, and no one even looked at him. He watched their faces instead. This close to the border there were quite a few people who looked like him and still some that looked like Merin and Bryce. There were people with darker skin than his that came from the most southern part of Hadran. He marveled at all of the people so consumed by their daily lives they didn't give a single thought to a small child traveling by themselves. Tiernan didn't mind, of course.

The further he went into the country the more he blended in, and the less people seemed to care about him. Soon, he moved off the paths to cut through the jungle. If he had any hope of finding Kor, he couldn't take the long way around. So into the jungle he went.

This was still the edge of the great forests that made Hadran lush and dense with vegetation. It wouldn't be too dangerous as long as he kept close enough to the city that he could easily find his way out if he got lost. Too deep in, and he wouldn't be able to see the sky enough to make sure he was headed in the right direction.

He traveled like that for two days, stopping only for a few hours to let a small fire keep him company when it was too dark to walk. In Kaybrum, it was almost never fully dark unless you were in the walls, but out here in uninhabited Hadran, he couldn't see where he was placing his feet.

He could have held fire in his hand as he walked, but that would be much harder to explain away than just a fire on the ground like he was camping out. Hadran was dangerous for his kind.

He placed the palm of his hand against the brand that marked him for execution. He took a deep breath and watched the fire. It surged and flickered with a fierceness that he wasn't used to. Maybe it was his memories projecting themselves into the flames, or it could have been the nagging sensation that whatever had caused him to lose control was still inside of him somewhere.

He felt his eyelids droop. They felt heavy, and he wasn't sure he could keep them open all night, but he didn't trust this fearful fire to be left to its own devices. He scoured around where he had stopped and found some rocks he could use to ring the fire in case it decided to try and spread while he was asleep.

In Hadran, he couldn't trust anything, not even his own fire.

It was still dark when he woke up, but the fire was still contained within his rock barrier. He took a deep breath.

He would find Kor today, and if he didn't, he would get closer to him. He kept walking. The sun rose slowly, illuminating his path. He had gotten further in the night than he had thought. He could smell the sea breeze. It stung his nose.

He rushed into the morning. When he found Kor, he would convince him to come back, and they would be able to go back to Merin and Bryce.

Tiernan broke into a run. The trees began to thin out even more, and when he broke through the clearing, he could see all of Porttown below him.

CHAPTER SIXTEEN
BRYCE

AFTER THE FIRST NIGHT IN THE SCHOOL, BRYCE NEEDED air. He needed space. The nightmares had made him toss and turn. As soon as one of the volunteers came to start breakfast, Bryce ran out the door. The first few steps, he gasped for air like he had been holding his breath for the entire night. Then he started calming his breathing. Deep breath in. Count. Let it out. Repeat. It helped separate the daytime from the night.

He headed to the garden. The plants rushed to him, but he pushed them away.

"Give me a minute," he told them with his thoughts, but he wasn't sure plants knew what a minute was. But they listened. They turned their faces back to the sun. Bryce climbed up into his favorite tree. The leaves surrounded him. They shifted and turned until they blocked him from view down below. He hadn't asked, but they seemed to read his mind.

Once he knew he was invisible to the passerby, he let the tears run down his face. For the first time since Kor left, he let his feelings take over. The leaves moved to catch the tears, and Bryce watched as they dropped from leaf to leaf until they hit the ground.

Korvo was gone, and he had left too much up to Bryce.

He had left, and there wasn't much hope he was going to come back. There was no way to reach him. He had left him in charge of people's lives. The last time he had done that, Tiernan ended up in a ball of fire just moments from death.

Something clicked for Bryce all of a sudden. If the room where the General had held him had messed with his magic, maybe the collar had messed with Tiernan's. What if he lost control? He was probably somewhere in the middle of Hadran, all alone.

The tears threatened again, but they did not fall. It was the time for action. And the first thing he needed to do was tell Merin.

A week went by. The school was running well enough, but he still hadn't figured out how to tell Merin about his powers.

He wasn't really needed throughout the day. In the mornings, he would stay with Merin while the kids worked on things connected to magic, but as soon as Hayden took over with everything else, he was out the door. Hayden had been coming most days as soon as they had reached the midmorning.

Some days, he didn't come, and Merin made do somehow. She hadn't asked Bryce for help, and Bryce wasn't sure if that was because she didn't want to bother him or if she didn't think he could help. And either way, he didn't really feel like finding out which one it was.

This morning, he was running to get supplies that Merin had asked for in the kitchen. Feeding hungry kids was a little more than they had bargained for, but Hayden had made it a little easier on them with the merchants giving them a deal. Bryce wondered how well they would be doing if it wasn't for Hayden.

"Well, if it isn't Bryce," Hayden said over the crowd that had gathered in front of the produce that Bryce had been sent to pick up.

"If you were going to be here, Hayden, why didn't you just bring this to the school when you came by? I have enough things to do."

"Like?"

"Work."

"Right. You know I still have a market to run? Things in the works?"

"Doesn't your family run the marketplace?" Now he was just being snotty because he could. Merin was grateful for Hayden being there, but Bryce couldn't let it go.

"I'm my fathers' only child, and someday this whole thing is going to be under my control."

"I'm sure you'll be very prosperous, but maybe make sure Merin knows you aren't going to be playing school with her forever."

"What are you saying?" Hayden asked.

"I'm saying you're going to run out of interest in Magics before too long. Everyone does. Once the headlines stop, people start letting things go back to the way they were. Convinced that by helping for two minutes they are good, just people. You're no different."

"But I want to help Magics," Hayden said. "I want to help you all."

"Sure. But you have a marketplace to run."

"A marketplace where I've allowed Magic business to happen and hired my own security to cut down on the amount of Watchers in this area. I'm not the bad guy, Bryce."

"Why?" Bryce asked, looking down at his feet. He couldn't understand this rich kid.

"Why what?" Hayden said.

"Why do you want to help us? What makes it important to you?"

Hayden looked around at the bustling marketplace. He started to explain, but Bryce stuck out a hand to stop him.

"If it's just about profits, you can save your breath."

"You think I'm a bad person for thinking of profit, but that's . . ."

"I don't. I mean, I did, but now, at least I realize that, in some way, we're all equal in your mind. All people are just dollar signs to you, and that includes me and Merin and all other Magics. You might be one of the few people I know who sees any sort of equality."

"You know—"

"I'm not done. It doesn't mean I like it. Or you. Your loyalty is always in question when you're following your own self-interests."

"That's a little unfair," Hayden said, moving toward him.

"Maybe a little, but not totally." Bryce looked at the bushels of food that he had come to bring back to the school. Hayden was helping, and as much as he hated to admit it, without him, they would have had to go begging to the Council for more funds, and with Kor's absence, the chances of them shutting down the whole operation grew significantly.

"If you hurt Merin in any way, or you let her down, I won't forgive you, and . . ." His fingers balled into a fist.

"I've already had you punch me once," Hayden said, putting up his hands in mock defeat. "I know the consequences, but I really think that someday you'll see I want to do more than just help with food and other easy things. Merin, she's—"

"Don't finish that sentence. I already know that she's brilliant, patient, and kind. She's amazing. I've known her for a lot longer."

"But you keep her at arm's length," Hayden said. His eyes had turned serious in a way that decrying his character had not.

"I do not," Bryce said, but he knew he was. He felt it when she snuggled close to him or suggested they walk through the garden when she had a break.

"All she wants is to understand you. She wants to be let in. No matter how dark it might be in that angry little brain of yours, she wants to see it."

"You don't understand," Bryce snapped.

"There's that line again. I don't understand. Merin doesn't understand. Let her understand, or you're going to finally push her away. Pushing people away won't keep them safe. Kor pushed you all away, and it hasn't made your lives any easier."

Bryce grunted.

"You don't have to listen to me," Hayden continued. "Push her away all you want. Just give some of us an opportunity."

Bryce's eyes snapped to Hayden's, and he grabbed the older boy by the collar of his shirt.

"You want to be a man of action now?" Hayden teased. "Then just do the action that's going to matter. Talk to her."

Bryce let him go, and Hayden smoothed out his collar.

"Now, this has been scintillating, but I have a very dull meeting to attend. Have a good day, Bryce."

Bryce watched Hayden disappear into the bustle of the marketplace. He took a few deep breaths before starting back with the food.

The baskets were full, and the wagon he used was not the best. It was a hand-me-down from Vycky, and the front left wheel seemed to move slightly off from the others. It would work for now, but eventually it would be another expense they would have to incur.

He should go by Vycky's for a few shifts to pick up some cash they could put into savings for when the wagon finally broke down. He got to the street that would lead him to Vycky's door, but his feet wouldn't turn.

Avoiding Vycky and the garden had become more of a routine than he wanted to admit. The plants connected with him in a way he worried might rip him apart. He used to have to find his connection to them before he could sense what they needed or get them to grow. After his stint in the prison the General had created, the plants reached out to him. Sometimes it felt like they were pulling at his magic. The light would swell inside of him, and he felt like he was bound to burst at some point. Even in Vycky's shop with cut flowers, he would turn around and buds would have opened that he hadn't intended. He wasn't losing control; he'd lost it. His inner light, normally vine-like as it moved through him, was more a waterfall of energy that sprayed and splattered wherever it saw fit.

He still needed to tell Merin. He hated to admit that Hayden was right. But he didn't need to tell her everything. She could live without knowing how they tortured him. That was all in the past, but in the future, she could be let into that.

It wasn't something he was looking forward to, but maybe she could at least understand.

CHAPTER SEVENTEEN
KORVO

THE SHIP WAS DARK, BUT THE SAILS SUCKED IN THE LIGHT of the moonlight. Korvo couldn't see what was being loaded, but he could see the flashes of swords and jewelry as people passed by him to load the ship.

Pirates, Kor thought. *How did I end up here?* He took a deep breath. His belly was full of food, and while the cards had been pulling for him to read them, he wouldn't let himself, lest it be something that made him turn around.

He couldn't let the General do something else. He had to finish this now before something worse happened. Gathering people in the East was only a recipe for disaster, and he had to get there, even if it meant going with pirates.

"Coming, Korvo?" Dacia whispered in his ear. He hadn't heard her approach him at all.

"Let's go." He made his way up the gangplank.

On the ship, things flooded back to him from his childhood. He had been raised on a boat. Running along the warm, sun-soaked boards. He looked over the ship he was on now. There was no sun, but there was still the feeling that something good was happening with the soft sway of the boat in low tide.

"How are we making it out of here?" Korvo asked, but Dacia had already moved on. She sent people scattering as she went. They ran to their jobs. Sails were hoisted. He heard the crack of the breeze against the sail.

"Aer would make a ship like this fly," he said to himself. Aer had never been out of the city. She said the wind brought her what she needed to know about the world outside of Kaybrum. He closed his eyes and imagined just for a minute what it would have been like to sail with her. The wind would have sprayed them as they raced through the waves toward whatever star he chose to follow. He could see her smile every time the sails went taught.

But here, even when the sails were raised, the breeze hardly lifted them at all.

"Why bother with the sails?" Kor asked when a sailor stood by long enough to listen.

"You'll see."

The breezes began to spin around them. Then the sails cracked and whistled until they were full. The boat jolted to life, and Kor had to blink to make sure his daydream hadn't come true. He pinched himself. He was awake. Barely in the night could he make out the person who seemed to be calling the winds. Dacia. No wonder people parted in front of her.

"She's a Magic," Kor said, but the sailor had already moved on. Of course she was. That's why they would be leaving at night. They would be able to move in and out of ports so much easier than anyone else as long as they weren't caught. Pirate was starting to sound about right.

"Impressed?" Dacia said when they had made it past the dock and far out into the open ocean. The natural breeze had caught the sails, and even without Dacia, they were moving pretty rapidly. Although, Kor could see what she had meant about this not being the fastest boat.

"I've seen something similar," he said.

"Should have guessed from someone who's so well-traveled." Now that they were out in the open ocean, sailors had started putting lanterns around the dock. Someone lit one near where Kor and Dacia were standing. Kor could see her better than he had before. She looked ragged. Her eyes had severe bags underneath them, and she was breathing heavily.

"Does it take a lot to move the ship?" he asked.

"Takes a lot to do anything these days," she said.

"I am well aware of how that feels," he said, holding up his hand in the light. She nodded.

"Why are you chasing that ship?" Kor asked. He had already thrown his hat into the ring; he might as well know what was happening on the ship.

"Their cargo," she said. Her voice had a slight edge to it, and Kor didn't want to press much further. It was awfully easy for someone to end up overboard. "Why do you want to go east?"

"Unfinished business."

"Right. Clear enough."

He was glad she didn't push any further. He wasn't really sure what he would say.

"There's room for you in the crew quarters. You've slept in a hammock before?"

"Of course."

"Great."

"Dacia, why am I here?"

"We're going east? I thought we just talked about that," she said.

"But why invite me if you weren't even sure I knew how to sleep on a ship, let alone do anything?"

"Cards are useful. Knowing what's coming out here can't hurt."

"Dacia," he said as she started to walk away. "Which way is my new hammock?"

"Right down the stairs there and to the left, although I wouldn't waste my time looking for a hammock that looks new. See you in the morning for a reading, Korvo."

Kor went down the steps. Out of the lights from the deck, he stopped on the stairs and let his eyes adjust. To one side was the galley. He could smell it before he could even see it. Salted meats and apples caught his nose immediately. The other side had twelve hammocks strung along the beams in the ceiling. Most of the hammocks had stuff tucked inside them from the different crew members. Some had blankets, others more personal items. Kor didn't look for very long. No need to make any enemies on the first night. When he got to the second to last hammock, nothing was sitting within the folds of the fabric.

"Guess this is home," he said, reaching up to tug on the support ropes just to make sure no one had loosened them to punish the new guy.

The ship rocked. Kor stumbled, and his arm ended up caught in the ropes.

"Not found your sea legs yet?" a voice came out of the shadows.

"Believe it or not, I grew up on a ship. It's just been, well, it's been quite a few years. I'll find them eventually."

"The sea never leaves you completely," the voice said. It was rich, and the slight southern Hadranian accent mimicked that of Dacia's.

"How long have you been sailing with Dacia?"

"The captain? Few years, now."

"And?"

"She runs a tight ship. Keeps a skeleton crew of people she can trust, and I've never been cross that I signed on."

"And she's a Magic."

"You noticed."

"Are you all . . ."

"Magic? No. Some are. Half, maybe."

"You?" Kor asked.

"Concerned you're sleeping next to a Magic?" The man asked, throwing his gear into the last hammock in the row.

"Oh no. In Hadran, it's just hard to tell who you can trust when you are Magic."

"Ahh, that's why Captain let someone new join. She doesn't often take kindly to strangers."

"I can see why."

"No, I'm no Magic. The sea is enough magic for me. Endless and unpredictable."

"A true man of the sea. I'm Korvo."

"Jaxson. Nicely met, Korvo."

"Nicely met."

"I'm watching the deck tonight for the middle shift. If you find you can't sleep, you can always come join me." He organized his stuff in the hammock. A small box was amongst the things he put into the space for keeping. "If you got anything you don't want to snuggle up to all night, there are some crates over there where you can put some stuff. It will be fine. No one ever puts anything of value in the common areas, so no one looks there for things either."

"Nothing to put, but thanks. I appreciate it."

Kor climbed into the hammock, glad now that Jaxson wasn't there to witness his awkward acrobatics. The sides of the hammocks hugged him tightly, and the sides came up over his face and blacked out the rest of the room. He heard a few people come down. Relieved from the launching of the boat, it would be time for most of the crew to sleep.

Kor listened as parts of their whispered conversations drifted to him.

"Captain says she's sure this time we'll get there."

"It's been a month since we last had any clue, why all of a sudden is she so sure of herself?"

"That's Captain's business."

They moved away so that Kor couldn't hear any more of the conversation, but other conversations followed. Enough to show him that this crew knew each other well. He was the only new person on the boat, as far as he could tell, and there was something that they were searching for.

Something in Sepsrym. Or something that they wanted to stop from getting to Sepsrym. He just had to be along for the ride.

The conversations drifted off to silence, and Kor was left alone with his thoughts as the ocean slowly rocked him back and forth. At first it had been soothing, a memory long buried in his mind about good times he had with his family, but soon those memories devolved into the rest of his past, which was a lot less calming and a lot more enraging.

He shifted around in the hammock, but there wasn't much he could do to change position. After about an hour, he'd had enough.

Might as well go work on my sea legs, he thought. He poured himself from the hammock as gracefully as he could and set back up the stairs. The night had grown cold out in the open water, and he shivered. While he may have grown up in a village of boats that sat in the ocean, he'd never spent much time out in the open ocean.

He walked up to the deck. The slow roll of the ocean rocked him as he moved. He had slipped the metal collar into his pocket just to make sure it was safe. It wasn't something he should let just any Magic touch without knowing what it was. And since his new bunk-mate had said most of the crew was magic, he might as well keep it on him. His hand slipped into his pocket. A jolt whizzed through him as his hand touched the wood of the boat. Images flooded his mind.

He looked out into the darkness, missing the edges of the buildings and walls of Kaybrum. He stared out into the nothingness for another minute, letting the images dance around him.

The wood was still warm from the sun, even though it had set quite a while ago. Wood has memory. He let his hand rest on the railing. Flashes of life sprung before Korvo. He had always been able to read wood this way, find the grooves and grain that told a story. But this wood also contained something that felt like the future.

He removed his hand. He was too tired to try and decipher the fates, and if Dacia was going to have him read the cards for her, he couldn't waste any of his magical energy on the future of a railing.

So instead, it was back to his terrible plan. Acting impulsively had never helped him in the past, and so he was not sure why he thought it was going to help him this time. He leaned down to put his head on the railing. One thought blossomed into his mind. The sun was brilliant even though it was still nighttime. The vision was all-consuming. And in that vision, one image stood out. Kor saw this ship. This railing. And Tiernan.

"You aren't losing your dinner over the side, are ya?" Jaxson asked, moving to stand next to Kor on the railing. Kor jumped. He leaned his back against the railing.

"No, I, uh." Kor tried to focus, but the blinding vision kept coming in and out of his mind. It had to be a look into the future. Did Tiernan follow him into Hadran? Had he somehow made it on the boat?

"It warps the wood," Jaxson said. Kor couldn't decide if he was joking or being serious.

"Yeah," Kor said, stumbling through the conversation. Why had the ship shown him Tiernan, and why had it been so clear? He could have reached out and touched him. Rarely did he get such clear snippets of the future. First the sailor, and now this. It was like the fates were opening their gates to him again. But even though it had shown him something, it was still a puzzle.

His fingers itched to get the cards out. He rested his fingertips on the edges of the cards. They whispered a million things much too quickly for him to catch.

"Hey, Jaxson, listen, is there any way someone else got aboard this ship after the crew was accounted for?" Kor asked, taking his hands away from the cards but careful not to let them touch the railing.

"You mean like a stowaway?" Jaxson thought for a minute. "People can be pretty sneaky, but I doubt it. With the amount of people coming and going, someone would have seen something by now. Why?" Jaxson leaned in. Kor could feel his breath a few inches away in the cold night.

"Just, you know, hard to be back in Hadran as a Magic." Why did he lie? It had just come out of his lips before he had even thought of it. He had to be pretty ashamed of his non-existent plan if he was worried about what a total stranger might think.

"Had it rough then? You look like you're old enough to have lived through the war."

"Lived it would be more accurate."

"Captain did as well. Never quite the same, as they say."

"Hard to be. Things like that change a person. Seemed like moving all that wind really took it out of her," Kor said, trying to change the subject away from something that was making his heart race.

"Right, well," Jaxson paused, ignoring Kor's comment completely. He rapped his knuckles against the top of the railing three times. "There is no way Captain's letting anyone who's going to hurt you on this ship, but if it makes you feel better, I can help you look around when the light breaks."

"No, thank you, though. I appreciate it, really," Kor said, taking a deep breath.

"Well, I don't trust you have found your sea legs quite yet, so best to keep an eye on you. You should probably head back down and try to catch some shut-eye."

Kor shook his head. "I couldn't sleep. I'll just sit out here and think for a while longer, but don't let me keep you from anything you need to be doing."

"Do you know how to coil rope?" Jaxson asked. He was a few feet across the deck, and Kor scrambled to be over by him.

"Haven't done it in a while, but I bet it will come back."

They worked in silence for a bit. The heavy rope was coarse in his hands, but Kor found his rhythm faster than he thought. Jaxson hummed to himself. It was a low noise. It seemed to move with the ocean and mix with the depth of the water. It reminded him of the calls of whales off the coast of Hadran. He wondered if they were there now, somewhere below them in the depths.

When there was no more to do, Jaxson leaned against the mast and pulled out a small knife and a block of wood.

"You whittle?" Kor said, looking over at the deft work Jaxson was doing.

"I think almost every sailor does. You?"

"I've been working on bigger things lately, but that really takes me back."

"It takes my mind off of everything."

"Everything?"

"Isn't it nice to just be without thoughts for a little while in the dark?" he asked. Kor couldn't tell in the darkness if he was avoiding the question.

"I can't remember the last time I whittled something."

Jaxson put down the wood. It caught in the lantern light. Kor could make out the edges of a fluke at the end of the piece. He had been making a whale.

"It's not healthy to be so focused all the time. I've told the captain that too. You and her are a lot alike. Like finds like. Water always calls to water."

"Does the captain listen?" Kor asked.

"She only sees the sea as a means to an end. A way to get from place to place. She doesn't take time to appreciate it. Not anymore. But the captain is a good captain. And I'd follow her to the ends of the Earth."

Dedication, Kor thought. He wondered if his people had ever felt like that. He felt the crease in his brow. He knew why Aer and Bryce had done what they had done. It didn't mean they didn't believe him, but facing this kind of loyalty just seemed like a slap in the face. Not only was he judging the loyalty of the people he loved, but he had left them to face the war of Kaybrum alone. He had left Bryce. Bryce had never left him. He was the disloyal one.

"Looks like you need this," Jaxson said, picking a soft piece of wood out of the basket next to him. "Need a knife, or is that one in your pocket?"

Kor glanced down just to make sure the collar wasn't visible.

"Relax, it's just a joke. I'll get you a knife."

Jaxson stood, his long legs unfolding until he was standing right above Kor. Somehow, seeing his height from the seated position made him seem like a hero from the sailor stories told on nights like this.

Heroes who sailed around the world, finding monsters in the depths. Discovering new places and bringing treasures back to their lands from far away. The type that flew through storms that would rattle most ships apart. The kind of heroes that never left the deck in times of trouble. But those stories were never about pirates, never about people who didn't have grand gestures in mind. Just because he looked like the childhood heroes he had pictured a thousand nights before bed didn't make him a hero of legend. He was just another sailor who was on the ship that was taking Kor to the East. Taking Kor to his mission. To the thing he had to complete. No one was going to save him.

"Here," Jaxson said, sitting back down. This time slightly closer to Kor. He smelled like the sea. Salty and calming. He handed Kor a knife. It was a small blade, no more than three inches long, and the handle was a dark wood that he had never seen before and smooth like it had been handled for years.

"Thanks," Kor said. He took a deep breath. And as he did, Jaxson started humming again. He listened for a moment before he put the knife to the wood. He let the piece of wood direct the knife where to go. It was soothing to work with wood again. He let his mind let go of the things that kept swirling around in his head. He stopped looking for a plan and an answer.

"That song sounds familiar," Kor said.

Jaxson just nodded as he continued.

Kor got the hint. He thought about the warmth in the sunlight at the workshop. He let those feelings drift through him. It felt like the night air pulled the worries out of him and let the unending ocean drown them.

Jaxson began whistling. Kor looked up. He had been so concentrated on letting the knife nick a little here and shave a little there that he hadn't realized how far he had gotten. In his hands and in the wisps of the rising sun, he had the rough outline of a bird in his hands. It was blocky, not something Gesepi would have wanted to put in his window, but it still looked—Kor thought about it—it still looked free. And it wasn't finished.

"Ready to turn in?" Jaxson asked. He held out a hand to Kor. In the light, he could see Jaxson's features better. He had a strong nose and brown eyes like the caramel heated on his mother's hearth for celebrations. His hair was pulled back into long dreads at the top, while the sides and undercut of his head were all shaved. His shape still very much gave him the body of a hero, but there was something in his features that just wasn't right. It wasn't that he wasn't attractive—because he was. Kor couldn't say he wasn't. Not even if he tried. But there was something like hurt. A hurt that no one in a story had ever dealt with. A history that did not scream of justice and treasure but hardship and making things out of nothing. Even the small scar on his cheek, right on his cheekbone, added to the story. *A story I'll probably never find out,* Kor thought to himself.

"Here's your knife," Kor said, handing the handle back to Jaxson.

"Doesn't look like you're finished," Jaxson said. "Hold on to it. We'll be on this ship a while more together."

Kor tucked the knife into the belt that held his pouch of cards. "Thanks." He held the bird up to the morning rays to inspect his work a little better. Could he have made something much better in the workshop in the sunlight and all the tools at his command? Of course, but it wasn't a bad start, and it gave him some relief to know that he would get to have more time to work on the entire thing. He hated feeling like things were left undone. Boxes still needing to be checked weighed heavily on his mind.

Jaxson's lips curled into a smile. "A bird, huh? Got something you need to escape?"

"Just listened to the wood," Kor said.

"Sure, sure. I get it."

"What does a whale say about you?"

"Just a love for the sea."

"So if yours can just be about a love for the sea, why do you think my bird says something about me?"

"Cause that looks like a Phoenix to me," Jaxson said. "But maybe I've been staring into the dark too long. I'd like to get some sleep before I have to report to the captain. You should get some sleep too. My guess is the captain will have you pretty busy."

The rest of the deck was coming alive now. The crew had woken from their sleep and started the daily process of running the ship. He stopped and watched them. There was a certain elegance to life on a boat. A certainty of what had to be done, and yet you were at the whim of the gods, being tossed around on a sea so deep with secrets it was impossible to know what was at the bottom.

By the time Kor got down to his hammock, Jaxson was already asleep. Kor climbed into his hammock and closed his eyes.

His dreams started normal enough. The beach, the smell of crab roasting on a fire pit, all the smells from his childhood. The faces he grew up by floated in and out of the scene. They laughed and sang. It was a memory, Kor realized, from when he was only about five. This was just a little bit before he would misinterpret the ice blue the cards showed him as the raging sea and not the General's warpath. But this memory, things were good. It was a celebration, something to do with the tides. The memory was faded. Like he was watching it through a bottle. It played out slowly in front of him. His father approached. Kor immediately recognized his dark hair pulled tight at the nape of his neck. The beard he grew had been cut short, as the men who had come back from fishing did for the celebration. His clothes were dyed red, and in his ears, he wore disks of shiny shells that glittered in the sun. He was smiling.

"Any luck telling me who's going to win?" his father asked. He rubbed Kor's head.

Then, the memory stopped. Like a light went out, the dream went black. For a moment, Kor wanted to go back to that memory. Back to the smile on his father's face. He hadn't thought of that smile in years. Mostly he remembered the sneer and the furrow that dominated his face when he kicked at him for his mistakes. The lack of any emotion at all when the General had paid him money for his child. Those were the things he remembered.

It was normal to think about his father, Kor told himself in the darkness of undreaming. He was on a ship for the first time in years, smelling the fresh air, and he had been back in Hadran. There wasn't anything else to this memory.

Slowly, the color returned.

This time, he was in Kaybrum, walking through the garden. The flowers were always less vibrant, but they still felt more like home than the cold buildings in the city. Aer thrived in the cold city; it was like she was born to stone and glass, but not Kor. He noticed a lump under the rose bush. Its flowers were more open and beautiful than those of the other plants, most of which were still buds waiting for a slightly warmer day to open.

As he got closer, he saw what the lump really was. It was a young boy. He had his legs pulled up tight. Even in his dream he could feel the fear and anger wafting off of the small boy. His energy was almost palpable. There were no tears on his face, just dirt and leaves, but there was such a fire in his eyes that Kor had to come closer. It was Bryce. The first time he had met Bryce. Why were his memories trying so hard to show him the things he didn't want to think about any time soon? Seeing Bryce again, not as the strong giant, built like stone he was now, but the small boy who was in the city and afraid and had found the one patch of dirt where no one would bother him. It wasn't until Kor was looking through his eyes in the gaze of a memory that he noticed how large the thorns on the plant had grown. That rose was keeping him safe, willing to scar anyone who came close to the boy. Bryce had always been powerful. His emotions were directly tied to the life around him. More than Merin or Aer or the cards who dealt with things that weren't alive. Bryce dealt with the living. He dealt with things that could also feel and could take his feelings and turn them into something real. Something that didn't have to hurt inside of him.

And yet Bryce was still hurting. Kor knew he had left him, and he wondered how large the thorns would be on the roses when Bryce saw him again. Did he understand why he had left? Or did it not matter if he understood or not because he had left? He had left like everyone else.

"Korvo," Aer's voice called. But she wasn't in this dream. She hadn't been in this memory. He had found Bryce alone. They had taken a few days to get to know each other before he had him meet Aer. Aer was sometimes too harsh and too fierce. It didn't always help for her to meet new people.

Why was she in this memory? Why was he seeing memories instead of dreams, and why did these memories have to come? Kor opened his eyes. He was swinging slightly in his hammock, rocking to the ever-pulling tide of the ocean.

The memory of his father made sense. That was something that he connected to the seas, but Bryce? Bryce would not like the ocean. Even though there were growing things in the ocean, he wouldn't like not being able to reach them. Korvo wasn't even sure he could swim. He was a boy from the countryside outside of the city. There weren't many lakes or rivers out there. But he had never asked. So much of their relationship had been about their hurting, their treatment, and Kor wondered if he really knew Bryce as well as he thought he did.

Had he even really talked to him about Merin? Did he ever offer advice or say something about him being smart? About young love? He wasn't sure. He didn't remember, but surely, he had. Right?

He looked over and saw Jaxson still sleeping and pulled out his bird carving. He wasn't going back to sleep when his memories were wreaking havoc on him. Instead he could just let his mind escape for a while. Jaxson shifted in his sleep, letting a soft grunt of satisfaction escape from his lips. Maybe he needed to be a little more like Jaxson and let go of the world. Maybe. But Kor felt the metal in his pocket as he reached for the knife. He still had work to do. Work that couldn't be forgotten so easily.

Instead, he got up and walked up to the deck. He leaned on the railing and watched the sea go by. The water changed colors as the clouds passed overhead, and the spray brushed his face, so he finally felt awake.

They were headed into the sun. Due east. To whatever waited for him in the land where the sun rose and magic was a death sentence.

"Korvo," Dacia called.

Kor looked up. She still looked tired. Under her eyes, a dark shadow refused to be touched by the sun's rays, and he could see the slight hang in her shoulders. Moving that much air had taken a toll on her. Kor reached down and touched the metal in his pocket. Would that make it worse for her or better? Did it matter? The collar was created by the people who supported the General.

"Captain," Kor said, giving a smart nod in her direction.

"Could you come to my quarters, please?" she asked nicely, but Kor could tell it was not an invitation. It was an order. On any ship, captain's orders were law. He headed up to the second layer of the deck, let his hands briefly touch the wheel, and then he followed her into her quarters.

Unlike the rest of the ship, which was seaworthy in every way, Dacia's cabin had small holes in the walls that let in the light. Kor wondered if they really let in the breezes. Aer wouldn't have liked being in the hold of a ship. Pitch poured into every crack to keep the water at bay would also mean that her winds would be trapped inside with her or outside without her.

"How can I help you, Captain?" Kor asked, taking the seat that Dacia gestured to. It was a small wooden chair, and Kor couldn't help but find at least fifteen things he would have changed about its design, but he didn't mention those to the captain in front of him; she had a much too serious look on her face.

"You're going east. Any particular reason?"

"Are we sharing our reasons now?" Kor asked. In the din of the room, lit only by the small cracks and the lone candle on the desk, Kor couldn't decide how to read her sudden openness.

"Private then?"

"Very." So private, in fact, Kor thought that he wasn't even sure about them himself.

"Can you read the cards for us?"

"Us?" Kor asked. He looked around, but there wasn't so much as a cat in the room.

Just then, the door opened, and Jaxson came to take a seat. He moved a few things out of the way on a dresser behind Kor and took a seat without a word.

Kor wondered if he had been waiting for an invitation to come in or if the two of them were just so in tune.

"Sure. What kind of reading? It helps to have a question in mind. It makes it easier to find answers. I'll be honest, though, things aren't as clear as they used to be." He held his hand out. Dacia nodded.

"We want to know if the cargo we are looking for will beat us to the East."

A simple question. Simple questions usually weren't that hard. Kor felt the pressure to use the collar in his pocket, but it might complicate the issue. Best to stick to what he knew for now.

He shuffled the deck easily in his hand. He asked Dacia to cut it, but it didn't really matter. Many people just felt like they were more connected to their destiny when they were directly involved. He wanted to make sure the captain felt respected.

The first card he pulled, he set down in front of them.

"Is it the cards themselves, or do you get feelings from them?" Dacia asked.

"See this card?" Korvo asked.

She nodded.

"Well it's more than just this card," Kor said, but he offered the card for the captain to study. When she reached for it across the desk, her pirate mark stuck out against her obsidian skin.

"So what else does it say?" she asked, putting it back in front of him. Kor closed his eyes. He put his fingers over the edges of the card. It lit up.

He thought for a moment. The messages were mixed, but somehow, he couldn't shake his presence in the images being shown to him.

"Pull another card," Kor said without opening his eyes. She must have as another card's edge slipped in under his fingers. Again, he couldn't seem to separate himself.

"Will it beat us to the East?"

"Yes and no," Kor said.

"What does that mean?" she asked.

"Easy now, Captain," Jaxson said in his easy lolling tone.

"It seems like some of the cargo is already there." What it was was still unclear. He had been hoping he would get some information to know what kind of crew he had gotten himself in with. "More is on the way."

"More?" Dacia said. There was that edge to her voice again. Surely more of whatever cargo they were trying to steal was going to be a good thing. Even if they couldn't take it all on board, they'd have more opportunities to take it. But she sounded, sad wasn't the right word, more like the wind was being pulled from her chest. Deflated. Exactly the way he had felt when Hayden had told him the General was going east. Like anything he could try was never going to be enough.

"I just read the cards," Kor said. They might feel the same, but that didn't mean he had started to trust them more. Especially when the cards insisted that he was somehow involved with this crew beyond the harbor in the East.

"Would details help?" Jaxson said. He had pulled the little wooden whale from his pocket. In the light, Kor could see the level of detail that he had created on the whale. It looked like if they put it into water, it would just swim away in the depths. Kor could see little barnacles and spots on the whale. Jaxson looked at it, but Kor could tell his eyes weren't focused on the piece but on the captain.

"Jaxson," the captain warned.

"More could be a problem for the crew, Captain. I think you both might think about dropping the mistrust. It's not becoming of either of you."

"He whittled with you, didn't he?" the captain asked Kor, and he couldn't tell if it was a joke or not, but somehow, he felt a little hurt that Jaxson might have sat through the night with lots of other people.

"Where are you headed in the East?" Kor asked to stop the line of questioning.

"Sepsrym," the captain said.

"Ahh, yes, I have to admit my geography lessons have been lacking in the last few years."

"The Eastern Capital."

"I didn't think I was that behind. The capital moved?"

"Renamed. The current emperor decided he wanted to honor his horse."

"He named the capital after his horse?"

"Better in his twisted mind than the possibility of where the old name came from."

"What could be worse than a horse?"

"Do you remember the old name?"

"Ignion." Kor remembered the big map on the wall of the Refuge. He had pulled it out of an office and put it up. At first, he tried to tell himself it was to teach Tiernan and Bryce about the world. But in the end, Kor spent most of his time trying to divide the world into places where he would be either hated or tolerated for who he was. He was always disappointed by how little there was that would welcome him.

"Does that name sound familiar to you in any way?"

"Should it?"

"Legend has it," Jaxson started, "that the East was first settled when a royal family split apart from the West. There was only one family that decided to break away from the West. But they gathered support as they traveled east. Eventually, they ran into the mountains that keep the two places divided. Many people tried to pass through the mountains, but few ever came back to teach anyone the way over. It was thought they never made it to the other side and that they were stuck on the mountain. But this group, which had grown large as they traveled, had slowed due to the number of people, and as the traveling group grew, the Western rulers began to worry that they were trying to amass an army against them. They sent their army after the traveling group. They had to choose. Would they stay and fight an army with peasants and craftsmen, or would they try to make it over the mountains and hope for the best?"

"Jaxson, the simple answer would have sufficed," Dacia said, but she didn't stop him.

He continued. "They chose to take on the mountains. Those mountains made the dreary days of winter in the West seem like summer in Hadran. But they soldiered on. The wind whipped at them. The snow clawed at their feet. Their teeth chattered. Until one of the leaders, who had been a duke or some other vaguely important man, realized one small boy in the group seemed immune to the cold. He walked with his hands loose, skimming the tops of snow drifts with his fingers. The duke called out to the boy and asked him why the cold didn't bother him. He said he had the heat of the sun inside of him."

"A Magic," Kor interrupted.

"Indeed. A Fire Magic, at that. The boy began to share his gift with the people close to him, and with his help, they found their way through the mountains into the East. In the East, it was still not an easy time. It had been long abandoned by the people who had used to live there. But the boy was able to help them clear land for crops, and when they finally reached the sea, the duke and duchess had found him indispensable. They decided to adopt the boy. And as they named themselves the Emperor and Empress of the East, he became the crown prince. His name was Ignion."

"That story could have been one sentence long," Dacia protested.

"Stories cannot be rushed."

"So they'd rather have their capital named after a horse than a Magic from some legend?" Kor asked.

"Yes, but that story has been twisted for years. They make the prince out to be evil."

"I've read that story. It did not make the favorites list among my . . ." he didn't know what to call the people he had left behind. They were family to him, but did they still think the same about him? "People," he finally decided.

"Ignion also is not the prince of the East in those stories. Sometimes he's from Hadran, sometimes the East or even the North," Jaxson explained.

"Anything to make people forget that there's a possibility that the rulers of the East are descended from a Magic," Dacia added.

"I see," Kor said. "So why Sepsrym? I can't imagine, as both a pirate and a Magic, you would be welcome there. Why not land somewhere with less security?"

"Cargo," Dacia said. "Besides, Jaxson here wants to see the sand towers."

"Sand towers?" Kor's vision came to mind. The endless beach, the running horse, the crow, and the Phoenix. Phoenix that became a crow.

"Part of the show of wealth. Hand sculpted 'without a hint of magic,' but I can hardly believe that."

Kor wasn't listening about the towers anymore. He was too caught up in what the future was showing him.

"Cards on the table," Kor said. He saw their eyes glance at his cards. "No, I mean, it's time to come clean. I'm headed to the East to stop the Hadranian General who captured me and tortured my friends. Something bad is happening in the East for Magics, and I have a feeling it won't stay just in the East for long."

Jaxson raised an eyebrow. Again Kor realized the gesture was meant for the captain. She sighed.

"Something bad is happening is an understatement. The cargo we're looking for." She glanced over at Jaxson. He nodded. It was the first time she had seemed unsure. "The cargo we are looking for are captured Magics. They've been bringing Magics from Hadran to the East for the last few months, and we finally got an ear into the travel plans, but now I fear it's more than we can even hope to take back with us."

"You're on a rescue mission?" Kor said.

"I think I've said enough for now. I'm going to need some time to think about what you've told me."

He didn't have to be told twice; Kor realized he had been told to leave. Jaxson followed him out of the room.

"You two seem like you're on the same wavelength." Kor looked up at Jaxson. It had been a long time since he had really looked up at anyone.

"Been on the ship a long time." Jaxson seemed distracted, more than he had before.

"How did a non-Magic fall into this, uhh, line of work?" Kor asked. He wasn't sure what he expected. If he wanted Jaxson to say that a ship was a ship and cargo was cargo, so he didn't have to worry about if he really cared about Magics. Like Kor had to think about when Hayden was around. He wondered if Hayden was still coming around or if Bryce had gotten too angry and they had fought. He wondered if Bryce could keep his temper. Without the Refuge, they could send him to the labor camps for something like hitting a man of stature like Hayden. But then again, he wanted Jaxson to care. To more than tolerate that he had his hammock swinging next to a Magic. That it wasn't just ship rules that allowed him to take orders from a captain with magic. And it wasn't just because Jaxson was handsome and funny. Was it so bad to want to be liked for himself?

CHAPTER EIGHTEEN
TIERNAN

TIERNAN HATED THE WATER, ESPECIALLY THE OCEAN. HE hated everything about boats, even though he had only been in one for a few hours.

Kor had been long gone from Porttown when he had gotten there. A few people had seen him, but Tiernan couldn't find any solid clue until he had stumbled into a sailor discussing their upcoming trip with someone else. They were putting the last few pieces of cargo onto the ship, so they were talking loudly to cover the distance between them.

"He said it seemed to be some sort of sickness. Seemed pretty reliable. Knew we were really going east as soon as he touched the cards."

"Still you really going to trust some Magic out on the docks? That's a man so desperate for coins he'd say anything."

"Why would anyone pretend to be a Magic?" The first sailor laughed.

Cards. That could be Korvo. And if they were headed east, Korvo might have found some way to sneak onto their ship.

Tiernan slipped by the sailors and scurried up the gangplank. Immediately he felt nauseous and weak. His legs seemed to buckle underneath him. It took all of his strength to get off the main deck and into the holds. If Korvo were here, he would find him down there. Then they could get off the ship before they ever set sail.

Tiernan headed for the cargo bay. Korvo could easily have hidden in one of the many crates on the ship. Tiernan headed to the first one. It didn't take him long to figure out the crates' lids were nailed down, and he had no hope of opening any of them on his own. But if they were nailed on, that meant that Kor wouldn't be inside them. He tried to quicken his pace, but it just made his legs swerve out from under him.

His throat started to scratch from the salt air.

"Kor?" he tried when he found one crate with a loose board. "Kor, are you here?"

No one answered. He pulled himself to the top of the crate and leaned in to see what was inside. The boat lurched, and Tiernan tumbled into the crate. The boat rocked forward. Had they set sail?

He had to get out of there. He tried to get out of the cargo box, but his wobbly feet couldn't find any traction. His feet kept sliding down something smooth and hard. He slipped again. His hands made contact with what felt like metal. He felt inside of him for a small amount of fire to light his way. If he could just see, he could still get out of there in time.

A small fire appeared in his right hand. Metal chains filled the box around him. His breath caught. His hand trembled, and the fire flared. He took a deep breath and let it disappear. No way he could get caught now. He just had to get off the boat. He scrambled up the pile of chains as fast as he could. He didn't bother trying to put the lid back on. He had to go.

As he ran, the ship rocked back and forth, making him cover twice as much ground as he weaved across the floors. He waited for the coast to clear along the stairs and made his way to where he could see the blue sky above him.

Except there wasn't just blue sky above them. There was blue everywhere. Porttown was disappearing behind them in the wake of the boat. The two masts were full of three sails, and they were moving at a speed Tiernan didn't know boats could move. He tried to take a step toward the railing, but his stomach heaved.

"Cabin boys aren't what they used to be," a sailor said from behind him. It was the same one that had been talking about Kor. "Better get it together, kid. It's going to be a long trip."

CHAPTER NINETEEN
BRYCE

WHEN HE GOT BACK TO THE SCHOOL, MERIN WAS DEEP IN teaching. His confession would have to wait. He sulked at the back of the room, half listening to the speech Merin was giving. Bethlem walked in the front door and waved him over. Bryce got up slowly and walked over to him.

"Something has come up," Bethlem said. His eyes stared down at the ground, and his hands twitched like he was looking for a glass to clean.

"What's come up?" Bryce said. When Bethlem didn't respond, Bryce leaned down so he could be in Bethlem's eye line. "What's come up?" He asked again.

"One of the kids," Bethlem sighed, "they've been arrested. I saw it happen in the marketplace this morning."

"Which kid?"

"Well, I guess he's not much of a kid. Thomas. He comes here most days. He's about thirteen."

"What was he arrested for?"

Bryce rubbed at the knot that seemed to have taken permanent residence under his shoulder blade. He had known, of course, that the school hadn't stopped arrests, but somehow he still felt blindsided. He had been at the marketplace just hours ago. How had he missed it?

"I'm not sure. I saw the arrest but nothing that led up to it. He was kicking and screaming about having control. I think his group of friends, some of them might have gotten arrested too."

"Well, at least it wasn't here. The school does not need any sort of reputation."

"Bryce," Bethlem took a deep breath. "You are his legal guardian."

"What?"

"Did you read any of the papers that Kor left you?"

"I've looked at them."

"Korvo has legal guardianship of all the kids who were originally supposed to stay in the school."

"So, Thomas?"

"Thomas is, by Kor's absence, your legal ward."

"What does that mean?" Bryce asked. His voice carried, and a few of the students turned to look at him. Merin frowned, and Bryce threw her a smile. She went back to teaching.

"It means you can demand a trial. With Merin's knowledge of the law and Kor's research, it will be the first trial a Magic minor has gotten in as long as I can remember."

"But—"

"This is our chance. This is our chance to get them to admit in a court of law that magic is not illegal and is not a reason for arrest. This could be it."

"What do I have to do?"

"You have to make the case."

"You remember that I can barely read and write my own name? Merin should do it."

"You are their legal guardian. That's the only representation they are allowed. Besides, Merin's father will be the lawyer on the other side."

"But he's not a court lawyer, right? He's more the guy in the background with the Council? Doing, doing . . ."

"After the mess with the Council, he's been working the courts again like he did when he was young."

"Shouldn't he be working with us at least a little bit? To, I don't know, make up for his part in the Operation Fire Bird mess?"

"I'm sure he doesn't think he's doing anything wrong, but it would be much harder for Merin to go against him. It has to be you, Bryce."

"I'm not even of age. Is it even legal for me to be someone's legal guardian?"

"Thomas is in your hands, whether you like it or not. You can do this. Merin and I can help, but you will have to go to court."

"Bethlem . . ."

"I have the utmost faith in you."

"Where do I even start?"

"I'd go talk to Thomas. See what you can find out."

"Right . . ."

"Visitor hours in the adult prison are today from five to six. See if you can have Merin take a break and come with you."

Bethlem left behind a sorry smile and a pat on Bryce's shoulder. Neither of which helped at all.

Merin looked at him across the room, and she raised an eyebrow. Telling her about the plants was going to have to wait. Again.

He waited until the kids were reading a story and the older kids had gone upstairs to rest before their nighttime work with the other teachers.

"We have a bit of a problem," Bryce said.

"I can read that on your face. What did Bethlem want?"

"Thomas got arrested. Maybe some others, he wasn't sure."

"But Thomas was doing so well. What happened?"

"Bethlem didn't know, but he can have a trial."

"Right because . . ." She stopped mid-sentence.

"Because I'm his legal guardian."

"It's going to be okay, Bryce. I'll help you study the law stuff before the trial."

He took her hands in his and took a deep breath. "You can help me beforehand, but you can't come to the court."

"I know that I can't stand there with you, but I can at least watch. We can leave Hayden or Bethlem in charge here and—"

"You can't come at all."

"Bryce, this is no time to get heroic and try to push me out of the way. You need me."

"I do, but Bethlem says the prosecutor will be your father, and I don't want you making him cut all ties with you over this. I know you haven't been going home very often, if ever. This would only make things worse."

"We have another issue," Merin said, letting her head fall back and staring up at the ceiling. "This means everyone will know Kor isn't just hard to reach."

"Right. No way around that. Things will get messy afterward. They might try to shut down the school."

"I won't let them. We just might be a little short of funds."

Bryce could see her mind had gone to calculating how they would make it through to the next few weeks. Her ability to think that far into the future amazed him. Kor had always been able to do it, but he could actually see into the future. Merin was just relying on her smarts.

"You might need to pick up some more shifts with Vycky, and maybe some other florists, if you can."

"Right," Bryce said. He scratched at his neck, and he could see her noticing. "Vycky hasn't been needing me," he lied. It was too much to put on top of all of this that he was losing control. "But I'll ask around. Let's focus on Thomas right now. Bethlem says we can go get his side of the story during visiting hours tonight."

"Okay, right after dinner, we'll go."

A student called for her on the other side of the room. He watched her smile bounce back to her face and heard her tone remain consistently positive throughout the conversation. He couldn't do what she did. He watched her for as long as he felt he could get away with before it started to be creepy and then went to collect his thoughts on the roof.

The roof hadn't helped reign in his thoughts, so Bryce paced until dinner had been served in the school. Everything was starting to fall into place with routines, and he realized how many of the older kids hadn't made dinner. Had they been missing more lessons than he had noticed?

"Are we ready?" Merin asked, coming to stand near him.

"Ready."

They walked quietly through the garden. Bryce had been avoiding it, but there was no quicker way to get to the other side of the city, and visitor hours were only so long. They had to make sure they had time to get some answers.

"You know, we should see if Hayden saw anything this morning at the market. He wasn't around for the lessons, so he must have been there in meetings. It is the first week of the month, after all."

"Still think Hayden is going to help every time we ask? If you haven't noticed, he's been at the school less and less."

"He still has a marketplace to run."

"So what are you going to ask Thomas?" Bryce said, changing the subject. Any time they started to discuss Hayden, the conversation never went the way he wanted it to.

Merin looked up at him and gave him a small smile. "*We* just ask him for his side of the story."

The prison was next to the Watcher's headquarters. Bryce felt the hair on the back of his neck stand up as they got closer. Merin moved closer to him. He could feel her arm getting closer every few steps. When they were close enough that Bryce could see himself in the reflection, he felt her hand against his. He grabbed it and gave it a short squeeze. He could do this.

"We're here to speak with Thomas. He was arrested within the marketplace this morning."

"Family only," The Watcher on the other side of the desk said without looking up.

"I'm his legal guardian," Bryce said, laying the paperwork from Kor out on the desk. The Watcher looked it over and handed it back.

"Visiting hours are over in forty-five minutes. I'll have someone go get him."

He moved from the desk with such excruciatingly slow speed, that Bryce could only assume he meant to waste as much of those forty-five minutes as he could. He ground his teeth together, trying not to let any of his anger seep out from his mouth.

When the Watcher returned a few moments later, he pointed Merin and Bryce into a room down a hallway. Tables were set up around the room. Only one of them was occupied. Merin and Bryce sat down at the table furthest away from the couple sitting on the other side of the room.

It took another fifteen minutes for them to produce Thomas. The adult prison clothes hung loosely over his small frame. He was just a kid.

"Thomas," Bryce said, standing when the boy came over to the table.

"Am I supposed to call you Dad or something?" he asked. "And does that make you my mama?" He looked at Merin.

"I'm trying to help you."

"Help me. I'm in an adult prison because you two had to shut down the Refuge."

"Had you ever been in the Refuge?" Bryce asked. "I see the way you look at it when you come to the lessons. You don't have the same look in your eyes as the others. You never stepped foot inside before we cleaned it up for you."

"Your point? This is the smallest pair of clothes they had after they confiscated mine to make sure there wasn't lice in them. The smallest pair, Bryce. I could fit into one leg of these pants."

"Believe what you want, but things are better now."

"Yeah, if things are so much better, why am I here?"

"That's what we are trying to figure out," said Merin. "Tell us what happened this morning in the marketplace."

"I was with my friends. We were checking out all the new shops in the marketplace. They've been opening like crazy. Only last week, there were half as many places. So we went to this one store that was selling some hard candies from the East. We were just messing around. We weren't the only kids in there. But, this," he held up his hand, showing off the black Raven's head tattooed over his fingers, "gives them a single reason to watch us."

"So what happened that caused them to arrest you?" Merin asked. "Tell us with the most amount of detail you can. Especially anything they said about your magic."

"Well, have you ever seen one of those candies?" Thomas asked, looking at Merin. She nodded. "There are crystals of sugar. Which are just fancy rocks, you know, and rocks are Farad's specialty, and so we were just seeing if he could change their shapes at all."

Bryce had seen those—they were on her desk in the morning a few days ago. Hayden must have dropped them off for her. They really looked like crystals.

"But why were you arrested?"

"The lady asked for details, Dad," Thomas said. "So Farad was messing with the candies, turning them into things like hearts, talking all about how he was going to give them to some girl. Then he knocked over one of the displays and this really large thing. A thing that holds flowers and stuff—"

"A vase," Merin suggested.

"Sure, it fell and just completely tore this beautiful tapestry. It was a nice one from down in Hadran with lots of colors and things. Surprising to find something so colorful in a place from the East, but it just ripped a hole in it. I couldn't just let it do that. For one, they'd make us pay for it, and even though I could make something like that in a matter of minutes, it would have been more money than I could make in a matter of weeks. And two, I felt like showing off. Farad was getting everyone to look at him, and I didn't want to fall behind. So I let my fingers go to work. Weaving is a cinch if you just connect to the Earth and all that. It just took a minute. I was almost done when Farad showed me one of the candies he had changed the shape of, claiming how he was going to get all the ladies, so I set the tapestry down on my lap and popped it into my mouth, just to see his face."

"And?" Bryce asked.

"Give him time," Merin said.

"We don't have a ton of time, remember, and I have to somehow argue in front of the courts in what will be a landmark case, according to Bethlem. I need more than just eating his friend's candy. Which I'm sure they didn't pay for. Not creating a stellar defense so far."

"But were you arrested for stealing?" Merin asked. "Didn't Bethlem say there was yelling about control? Control of what?"

"That's what I've been trying to tell you. I tried to finish what I was doing, but the strings weren't laying right anymore. They felt like they were expanding and changing colors. The tapestry all started to change. And then the shopkeeper started yelling. And the next thing I know, two Watchers are pulling me out, telling me I'm being arrested for losing control of my magic. And that brings us here."

"Did you lose control?" Bryce asked.

"No. Well, I don't know."

"You don't know?" Merin asked.

Bryce looked away from both of them. He knew the feeling far too well. It made him feel like, somehow, part of him was trying to sprint away from him while he was standing still. But it wasn't him. He wasn't trying too hard or attempting anything that should have caused it. It had gotten to the point where even touching plants was making him sweat.

"Bryce?" Merin asked. He shrugged her off.

"Is there anything else you can remember?" Bryce asked.

"I don't know what happened to Farad and the others. But I heard a loud crash when they were taking me out. That's all I know."

"Time's up," the Watcher said, grabbing Thomas's arm and pulling him back out of the room. He may have been a snarky kid, much like Bryce was when he was Thomas's age, but when the Watcher grabbed him, all Bryce saw was a small kid who was in way over his head.

Bryce worried that he would see the same thing if he looked at himself in the mirror.

CHAPTER TWENTY

MERIN

HAYDEN HAD ASKED HER TO COME OUT AND MEET HIM. SHE didn't mind the break from the school, but she should have been working with Bryce on the law books. She had gotten Rachael to send more from her parents' house. They had been delivered to the school that morning, and she hadn't even gotten to see if any of it would be useful. The books were thick, and the writing was small and crammed together. They even smelled in a way that screamed that most people shouldn't look at them.

Bryce would just sit there staring at them. She wasn't even sure he would get up the nerve to open them without her there, but Hayden had insisted.

So here she was in the middle of the evening, heading toward the marketplace that should have shut down hours ago, but people were still wandering through. Some of them had packages under their arms, and others just seemed to be reveling while walking by the shops, welcoming them with open arms. Extending the hours of the marketplace had probably been Hayden's doing.

Every few people that passed her, she caught a familiar flash of the black tattoo. Some were on hands, arms, ankles, and necks. There was something that always seemed to mystify her. The tattoos were done by the government, but there didn't seem to be any connection in how they were done. Some were able to be covered up easily, and others, not so much.

She got to the address the messenger had delivered on a scrap of paper that looked like it had been ripped from a notebook in a moment of inspiration or worry.

It wasn't much, not the flashiest set of offices or gaudy in any way. In fact, if she hadn't been given an address, she probably wouldn't have been able to find it. It was set back from the street, and the door was the same boring shade of once-painted wood as the rest of the building. Everything just faded into the dying light.

She knocked on the door.

"Hayden?" she asked when the door didn't open. "Hayden? It's Merin."

"Let yourself in," he called from the depths of the building. She turned the handle. It creaked but gave way. She wasn't sure why she felt a sense of dread coming from the building. It was just Hayden.

"Hayden?" There was no answer, but a flurry of footsteps and paper came from a room down the hall on the right-hand side. She headed that way.

Books surrounded Hayden in a ring of disarray. Half of them looked like the law books that she had left with Bryce, but the other half had a newness to them that made her pick them up. She leafed through one that was closest to her. It was all in Hayden's scrawling handwriting. Journals.

"Hayden? What did you want?" She put his journal back in the mess where she had found it.

"I don't want anything. I need to tell you something." He was scribbling in another notebook.

"Something that couldn't be told to me tomorrow at the school?"

"One, no, it could not, and two, I'm not sure if I can come by the school tomorrow."

"Meetings?"

"Huh?" He still hadn't looked at her.

"Do you have a meeting tomorrow?" She tried to make herself clear. Whatever he was so excited or nervous about had him really distracted. She still wasn't sure how he was even feeling. Just that he wasn't his normal calm and cool self.

"Yeah, yeah, meetings," he said, but she wasn't convinced that he had really heard her at all.

She walked over to him and put a hand on his arm. She took a small breath and let her magic run through his veins, imagining it trickling around his body. His arm relaxed, and she let go.

"Why am I here?"

Hayden looked at her for the first time. His eyes were clear. He opened his mouth a few times as if to speak and finally remembered to take a breath. Then he started talking rapidly. It missed his normal, carefully contemplated cadence, and instead, it was just a whirl. Merin wondered if this was what it was like inside his brain. Everything was going a million miles a minute. Everything was connected in some larger net that only he could see.

"I figured it out," he said, taking a breath for the first time. She realized it was the first thing she had actually understood. "I figured it out last night."

"Figured out what?"

"What they were doing to the Magics in the Refuge. Why they kept all that information on Bryce and the others." He paused, but not long enough for her to say anything; he just plunged ahead.

"It was all an experiment. It's like you told the kids the other day at the school about the jackets from Hadran. How they had opened the connection that you all have to the world. That was the piece that finally made it make sense. And I found it in this journal." He held one up to her face, then took it back and looked at it. "Well, not that one, but one of these. I just had it. But they were experimenting with control. What was enough to open the control, and how much stress it took to shut it off. They were trying . . ." He was flipping through pages at what seemed random.

"They were trying to figure out how to turn our magic off?" Merin took a step back. Her arms snapped around her chest like she could protect that inner light from the outside world. "Hayden, how did you figure it out?"

"It was something that had been bothering me in Bryce's file. In the notes, there were a bunch of numbers about blood."

"Right. They took blood. They had knocked him out with gas." She had read that portion multiple times despite feeling like she couldn't breathe when she read it.

"You see now why I couldn't tell you any of this at the school," Hayden said. He was still rifling through notebooks around his desk. His hair was tumbling into his face. She was sure now; this was the real Hayden. This was the Hayden that got too into stories he read to the kids at school, even though he said he hated them. This was the Hayden who saw the whole world as a puzzle that he could solve if only given enough time.

"What do you want to do with this information?" Hayden said suddenly. His eyes were alight like he had some great ideas. "I've been thinking about it, and—"

"I don't want to do anything about it. I want to bury it so that Bryce never hears of it. It was bad enough someone learned how to bypass our controls, but to take it away entirely?" She slammed her hand down on the desk. "That's like asking him to suffer his whole life, to be treated less than human, and then not to have anything to comfort him in the end. If you saw the way Bryce looks at plants, he truly understands them. It used to be the only thing that made him smile when I first met him. The only time he would smile was when we were in the garden. Everything else was anger and fights. If you took that away from him, he . . . he . . ." She didn't want to finish her sentence.

"Not to be blunt, but wouldn't it make him just like everyone else?"

"Do you have a number?" Merin yelled. She felt her blood boiling up and around her. She stared at Hayden. "Do you have a file from a prison?" When Hayden just looked blank, she flicked one of the many journals to the floor. "Bryce will *never* just be like anyone else. That's what you don't understand."

Hayden stared at her for several seconds. His eyes flicked back and forth across her face. She could tell he was letting ideas connect throughout his mind. He was thinking. Kor was a planner. He made lists and kept detailed records filed away in different formats. He formed chain reactions of favors that had to be precisely followed in order to get the ball to roll an inch. He never acted without thinking, but Hayden was different. He also saw the world in the same puzzle pieces to be solved, but it was clear now that Hayden didn't sit and wait to plan. He created his connection as he went like a spider making its web. And he hadn't thought this part through.

Hayden took a deep breath and pushed his hair back into its proper part.

"Clearly, I've upset you, and that wasn't my intention," Hayden said. His calm exterior settled on him like a mask. She took that as her leave to go.

"Merin," he called as she turned to go out the door. She looked back. "Your magic is wonderful. You aren't like everyone else either."

She nodded, but his words dredged something up deep inside her. If somehow tomorrow she woke up with no magic, she could return easily to the world where she had lived the majority of her life. She could return to her parents. They'd be relieved. Her father would look her in the eye again. Her school would welcome her back. Her friends would probably just regard the last few months she'd been missing from class as a rebellious vacation. She could slip back into the world she knew easily. She looked down at her hands. For no other reason than the fact that she didn't have the tattoo that all other Magics had. The thing that would forever mark them as different even if they no longer had magic.

She looked at her wrist and traced the outline of a Raven's head along her pale skin. She needed it. She needed it to understand Bryce, but more she needed it for herself. To make it clear to herself that she belonged.

She stopped by one of the stores that was still open. She looked around for a minute, barely glancing at all the wares. She was only looking for one thing. She found paint and brushes in the corner. She got the blackest ink she could find and a thin brush.

She would decide where the tattoo would go. It was a luxury that Magics didn't get, but she wasn't sure how to go about procuring a tattoo on her own. If she went to the government, there may be fines or questions, or even imprisonment. She wasn't sure. Magics always had the tattoo. It was too hard to hide who they were. It hurt to not use their magic. She had been lucky. And even now, she was lucky. She purchased the ink, still lost in her thoughts.

She headed for Aer's apartment; it still wasn't a place that she could call her own. Still wasn't a place she felt totally comfortable. She looked down again at her wrist, but maybe with the mark, maybe then she would feel like she truly belonged.

Back at the apartment, Bryce was fiddling with the law books. He had opened a few but to random pages. Merin felt guilty for leaving him for so long.

"Did you get everything settled at the school?" Bryce asked. She tried to hide her guilt over lying to him by nodding.

"Great. We have a few hours before I'll need to go back."

"I asked Bethlem to stay over with the kids tonight," she said, sitting down and opening the book nearest to her. Unlike Hayden's scribbled journals filled with ideas all mixed together in a light sense of excitement, these books made her eyes feel heavy as soon as she opened them. "I figured this might take us a while," she said. She ran her finger down the table of contents. Even the insides of the books felt dusty and old.

She read to herself, and she watched Bryce flick the pages out of the corner of her eye. His life would have been so different if he had been born without magic. A happier life, full of family. He would be sitting around a dinner table with his parents, talking about the farm, not trying to learn the law to help a kid he barely knew.

"Do you want me to read it out loud?" she asked. He shrugged his shoulders. "I'll stick to the things that seem the most relevant."

"Can I help?" Bryce said, "I'm feeling pretty useless."

"Search the books for anything that mentions magic. It should be in the table of contents."

They scanned their respective books in silence.

"Ahh." Merin looked up over to Bryce. "I think I found the law they say Thomas has broken." She read slowly and carefully. "'MC24 Section 6.1b Magic, Control. Any Magic who has been found to be out of control of their magic is seen to be a danger to the commonwealth of Kaybrum and will be sentenced to prison or labor camps until they can adequately control their magic.'"

"And what does 'adequately control their magic' mean?" Bryce asked. His voice shook, and Merin wondered if he was concerned for Thomas. It did sound like the boy had lost control for a moment. "How do they decide what is out of control and what is in control? They could keep you locked up forever."

He laid his head down on the book he had in front of him. He placed his hands on top of his head.

"We can argue he wasn't out of control."

"There's no *we*, Merin. It's just me. And I don't have the words. I . . . I need to." His words softened. Merin heard the tears he was trying to hold back.

"I think you should go lie down for a while. I'll read the rest of this," she said. "Get some sleep in a bed that's not inside the Refuge for once."

He shook his head but eventually relented. She waited until she could hear his breath even out. It was probably the first time that he had gotten any real rest in weeks.

She checked again to make sure he was asleep. Letting her fingertips graze across his forehead. He nuzzled into her fingers, and she blushed.

Now that she was sure he was asleep, she got the paint out of the bag from the market. She dipped the paintbrush into the paint, and with just a moment of hesitation, she started drawing the Raven's tattoo onto her wrist. When it was done, she rolled up Bryce's pant leg to compare the two. His was old now, faded and warped as he had grown over the years. Hers was dark, and the paint was still wet, but it looked right. She could take a needle and poke it in herself or find someone to do it for her. There were Magics who could move ink. There was even a student in the school she could talk to in the morning. The black ink stared at her, but she didn't have time to just stare back at her wrist. Thomas needed them.

She went back to the table of law books and sat down, careful not to smudge the new ink on the old books. She read through as many different scenarios as she could. There were no cases where Magics had successfully defended themselves against the claim that they were out of control. There had been so few trials against Magics. The older the book, the more cases of trials, but they disappeared throughout the years. No wonder no one seemed to know about them. The Magics of the past had probably given up hope, and eventually no one remembered. She had only come across the fact that family could present a case for them randomly when looking for something else for Kor when they were smoothing everything over with the Council after Aer's rebellion. She never thought to look for actual cases.

Only family was able to argue for the Magic. The Magic was not allowed to speak for themselves. It seemed that sometimes they weren't allowed in the courtroom, depending on the level of fear from the court. They were tried by a single judge. She thought about the fact that her father, who had been a lawyer for decades, was going up against Bryce, who, after one paragraph of law, had fallen into the deepest sleep she had ever seen him take, and she realized this was going to be a much harder fight than she thought.

Why hadn't Kor left her in charge of the kids? Sure, it probably would have hurt his feelings, but she could do this. She could never ask Bryce to give up the kids. It made him feel useful and honored. The idea came to her in a flash. The law said family members.

She shook Bryce awake. His fists rose to cover his face.

"It's just me," Merin said. Bryce untensed. "We need to talk."

"That doesn't sound like something I'm going to like."

"I'll give you a minute to wake up. I'm going to need your full attention. When you're ready . . ." She wandered back to the books.

Bryce stretched and grabbed a glass of water before he sat down. She tapped her finger on the paragraph explaining the family member angle.

"Hey, before," Bryce said as he sat down, "there is something I need to tell you."

"Well, first, I need to ask you something." She pushed the book over to him and tapped the paragraph. "Read this first."

He grabbed her arm. "What is that?" His eyes focused so clearly on her wrist.

"It's not important. Focus on what I'm trying to tell you."

"It is important," Bryce said, shaking his head. "Why did you do this?" The ink smeared, and his furrow lessened a little.

"I'm tired of being different." Merin pulled her wrist toward her body.

"Do you know why they mark us?" he asked.

"Because it shows—"

"Why they mark us where they do? Why, unlike a pirate brand or a criminal tattoo, Magics' tattoos are all in different places? Why mine is on my leg and Aer's was on her neck? Do you know why?"

"I . . . I don't."

"Because we can never remove them. If a pirate wants to escape their life, all they have to do is cut off their hand. They'd survive. Some of them might even be able to keep most of the hand, but Magics, they place it where they place it so that a Magic can't complete the connection with the elements. Aer can't talk with the winds if she has no neck. Kor can't read the cards with no hands, and I couldn't connect to the Earth without both feet on the ground. Sure, we'd live. We might still be able to connect in some way like Kor can. But it wouldn't be the same. It would be a strain. You can tell something is missing for Kor. I bet he hasn't been truly happy since that acid hit his skin. That mark is control."

"But you show yours off with pride?"

"Pride. Sure. Kor taught me that much, but there is nothing I can do about it. I have one. I didn't get a choice. You have a choice."

"Right, and I have a choice to show you that I understand and I'm with you always."

"Do you think I don't know that? I've seen what you've done. You've given up your life, your family. I know you say you can still go home and that things will work out, but we know you haven't even tried to reach your parents in weeks. Rachael has brought all these books to us. You haven't stopped by your house in longer than that. You've poured yourself into the school, but I know you miss your own lessons. I know you want to go home."

"I don't want to go home."

"Merin, I want to go home, and my parents didn't protect me, but sometimes, especially since Kor left, I've wanted to go home and just sit in the fields for a few hours. You have a choice. Don't do it, Merin. Don't let them ink something on your skin that tells them how they can control you." He reached down and smudged the ink that had mapped out where the tattoo would go. "I know who you are, and so do you. You don't need ink to tell you to have pride in yourself."

She snatched her wrist back and looked at the Raven's head smudged on her wrist. A single tear rolled down her cheek.

"Tiernan's Raven is on his heart, right next to the Phoenix," she muttered under her breath.

"Exactly, because Tiernan is fire." Bryce laughed just a little. He got up and got a wet towel. He gently rubbed the paint from her arm.

"Well, this is either a great time or an awkward time," Merin said, "but will you marry me?"

"I'm sorry, what?" He pulled back from her.

"Anyone who is family can defend Thomas. It doesn't have to be you."

"But your father?"

"Actually, it may throw him off more if it's me. You, he may want to destroy even if he believed you were right. He's not your biggest fan. Besides, you said it yourself: I haven't been home in weeks."

"And somehow that's going to change if we get married?" Bryce dabbed at his temple with the wet towel, smearing black ink across his forehead.

"This is stressing you out. I'm not trying to add more to your plate. Let me help, Bryce."

"And I don't have to go to court?"

She could see the relief begin to win over the surprise on his face.

"Well, I'm glad that marrying me is good for something." She laughed. It was an awkward request.

"Merin—"

"We can just be married in the courts, not like under the eyes of the Twelve Gods. It can just be for the time being until Kor comes back."

"Merin, I love you. I love you because you're smart, patient, and kind. I love you because you do what's right. I think I can handle being married to you for whatever reasons the world presents me."

"Bryce, I . . . I . . ."

"When?"

"When what?"

"When should we get married?"

"Before the court case, so before next week."

"How about tomorrow?" Bryce suggested.

"There's paperwork, but I bet Bethlem could help me push it to tomorrow night."

His face fell. "There's something I need to tell you first. It's only fair. There's something wrong with me." Bryce looked anywhere but at her.

"What do you mean?"

"I've . . . I've been losing control of my magic." He rubbed at the back of his neck.

CHAPTER TWENTY-ONE
KORVO

STORMS COME FROM ANYWHERE OUT ON THE OCEAN. THEY come fast. It had only been a matter of hours after Kor read the cards within Captain Dacia's quarters when the sky began to darken. It should have been midday, but the light faded quickly. Lanterns were produced and spread around the deck of the ship. Once it started raining, they would work in the dark, and depending on the ferocity of the storm, it may be a matter of moments or hours.

Kor felt the first splatter of rain hitting his face. *Best to get out of the way and let the crew work.* He started to head down into the belly of the ship, but Jaxson called out to him.

"We could use an extra pair of hands," Jaxson said. Kor turned around and headed back up the stairs.

"I know enough to be barely helpful, but if you need it," he said. The ship rocked, and Kor wobbled on the deck. Jaxson held his hand out, and Kor grabbed it. "Like I said, barely useful."

"And like I said," Jaxson straightened Kor's rumpled shirt, "we run a skeleton crew. Any hand around needs to be put to work."

Kor looked down at the hand he had given Jaxson, who rubbed at its disfigurements.

"Every hand is useful to us," Jaxson said, bumping Kor with his shoulder before heading on. Kor followed him. The boat creaked and rocked as the waves around it began to grow. They weren't big

145

enough to crest the sides, but even small waves like this could be dangerous. The wrong step could send him over the edge.

"Here," Jaxson said, throwing him a rope. "You remember how to tie one of these?" Kor blinked. He looked down at the rope in his hands and then looked over to Jaxson, who was securing one end of the rope around his waist and the other along hooks that surrounded the main mast. "Can't catch you every time you stumble," Jaxson teased.

Kor nodded and tied his rope around the hook next to Jaxson's.

"It's got to be tied tighter around your waist," Jaxson said, pulling the rope tighter around Kor's middle. Jaxson was starting to have to yell to be heard over the wind. "Ready to climb?"

"Climb?"

"We have to get the sails up."

"Up? In this wind?"

"Captain's orders." Then he started to climb. Kor followed him. Rung over rung he let himself up like the side of the Refuge he had climbed so many times. He shivered as a blast of the ocean air shot through him.

"Aer would be laughing right now," Kor said as he steadied himself.

"What?" Jaxson called. He pointed at his ears. "I can't hear you."

Kor waved him off. There was no use trying to explain it while yelling over the winds. Jaxson shrugged and kept climbing.

They had reached the next level. Jaxson slipped over to where Kor was and stood near him.

"What were you thinking about?"

"When?" Kor asked.

"When you were climbing up here. You seemed awfully distracted for someone climbing in the midst of a storm."

"My friend Aer, she had wind powers like the captain. She would have laughed at me being blown about in the winds. She would be climbing as high as she could, conversing with the wind throughout the entire storm."

"Had?"

"She died recently saving the small boy I was trying to protect from the General."

"The General you mentioned this morning?"

"The same."

"And Aer was a friend?" Jaxson asked.

"She was . . ." he paused, trying to describe Aer. "She was my oldest friend, and sometimes she was more . . ." He let the rest of his thoughts fly out of his head with the wind.

"Captain says those that speak with the winds are never lost," Jaxson said, looking out to face the storm. Rain splattered on his face, but he kept staring out into the distance. "The wind keeps them around forever, taking their memory around the whole world."

"So you're telling me this wind *is* laughing at me." Kor looked out into the darkness of the clouds that had gotten very close now. "Thank you, Jaxson."

He simply nodded and went back to work. Kor tried to keep up with Jaxson's deft hands and his decisive movements, but it was clear this was nothing new for Jaxson, and Kor was trying to reawaken muscles that had long since fallen dormant. He closed his eyes. It had been almost a decade since he had been on a ship. The moment he closed his eyes, the boat below him rocked severely to one side. His eyes flew open.

"Are we going to try to outrun this storm?" Kor asked, tying the last bit he needed into place. Jaxson smiled. It was a wicked sort of smile that made Kor smile as well.

"You'll see."

Kor looked up. The darkest of the clouds were over them now. Thunder was rumbling loudly enough that it shook Kor's teeth. There was no way that Dacia had enough power to beat this storm. It was moving quickly and only getting stronger. Waves crashed onto the deck, drenching Kor from head to toe. He was happy to find the rope was still tight against his waist.

"We'll never outrun this," Kor yelled at the top of his lungs. Lightning crashed as if to accentuate his point.

"You're right," Dacia said, coming from behind him.

The sails were whipping themselves into a froth, and Kor was sure they would start to rip any moment now. The lanterns had all been knocked out by the waves or the rain, and it was dark along the deck.

"The sails are going to go," Kor said.

"You've been on land too long," Dacia said. Lightning flashed again, revealing the captain's face. There was a line in her brow that

Kor couldn't quite place. Her voice was filled with a sense of levity like Jaxson's smile earlier, but her face was filled with creases that looked like they were holding that levity to her face like a mask.

"This storm is moving faster than us. It's going to batter us until we're all broken and bloody floating in the ocean."

"There's a shorter way," Dacia said. She whistled, and the crew snapped to attention.

"And how is that?"

"Through," Dacia said. "Now move over. It's time for this captain to work."

She walked slowly, but Kor noticed that she didn't falter a step when the boat rocked beneath her. She stood under the main mast.

"Let's go," Dacia said. The crew all moved at once. Hardly a word was said between them.

The ocean fought them every step of the way, but the ship slowly turned. They were face to face with the raging storm. The wind whipped around Kor, causing his eyes to tear. His tears were part of the ocean now.

"Now," Dacia yelled. Everyone braced for impact, and Kor only barely grabbed onto something solid before the boat lurched. Dacia had called the wind into the sails. It was flooding them, pushing them through the storm. The boat jumped, but the sails were solid. They flew toward the clouds. It got darker. There were no lights.

It felt like he had been swallowed, and he would have thought time stopped if he wasn't still being pelted by rain and ocean spray from every side. He heard the sails snap. Dacia was losing them. They were nowhere near the end of this storm. Kor felt his way toward the mast. He didn't have a plan of how to help, he hadn't had a plan this entire time, but he had to act, so his feet kept going forward.

"Dacia," he screamed, the winds howling around him.

She made no noise. He climbed closer to her. He hooked his arms into the rungs of the ladder to get to the next deck of the ship. The storm sent him slamming into the side of the deck.

"Captain," he heard right above him. Kor was sure it was Jaxson, but it was still too dark to see. "Captain Dacia," Jaxson called. The sails now were being blown the opposite way. The storm was winning.

"Jaxson," Kor yelled. "Jaxson, that song you were singing earlier. It's a song of the winds. Maybe it will help."

He wasn't sure Jaxson had heard him, but the sails had stopped sputtering around. The ship had stopped jerking from side to side.

They were moving through the storm again.

"Jaxson, keep it going." It shouldn't have been working; Jaxson didn't have any magic, but maybe it was helping Dacia maintain what little strength she had left.

The sky was beginning to lighten.

Kor could see Jaxson bracing Dacia, whispering in her ear. They looked alike, Dacia and Jaxson. He hadn't noticed it before, but braced together, it made a lot more sense. They had the same eyes.

They were nearing the edge of the storm. The light had returned, and the wind was no longer whipping at him. Kor realized he had been squeezing the metal rung with his arms as tightly as possible. There would be bruises along his elbows; he could already feel them forming.

Now in the light, he could see Dacia clearly. She was having trouble breathing. Her whole body heaved each time she breathed in, trying to help her lungs pull air into her body. Jaxson had his forehead pressed against her temple.

"Jaxson," Kor called. He climbed up the rest of the way. His arms ached, but he rushed over to them.

"Help me get her to her quarters," Jaxson said.

Kor nodded.

"Just help me get her on my back. I'll carry her down."

Kor helped Dacia stand. She was lighter than he thought she would be, and she felt bony. He steadied her as Jaxson shifted her onto his back.

"I'm not a child," Dacia said with gritted teeth, but she let Jaxson wrap her arms around his neck.

"I know. This would be a lot easier if you were," Jaxson said, but he let her go at her pace.

The rest of the crew was working diligently. No one seemed to be watching as their captain was taken down to her quarters. This must not have been the first time.

They went about their business like nothing was happening. They were almost too convincing.

When Dacia woke up, Kor was sitting next to her. She blinked at him a few times like she was trying to place him, but eventually a look of understanding washed across her face.

"Korvo," she said.

"Captain," he said, bringing her a glass of water. "That was impressive."

"It would have been."

"What's happening with your magic?" he asked. He should have seen it before. It wasn't that she wasn't a strong magic or didn't have a lot of control; it was like her magic was disappearing.

"Too long of a story," she said. She turned her head away from him, avoiding his eyes.

"Then let's start with a shorter story," he said. "You and Jaxson, you're siblings, aren't you?"

"Jaxson is my older brother."

"He calls you Captain?" Kor said.

"I am his captain."

"Fair enough. Are you trying to keep it a secret?" Kor asked.

"No. Everyone figures it out eventually. We look enough alike."

Kor looked her over. How could he have not seen it before? Their skin was similar in color, a dark black that seemed to echo the depths of the ocean. Their eyes were amber gold. She had just been brash, and he was so mellow. But his smile and her laugh were cut from the same cloth.

"What happened out there?" Kor asked again. Dacia looked at him and sighed.

"The culmination of a lifetime of misfortunes."

"I have my own," he reminded her.

"Of course."

"I can be relentless when it comes to gathering the information I need, so you might as well tell me now. And honestly, I'd probably just be getting into your crew's way."

She sighed. "Jax and I. We lived in the south. The very tip of Hadran. Our family were merchants. Trading with places like your Kaybrum and the East. Jax was meant to take over the business, but there was a ship, at the end of the war, that took me. Made me work for them by blowing them wherever they told me to go. There was no rest for the wicked, they told me, and I could feel it." She pulled her hand close to her chest. "I could feel my magic just sputtering. We were dying. There wasn't much left of us. Jax found me. There was a fight. Jax knows this part better than I do. I was barely conscious. Turns out the ship belonged to big money. They banned our family from all of the ship routes. Jax tried to do other work, but his heart belongs in the sea."

"So you became pirates."

"I went looking for revenge. I gathered a crew, and I went looking for that ship. The law wasn't going to help, and I decided to take it into my own hands. But when I found them, I couldn't do it. The lightning I had seen so many times in my dreams, I couldn't bring it down about their ship. Instead I took the Magics that were aboard. Some of them are still here. When I got back to shore—"

"You were labeled a pirate."

"Steal cargo and get yourself a few marks to go with it. Matches the look a little. I feel like it says more about me now than the Raven's head. You've seen what doing magic does to me. How did you know about the song?"

"Heard it from Jaxson while he watched me coil some rope."

"But how did you *know*?"

"I'd heard it before. My friend, Aer, sang songs like that all the time."

"Is Aer the friend Jax was just telling me about, a Wind Magic, and . . . something more?" She laughed.

"When did he tell you that?" Kor asked.

"We find storms give us a chance to talk without people hearing."

"So you're talking about me," Kor said.

"We've been around the world with the rest of this crew. Who else are we supposed to talk about? Besides, my brother seems to have a special interest in you."

"Special interest?"

"I'm trying to tell you that he likes you, and I'm trying to gauge your reaction to see if I can tell him to tell you. I'm just too tired to do it more subtly."

"I'm not sure I'm ready for that." Kor's eyes drifted from the captain.

"Not ready, or not interested?"

"Not ready," Kor said. He was sure of it this time. Aer flashed through his mind. The curve of her smile on the rare occasion she laughed. Jaxson's softness was nothing like the angular lines of Aer's face. She looked like electricity had been forced to take human form. Jaxson was like fabric that had been left in the sun. Soft, sturdy, but supple. Aer's hair had glimmered in the sun while Jaxson's dreads floated around him in the soft lantern light. Aer was abrasive, and Jaxson seemed to go with the flow like the waves of the ocean. They were so different. But passion, purpose, and beauty. They both had those things in spades.

"I'll have to let him know," Dacia said. She began to cough. Her body convulsed, and she hugged her stomach in.

"Can I do anything?"

"You got some healing powers?" she said between groans.

"No," Kor said. "This is all from them running you ragged on the boats?"

"Yes and no. Somewhere along the way, there was this—" she coughed again.

"Let me guess, some metal or fabric with metal in it that they made you wear."

"How did you know?"

"Whatever they used on you, they perfected it. They sent some to Kaybrum. That's what happened to my friend. The stuff made her power run so hot."

"It killed her?" Dacia asked.

"We couldn't get it off. She chose. She chose to save a little Fire Magic instead." His throat was raw, and he felt a little rim of tears trying to push their way out of his eyes. He blinked them back in the dimness of the room.

"I see. How's the Fire Magic doing now?"

"Probably hates me now. I left. I stopped thinking and let my anger pick up my feet to chase after the General. I just left him in Kaybrum with everybody else."

"But how's his magic?"

"That boy has magic control like I've never seen. He's scared now, but he's seen a million things in his short life. I don't know if one more would really damage him all that much." He tried to end it with a laugh, but it got caught in his throat and came out as more of a sob.

"You can still see the scar it left around my neck," she said.

"Everything does some damage. Even if you can't always see it." She coughed again. It took a few minutes before she could speak. Kor waited. "And sometimes, it's pretty obvious."

"Does the crew know?" Kor asked.

"They pretend they don't, but they do. Everyone has heard me cough my insides out after I have to use my magic."

"And the crew," he said, coming closer, "do they know what you are really trying to do?"

"You mean, do they know what the cargo is?"

"Of course. That's why they all signed on," Kor answered his own question.

Kor leaned against the wall. Looking out the window, he could see they were far from the storm.

"I left my crew at home. I left them a note, and I ran." He let his head thump against the wall.

"Sometimes a captain has to make a decision."

"Sure. But what decision did I make? I had no plan. I just wanted revenge. Revenge for what the General did to Tiernan, to Aer, to me, and all of the other Magics in Hadran. I normally plan things out. It took years of plans to destroy the Refuge—" He faltered. Dacia wouldn't know what the Refuge was. "A torture prison for underage Magics."

"Did you always have a plan? Did you wake up one morning and say, here is my ten-step process for destroying a prison? Or when you started, did you just want to rage with the fire of your frustration and let it burn a path for you?"

Kor hadn't thought about that in a while. His world had been ruled by the to-do list. By walking the tightrope of keeping everyone safe and getting something done. He had colored within the lines for years; it was hard to remember that, at one point, he had wanted everything to go up in a blaze. He had tried to separate himself from the Korvo out in the jungle, who had wanted to wage war, and the Kor who had found himself in Kaybrum, making a difference where he could.

"You wanted it to burn then, just like you want it to burn now. You just had a lot longer to figure out what was happening then. You played a slow game. One game piece at a time, but now the game board has switched and shifted. You have the same zest I bet you had back then. I can see it across your face right now. Nothing's changed, Korvo. You just haven't found your plan."

"I found you guys," he said.

"And that's probably good enough for now. We have a few more days to make a plan before we hit Sepsrym, and then we can make a new plan once we hit land."

"I still feel bad for abandoning them."

"But did you abandon them or just delegate some of your work to a crew that can handle themselves in a storm?"

Kor closed his eyes. He had written the letter in a bit of a rush, but he didn't regret what he had said. He had always trusted Bryce and Merin. He had sent them to find Tiernan in the very beginning. Sent them to gather people to make them understand what was happening at the Refuge. Bryce had convinced the Council. Merin had stood up to her non-Magic friends. He trusted them. They were small, but they operated as well as this crew. They were just miles apart.

"If you don't mind," Dacia said, "I'm going to take a quick nap before we get back to work."

"Of course." He turned to go but turned back to look at her. "Thank you."

She smiled at him. "And you promise you're just not ready?"

He nodded.

CHAPTER TWENTY-TWO
TIERNAN

THE LONGER HE WAS OUT AT SEA, THE WORSE TIERNAN felt. The salt pushed at his temples like knives, and the rolling of the ship made him feel like he was constantly spinning. And the worst part was, it had become clear that this crew was not a fan of Magics, which made it hard to practice with his fire.

Samuel, the cook, whom he met first on the boat, had taken a liking to him, and had let him come work down with him when the captain didn't need him to scramble up the riggings to suffer the ocean from a much higher height. As much as he could, he lit the fires when the cook wasn't looking and played with the fire when no one else was around. But even when he could use it a little, it was still a risk. Fire on a boat was a danger—fire that he wasn't sure he had total control over, that was even worse.

He was letting a small flame dance around his fingertips when he heard the sailor coming down the steps. Tiernan could always tell it was him because he walked with a lurch, kind of like Bryce did when he was in the gardens. Like his feet were too heavy to pick all the way off the ground. Tiernan wondered if the cook did it to keep grounded on the ship.

"You'll be happy to hear," Samuel called down to him. Tiernan tried to make the fire disappear like always, but it wouldn't go. He shook his hand, but the fire wouldn't let go. He placed the tiny droplet of fire onto the bottom of a loaf of bread near him. It scorched the edge of the bread, but it finally went away.

Samuel ducked his head into the kitchen. "Did you even hear me?" he asked with a chuckle. Samuel was a kind man. He was from the North. Tiernan figured maybe North of Kaybrum as his accent was stronger on the consonants than anyone in the city that he had heard. He looked more like Bryce. Brown hair, gray eyes. It made Tiernan trust him at once, which he knew was stupid, but he missed Bryce.

"Sorry, Samuel. I only heard a bit."

"You're still learning, kid. I don't expect you to always get it the first time. You're already the youngest cabin boy I've ever met, but you sure are a fast learner."

"What was it you were saying?"

"We're making landfall tomorrow morning. Picking up cargo."

"We're in the East?"

"Had to go south first. Picking up something really special's what I've been told."

"Where in the South?" Tiernan asked. He vaguely remembered the map that Kor had put up next to the table where they ate. He couldn't remember if there was anything more south than Hadran."

"Cooper's Town," he said, slicing an apple and eating the piece off of the knife. "Not much down there. A few mines, I suspect. So maybe we'll be hauling up gems or gold. Wouldn't mind sneaking me a pocket full of that." He looked over at Tiernan, who had lost some of the color in his face. "Of course, I won't. But can't a man dream? Enough money, he could get his own ship. Hire someone else to do all this cooking."

"Cooper's Town is in Hadran?"

"The very bottom."

Any color left on his cheeks drained into the wooden planks below him. He couldn't get off the boat. Even if he could get over the idea that he was abandoning Kor, there was no way that he could get all of the way from the bottom of Hadran back to Kaybrum. His heart sank. Could he even step off the boat when they were in the harbor? Was that too much of a risk? If he was stopped, he would be sent back to prison.

He looked down at the burnt bread next to him. Which was worse, this horrible ship or the prison he had lived in for years? He shuddered. He would take his chances on the ship. At least it came with the chance to find Kor.

"You still cold?" Samuel asked. "Ocean air just hasn't sunk into your bones yet?"

"Not yet, I guess," Tiernan said, but he knew it would never happen. Fire and water just don't mix.

"Maybe it's better that you get off in Cooper's Town. You can probably catch a caravan going back to Porttown or where it is you came from. Plenty of work for a lad like you."

"I think I'd like to see the East," Tiernan said.

"Oh, I don't blame you. It's a sight. None of these little ports can hold a candle to where we're going."

Tiernan got up, and immediately, the world rocked beneath him. He slipped down to one knee.

"Maybe it's best that you stay out of the way when they load the cargo," Samuel said. "You can stay down here or maybe even explore Cooper's Town. With the pomp and circumstance the captain's been taking with this voyage, I bet it will take quite a few hours before they're ready to take off again. Might be good for you to get some time on land at least."

Tiernan nodded. Land would be good, but Hadran? He had barely convinced himself to cross the border and wander through the forest. He had felt like he needed to hold his breath in Porttown, but at least he knew he could get back to Kaybrum from there, and Bryce and Merin would know where to look. If he somehow got stuck in Cooper's Town, he'd never get back. Tiernan ripped a piece of the burnt bread off and ate it to try and mask the tears that were brimming in his eyes.

"You best behave yourself," Samuel mocked. He pulled a small silver coin out of his pocket and handed it to Tiernan. "Go get yourself something to eat once we hit the dock."

Tiernan held the little coin in his hand. It didn't matter that it was the smallest and least valuable coin in all of Hadran; it was the most money he had ever had. He held it with reverence.

"I can't," Tiernan said, trying to hand the coin back.

"It's nothing," Samuel said. "Besides, I'm avoiding anything that I didn't make myself."

"You're cooking isn't *that* good," Tiernan teased. Samuel smiled and laid a hand on his head.

"I got my cards read by a Magic before we left. He told me he thought I would get sick. He saw a vision of me holding my stomach. So I'm just hedging my bets. If I make myself sick, I got no one to blame but myself now."

"A Magic?"

"You know they ain't all that bad. I know people think they're dangerous, but it's not like he was shooting fire out of his hands or anything."

Tiernan curled his fingers into his palms, worried somehow Samuel would be able to see his magic if he saw his fingers. He felt his nails digging into his skin, but he held them tight.

"He just looked like anyone," Samuel said, staring down at his own hands. "In the Northern Countries, magics live freely."

Tiernan studied Samuel's face. The older sailor looked like he was longing to go back to the North. Tiernan, for a split second, thought about showing Samuel what he could do, but he couldn't seem to convince his fingers to move. Then Samuel looked down at the knife he had set out to make the evening meal. The moment passed.

"Best to get to work. This crew is going to want to eat a lot this morning as we'll make landfall before breakfast. You best get to peeling them potatoes."

Tiernan pocketed the coin Samuel had given him and sat peeling the potatoes while Samuel sang to himself as he made the rest of the food. Sea shanties, easy songs with a rhythm that seemed to make the pile of potatoes go by much faster.

Samuel was the only thing that was decent about this boat, and he had been right about the crew being hungry. Being at a port meant that no one was worried about running out of food in a few days. They could pick up more tomorrow, and so the crew ate and drank and kept coming back for more. Tiernan spent all evening running down to the galley and back to the men around the boat. He filled cups, peeled a few more potatoes, and worked and worked until he was tired.

When they finally shut down the galley, Tiernan had caught the excitement of the crew. There would be land tomorrow—and valuable cargo. And while all of the other crew members were excited that they would be off to the East, Tiernan's excitement didn't get much past land. It was hard to think about anything, really, when everyone was in such a good mood.

He fell asleep holding the silver coin in his hand.

In the morning, there was a perfect indent of the coin that ran along his lifeline on his palm. All of the men were already out getting things done. They were docked by the time Tiernan made it above deck. Boxes were going out, and the men were moving quickly. He hoped there might be extra time to run through the town.

There were dozens of ships docked near them, and they were all larger than their ship. Tiernan wondered if those ships were any better out on the ocean than theirs. He looked past the ships to the town itself. It was busy and full of people. Cooper's Town was bigger than Porttown, but not like Kaybrum. Kaybrum was hard. Metal and glass seemed to be the favorite materials of everyone who lived within Kaybrum. Everything creaked or gleamed; nothing was just soft. Looking into Cooper's Town he saw just that. Softness. Intricate pillars made of mud bricks adorned large stores, and thatched roofs lined the walkways. Driftwood made its way into different forms of decoration, furniture, and buildings. It was welcoming, as if inviting him to take a load off and stay a while.

Tiernan shook himself. He couldn't get caught up in feeling like he belonged somewhere that would track him down and put him back in a cage to wait for his own death. He felt the coin that was still in his hand. He could take a step into that world, but he couldn't stay.

He weaved through the men who were swarming over the deck like ants on sugar. Barrels and boxes were moving at alarming speeds. Tiernan wondered if the chains he had found when he first boarded were being taken off the ship. In some way, the thought of those chains disappearing made him breathe a sigh of relief, but knowing they were being dropped off somewhere else in Hadran, the only thing he could think they would be used for was to catch kids just like him. He needed to stay focused. Get off the boat, find something to eat, enjoy the feeling of the earth standing still beneath him, and then right back here so they could take him east and to Kor.

He teetered down the gangplank, watching where the water splashed up the piers holding the docks out of the water. He hadn't seen anything for the water to crash against besides the boat for days. It was comforting.

And the ground was so nice. He felt stronger somehow, like his mind could finally process the world in real-time. His body, still reeling from the boat, felt like it was swaying. He took a few steps, but his feet held firm beneath him. He grinned and ran through the marketplace that made its way round the docks. Stalls called to all of the sailors in the port.

Some were offering food or clothing. Tiernan saw a booth offering new leather boots and hats of all different kinds and sizes. He wondered if the captain would be able to pass up a new hat. He seemed to pride himself on the purple monstrosity he wore with the large white feather in the band. Some of the other booths just seemed to have nice-looking ladies in colorful dresses. Tiernan ran by all of those.

He let his nose guide him to something that he couldn't resist. A silver coin wouldn't get him much, but it would get him something warm.

"Roasted corn," a booth called.

"Palmosos," cried another. That booth smelled so good Tiernan had to slow down. They had fried dough that was stuffed with meat. He walked up to the lady and handed her the silver coin. She handed him two. He smiled at her and went on his way. He had accomplished his main goal. He looked back to make sure he could still see where the ship was.

The first palmoso disappeared in a few bites. It was fresh and didn't taste like it had sat in the belly of the ship for weeks. And best of all, it wasn't dried, salted, or any form of potato. The second one, he savored. Bryce had taught him that. He frowned. He missed Bryce. What if Bryce was as upset with him as he was with Kor? At least Kor had said goodbye. How long had Bryce waited for him before he realized where he had gone? Suddenly the palmoso lost a little of its appeal.

Tiernan walked, holding the half-eaten fried dough in his hand. He could see the men were still streaming along the boat loading and unloading all of the different pieces of cargo. He had some time. He walked back through the market this time, taking in the sounds.

For so long, there had only been Samuel's sea shanties or the captain's yelling. And always, always the ocean. Now he listened to the chattering of all kinds of people. There were a few kids in the street. Tiernan didn't have to look hard to find scattered black tattoos popping up on their bodies.

Most Magics had the tattoo somewhere easily visible. He placed his hand over his heart where both his Raven's tattoo and his Phoenix brand were. His never needed to be visible; he was never meant to live out here, not even on the streets.

He walked over to the boy on the street that looked nearest to his age.

"Here," Tiernan said in Hadran. It felt so strange to use it after all of this time.

"Why?" The boy asked, giving the treat a suspicious glance. Tiernan didn't miss the boy's mouth opening and his hand moving toward the treat.

"Why not?" Tiernan asked. He shoved the still-hot palmoso into the kid's hand. He wouldn't try to have any more conversation. It wouldn't help either of them in the end. Kor would have. He would have figured out how to help this kid with dirt streaked across his dark features, but there was nothing Tiernan could do but risk himself. Tiernan squeezed his eyes shut as he headed back toward the ship. A couple bites of something nice would have to do for now.

There was no reason to stay out any longer. He treasured every step that he got on solid ground, and before he headed onto the weathered, wooden dock boards, he grabbed a rock to keep in his pocket. Maybe it would help center him. Probably not, but it couldn't hurt.

He felt ill immediately after getting back on the ship, so he went straight down to the galley. If Samuel was out, he could play with fire for a few minutes and try to make himself feel better.

"You're back?" Samuel said. His shoulders drooped, and his smile was far from the corners of his mouth. He rubbed at his eyes, which Tiernan noticed were rimmed with red. Where had he been?

"Thanks for the coin. It really helped to get the sea out of my lungs for a few minutes," Tiernan said, taking his normal spot, ready to start peeling potatoes. The men had worked hard, and they would want to eat tonight. He wouldn't get to play with fire until later, but at least Samuel's songs would make the first few hours back on the ship go by fast.

Samuel just nodded to Tiernan and went back to what he was doing. Tiernan waited for the songs of drunken sailors and mermaids in the waters, but they didn't come.

"Samuel, you're not singing," Tiernan said after a while.

"Right, sure." Samuel sighed. He rubbed the back of his hand against his eye, and then, in his low and rumbling voice that sounded like boulders bouncing down a mountain, he started singing a slow song.

Tiernan didn't realize he was crying until a tear fell onto the potato in his hands.

CHAPTER TWENTY-THREE
BRYCE

"I'm not signing off on this," Bethlem said when Bryce and Merin told him the plan.

"I'm not asking you to, just to figure it out," Bryce said.

"Bethlem, it's for the best," Merin explained.

"Wouldn't you rather have Merin arguing in court?" Bryce looked hard at Bethlem.

Bethlem shook his head and rubbed at his eyes. "What about your father?"

"It's what's best," Merin said. Bryce smiled. She had gained so much confidence in the last few months. She stood straighter. She looked directly into people's eyes. She spoke first in meetings about the school. And despite telling Bethlem it was just for the court, Bryce couldn't help but feel like the sun was exploding in his chest because he was getting to marry her. Maybe it was just a piece of paper, but it felt a little like she couldn't just slip away from him.

"I'd like it on the record for when Kor gets back that I didn't have anything to do with this," Bethlem said, shaking his head. But Bryce knew they had won. Bethlem whistled, and a messenger popped out of the back rooms. They often gathered in the back rooms, waiting in between jobs. Bethlem whispered to the messenger for a minute.

"It's done," Bethlem said, sitting down at his bar. Bryce had never seen him sit down, not even when everything had gone down with Aer and the Hadranian General. A little dramatic, but Bryce got the hint. This wasn't something to mess with, but he wouldn't mess it up. He couldn't mess it up.

"When?" Merin asked.

"They'll come get you at the school," Bethlem said. He waved his hand at them, and Bryce knew they had been dismissed and didn't want to cause the old man any more stress.

"Come on," Merin said. She pulled at his hand, and Bryce turned to go with her. "We still have more work to do before court."

Bryce nodded, but he couldn't help feeling like things were going to be fine. That feeling floated in him the entire day. He took over lessons at the school for the day. He even risked using his magic to show the kids some of the things he had learned about his connections to the earth, and he gave a history lesson on the Raven's head tattoo. The anxiety that had been gripping him seemed to ease a little when he could sneak a glance over at Merin nose-deep in a book and remember that in a few hours, they would actually be married. Even if it wasn't for real.

After dinner, a messenger appeared at the door. Bryce felt his heart beat a little faster. He caught Merin's attention and nodded toward the door with his head. She nodded and sent the little child she had been speaking with running off to bed.

"Where are we going?" Merin asked. Bryce shrugged. He hadn't bothered to ask.

"The Council building is closed, and they might not have agreed to it anyway," the messenger said. "A few clerks are still around in the records hall, but we have to get there before they leave."

Merin nodded. She grabbed Bryce's hand. It was warm and soft. Small but powerful. Without even using an ounce of her magic, the touch of her skin calmed him. Her pulse was calm whereas he could feel his rushing.

They walked quickly through the streets. Bryce would have preferred to run, giving his heart a reasonable excuse to be beating out of his chest, but he walked. The clerk's office was mostly dark, and Bryce worried that they were somehow too late, but when the messenger pulled at the door, it opened easily. Merin ducked into the dark hallway, and Bryce followed her. The messenger pointed down the hallway.

"Third door on your right."

"Thanks," Bryce said.

"I guess congratulations," the messenger said with a shrug.

Bryce smiled and waved at the messenger. He nodded and headed back out into the evening.

"Thought you two would never make it," Hayden said, greeting Bryce at the door.

"What are you doing here?" Bryce asked.

"It's like you think I don't know everything that goes on with the clerk's office. Who do you think I have all of those meetings with all of the time? I just happened to be working with Servil here when a messenger came asking for a favor."

"A favor from *him*, not you," Bryce said.

"Favors all around. Bethlem needed a favor, Servil owed me a favor, you needed a favor, I produced a favor. Everyone goes home happy. Or, I guess, in this case, you go home married. He didn't really explain why, though. You didn't get Merin pregnant, did you?"

"What? No." Bryce felt the warmth of the blush across his face. Hayden laughed. The blush only burned more.

"Let's not waste any more of Servil's time," Merin said, stepping in between them. Bryce noticed there was a rosy sheen on her cheeks as well.

"Not much to do. Sign a few documents. I stamp it. It goes in the books," Servil explained.

"Not very romantic, Bryce," Hayden teased. "You could have done so much more. Flowers, rings, a feast, fresh clothes at least."

"Let me guess, all things I could have purchased from someone in your marketplace?" Bryce snapped back.

"Well, we are open late now. I could just run over and grab a few things."

"It's fine," Merin said. "Servil, just show us where we need to sign."

Bryce couldn't help but think she was a little cold. This had been her idea, but what if she was regretting it?

Servil grabbed some papers and showed Merin where to sign. She picked up the pen to sign. Her hand shook. From regret? Happiness?

She handed Bryce the pen and gave him a small smile.

Servil pointed at the thin line where he was supposed to sign. It was next to Merin's loopy and curvy signature. Hers screamed grace and lightness. His was heavy-handed and crooked. The letters were all different sizes, and the Y was angular and crammed next to the R like it was trying to steal its wallet.

Bryce handed the pen back to Servil. He put it down on the desk and took out a stamp. It was a heavy-looking thing—formal in a way that a stamp that sealed their fates together should be. Servil rolled the stamp in red ink and then pressed it slowly onto the paper next to their signatures. When Servil removed it with a flourish, the city seal was clear: heavy walls encircling the leaves that represented the garden in the middle. Bryce had always liked the seal, but he had never liked it more than now.

"Done. It will be filed by morning."

Merin nodded. She wished Servil a good night, and soon they were out into the evening. It was still light out, being early in the summer, but Bryce looked around.

"I'd probably better get back to school. The last lessons of the day will be wrapping up, and I'll need to get the kids settled in," Bryce said.

"Bethlem's staying at the school tonight," Merin said. She glanced away from him. Pink sprang back to her cheeks.

"He is? Why?" Bryce asked. He wanted to grab her, to hold her tight against him, but he couldn't let his head get ahead of him.

"I thought . . . I thought we might want to spend some time together."

Bryce couldn't help but smile. "He agreed to that?"

"He didn't suggest it or anything." She looked down at the ground.

An awkwardness had crept into the conversation. And it stayed with them long after the door to the apartment had closed behind them. All Bryce wanted to do was look at her, but he couldn't seem to bring his eyes to hers.

"Being married . . ." Merin started. "It means you could live here."

"It does, but Bethlem's not going to start living at the school. He's got his own wife."

"I could start living with you at the school."

He didn't want her to spend the night there. Not yet. He didn't say anything.

"I guess we should take advantage of tonight then," she said, finally stepping toward him. She put her hand on the side of his face, and he leaned into it. His arms wrapped around her, and he bent his head down to kiss her on the forehead, but she moved to kiss him on the lips.

All the awkwardness of a few moments ago had disappeared. It didn't matter what anyone thought or what had brought them to this moment. He wanted nothing more than to be with her every second of every day.

He pulled away from the kiss. "I have something for you," he said. He reached into his pocket. He hadn't had the nerve to give it to her before. He opened his palm so she could see the smallest gold ring.

"You don't have to wear it," he said when she picked it up. "I didn't have a lot of time to save up, so I only had what I've saved from working at Vycky's." He felt himself rambling. Still waiting for her to say something. Instead she slipped it on her left ring finger.

"It's perfect."

"I love you," Bryce said. The words had been bubbling in his stomach all day and finally burst out. He had been trying to keep it business, to keep it the formality that they had attempted, but he couldn't keep it in anymore.

"I love you, too."

"I would have asked you, you know. When we were older. For real. For the law and the Twelve Gods and everyone in the whole world."

"I know. Now we just get more time together." They both looked at the ring on her finger. Bryce carefully threaded his stocky fingers through her graceful ones. The thin metal felt strange on her hand, but it made him happy.

"I know this was just a formality—"

"Bryce," Merin said. She looked at him with her beautiful blue eyes. "Just kiss me."

He did. And if it were up to him, he would never stop.

CHAPTER TWENTY-FOUR

TIERNAN

"SHOULD I THROW THESE OVERBOARD?" TIERNAN ASKED after he found a few potatoes that had rolled behind a barrel that were halfway to growing a brand-new set of spuds.

"Nah, hand them here."

"We have plenty of food for the crew," Tiernan said. Samuel had been very careful with the portion sizes since they had left port. Tiernan figured it was just because they were going across the ocean to the East with no stops in the middle. "I'm not sure we should eat sprouted things."

"Aye, it's food they won't miss."

"So you do want me to throw it away?" Not that Tiernan wanted to go up on deck where the waves from a storm were splashing the deck every few minutes. "I don't have to do it right now. I can wait till the storm has ended."

"Pass them here," Samuel said. Tiernan gave up on it making sense and chalked it up to just another thing about boats he would never understand. Samuel began to sing the sad song again as he peeled the sprouted potatoes and removed the eyes.

"Could you sing a different song?" Tiernan asked. Every time Samuel sang it, it made him sad, and without being able to use his fire to comfort himself, he would prefer not to feel that way.

"When I finish these, I want you to take them down to the hold."

"The hold? Is someone guarding the cargo? Was it jewels?"

"No, lad. But I think it's time you learned something about the sea."

"I have learned enough for a lifetime. Thank you."

"Then about life then. About how this world works. About why men sing sad songs."

Tiernan knew exactly why people sang sad songs. He doubted whatever was in the hold could rival what he had lived in his life, but Samuel was set on it, so down into the hold he would go. At least if he was alone, he might be able to use some magic for a moment.

"If anyone asks, you're sneaking this food for yourself," Samuel said after he bundled the hot potatoes in his kerchief.

"Food theft is a day in the brig," Tiernan said. More than one man had ended up there on the journey.

"I'll vouch that it was just scraps. But I promise it's better that way, even if it means a day in the brig."

Now Tiernan was more confused than ever. Maybe giving potatoes to the hold was a thing the Twelve Gods demanded. Maybe that's why they never seemed to answer his friends' prayers. They were seriously lacking in potato rituals. Samuel was a religious man; he might consider upsetting the gods worse than the brig.

"Off you go now, boy."

He made his way up top to the deck. The galley didn't connect to the rest of the ship's underbelly. As Tiernan slowly made his way across the ship, he saw that the storm had begun to close in on them. He prepared himself for the acrobatics his stomach would be performing the rest of the night.

When he climbed down into the ship again, he was already soaked from the rainwater. If he was never on a ship again, it would be too soon. He loved Korvo, but this was a part of his life that Tiernan would never understand.

He crossed the barracks with the hammocks swaying with the ship. No one seemed to give him any attention. Storms meant one of two things. Hiding out in the ship until it passed or fighting the gales on the deck.

"What am I supposed to do with this?" Tiernan said to himself as he reached the sturdy door that marked the hold. This was where he had gotten stuck when he first came onto the boat, and knowing there had been a box of chains in there, he hadn't come back since.

He opened the door slowly. A wave of stink hit him. This was not the smell of dried meat or spices. He knew this smell. It was prison. It was people.

The ship rocked, and the lantern near him flickered out. Tiernan was in the dark now, with only the smell of people and hot potatoes to guide him.

"Is that food?" he heard someone ask in Hadran.

"Probably just coming to torture us. Don't get your hopes up," another voice replied in the dark.

"Who are you?" Tiernan asked.

"Prisoners," the second voice said. It came from Tiernan's right. "I think that's obvious."

"Why?"

"Why are we prisoners, or why is it obvious?" the first voice asked.

"Why are you here?"

"Magics being taken to the East. I can't imagine it's going to be for a holiday. Although what is one prison to another?" The older man tried to sound nonchalant, but the echo of the chains as he moved made it sound hollow.

"Magics?"

Tiernan let a ball of fire roll onto his hand. The faces were illuminated now. Ten people. Ten Magics along the edges of the hold. They sat with their hands and feet chained to the wall. Now it wasn't just the ship that was making Tiernan's stomach turn.

"What you got there?" The first voice asked. He was a younger boy. Probably thirteen.

"Potatoes." Tiernan handed them over. The boy took one bite and passed it to the next person down the line.

"And the fire?" The older man asked.

"I'm a Magic, too."

"I can see that. I wouldn't let anyone on this ship catch you with that. You'll be down here with the rest of us."

"I can get you out. I'll get you out."

"And go where, little one? We're in the middle of the ocean. By the time we get to the East, we'll be too tired and hungry to fight."

The ship began to rock in earnest. Crates began to slide a little around the middle of the room.

"There's a storm. We could use the noise as cover," Tiernan suggested.

"Cover for what?" a sailor's voice came through the door. "Is our little cabin boy going to hurt some Magic scum? And just when I thought they had started making them too soft."

"Go, little one. Thank you for the meal." The man smiled at Tiernan. "Now put your fire out."

"But, I—"

"We are safer with you out there than in here with us." Tiernan extinguished the flame, plunging them back into darkness for a moment.

The sailor came in through the door, bringing a lantern with him. He had been drinking; Tiernan could smell the alcohol from where he stood. The crew would not be happy. Everyone was supposed to stay sober for storms. The last thing they needed was someone to get washed overboard or be unable to tie something down properly. That was it.

"I just came to make sure everything was properly tied down," Tiernan said.

"Oh, we got enough chains on them to keep twice as many of them in check. They ain't going nowhere. Captain says we have to just leave them alone, but a storm is the perfect time to make them scream."

"Captain won't like it if I report you've been drinking and disobeying orders."

"You worthless brat. On my ship, cabin boys knew when to keep their lips shut."

"We aren't on your ship. You are not captain. You are not first mate. In fact, I hardly know who you are, so I doubt the captain will have any trouble leaving you once we get to port. Or be sad if someone pushed you over the railing for drinking during a storm."

"You threatening me?" The sailor loomed closer. In the limited lantern light, Tiernan didn't see the man's hand until it struck him across the face.

"I'm just stating facts, sailor." Tiernan stood up. The man raised his hand to slap him again. Tiernan caught the hand before it hit him. Without thinking, fire sprung to his hand. It encased the sailor's hand in a ball of flame. He yelled.

"You're one of them. A dirty Magic! I should have known. Kester! Kester, get in here."

Another bumbling sailor came inside. He must have been keeping guard. Tiernan should have known that idiots like these never came by themselves. They always needed someone to fan the flames for them to do something stupid.

"Get the captain! The cabin boy's a Magic."

Tiernan heard Kester's footsteps as he ran toward the deck. The larger sailor pinned Tiernan's arms behind him. He could burn him again, but that wasn't going to get him anywhere. The Magics were right. There was nowhere to go. Not in the middle of the ocean.

It didn't take long to find out that the captain hated Magics more than he hated drunkards, and Tiernan was hauled up in front of the crew. They tied his hands in front of him.

Whispers darted through the crowd, barely audible over the screaming winds. "He doesn't have a mark," Tiernan heard someone close to him say. They searched him then. Finally, the captain pulled his shirt over his head. It stuck on his arms where they were tied, but the damage was done. Both the Raven and the Phoenix were visible to the entire crew.

They threw him in the brig.

"We'll put you down with the others when the storm passes," the captain said before he spat on the ground near Tiernan. When the crowd had thinned to go back to their posts and Tiernan thought he was alone, he curled into a ball. He had been trying to save Kor and had just ended up getting caught—again.

"I would have never . . . if I had known," Samuel's voice caught in a sob.

"You wouldn't have let me work?" Tiernan said. There was no point now in watching his tone. The damage had been done.

"I would never have sent you down there. I would have protected you. Can you forgive me?"

"Why? Why would you have protected me?"

"Because now you know why grown men sing sad songs." He brushed the tears from his eyes.

"Thank you for giving them the potatoes."

"I'll bring as many as I can." He stood and wobbled a little. "I guess that Magic on the docks must have been real."

"Why?"

"Because I have never felt more sick to my stomach than I do now."

"I think that Magic was my friend, Kor. He's going to find us in the East."

"I hope so."

CHAPTER TWENTY-FIVE
MERIN

THE COURTROOM SMELLED JUST LIKE SHE REMEMBERED when she had come to watch her father work when she was a little girl. It was musty and old like the law books they had been reading. Just being in the room made her feel like she had to walk quietly and speak softly. There wasn't much difference between here and her childhood home. Besides the smell.

She hadn't set foot in here in years. Ever since her father had become the full-time lawyer for the Council, he had stopped doing trials. She had never been on the floor. It was reserved for the lawyers and the judges. A Watcher sat to her right, and she was glad that she was the one doing this.

That is until her father walked in from the side room. His eyebrows were knit tight, but he wasn't wearing his best suit. He looked tired. For a split second, she wanted to walk to him. Let her magic soothe out the knots he was always getting in his back from sitting over a desk. She took a fateful step toward him, and then they opened the door and let Thomas in.

He looked gaunt. Where a few days ago he was full of vigor, he seemed empty. He was ghost white. The shirt he wore was torn and ripped in places all around him.

"Thomas? What happened?" Merin whispered.

"I can't say," he said. She watched his eyes drift over to the

Watcher in the corner and then over to her father sitting down and putting his papers all in order.

"After?"

"Either I tell you after, or it doesn't really matter," Thomas said.

Merin swallowed.

The judge came in. They stood.

"I can't remember how one of these goes," the judge said. He looked around the room. Merin's father chuckled.

"We won't have to get very far," her father said. "Only a family member or guardian can stand in on one of these trials, and looking at the paperwork, it shows that this Magic has been put under the power of Bryce Segal. This is Merin Pomry. As much as I might want, she can't stand in."

"Your honor," Merin said, taking a deep breath. She refused to look over at her father. She didn't want to see his face. "Council must not have seen the paperwork that Bryce Segal is my legal husband. Therefore, I am family."

She sat. She could feel her father's eyes boring into the side of her head. She stared down at the table. *Don't look.* Her stomach churned. She didn't regret it. This would have been too much for Bryce, and he had already had too much happen to him.

She didn't need to face torture or get any sort of tattoo. This would be how she could show him she was in, no matter what.

"I assure you, your honor, there has to be a mistake," her father said, sputtering.

She grabbed a copy of their license and presented it to the judge.

He poured over it. "It appears fully legal to me. Let's proceed, then. Mrs. Segal, you may start."

She took another deep breath. She glanced down at the notes she had written out, but she had memorized them. She was glad they had allowed Thomas in the building; they didn't have to, but his disheveled look would work in her favor.

She stepped away from Thomas and walked to the podium at the front of the room.

"Thomas was arrested for being 'out of control' of his magic. Someone who doesn't know what kinds of ways his soul is able to connect to the power of the Earth made a decision that he was out of control. It is a law that has been used to keep Magics like," she glanced over at her father, "like Thomas and I under the whim of the court system. But I ask you, what is control? And how do you determine control? You can't. Fire is out of control when it sweeps through a town, hurting people, burning down buildings, and running amok. A drunk is out of control when they're throwing bottles at others. There are no *legal* specifications about the definition of control." The words had been practiced. They came out of her with ease and confidence. When she was done, her father spoke.

His words were about the facts. Who had been where and what property had been damaged. Merin could tell he was not completely focused on the words.

The judge called for silence.

Merin stood tall, but this was not a normal part of the trial. It could mean anything, and she doubted she would be able to stop it if it came down to it.

"I think I've heard enough for today but not enough to proceed with this trial outright. I am releasing the Magic into his guardian's custody until a further hearing can be set."

Merin looked down at the sitting Thomas. He hadn't moved or reacted.

"You are getting to come home with me," Merin whispered.

"So I'm innocent?" Thomas's eyes filled with hope.

"Not quite yet, but we're getting there. And you don't have to spend another night in prison."

Thomas nodded slowly. The Watcher escorted him out the side door in order to collect his things and have the chains removed. Merin would meet him out front.

Merin walked out of the courtroom. She tried not to look at her father, even though her eyes were trying hard to catch a glimpse of him in their periphery.

"Merin," her father said, grabbing her arm. "I'm . . . I'm proud of you."

"That won't make me come home." She saw the little ray of hope dwindle in his eyes.

He sighed, "I thought that might be the case. Then I should warn you. This was not the first case I've been handed like this. It seems whatever happened to Thomas, and I know something really did happen, it's happening to people across the city. I have five more cases in the next two days that all list Bryce as the only member of kin."

"Five?" She couldn't keep the school running and be at every one of these trials. She had maxed out her favors with everyone in the last few days. Hayden couldn't spend more time. Bethlem had already left his bar more than he ever had in the past. She could go to one, maybe two. But—she watched as Thomas was greeted at the door by his friends with laughter and hands on his back—how could she choose whose trials to attend?

"Something's happening, Merin. Something is causing the Magics in the city to lose control."

Merin immediately thought of Bryce. He had been careful, but even being in the garden caused him to break out in a cold sweat.

They had to talk to these other cases. Figure out if there was something in common. If there was something messing with their connections like they were with Bryce. Or if there was something that had already happened to them that was finally kicking in. She had to talk to Hayden. And to Bryce.

He'd have to go to court after all.

Bryce was waiting for her in the school. The students were busy with the books he had handed out from the shelves. She noticed he hadn't passed out the *Little Fire Prince*. She didn't blame him.

"How was it?" Bryce asked.

"Thomas will be here soon," Merin said, sitting down. Adrenaline had been keeping her up, keeping her going, but now that it was finally done, she felt the ache in her legs like there wasn't enough blood getting through them; she felt her head tense at the temples, and her eyes were drooping.

"So things are okay?" Bryce said, coming to stand next to her. She forced herself to look up at him.

"For now. We won a battle," she said.

"So that's good. Why do I feel like I don't like what's coming next?" Bryce asked.

"I talked to my father."

"And?" Bryce's eyebrow tilted up.

"We're all right." She still wasn't sure what Bryce expected. She was tired, but she made a stab in the dark. "I'm still going to be staying at Aer's, but I might not wait till I know they're out to go get more clothes." Bryce seemed to relax with that.

"And? I know there's more."

"Exactly."

"Exactly what? Time to start making some sense here, Merin."

"There's more cases. At least five, my father said. All kids with your name attached to them."

"Well, you'll handle them like you did today."

"I can't. I didn't even win today. We have to go back. And there's more than one judge in the city. Some of the cases are at the same time. I can't be in two places at once."

"And they won't reschedule?"

"They don't want us on their schedule in the first place. They won't make exceptions for us."

"So . . ."

"You'll have to go to court. It's the only way."

"What about the school?" Bryce asked. He looked around. The kids were working independently, but that wouldn't always work. They were about four people short. "Can we leave them for a trial?"

"And if the city comes by and sees that we aren't here, we'll lose this place faster than you can make a flower bloom."

Bryce pulled away.

"I didn't mean . . . I just . . ."

Bryce saved her from her embarrassing stumbling of words. "We need to talk to Bethlem."

"I already did. He's willing to take a few more night shifts after the bar rush slows down. He's training some guys to work the bar for when he opens a second location in the marketplace, but that just gives us time to work on a game plan. It doesn't make the days any easier."

"I can't go in front of the court. You look exhausted, and you've been there before. They respect you. I won't win the cases. How do we pick who gets me and who gets you?"

"There's something worse," she said, rubbing at her temples. She wished she could heal herself, but she couldn't.

"Should I get a cool cloth?" Bryce said. She nodded. Him running to the kitchen gave her another moment to get her thoughts together.

The rag he handed her was dripping, but she dabbed at her forehead with it. It helped clear her mind a little.

"Should I sit down?" Bryce teased, his signature smile spreading across his face. She stared at him a moment.

"Bryce," she said, "they were all arrested because their magic is out of control."

"But you know that's just a rule they can throw around so they can take us whenever they want—"

She put her hand up. "This time, I think it's true. You heard it yourself. Thomas told us he didn't know he was doing it and . . ." she trailed off. She didn't want to say the words out loud.

"And *I'm* losing control." Bryce said, pulling a chair over to sit next to her. "What's happening?"

"I don't know. I figured it was because of the General that your magic was changing, but Thomas wasn't ever in the Refuge when the General was around. And the others, all at the same time. Something is happening."

She pressed the wet cloth to her eyes. The pressure helped her think, but the tiny droplets of water rolling down her arms distracted her enough that she couldn't put the thoughts that were buzzing around in her mind into any sort of plan.

"Merin?" a little voice asked from beside her. "Will you help me?"

Merin paused and looked down at the book that had been shoved onto the table in front of her. The text was small and was probably too advanced for a student that age, but she pointed at a few pictures.

"What do you need?"

"In this picture, this man works at the Refuge?"

"Why do you ask that?" Merin asked, The picture was a man taking notes of something that was bubbling.

"That's what they did, but I don't know this word." She pointed at the book again.

"*Alchemist*. It's someone who studies the world around them."

The little girl nodded a little, but she still had a frown on her face. Merin wanted to help her, but she had just made a plan.

"Bryce, I have to go. I'll send Bethlem again tonight if he can make it so we can get started."

"Merin?"

"I'll explain later."

She rushed back out the door and into the afternoon. She had to find Hayden. She headed to the marketplace.

He wasn't walking around the stalls, and no one had seen him for a few hours, but eventually, she was pointed in the direction of the warehouses where he often took inventory. She headed there. The doors were open, and she let herself in.

"Hayden? Anyone?" No one answered. The warehouses were labeled with cheaper versions of the signs swinging in front of the stores outside. She spotted one for Gesepi's.

Immediately she, felt the void of Kor deep in her soul. Just having him around would make this all easier. There would always be one of them at the school. He would know who to talk to.

Gesepi's space was almost empty. She wondered how much of that was because of all the wood Hayden had sent to the school. How much had Hayden spent on the school?

She walked deeper into the space to see if she could find anyone who could help her find Hayden. There was just a desk with a few notebooks, and by the handwriting, they were Hayden's. She flipped through them. They all spoke about the research at the Refuge. There was new information here. She had read Bryce's file so many times she recognized when something wasn't about him. Hayden must have been interviewing other Magics or had found some other files somewhere.

"Great minds think alike," she said to the dusty warehouse.

"Merin," Hayden said, appearing out of the depths of the warehouse. "To what do I owe this surprise? I thought you were due in court today."

"Today. Tomorrow. The next day."

"Not going well?"

"Yes and no. It went fine, but now we have a bigger problem. I think you might be just the person to help me fix it."

"And how's that?"

She explained what she had heard at the courthouse. She left Bryce's control issues out for now to let him maintain some privacy. "And then I came here," she said, "and it seems like you are already looking more into it."

"I have been," Hayden said, looking at the notebooks.

"We have to figure out how to help. Use what we know about how they tortured those poor Magics to help them now. We can do that, right?"

Hayden ruffled the corners of the notebook. "Probably."

She could see he was tracking his thoughts like he was reading all of the notebooks he had written in at once.

The next morning, she turned over to find Bryce asleep in the bed. She studied him as he slept. He must have come over after the morning shift had arrived at the school. She let a finger trace the lines of his face. He stirred awake.

One glance at the small sunbeams on the wall, and he pulled himself out of bed.

Merin let herself sink into the warmth of the sheets even as Bryce got up.

"I have to go to court today," Bryce said, standing and looking at his wrinkled clothes.

"I know. You'll do fine. I've gotten as much information as I could about the laws. If you remember even part of that, the kids will be okay. You just take a breath before you start yelling."

"I won't yell." He lifted his shirt to his nose for a smell and grimaced. "I can't wear these though. Did Kor leave any clothes here?" Bryce asked, looking around.

"In the top drawer of the dresser there." She pulled the sheets around her.

"This one?"

She nodded.

As he opened the drawer, the wood squeaked a warning, but it was too late. Bryce stared down at the open drawer. Merin sat up. She had hidden his file, right? She hadn't looked at it in quite some time.

"What in the Twelve Gods is this, Merin?" He held the folder in front of him.

"Bryce, I can explain. I just didn't want you to see it. I thought it might make things worse, and you were doing so well."

"I could understand that if you burned it. But keeping it in a drawer? Did you . . . " He picked up the file. A loose paper fell from the stack. "Did you read this?"

"I . . . yes. I did." Her chin dropped to her chest. "You kept saying I didn't understand. I just wanted to understand what was going on with you."

"I told you to leave it alone. That there were things I never wanted to share."

"But you were pushing me away again. Pushing me away and not letting me help. You can only fight demons on your own for so long."

"But they are *my* demons, Merin. Mine. There's a reason I haven't told you all these things. There's a reason I didn't want you to know what they did there because what if you couldn't go back in there? What if you couldn't teach in the school? Or what if you couldn't look at me the same?"

"Bryce, of course I would look at you the same. I knew bad things had happened. I just didn't realize . . ." A sob caught in her throat that she had been holding in since she had read the pages.

"Hayden and I figured it out," she said in between sobs. He hesitated but came toward her.

"You showed them to Hayden? How could you?"

"First, I wanted him to understand us. Understand what the school was, he didn't know. How could he? But, there's something I'm not sure you even know. Or maybe you do. You keep a lot of things bottled up. But I had Hayden read it again. If we hadn't burned the other files, I would have looked at a different file, I swear, but Bryce, they were experimenting on you."

"Yeah, different ways to torture us. I was there, and I wasn't the only one. It's right there in file 3571."

"All of you. And not just ways to torment you. Bryce, they were messing with your magic. The connection you have with the Earth. I think . . . I think they were trying to figure out how to take magic away from us."

"Well, they obviously never figured it out." He turned away from her, but she could see he was staring at his hands.

"It's like that fabric from Hadran. It messed with your connections, right? You said it yourself. You're having trouble controlling it. I see you avoiding even the flowers Vycky brings by, and I notice when you haven't been near the garden in days."

"So?"

"Kaybrum was doing similar experiments, but they were just going the opposite way. Instead of exploding the control mechanism, they were trying to turn it up so much that it choked off the connection. I've asked Hayden to see if he can figure out how to help the Magics. Maybe if we can slow down the court cases."

"You asked him to keep looking?"

"We need as much help with these cases as we can get. Now, the three of us can figure out what to do with the information together. It's your file, Bryce. I had no right to read it. I had no right to share it with Hayden. You can be mad at me for that."

"You lied to me." His fists balled up. "For this long."

"It wasn't a lie. I just . . . I didn't know how to tell you, and with all of the things going on with the court, I didn't want to burden you or make you relive those nightmares. You were doing so well."

"I . . ." his left fist tapped the table a few times, "I love you. I am angry. I should leave right now, but I can't. I want to find some reason to walk away, but I can't. I just want to wipe those awful things you read from your mind. I wish I could have comforted you every time you had to read one of those sentences. I want to be the one who helped you figure out something important, and I don't think we should let Hayden continue. We need to figure this out on our own. Magics will figure it out together."

"We will. I'll make sure Hayden doesn't get too far."

CHAPTER TWENTY-SIX
KORVO

Sepsrym appeared at first to be a paradise. The streets were clean and even. Wagons pulled carts through the wide paths with ease. But as Kor looked closer, things seemed like they had been polished with nothing more than spit. People kept their eyes down as they walked. A few here and there greeted each other on the street, but mostly, people trudged around the city as if their lives depended on blending into the sandstone walls.

Right before they had made landfall, Dacia had asked him how long until the other ship got there. The cards were clear. They had until the day before the new moon. Two days. Two days to make a plan, or two days to get better at flying by the seat of their pants. It didn't seem like nearly enough time for either option.

"Do you need to go see the captain?" Jaxson had asked, leaning over Kor's hammock that morning.

"For?" Kor asked. He was still groggy from the deluge of nightmares he had faced throughout the night.

"The Magics cover their tattoos when we reach port," he said. "Captain bought some special paint a long time ago to hide her scar. It works great on the other bits we have to sometimes hide."

"I think I'm all right," Kor said, lifting his mangled hand up for Jaxson to see. Underneath all the scar tissue, there was a Raven's head, but it was missing anything that was immediately recognizable.

"Why a Raven?" Jaxson asked, taking Kor's hand in his own and looking at the remnants of the tattoo that sat between his thumb and finger.

"That's what you want the answer to? Not, why my hand looks like that?"

Jaxson shrugged. "We've all got stories. Sometimes it's just better to let them come out when they want to come out. But information is always good."

"The Raven used to be synonymous with magic. I can't tell you why. There's not a lot of great reading on magic lore, but what I pieced together is that the Magics from the stories had Ravens, and that's how they all communicated. They would put Raven feathers in their hair or their belts and pass through the world mostly undetected. And when the East turned on the Magics, they used their own symbol against them."

"You know a lot about Magics," Jaxson said, letting his fingers drag over the lines in Kor's palm.

"I've pieced together a lot over the years. And when you hear bits of the same rumors from Hadran and Kaybrum, you start putting the puzzle together."

Jaxson grunted a response. But in that, Kor could hear his approval.

Even when he was walking through Sepsrym, that conversation made the worst of the scenery fade into the background.

As they walked, the words on the beautiful buildings read things like Office of Control, and the signs on the street told Kor how to report magic in three different languages. He had to focus. They only had two days to figure out how to stop whatever it was the General had been brought back for, and the first way to do that was to find the General.

Jaxson trailed behind Kor. Kor didn't bother to turn around and look; he could feel Jaxson's eyes on him. If he got any clue about the General, Kor was to move away immediately and signal Jaxson. He couldn't risk getting caught.

Kor knew he could have used the collar and the cards, but he felt his magic so differently here. And the East was not the place to misunderstand magic. So, they walked through the city slowly. Both listening for any murmur of conversation that might lead them in the right direction. The streets were too quiet. Even though many people were out, they all seemed to be so absorbed in their own business that they had no time for rumors or gossip.

Without rumors or gossip, everything he had accomplished in Kaybrum would never have come to fruition.

Jaxson slipped in next to him while they browsed a market stall that sold boots and other leather goods. Jaxson looked at the money purse while he chatted. His face was blank, and Kor tried to match his emotionless stare, but it felt nice to have him standing next to him when he was just beginning to think things were hopeless.

"Anything?" Jaxson asked. Kor shocked his head no. Jaxson picked up a different coin pouch. He looked it over diligently.

The shopkeeper came over to stand near them in the hopes of a sale. Kor moved to the other side of the stall. Nothing caught his attention on display, but a small leather cut-out that was sitting on the shop 's bench drew his eye. It was leather pieces cut to look like a highly detailed feather. Kor wondered how long it would have taken the artist to cut out each little sliver of the feather by hand.

"I'd better come back," he heard Jaxson say. "It's almost my shift to watch the ship in port, and my captain will tan my hide nicer than these purses you have. I'll be back, though. Been doing some trading down south, and Captain's promised to fill the coffers."

Kor couldn't see the man's face, but he could feel his whole demeanor change. Maybe people knew what was happening in the South. Maybe that's why everyone seemed to keep their heads down.

Jaxson left the stall, and Kor spent another minute or two browsing before he left and exited the other direction. The shop-keeper had not approached him. Kor was used to people avoiding him, his hand, and his magic. But this seemed different. It was like the man had frozen after Jaxson had spoken.

Kor glanced at the leather work on the workbench. A feather. A black feather. Could he possibly be . . . he didn't let the thought finish. Of course, he was looking for some sort of a resistance to help him. He felt alone and lost without his people and his plan. He was seeing things that probably weren't there.

"Hold it right there, Magic," a voice demanded from the street. Immediately, Kor froze. Maybe there was enough of the tattoo on his hand after all. He turned slowly, but there were no men standing behind him. Instead, they were standing in front of a young child. Older than Tiernan; younger than Bryce.

"You can't take—" the young girl started to say. Her defiance reminded him of Aer and Dacia. But she never got to finish her declaration. Suddenly they were on her, three grown men wrestling her to the ground.

Kor caught bits of what she was saying. "Where," and "others" drifted over to him, but the rest of the conversation and any answers she might have given were lost to the morning.

Within a minute or two, they had removed her from sight. The marketplace seemed to double down on the lack of eye contact. Kor realized he hadn't moved in the last few minutes, but neither, it seemed, had anyone else.

They had, however, begun to whisper, and whispers were information. And as Jaxson had said, information is always good.

Kor hung on every word that he could, but folks seemed to want to talk only when they thought no one could hear.

After the crowd had thinned for the midday heat, Kor returned to the ship. It only took a few more minutes for Jaxson to return as well.

"Tell me what you heard," Kor said as a way of greeting.

"Not much. That is the first time that's happened in recent memory. Magics were scarce."

"I heard about the same, along with enough platitudes that 'if they just kept to themselves, they would be fine. They had to go about bragging.'" Kor said. Jaxson rolled his eyes.

"I also heard one extremely pleasant old man talk about how he was glad the country was finally doing something about the infestation problem," Jaxson said.

"Infestation? They know Magics have always existed, right?"

"Of course not," Jaxson said. His face was the usual blank slate that Kor tried to puzzle out. "But they do seem to know that the all-powerful ruler of this place is meeting to discuss the problem."

"Well, at least we haven't missed whatever it is they are going to decide to do."

"We?" Jaxson asked, his face still infuriatingly unreadable.

"Is your plan still just to take the Magics from the ship that we can't even find and fly as fast as you can back to Hadran? Do you really think that's going to be enough? That there aren't going to be more ships? That they'll be safe in Hadran?"

"We can go north," Jaxson said. Something about the pull in his words and the slightest deviation from his effortless face made Kor realize *he* was included in that we. That the "we" Jaxson was talking about may not have included anyone else on the boat. Kor found himself wanting that we. Needing that we. He swallowed.

"I came to do something about it. We have to find out about that meeting."

"Then we find out about the meeting," Jaxson said.

Bits and pieces rolled in from everyone else who had gone into the city, but things still weren't clear.

"You have to play it smart, Kor," Dacia said when he began pacing in her quarters.

"You were the one that told me it was okay to want to burn everything down," he said, not stopping his relentless pace around the room.

"I told you that it was part of the process, but now is the time to plan carefully. I don't want you barging in there and announcing our presence."

"I need to get into that meeting."

"Then plan, Kor. Show me what you got."

He stopped pacing finally and sat down. He took a deep breath and brought out the cards, laying them out in a circle. He stilled his mind before he began to flip them, then studied them in silence. The pictures swirled around in his mind as he sorted through the images. He heard Aer's voice in the back of his mind asking questions, helping him line up the pieces of the puzzle. He hadn't heard her voice in a while. His heart sank.

"You got it?" Dacia asked, looking over at him.

"The palace. Tomorrow night," Kor said. Then he turned and walked out of her cabin. He needed to be in the air. He needed to be around Aer.

No one batted an eye as he climbed the mast. He looked down at the boat bobbing up and down with the whims of the ocean. He looked up. Nothing but blue skies. He would have liked at least one cloud so he could see the speed of the wind so high up in the air. He waited, but there were only gulls drifting lazily on the soft winds.

"You're out there?" Korvo asked the sky above, his fingertips itching to touch the collar stored in his hammock below deck. "I need more than my own words talking in your voice. I need a plan."

He let the visions he had pass through his mind as he watched the gulls gliding on the winds. The palace. He could sneak in as a guard or a worker, but in the palace, there wouldn't be very many Hadranian people, and not knowing the customs, he would stick out. He had never been one for acting. Where would he not stick out? How could he get in? He searched his mind for more information. He looked at the gulls; they pulled at the edges of the warm air that lifted them up in big gusts.

He watched them arch around each other. Completely oblivious to the world below them. That was it. It was obvious. He didn't need to go through the front door. He had spent so long in Kaybrum making sure he was allowed to come through the front door that he had forgotten what Aer had clearly realized. No one needed to invite them in. And with the palace, he could come in from the air. From above, Dacia could help. It would be a lot to lift him, and maybe Jaxson, so he would need to work fast.

Step one, Dacia would use winds to lift them into the palace grounds. Kor could find his way through the palace to the meeting. It would be somewhere secluded. Step two . . . he stared at the gulls again, hoping more of Aer's wisdom would rain down on him. The gulls swooped low, cawing at him. Kor pulled in his legs. He needed wisdom to rain down, not gulls. He let his forehead rest on his knees. Step one was clear. Step two was less so. What would he do? Gather information? What did information do for him here? It might help him find some Magics and what they were up to, but he had no pull here; no one would listen to him, and if the mutterings in the street turned out to be nothing, no one would help him. The leather feather from the marketplace flashed in his mind. He shook his head. He couldn't let himself hold out hope.

Aer wouldn't just collect information and sit on it. He had to learn to think like her. Step two suddenly became a lot clearer.

"Tired of being alone?" Jaxson asked from halfway down the mast.

"Never alone," Kor said, but he popped his head up and beckoned for Jaxson to join him. It was crowded for two, but there was enough room for both of them as long as neither tried to move around too much.

Their knees touched.

"Dacia said it seemed like you wanted to be alone for a while," Jaxson said.

"Yeah? Why'd she say that?" Kor said, staring out at the ocean.

"Because you ran out of her quarters. And since you climbed up here, when you never like anywhere where you might get cold, I can only assume you were thinking about Aer."

"I . . . I was also thinking about a plan," Kor said. He dropped his head again and scratched his ears.

"I can back off, you know," Jaxson said. It was so sudden Kor didn't have a response.

"It's not that."

"But you came up here to talk with her," he said.

"I did. I . . . Aer was my best friend, and together we fought in Kaybrum for everyone. It feels wrong to be doing it without her. Back in Kaybrum, I had the school. I had a plan. There was a next step, a step that had been around when she was, but once we were finished, I just felt lost. Like I couldn't go on in Kaybrum without her, you know? I had to leave."

"Because of the General?"

"Yes, and because I felt like there was no other choice. I couldn't stay there, but I couldn't tell Bryce and Merin that. I was running away without a plan. And I could pretend it was about the General, the cause of everything, but when we were this close, I can't pretend that was what it was all about."

"So you had to come up here and figure it out."

"Yes, but I have a plan now."

"And?"

"It felt like she showed it to me. Like she told me it was okay to start over." He looked down at their knees.

Tentatively, he put his hand on Jaxson's knee. Neither of them moved. They sat and let the breeze whisper around them.

"What's the plan?" Jaxson asked eventually.

"We get into the palace from above." Kor described his plan while Jaxson watched the gulls fly around.

"You think she can move both of us?" Jaxson asked quietly.

"She moves this whole ship," Kor said.

"And then she's tired for days at a time. She just moved the ship the other day. And if we find any Magics, we're going to have to move the ship again."

"I . . ." Kor wasn't sure he should tell Jaxson about the collar. He swallowed. "I have something that might help. Or hurt." He told him about the collar, what it did, where it came from.

"I won't give that to her," Jaxson said. "It might burn her up even faster than I thought possible."

"I thought that would be your response. I can go alone," Kor said.

Jaxson shook his head. "I might not be willing to let her use the collar, but I'm not going to let you go alone. They might recognize you and capture you before you can get any word back to us."

"I don't think we can risk it without help from Dacia."

"I'll ask the captain."

"Jaxson, why do you always call her captain?"

"She's the captain. It's her ship." He shrugged and started down the mast, but before his head disappeared below the platform, he stopped. "And I like to remind her that she's strong." He climbed down, and Kor watched him easily move across the deck to the captain's quarters.

That night, Dacia followed behind them. She had changed out of her normal clothes and into a drab dress. At first, Kor hadn't recognized her, but her tight curls peeked out of the kerchief she had placed over her head to match the local customs.

There were people out and about in the marketplace, but near the palace walls, the crowds thinned to almost nothing. They walked slowly until they found a place where no one could see them from the main road.

"You boys ready?"

"At your leisure, Captain," Jaxson said.

"I'll send Kor over first," she said. Pain rippled over her face as she called the winds to her. They bucked and pulled as she tried to pull enough together for the lift. After a few seconds, sweat dotted the edges of her forehead and dripped to the ground.

"It will only hold for a few moments," she said without opening her eyes from the concentration.

"What do you need me to do?" Kor asked.

"There's enough wind to sort of boost you up. I won't be able to lift you both. Just trust me that there's enough to hold you if you step right there." She pointed with her finger.

Kor took a breath and then jumped where Dacia had pointed. He felt the surge of air that pushed him over the edge of the wall. The air swirled around him. It sucked his breath from his lungs, and it took him a minute once he was over the wall to feel like he could trust breathing again.

He waited for a minute. Two minutes.

"Jaxson? Dacia?"

There was no answer but a small rush of the wind. Kor pressed his hand against the stone wall.

"I'll do it on my own," he whispered as loud as he dared.

He made his way into the castle. It was dark now and that meant there were lots of rooms that were encased in shadow. He moved from space to space toward the hallway that seemed to be where the lights were concentrated.

"This will fix the problem once and for all," a voice said from down the hallway.

"Are we so sure?" That was a voice Kor recognized. The Hadranian General. A voice that had haunted him for almost a decade. It made him stop in his tracks. Kor had known he was going to be there, but it still felt like a stone being dropped into his stomach.

"I know the last plan had, well, unideal results," said the first voice. Kor crept closer. "This time, we get to the source. We can finally get rid of the Magics forever. It doesn't matter if we turn the people against them. Now we can eradicate the entire possibility of magic."

Get rid of the possibility of magic. Kor's heart beat so hard he pushed his hand against his chest, just trying to calm it down. It didn't seem to work.

He wished Jaxson or Dacia was there. Someone who could make him feel like he wasn't drowning.

"We've been testing it for years," a new voice said. Kor was close enough to see them now. The new voice was sitting with their back to the doorway, but Kor could just make out the Hadranian General sitting to their right. "It's almost ready. Our last shipment arrived tonight. The last round of testing will begin when they are good and hungry—and obedient. A week or two in the caves will make them pliable."

"I still don't think it's enough. You haven't been to the North in years. People there don't see Magics as abominations. Some of them, some of them even wish they were Magic. It's going to take a lot more than just stripping them of their power. People there will rebel. I've seen Kaybrum turn over a single Magic. Just one, and they crumbled. You have to turn them against them. Then they'll beg for us to come in. Then we can do more than just get rid of the Magics. We can finally make some headway in taking over the North like we did the South." Kor couldn't see his face, but the amount of silk and gold piled around him made it exceptionally clear that the emperor himself was trying to destroy magic.

"What do you suggest?" the General asked.

"Just let me keep doing what I'm doing, and the North will crumble into our hands."

"There's still the problem with the cough," interrupted a man he couldn't see.

"You have a ship full of Magics to get it right." The emperor tossed his hand around like it was not important. Kor could feel his breath coming in sharp bursts, and his hands clenching. He moved away from the door; he had heard enough as it was. He didn't need to risk his anger getting him caught.

Now he just had to find out where these caves were. He moved back through the castle. He found a staircase that led down. Dungeons would be a good place to start looking for caves.

The stairs continued down for a long time. All the light from the windows above had long since disappeared by the time Kor found something resembling a door. He placed his hand on it. Even without the collar, he was starting to get more images from things around him. The door screamed of people's pain and desperation. Added to the sound of coughing he heard faintly behind the door, and Kor knew he had found the right place.

He eased the latch on the door so it would open quietly. He had no idea what he was walking into. There could be armed guards or bodies strewn about.

He slipped into the room. The walls were carved out of rough stone, a far cry from the smooth sandy towers above him.

A little light from a dying torch brought the room into focus.

A guard was there asleep on his chair, and tunnels branched out behind him. The coughing had gotten louder from one of the tunnels. It must be where they were holding the Magics.

Kor walked past the guard. He kicked a tiny pebble, but the sound echoed throughout the cavern. The guard stirred. He blinked a few times before slowly going back to sleep. Kor let out the breath he had been holding. He wasn't going to be able to do this alone. He would need help. Slowly, he slid his fingers over the guard's set of keys and pulled them from his pocket. There were multiple keys, and Kor hoped one of them would open a back door to the palace. Dacia would not be able to lift him again; that was obvious. Unless he gave her the collar. *No,* he interrupted his own thought. He had the keys now. They would be able to come back in.

Taking down the General would have to wait. These people needed them now.

Jaxson insisted on coming with this time after Kor had filled him in on what he had seen.

"I'm glad you didn't try to rescue them all by yourself with no way out."

"How many do you think we can sneak out at a time?" Kor asked.

"Ten seems to be the limit, to be honest. More if they are in good health, less if they are sick or injured or children. Kor—" Jaxson nodded over to a group of sailors that were walking by.

Kor's hands were firmly stowed in his pockets. One hand wrapped around the keys and the other around the collar. It was late, the ships were quiet for the most part as the sailors on shore leave fluttered about and the rest took to sleeping on the boat. No one would likely overhear them, but it was best not to chance it.

Kor kept his head down as they passed by.

A bump to his shoulder made him look up. A sailor had wandered into him. The walkways around the docks were wide, so the man must have been pretty deep in his cups to have run into him.

The man muttered what he assumed was an apology as he

sauntered away. He had looked familiar, but after days of combing through the city, Kor was sure he had probably seen every sailor on the docks multiple times. He followed the man's trajectory with his eyes. He knew he had seen that ship, though. It was the one they had been chasing since Porttown.

He nodded for Jaxson to look.

"We just missed them." He shook his head.

"At least we know where they were bringing them. It's just an extra step. Or maybe we can rescue more this way."

He went to take his hand out of his pocket and place it on Jaxson's shoulder. But the cold ting of metal met his arm. In his pocket, there was a new key. It wasn't old and iron like the rest of the keys. This one was new and it hadn't been in his pocket when he left the Black Phoenix.

"Jaxson, I think that man just gave me a key."

"That drunk? Isn't he headed back to *that* ship?"

"Maybe." Kor put his hand back in his pocket with the collar. He lifted the wrap on it so just his pinky finger would touch.

The man's mumbled words became clear.

"Please help them."

At the back door, it took a few tries, each key grinding at the lock until one of them finally snapped it open. Jaxson gave Kor a small smile. Kor nodded, and they plunged into the darkness together.

The door was locked this time, and there was no guard on the other side. Kor gave a silent hope that the guard had not been thrown into one of the cells down in the tunnels for losing the keys.

"Be prepared," Kor said, whispering into Jaxson's ear. "We don't know what kind of shape they are in."

"I'm ready." Jaxson put his hand on Kor's shoulder.

They walked toward the tunnels and followed the hollow cough down to the right. Kor slipped the keys into the cell door until he found the right one. It creaked when he opened it.

Twenty pairs of eyes all turned to look at him. One set of eyes was unmistakable.

"Tiernan?"

"Kor?"

The little boy moved to grab him, but a chain around his ankle stopped him. Kor felt bile bubbling in his throat.

"What are you doing here?" Kor asked in disbelief as he moved closer to the boy so he didn't need to speak anywhere above a whisper.

"I'm looking for you."

"In a prison?" Kor asked with a laugh.

"Based on our lives, it wasn't a bad bet," Tiernan said. Kor hugged him. He was still as small as he remembered, but he wasn't too skinny. The prison must be a new development.

"I'll get you out," Kor said, reaching down to the chains. None of the iron keys matched the locks around his feet. He tried the other key. It turned easily.

"Can you take everyone?" Tiernan asked. Kor looked around. No. They couldn't. There were too many. And in the shape they were in, he wasn't sure they could take more than five. They had to move quickly and out of sight. Get back to the boat, hide during the day, and come back for more when they could.

"No." There was no need to lie to the boy. He had seen it all. "We'll come back for the rest."

"I'll stay."

"You will not."

"If you can't take everyone, I'll stay."

"It could be days, weeks even, before we can come back for another round of you," Kor said. "You come tonight."

"I'll stay."

"Tiernan, I am your legal guardian, and I say you're going."

"Take them," he pointed to a group that was huddled in the corner. "Whatever they're doing to us, they did it to them. Their magic doesn't seem to work anymore, but mine does. It might work too well." He looked at his hands. "I can still fight. Take them."

"Kor?" Jaxson hissed from the door. "We only have a few minutes."

"I'm moving." He took one long look at Tiernan. It hadn't been more than a few months, but the scared face of the little boy Bryce and Merin had plucked out of the Watcher's grasp was gone. He was still small. Much too young to be deciding to stay in a prison willing to fight.

"It's okay, Kor. I know you'll find me, and I'd rather not spend any extra time on a boat if I can help it."

"Right," Kor said. He felt the threat of tears against his lower lids, but he looked up and blinked them away. Then he closed the ring back around Tiernan's leg.

He went over to the huddled mass of bodies that were cowering as far from the light as they could be.

"Come on," Kor said as he started unlocking their shackles. "You're coming with me."

They didn't need to be told twice. No one even spoke. They got up, still close together, and made their way out the door. Jaxson led them, and Kor stayed back to lock the door behind them.

"We'll be back," he whispered to the prisoners left in the room.

"I know," Tiernan mouthed back at him.

Kor tapped the door once and then followed Jaxson out the door.

They moved quickly. The streets were mostly empty, but anyone on the streets could ruin everything. The streets were clean, and there weren't a lot of large crates or anything discarded that they could hide behind. Kor made them walk in twos and threes, spaced out. Jaxson was at the front, and Kor made up the back. They tried to move inconspicuously without leaving too much of a gap between them all. A few times, Kor turned a corner, and he couldn't see the group in front of them, let alone Jaxson. He felt the familiar bile from letting a friend put themselves in a dangerous situation. No, it was more than just that. He felt the panic of losing someone again. Someone who understood him. Someone he could let see everything.

His heart beat so loudly, he worried it would give them away. The man next to him looked at him with fear. Kor flashed his practiced smile that said everything was okay, but he knew his eyes didn't reflect it at all.

They rounded another corner, and Jaxson came into view for just a second. He was looking into the window of a shop with his female companion. He smiled and nodded like he was out shopping for the girl's new outfit. Kor took a breath.

He headed down a different street. They couldn't all approach from the same side. An outsider passed by. Kor struck up a conversation with the man next to him.

"Sure is clean around here. No wonder the captain wanted us to take that bath."

The prisoner he had just rescued looked at him sideways, but Kor flicked his eyes toward the man on the opposite side of the street.

"You'd think being surrounded by the water," the man started. It was shaky at first, like he was trying to remember a life he had once lived, but soon the words came easier. "We'd smell a little better."

"Speak for yourself," Kor joked. "I think I still smell like a bucket of roses."

"Roses left out in a bucket of fish, maybe," the man joked.

Kor sniffed himself for effect. The conversation seemed to be working. The man across the street gave them a look and turned the other way. The look on his face didn't scream that he was going to search out the authorities, but it did say he wanted nothing to do with two smelly sailors who had probably squandered their money on something much less savory than a bath.

"Best not to keep the captain waiting." Kor kept the details vague. There were hundreds of ships in the port. Many of them would have Hadranian sailors mixed in with them. He had no extreme markings, and both of their clothes were old and tattered. They looked the part.

The old man beside him began coughing. Kor grabbed him and held him upright.

"The sea will clear it up," the old man said, but Kor saw a trickle of blood on the corner of his mouth.

Even though they had been in the back when they left, they weren't the last ones on the boat. A couple of men had been stuck for a few minutes chatting with a passerby about an argument. But eventually, they were all there.

Ten people. Ten Magics that no longer had any connection to the elements.

Kor and Jaxson helped them onto the ship. Many of them were coughing, just like the man that had walked with Kor. Kor saw the flecks of dried blood on their clothes.

He leaned his head against Jaxson's shoulder when he came near.

"I'm out of my depth here," Kor said.

"Just move. It's about to be light, and it's time to go."

"We can't do this alone, Jaxson. They need help."

"Help? We need a miracle. They're going to find where we're hiding the ship during the day. And sick people should not be on boats."

"We need help."

"We're in the East. Who is going to help us? You'd just set off the dominoes racing toward us."

Kor spun around. His eyes were tight, and he looked at Jaxson for something that said he wasn't blaming Kor for this.

"I'm not blaming you. I'm not saying this is your fault. The dominoes were set. Things were going to fall. I knew it. Dacia knew it. We aren't going to leave you, and we won't leave Tiernan and the others."

Kor sucked in a breath over his teeth. Poor Tiernan was still waiting for him in that prison. If they figured out how they got in, they might move him. But he had refused to come. Kor had abandoned him again.

"Get on the boat," Jaxson said.

"Give me five minutes. I need to send a letter," Kor said.

"To who?"

"To the only people who can help us."

He ran back toward the docks and flagged down a messenger.

"What can I do for you, sir?"

"I need to get a letter to Kaybrum."

"Sure." The messenger searched around his person and found a piece of paper that had seen better days, but it would do. He didn't have time to find anyone else.

He glanced over his shoulder. He could see Jaxson waiting for him on the ship, or maybe he wanted to see Jaxson on the edge of the ship. It was too dark to really see.

He wrote quickly.

The Newest Kaybrum Public School, Care of Bryce and Merin. He knew better than to write to the school for Magics. This was the East after all. *Help is needed in remedying the current situation. Please send help immediately.* He needed to let them know to send Merin. Bryce would want to come, but he needed someone who could heal. *How is the cough you've had? I'd love to know your doctor's name. I could use one,* he wrote. He hoped they would understand. He signed it Kor and almost handed it back to the messenger, but wrote underneath his name, *By the way, I got the package you sent.* He had to let them know that Tiernan was with him. Even if he hadn't fully saved him yet. He knew Bryce would be wrecking his brain over Tiernan running off.

"Kind of a weird letter to need to write in the middle of the night," the messenger said, looking it over.

"Just needed to send it."

"I'm not judging. I just don't get a lot of business letters in the middle of the night."

"You can get this to Kaybrum?"

"It will be there in a matter of days. A group's going over the mountains starting in the morning, so you have good timing."

Kor nodded and, with nothing to add to the conversation, made his way back to the boat as quickly as he could without attracting any attention.

CHAPTER TWENTY-SEVEN

HAYDEN

HAYDEN BOUGHT HIMSELF A CUP OF THE STRONGEST TEA that was sold in the marketplace. It was the only thing that seemed to slow his mind down long enough to focus on anything other than the experiments on Magics. He breathed in the hot steam for a moment before letting his mind drift to where it was always coming back to.

No wonder Bryce is always angry, Hayden thought as he poured through his notes again looking for something new. If Magics were being affected by these experiments, it meant they really were messing with their connections to the elements. He had interviewed the kids who were still in jail waiting for their trials. It was amazing what flashing his family name and a few coins would do to get him in the door. It was worth it.

His desk was covered with notebooks and pages of crumpled ideas that weren't bad enough to be thrown away but not good enough to let stay piled neatly into the notebooks. It was hard to let go of anything, though, when it was this important.

"Hayden," Father Marco said.

Hayden jumped.

"How many times have I told you to keep this desk clean? It's worse than before."

"What are you doing back? You were going to be in the North for a year." Hayden sputtered.

"Is that how you typically greet people?" Marco asked, his brow raised.

"Sorry, sir." Hayden tried to snap back into the perfect son form, but he had not had nearly enough of the tea for that to happen. He felt his fingers twitching. "Welcome back to Kaybrum. Is Father Christi here?"

"No, he carried on to the North. I had to turn around."

"Turn around? Why? Are you all right?"

"I am fine, but my investments in Kaybrum, they are not looking so good." His eyes glared deep into Hayden.

"The marketplace is growing continuously," Hayden stammered.

"And yet large sums are walking right out the door. Profit is disappearing from the books."

"You think someone is embezzling money?" Hayden asked. Marco did not answer. He stepped lightly over the notebooks stacked on the floor and swept the papers in the chair onto the floor. He sat.

"No. I don't think someone is embezzling money, but I honestly would have preferred that." His voice was devoid of any emotion. "An embezzler I would have just sent to prison. One letter to the Watchers and it would be done. I wouldn't have had to come back to Kaybrum. A faulty heir, though, that I had to deal with personally. Do you care to explain yourself, Hayden?"

"What are we talking about?" Hayden said. He knew better than to admit fault without knowing exactly what the other person knew. It was basic business.

"First, the Nagely family paid for the removal of Gesepi's overstocked wood. I could see how that could be a decent decision. With the market growing, you would want the storage space for new goods. But why, Hayden, has the Nagely family been subsidizing large orders from the grocers, and other stores around the marketplace?"

Hayden's heart sank. He felt his chest deflate. He would tell the truth, but his father wasn't going to like it.

"I was helping the new Magic school."

"You were *helping*. Dear gods, boy, I thought I raised you better than that. And Magics of all people."

"They are just children, and they have suffered so much."

"I don't care if they all lost their legs," Marco snapped. "They are not our problem." Marco pushed the notebooks off the desk. Hayden watched them with his eyes, willing them to land in some semblance of the order they were stacked in. He didn't dare move.

"Charity is good for a business's image," Hayden tried in his best business voice.

"There is a difference between a charity that will actually help this family and one that will suck this family dry. You never choose something controversial. Magics, my gods."

"Magics have been helping to fill our coffers with their new business in the marketplace. We want to make sure they think they are on our side. Merin and Bryce—"

Marco laughed. It sent a shiver down Hayden's spine.

"You know their names?"

"Yes, Father. I know their names. I've helped at the school. I teach there. They are my friends."

"Friends? Hayden, please. Friends are people who can help you. Mutual help. What have they done for you? For this family? I expected better from you."

"They are my friends. The only ones I really have, thanks to you."

"I have given you plenty of friends. Proper friends. Friends you don't deserve. Just like you don't deserve the Nagely name."

"You've given me business contacts." Hayden heard the edge in his voice. He wasn't sure if it was anger or tears that were about to burst from his eyes, but he knew neither one would make this go any better. "I have done enough for this family. I have proved myself over a thousand times. First in the North, and now in Kaybrum."

"You have a long way to go, and this little setback won't make it any easier."

"What are you going to do? Un-adopt me? Send me back to whatever poor family you purchased me from? I'm sure that will look great for you."

"Shut your mouth, Hayden. You are talking nonsense." Marco rubbed at his forehead. Hayden could feel his heart pounding in his chest, but he stayed quiet.

"You had better find some way of profiting off this relationship, or I will send you far away."

"To the North again?" Hayden asked. Marco looked up at him through his furrowed brow.

"The closest you will ever be to Kaybrum and these Magics will be the furthest island in the Langburn Peninsula. You'll be living your life in exile on some island so deep that everyone will forget about you. That's the beauty of adoption, Hayden. I can always get someone to replace you."

The words hit harder than Bryce's fist. It sucked the air right out of him.

"I have eyes and ears everywhere in this town," Marco said, standing up. He plucked at the edges of his sleeve so his shirt lay flat. "Figure it out, Hayden. Now, I must catch up with your father. You know he doesn't like to be on the roads by himself."

Confusion and curiosity spread through Hayden. He couldn't help himself.

"How are you going to catch up on the road?"

"See, Hayden, if you had been keeping your mind involved in business and not these so-called friendships, you would know that the East has invented flying contraptions that go three times the speed of road travel."

"Flying contraptions? Do they use Magics?"

"I didn't ask. Now I must leave."

Marco turned and started out of Hayden's makeshift office. When he reached the door, he turned around and paused.

"Hayden," he started.

Hayden couldn't help but feel a small glimmer of hope rise in him.

"Clean up this office."

Once his father was out of sight, Hayden slumped to the ground in the midst of all of his notebooks. He didn't pick them up like he knew he should. He couldn't get himself to do anything. But while his body was completely still, his mind was racing.

CHAPTER TWENTY-EIGHT
MERIN

"HEY, MERIN," BRYCE CALLED FROM THE FRONT DOOR.

"I'm in the middle of something," she said. Reading lessons had finished for the day, and the students were being taught about business or trade skills. Actually, she had lost track. If it wasn't for Hayden and his group of volunteers, she would have never been able to keep everything running. The court cases had started ruling her life. In between lessons and keeping on top of the finances of the building, she was studying the laws and writing arguments for upcoming cases. While they had gotten several kids released, some of them just for temporary orders like Thomas, not all of the cases had been going well. People were still biased. There was a long-running societal distaste for Magics, and some of the judges probably weren't aware that they were making decisions rooted in systemic problems and not on the facts in front of them.

"You got some sort of message thing," Bryce said, bringing it into the room.

Just seeing him made her relax a little. She knew that they were only married because of the court cases, but being around him felt like home. It made her feel brave. Warm. It reminded her to keep the light inside of her burning.

"Probably from Hayden," she said, gesturing for him to put it on the desk in front of her. "He's been meeting with connections from the North all week. He's probably just apologizing for not making it to his lesson."

"Does he normally send you leather-wrapped messages? Seems a little overkill when you could just send a note with one of the kids around town for a few pennies."

"Leather-wrapped? Court summons, maybe?"

They had been waiting to hear about the continuation of Thomas's trial. It kept getting pushed and pushed, but if they could get this one settled, they would have a better chance with all of the others. Law was set mainly by precedent, and since there was none, Merin had the chance to make history.

"Better open it."

Bryce untied the leather cords holding the letter in place. His eyes glanced over the first few words, and he dropped it on the table.

"What? Did they set a date? Bryce, did something happen?"

"He's not dead," Bryce said.

"Who's not dead? Were we expecting someone to be dead?" Some of the kids had been beaten up while they waited for their trials, but death? Death was not something she had expected. And more, the relief washing over Bryce's face did not match any of the scenarios she was imagining.

"It's from Kor." Muscles relaxed around his jaw that hadn't relaxed in months. She picked it up and read the first line.

"'The Newest Kaybrum Public School: Care of Bryce and Merin.'" She didn't read further for a minute; she just enjoyed the relief she was feeling from seeing his handwriting. From knowing that he wasn't captured.

"Is he coming back?" Bryce asked.

"You didn't read it?"

"I saw his handwriting. I recognized it immediately." He blushed. Merin didn't blame him. It was overwhelming knowing that he had left, but it was almost equally hard to deal with the fact that he had finally contacted them. Right as they were about to fall apart at the seams. He hadn't abandoned them.

She read the rest of the letter out loud.

"What does it mean? Neither of us has had a cough. We don't have a doctor. We just have—"

"Me," Merin said. She re-read the letter, looking for all the hints. "Show me the leather again."

Bryce handed her the leather packaging. She unfolded it. She was looking for something to show its point of origin. Sepsrym Port Delivery. *Sepsrym.* The East. She glanced at the map above her desk. He had made it to the East.

"Something is wrong," she said finally.

"I got that. He's not making any sense."

"He's in the East. He probably couldn't risk anyone intercepting his letter. Look at what he called the school."

"We *are* the newest public school," Bryce said.

"But what would Kor call it if he was standing here with us?"

"The School for Magics. But what about the cough? The doctor?"

"Bryce, I think he needs me to go. Someone must be hurt."

"They can find another doctor. I am not letting you go to the East by yourself."

"Kor needs us."

"Kor already needs us here." She heard the whisper of desperation in his voice.

"You're right. We have cases." She shuffled the letter to the side and picked the case book back up. Bryce settled into a chair, but she noticed his eyes wouldn't fully leave the paper.

"Do you think he means Tiernan?" Bryce asked finally.

"We haven't sent him anything else. We weren't even sure he had made it to the East."

"What if Tiernan is the one who's hurt? Maybe we should both go."

"These cases aren't going to try themselves," Merin said, but she couldn't force herself to read another word. In her mind, she was already thinking of how they could get to Sepsrym. The mountains would be the fastest route, and at this time of the year, it would be rather mild. She would have to get Bryce some warmer clothes. She'd have to go see her parents.

"You've never been out of the city," Bryce said as if he could hear her thoughts. "I should come with you."

"You're right. They can find their own doctor," Merin said, trying to reassure the furrow that had fallen onto Bryce's face. She couldn't leave. She'd never even been outside the wall. How was she going to travel all the way to the East and then find Kor? They were already swamped as it was. *Kor made his mess,* she thought, some of the anger she had been bottling up finally cracking through the top. He had made this mess and whatever mess was in the East, and that didn't mean that they had to drop everything to fix it.

"You should go," Bryce said. His tone did not match her feelings of resentment.

"Bryce, I know you feel responsible for what happened to Tiernan before, but if he's with Kor, they'll figure something out. We have too much to do here. What happens if they schedule Thomas's case before we get back?"

"*You* should go. Alone."

"Alone? Bryce, we stick together." Now she could hear the fear in her voice. She'd been so consumed by the constant stress that this new tidal wave of emotions felt like it might drown her. She wanted to cover her ears and sink below the desk.

"I won't make it past the border," Bryce said. "Even if we could go, we'll be searched. I'm marked. You aren't. I have a criminal record. You don't. You have family clout. I have nothing to my name."

"My name is Merin Segal."

He cupped her chin in his hand. His eyes looked straight into hers so intensely she had to look away. He rubbed her cheek with his thumb. "You are the smartest person I know. You are everything. You are my everything. But Kor wouldn't have risked writing unless something was really wrong. He went this long without telling us what was going on. He needs you to go. Not me."

"I can't do this without you," Merin said, but she was already calculating her rate of success in her head. Thinking of all the notes she'd need to leave for everyone. "And what am I going to do, just leave you and Hayden to kill each other?"

Bryce laughed. He flicked a tear from her cheek. "Don't worry, if it came to a fight, I'd win."

"I know. But then how will we afford the food if he's dead?"

"You're going. I can see it in your face."

"I don't want to leave you." She didn't have to finish the thought. *Not like Kor did. Not like Tiernan and Aer. Not like your family.* What they had was something different.

"There's a difference. I'm sending you. I'm asking you to go. To help our friends in whatever way you can."

"I've never even been out of the city."

"I've never run a school."

"You're being too calm about this," Merin said. He was alarmingly quiet. There was no fight, no angst, no rage. Maybe he was too defeated to fight. Her bones felt heavy, like the weight of the world was pressing her down into the floor.

"You'll leave me a list. I have Hayden. As much as I hate to admit it, he's been useful."

She rested her forehead on his chest. They stood like that in the office for a moment. She was trying to memorize the moment: his warmth, his heartbeat, the sound of his breathing, the way his arms felt. She was desperate to take it all in.

"I'll write."

"Not too much," Bryce said. "It probably isn't safe. Besides, I have enough reading to do as is."

He kissed her forehead then. She pushed into his chest once more and then stood straight, putting on her bravest face.

"I need to go see my parents. I should probably patch things up with them in case—"

"In case it's a while before you see them again." Bryce finished for her. She could tell he didn't want to think about the danger of going East. She didn't really want to think about it either. But he was right. It wouldn't be safe for Bryce, and if Korvo was found out, it wouldn't be safe for him either.

Her parents' house loomed now. Everything felt big. There was too much space. Too many places to put things just to put them there. She had grown more accustomed to Aer's apartment then she thought. She realized she'd even finally started thinking about it as her own.

Rachael was humming in the hallway, but Merin wasn't ready to talk with her yet. She wasn't ready to hear about what a stupid decision she was making. She was ready to hear about how she should come home and how she was hanging out with the wrong people and how she needed to think about her future. She was not ready to hear the truth that she wasn't ready for the outside world. Her parents might not see it, but Racheal would.

As she walked toward her father's study, she traced her hand on the wall. She hadn't known anything besides the world of her parents until she met Kor and Bryce.

She had been walking in the garden. Some school project that had seemed boring at the time, so she was taking her time. Her classmates were all ahead of her. Sketching flowers or leaves, but she was focused on the two boys talking off to the side of the path. One of them was up in a tree. His legs hung down from where he sat, and he had wrapped his arms around a branch. The older boy was leaning on the trunk of the tree.

Merin remembered wondering why they weren't in school and thinking they were some sort of delinquents. She blushed at the memory. Ignorance had made her blind once, but she reminded herself that people were supposed to change. And it was okay to not think the same things she had thought in the past. It didn't make her a bad person because she had once thought that. She knew better now. Wasn't that what Bryce was always saying?

The boy leaning against the tree had called out to her. That was the first time she spoke with Korvo, but it was the other boy that struck her. And when her skirt had gotten caught in the thorns, it was Bryce who had helped her. And now she was leaving Bryce to go find Korvo. She was leaving the walls of Kaybrum. Leaving this shelter behind.

Her father's study door was open. She peaked her head in, trying to see if she could tell what sort of mood he was in. She had thought about just lying and saying she was going to be busy and wouldn't be able to come by. It's not like she saw him outside of the courthouse anyway. But when she wasn't there for the trials, it would be suspicious, and she didn't want them sneaking around Bryce. He didn't need to be worried about covering up her disappearance. They had covered up Kor's for long enough.

"Father?" she said when she didn't see a deep crease in his forehead.

"Merin? Come in."

She followed his instructions and sat down opposite him at the desk. It had been such a long time since she had done this. He was usually asking for her magic to help him or trying to get her to leave. But now he just looked at her from across the large desk.

"I'm not going to be trying any more Magic cases."

"You're not?"

He shook his head. "I'm taking a break from them. I was actually going to tell you. I was writing a letter." He pushed the letter over to her. It only had a few lines written.

"But why?"

"Just doesn't feel right anymore."

"It felt right before?" she asked, but she knew anger had no place in this conversation.

"I was wrong. I see that now. I did wrong to you and your," he paused, "friends. I don't agree with how they handled things. And I thought I was doing what was best for you, but I can see now that I was wrong. All your life, I've been trying to keep you safe from something."

"I know."

"But what I was really doing was hiding you. I should have been fighting for Magics, not trying to keep you from them."

"What will you do now?"

"I can't work for the defense. My license doesn't let me operate in that way, but I could lend you my knowledge."

"You'll have to lend it to Bryce." She didn't wait to see his reaction to Bryce's name. Even though he had just apologized of sorts, it didn't mean he felt better about the fact that they had gotten married without permission. "Something has come up," she said, "and I need to go to the East." Best to keep her answers short and vague. Not that she had much more information to go off of. She knew where and that Kor needed her ability to heal, but that was it.

"The East?"

"I'm leaving soon."

"That will kill your mother."

"You can decide if you want to tell her or not. I will try to be back before she notices. It's not like I've seen her much these past months."

"Your mother feels like she's lost her daughter already."

"She only lost the daughter she was trying to make me be. If she wants to understand, I would be happy to explain. Later. But right now, I have to finish packing."

"Right. Well, you can do anything, my dear. You are so smart, and you have proven you are braver than your father. Be careful in the East. If being a Magic here is dangerous, there it is almost a death sentence."

Merin nodded and got up from the chair. She gave her father a long sympathetic look, and then walked out of the study, closing the door behind her. She didn't want to hear if he called after her. She had not been prepared for him to admit all those things, but she also hadn't realized she had only come to see him and not her mother.

She walked the short way down to her bedroom. Nothing had changed about it. Sure some of the clothes she had last left out had been put away, but there was nothing there to show that her life had changed much in the past year and a half. Nothing that said she was capable of running a school and practicing law. Nothing that showed anything but memories of family she barely knew and a world she barely existed in.

As she gathered some clothes and shoes, she looked over the dolls that stared at her from the walls. Years of presents from relatives she barely talked to. Her parents had kept her from them because of her magic. For her safety, they had said. After all, some of them still lived in the East. *Right,* Merin thought, *the East.* It would make it much easier to gain access to the country if she had a reason to be there. A reason for the people to not look twice at her.

She pulled some of the dolls off the shelf. Underneath were old cards where aunts or uncles had signed their names. Sometimes they shared a little about her cousins. She searched through them until she came across one that still had an address attached for an aunt with a cousin about her age.

Merin stuffed the letter into her bag and tossed the dolls back onto the shelf. They were crooked and slightly falling over, but somehow, it looked better to her. It looked changed. She had changed, and something in this house should recognize that.

Then she slipped out the back door of the house and headed back to the school.

Bryce was there waiting for her. There were still classes going on for the older kids. Lessons on different skills and trades to teach them about business. This had been Bryce's idea. Hayden was working with some of the kids who had first seemed so reluctant to be there. They had started out scared of every noise, but now they were eagerly listening to Hayden talk about the marketplace. Hayden glanced up and gave her a quick frown.

"I told him," Bryce said.

"You did?" Bryce rarely talked to Hayden if she wasn't there.

"I thought it only fair that he knew why he was stuck with me."

"No one is stuck with you."

"You're leaving in an hour." He said it like it was a fact and not a question. "I found, well I asked Hayden for help, but I found you passage through the mountains with one of his supply runs."

"I love you," she said. She wasn't sure why. The gratitude of him helping and sadness of leaving him just seemed better boiled down into that one sentence.

"I love you too."

He grabbed her hand and pulled her into their office space. He pulled out a chair, and she sat. He sat down on the ground next to her and leaned his head into her lap. She let her fingers run through his hair. It was softer now than when she had first met him. Probably sleeping somewhere other than the dirt helped that a lot. He was taller. He was less angry, or maybe he was channeling his anger in other ways besides fighting. She could feel how tense he was. How nervous. It didn't take much of her magic to know those sorts of things. She ached to ease the tension she could feel, but she knew she shouldn't. Not unless he asked. Not unless he invited her in.

His cheek rested on her leg. Silence fell around them. What could she possibly say right now?

"You should be careful traveling," he said finally. "People outside of the city, they can be desperate. They won't care who your family is. Don't judge them too harshly. They're just trying to live."

"I wouldn't."

"I know nothing about the East. Or mountains."

"I just know what I've read in books. I'm sure Hayden's company will have some knowledge though. I can rely on them."

"Don't trust them too much."

"Still don't trust Hayden?"

"I don't trust any non-Magics."

"Except Vycky and Sylvia, and you have to admit Hayden's been helping."

"Still, it's best if you hide your gifts."

"I never thought I'd hear you say that."

"I never thought I'd say it. I just can't . . . If something . . ." He faltered. "You need to come back, you know."

"I know. I will. And I'll find Kor and Tiernan. I'll let them know you're all right."

"Am I though? This whole day, I've been looking around the school. Looking at the trial documents, everything. The letters swim in my eyes after just a few minutes. I can't go more than an hour or two without snapping at Hayden. Your dad's going to rip me apart in these trials. And I bet he won't even feel bad about it."

"He won't."

"I told you—"

"No, he won't defeat you. I just talked to him. He told me he isn't prosecuting anymore."

"So the trials?"

"They'll still happen, but someone else will be on the other side. He said he wants to help our side." She didn't tell him that he hadn't exactly agreed to work with Bryce, but she wasn't sure having them work together was the best idea anyway, and letting Bryce know that her dad wasn't sure about him would only fan the flames. Hayden was bad enough, but her father? That might drive Bryce insane. Although she had, at times, imagined how satisfying it would be to see Bryce punch her father, she didn't really want it to happen. At least not while she wasn't there.

"Hmmm," was all Bryce said.

"You'll be fine. Kor trusts you. I trust you. Who knows how long I'll be gone. It might just be for a couple of days."

"Or months."

"I'll write."

"Too dangerous, remember." He said it quickly, but his eyebrows twitched betraying the fact that he didn't want it to be true. He didn't want to be completely alone.

"I'll find a way, just like Kor did."

"Just don't make whatever code you write too difficult to figure out. I'm still working on the words, you know."

Somewhere in the school, a clock chimed. He nuzzled against her leg, then stood up. He took her hand and shouldered her bag.

"I'll walk you to the market."

They held hands the entire time. Softly leaning against each other. Merin again tried committing everything about him to memory. Everything about his walk. His warmth. The feel of his skin where his shirt sleeves were rolled up, brushing against her wrist. The quiet of his breathing. She closed her eyes and took a mental picture of everything around her.

"Go see the world," Bryce leaned into her ear and whispered.

"Take care of our world," she whispered back. She kissed him on the cheek. He held her forehead to his lips.

"Come back."

"I'll always come back to you," she said.

The market was busy, and people were still packing the last of their things into their wagons. Horses were whinnying to get going. A young woman who looked to be about the same age as them came and greeted her.

"You must be Merin. Hayden said you'd be coming with us to Sepsrym. You'll be bunking with me. It will be nice to have another girl along. It's been such a long time since my older sister used to come with us."

The words drowned out as Merin looked back for a last glance at Bryce, but he had blended into the shadows. She turned back to the girl.

Her face was spotted with freckles, and her hair was a familiar bright red.

"Are you Vycky's sister?" Merin asked.

"You know my older sister? That's so great. See it's like we were meant to get along. Here, let me show you where to put all of your stuff. My name is Arya by the way."

Arya led Merin to the back of one of the smaller wagons. She opened the back lock with a series of quick flicks of her wrist. Inside there were cots laid out and small boxes at the bottom of each cot.

"You can put your bags in there. You can lock it too if you want, but I won't steal anything from ya, and Dad always has a lock on our wagon. He can be a bit overprotective, but before he made the switch to merchant, he used to run with a group of traveling performers.

People were always trying to sneak into the girls' wagons. Make all the boys fall in love with them on stage, you know, and they'd think it was real. Like it was only for them. I wish I could make someone feel that way."

Arya spoke so fast that Merin hardly had time to think about the fact that she was actually leaving. It was happening.

"How many times have you been to the East?" Merin asked.

"A few times a year since I was seven. Well, not that much lately. They seem to be really turning inward. They don't want things made outside of the East anymore. But Hayden always figures out a way to get business."

"You know Hayden well?"

"About as well as you can know your boss. Before he was our boss, he used to sometimes hang out with us before his Dads sent him North to learn about the trade side of things. He's between my sister and me in age. I'm just glad she was never interested in him. It would have broken her heart."

"Why?"

"It turned out well in the end, I guess. Vycky met her wife, but Hayden, he's a genius, but he does not really understand people. When they were small, everyone here was trying to push for them to be together, you know. It would have been a big step up in the world for someone from our group."

"Are they all family?" Merin asked, looking around.

"Nope. Well, not in the sense that you probably think. They are *my* family, just not, you know, blood. Hayden didn't tell me why you needed a quick passage to the East."

"Visiting sick family." Vague answers were always best. Stick to the vaguest of truths, and you could never be caught in a lie. Kor was family like the people in the caravan were Arya's family. "I have to admit," Merin said, "I'm nervous. I've never been out of the city before."

"Never? Not even on a school trip or something?"

Merin shook her head. The only trip outside of the city her school had ever gone on was to the lake. It was early, when her magic was just starting to work, and she was having trouble with water. Her parents didn't let her go.

"Well, you are in for a treat. We have a few stops to make

tomorrow in the farmland to fill the last few wagons. The East still goes crazy for their food, so we always pick up more than is ordered. Then we can sell the extra at double the price. That was Hayden's idea."

"When will we make it to Sepsrym?"

"A week. I sure hope your family isn't so sick you are worried about making it there in time."

"Oh, I hope not. Like I said, I'm just nervous."

"Stick with me." Arya smiled brightly and linked her arm around Merin's elbow.

They were rumbling down the road toward the mountains in minutes. Towards the East. Arya kept chatting about all the great things they would see on the way. But the days she seemed to think about as fun adventures just seemed like life sentences to Merin.

The cart rolled to a stop.

"We're stopping already?" Merin said, looking out the little window on the side of the wagon.

"Of course. It will take a few minutes to get out of the main gate."

"The main gate?" She hadn't realized they were still in the city. She felt foolish and naive. It was the same feeling as when Bryce told her she didn't really understand what he had gone through—what other Magics had gone through. There was a sense of shame for somehow not having this information. That people would think less of her for it.

"Right, you said you'd never been outside. You should climb up." Arya gestured to a door in the ceiling. "I'll give you a boost." Arya knelt down on her knees so that Merin could step on her back. It gave her plenty of room to get up and open the little flap of a door. Its hinge creaked as she opened it slowly. The wall was huge. She knew that. She had been inside the walls. But somehow, as they passed through the gate, it felt like the sky disappeared for much longer than she had thought possible. When you were inside the city, it all felt normal to feel the crushing hugeness of the walls around you. Somehow, what was so big, so dark, was also so small and confined. But outside, she felt like she was going from one life to the next.

Not hiding in something but moving through it. Finally, the other side came into view. The green hit her eyes like a blast of water. The fields were lush and stretched on for miles, dotted only occasionally by a barn or a small farmhouse. Livestock roamed in wide pastures.

"It's like a picture book," Merin said as she looked down to Arya, who was starting to shake under Merin's weight.

"What do you mean?" Arya said as Merin stepped down to the floor.

"There's just farmland. No big buildings, no city."

"Well, these farmers come into the city when they need things. We'll see towns outside of the city. Just not this close. Cities happen where people need them."

"I wish Bryce were here. I think living in the city has drained him. There are too few plants to spend time around."

"You know Bryce?" Arya blushed.

"Yeah, I work with him at the school. He's my very best friend. He's—" It wasn't that she was ashamed that on paper they were married, but the girl's blush told Merin that she had a crush on Bryce. Telling her new roommate her crush was off the market might not make for the best living conditions.

"Isn't he just dreamy?" Arya giggled. Merin nodded. It had been a long time since she had just chatted with someone about something that wasn't about Magics, politics, or trials. It had been a long time since she had a friend, and she wasn't sure that any of the friends she had grown up with were really her friends anymore.

"You know him through your sister?"

"Yeah. Pa got hurt a few years back, and I stayed with Vycky for a while to take some stress off of him while we weren't traveling. He used to help at her shop. Now, whenever I visit and he's there, he still remembers my name. That's kind of nice when you're out on the road with people you only ever see once in a blue moon."

"Do you meet a lot of people on the road? People you see more often?"

"Pa, sure. We usually make the same stops, and he has people that he goes way back with. That's how he knows how to get the best deals and is still able to get through the mountains. But there aren't many people for me to hang out with. Pa says I'm not old enough to do more than just listen to business conversations—even though I totally am—so there's a lot of downtime for me."

"What do you do?"

"Mostly explore the marketplaces we stop in. Find things I like." She pulled out a large box from the identical trunk next to Merin's. "These are some of my treasures." She pushed the box in front of Merin.

Inside were scarves woven with what looked like metal fabric, colors chasing golden threads through the patterns. There were rings of the thinnest metal twisting over each other in a way that made it look like they were trees that were alive coming together. There were a few books, their covers tattered and torn on the edges, well-read. Various other things caught glimpses of light as they tumbled around the box while they made their way along the winding path through the wider world.

The box of trinkets and treasures made Merin's heart ache for two things. One ache for the world that she had never actually experienced. Looking into the box was like looking through the books she had read a million times and seeing them come to life in front of her. In a way, she was jealous of Arya for being able to see the things she had only dreamed about. But she also ached to share all of these new discoveries with Bryce and Kor and Tiernan and Aer. Aer had never left the city. She had never wanted to. Kor and Tiernan had come from another place. How great would it be to go with them to Hadran and see it with their eyes? Well, if they weren't being hunted and marked for execution. But there was also Bryce. Bryce, who she wanted to share every thought with. She felt the urge to start writing him a letter now. About going under the gate. About seeing the fields. About how she was feeling at this very moment.

It was enough to make her choke up.

"Do you not like it?"

"I love it. I want to explore all these places with you," Merin said. She handed the box back gently to Arya. "I just miss my family already. It's been a big night."

"Well, then, let's get some sleep. When you wake up, we'll be in the next town, and then we'll get to do some exploring on our own."

Arya grabbed Merin's hand and held on for a second. Merin let the tiniest bit of magic trickle into the girl. She seemed as genuine and happy after that as she had before. Merin felt another twinge of jealousy but also hope. Hope that she could have at least one friend so things could be bright and sunny again.

Sleep did not come immediately to Merin. She turned away from Arya, who had taken to reading one of her worn novels by candlelight. It wasn't that the light bothered her; it was that she didn't want Arya to notice she was still awake. She didn't want her to ask what was on her mind.

If Arya liked Bryce, she would know that he was Magic. You couldn't know Bryce, especially in Vycky's shop, without knowing about his magic. But they were headed to the East. It was probably better that fewer people knew what she truly was. It could only get her new friend into trouble.

And trouble was brewing everywhere. Hayden had promised he had dropped the whole thing with the experiments, but maybe he was still working on it. He was always still working on things. Maybe Bryce could set him right. Or not. There were too many things she still didn't get about either of their behavior. It was enough to drive someone insane.

She breathed deeply, but sleep would not find her. She thought instead about the farmland they were driving through. The rolling green pastures and the crops that were growing. She imagined herself as a small stream drifting through those pastures and making them grow. Making them feel better and strong. Finally, sleep found her, but her waking dreams did not follow her into the world of sleep.

Arya shook her awake.

"Come on," Arya said. "We're almost there."

Stiff after a night on the hard cot, Merin stretched. Arya was already dressed and ready. She had a light dress on and a leather bag that crossed her chest. Merin suddenly felt self-conscious about her own clothes. Even the simple things she wore to the school felt out of place outside the city. She rummaged in the clothes she had brought until she found a plain brown dress.

Then she followed Arya outside of the wagon. True to her word, the minute they stepped outside, Arya locked it up. She gave Merin a wink and grabbed her wrist. Merin raced along with her. The town they had come to was small. It was nothing like Kaybrum. There were walls around it, but they appeared to be long-forgotten remnants of years past. There were no guards manning gates or tall buildings. The town was clearly all made of wood—not the glass and metal monstrosities she was used to. Things were less foreboding here. She walked by a sign that reminded Magics that the use of magic in the market square was illegal. Well, at least in some ways, it was less foreboding. Merin felt exposed in a way she never had before.

She trailed behind Arya, who flitted from one stall to the next. Some of the villagers recognized the people in their caravan, but no one stopped to talk with Arya, and they barely acknowledged Merin. She was just some stranger passing through. She wasn't sure if she liked that or not.

There weren't any things that seemed like they could be treasures. Mostly people were selling the produce they grew, the eggs they collected, the jobs that needed doing. She saw farriers and blacksmiths. She stopped to glance over the carpenter's little carvings. None of them seemed to have the same realness as Kor's did.

Arya stopped for a minute over a blanket. It was deep blue. Merin knew that color had come from the East. It was made from shells found in the shallow waters near the shore. She had read about it in books. She had seen the color, of course, in places around the city, but somehow, seeing it out here, knowing that someone had probably bartered for the dye and taken it home to work it into the wool they sheared from their sheep, it was just more real.

Arya exchanged some coins for the blanket and came back to Merin. "I know where we need to go next," she said, grabbing Merin's wrist again. "Come on. My treat."

Merin realized at that moment that Arya had no idea who Merin was. Who her parents were. Where she was from in the city. All she knew was she knew Bryce and Hayden. That could put her in literally any position in the city.

"You have to try these," Arya said, handing her a berry dumpling. Merin took a bite. It tasted like home. Not home with her parents, but home where she was soft and free. It felt a little like Bryce when he was falling asleep against her shoulder. Heavy but comforting.

"These are delicious," Merin said. She looked over at the stall Arya had come from, and she almost choked on her pastry.

The sign was clear. Segal Farms. *Segal. This could be Bryce's family.*

"I'm going to go find Pa for some business," Arya said. "Do you want to come or stay here?"

Merin barely heard her. "Stay," she finally murmured. She couldn't take her eyes off the sign. *Segal.* She moved closer. The woman behind the counter of pastries had soft gray eyes like Bryce. Her hair was graying. A small streak blended into her brown hair. Hair that looked like Bryce's. His mother. She had to be. Or aunt, maybe. Merin tried to shake herself. These people could have nothing to do with Bryce. *Or they could be your in-laws,* a little voice told her.

She moved toward the booth. Bryce rarely talked about his family. When he did, he didn't give much detail. It had been years since he left the farm to come to the city.

"May I buy a few more of these delicious dumplings?" Merin asked after a few more minutes of working up her courage.

"Of course," the lady said. She looked up then and stared at Merin. "Well, aren't you a beauty?"

"Thank you, ma'am," Merin said. She couldn't help the blush that formed on her cheeks. She waited while the woman puttered around for a small wax paper and gathered up the pastries. They were fresh, and she caught the aroma of more baking in the little brick oven in the back of the stall.

She had so many questions. So many things she wanted to ask. Did they live here? Did they miss Bryce? Did they talk about him?

When the woman handed her the pastries, Merin noticed the bracelet the woman was wearing. It was a dark circle of metal. Iron, maybe. It signified the death of a child.

"I'm sorry for your loss," Merin said, pointing to the bracelet.

The woman sighed. "Yes. Well, I still hope he's out there somewhere."

"What happened?" Merin asked.

"Sarah," a man's voice called from behind the oven. The woman looked down.

"I really should be off. The next batch will be done soon."

"Of course. Thank you for this." Merin left the coin on the counter while the woman bustled away.

She had said she was hopeful that he was still out there somewhere. Bryce. Behind the oven, a man stood up. He was a little shorter than Bryce. His skin was a much deeper brown. As though he was being slowly baked into the clay of the fields he worked in. His lips looked similar, but there was no trace of Bryce's wild smile or his soft, thinking face. This man had become hardened by the sun or by life in a way that Bryce hadn't. But there was no doubt in Merin's mind that they were related.

Maybe there was a chance for Bryce to reconcile with his mother. She fought the urge to write a letter now. Telling him everything she had seen. She'd been out of the wagon an hour. One day into her trip, and she already felt like she could fill one of Hayden's notebooks with what she had seen.

She walked now, taking small delicate bites from her pastry while she looked over the trinkets on shelves and things. She wanted it to last.

"There will be other marketplaces. The ones in the East, they're the best," Arya said, popping up behind her out of nowhere. "You don't have to find the perfect thing here."

Merin saw that Arya had a whole bag of things. The blanket she had seen earlier, but also a few new books and something that looked like a musical instrument made of small pipes.

When they got back to the wagons, the rest of the adults had finished loading and unloading everything they needed. They were ready to be off again.

When they hit the road, Arya showed her everything she had found.

"This is for you," she said, handing the blanket over to Merin. "It's not just regular wool. It's thicker. I figured since you've never left the city, you've probably never been anywhere as cold as the mountains. It will keep you warm. Well, warm enough, at least."

"Thank you," Merin said. She wrapped it around her shoulders. It was soft and light, and she wondered how warm it could possibly be, but she would take Arya's word for it.

"I saw there were some books in your bag," Merin said. "I can't believe you can read while we jostle around like this."

Arya shrugged. "You get used to it. Besides, people rely too much on their eyes for balance. That's why people get motion sick. You have to rely on your inner ear."

"How do you know that?" Merin asked.

"My mom. She was blind."

"Was as in she can see now or was as in . . . ?"

"As in, she's no longer with us," Arya said.

"I'm sorry to hear that. When did it happen?"

"I was young. Seven, I think. Vycky had already started living in the city." Arya's face darkened a little.

"I didn't mean to bring up something painful. We can talk about something else."

"It's all right. Pa and Vycky, they don't like to talk about it. I haven't gotten to talk about Mom in forever. She knew how to play every type of these," she pulled out the pipes for Merin to see better. They were small, wooden pan pipes. "She could do anything with music. Play anything. It was probably because she was so in touch with her hearing, but I think she would have been like that even if she hadn't been blind. It was just her magic."

"Magic?" Merin asked.

Arya didn't answer. She just blew into the pipes. It sounded less like a musical instrument and more like the exhausted sigh of some large animal. Arya frowned and looked into the pipes as if they held the answer.

"More practice," Merin said. Arya nodded.

Merin pulled out a book she had brought along and opened it in her lap. The first minute she felt fine, and then the words just seemed like they were swimming on the page. She closed the book and rested her head against the wall of the wagon.

"I guess I rely on my eyes too much," she said.

"I can read to you," Arya offered. Merin wasn't sure how else they would pass the time, and all the topics of conversation she had brought up seemed to just make the young girl sad. Merin agreed.

Arya picked up one of the tattered books from her box and started at the very beginning. The words came easily, likely because they were half memorized. They passed the afternoon this way, in a gentle peace that had been recently lacking in Merin's life.

CHAPTER TWENTY-NINE
BRYCE

BRYCE HADN'T BEEN ABLE TO WATCH MERIN WALK AWAY, but he had stayed nearby until the last of the wagons turned down the road. Keeping just out of sight, he made sure she got off without a hitch. He wondered what she was seeing now. The green rows of the farmland. Would she know what she was looking at? Would she be able to see the different types of plants, or would it just be a sea of green for her? He wished he could see it with her. He almost wished he could have slipped into the last wagon and gone with. Arya probably wouldn't have minded. She was always happy to see him, but she seemed happy to see everyone. Merin would be fine without him.

But would he be fine without her?

"Merin already gone?" Hayden asked.

Bryce hadn't noticed him approaching. "For an upper-crust city kid, you do sneak up on a person good," Bryce said.

"Got to be able to catch a thief in the act." Hayden laughed.

Bryce's blood boiled. He had learned how to become invisible in the shadows for his own safety. Hayden had done it for profit. Bryce glanced back to where the wagons had disappeared. It hadn't even been ten minutes without her, and he was already thinking about how to fight Hayden.

"She's gone," Bryce replied curtly. He took a deep breath. "Thank you for getting her a spot with them."

"It was nothing," Hayden said.

"I have things to do at the school," Bryce said. He turned and started down the path he had come with Merin, embracing the darkness, slipping into the tiny shadows of the buildings, and disappearing. It took him longer to travel that way, but he wasn't ready to face the world alone. As long as he was walking slowly, there was a slim chance that Merin would be waiting for him on the other side of the walk. With every step, reality became closer and closer to being real.

The night felt dark. Alone again. He walked to the garden once the kids were asleep. This was the place he had come to in the city when he was alone for the first time. Years ago when he first fled from his family. Fled wasn't the right word. When he left his family, tired of the stares and the snide comments and the ignoring they did. It was not a hard choice. He was already alone there.

The Refuge had found him first. He spent his first night in Kaybrum there. He remembered at first feeling grateful that someone was taking him off the street, but then they took him to the station house. They told him he had broken some laws. It was all a blur. He was put into the system. That was the first time.

His file started then. He wondered how Merin had reacted to that. That he had been so young. What had they written in the file the first night? Had they described him? Skinny, small. Covered in snot and dirt. He wasn't angry then. He was scared. That next morning, when they dumped him back out on the ground, that was when the anger had started. Being around his family, it had felt like maybe they were just out in the country. He had thought big cities would mean more people, more acceptance. But it hadn't.

Kor found him that morning. He had been kind. He asked his name. He asked what kind of magic he had. He read the cards for him. He got him breakfast from the bar. He took him in. There were still many nights that he slept in the garden. But he knew Kor wouldn't let him be alone ever again.

Yet here he was, once more alone in the garden. The plants twisted to come toward him. The connection he had with them was different. It was like they were trying to talk to him. Call back to him. Tell him he wasn't alone. He had them. He had them, and they would always come to him.

For the first time, this new power felt comforting. It didn't feel like he was losing control. It just felt different. Like the connection had changed. Shifted somehow. He reached out to stroke the leaves of the nearest plant. There was so much the plant wanted to share. It trilled to him about the wind. About the clouds and sun. About water. About the changes in the soil. About the people who had walked by. It wasn't clear. They weren't words. Plants didn't use words. That would be silly. But they were alive. He wasn't alone.

He walked slowly through the garden, touching this plant and that. Slowly trying to make sense of what they were all trying to show him. It wasn't something that was easy. Some things were easy. Trees had the most memory. They showed the most thoughts. It was like Kor said: they had deep connections to the earth. He could always read a tree slightly like he could read the cards. They were connected to water and memory and earth and air. They were the best connection people had to the elements besides magic.

He left the garden feeling a little less sad but more daunted by what came next. Running a school and freeing people from the oppressive trial system that was built to keep them down. And he had to do that without losing his cool. No big deal. Kor believed in him, and Merin believed in him.

He got to the door of the school. Most of the lights were off. A few in the upper floors, where the older kids might still be up, were on.

He climbed the staircase trying to keep his thoughts from leading him to a meltdown. The good feeling from the plants was gone. Forgotten in the dead of this place.

The dead.

He went back down the staircase and out into the courtyard. He had burned the ground around where the plants wouldn't go. He had considered it done. What else was he going to do? He could hardly dig up the bodies or find out their names and engrave them on a large stone. He sat in the middle of the circle he had dug. He called to the plants. They came. Slowly at first, then quickly. He prodded them, but they weren't worried any more. They sent roots toward him.

Whatever had been poisoning the soil was gone now.

Not that he needed one more project. But he could finally plant the garden he had wanted to plant so long ago. At least there was one thing he could do here. He asked the plants to watch the school. Then he headed back inside.

CHAPTER THIRTY

MERIN

THE MOUNTAINS LOOMED IN FRONT OF THEM LIKE GIANTS stretching all the way up to the sky. Their summits were lost in the clouds that encircled them. Merin felt cold just looking at them. She pulled the blanket Arya had given her around her shoulders. It did help keep the chill at bay.

"Is there a path to get through there?" Merin asked. She knew there had to be. Arya had taken this trip a hundred times in her life, but looking at the tall spires of rock and snow, she just couldn't imagine a way through. She felt like they would swallow her the moment they went beyond the opening.

"Of course! It won't even be too snowy this time of year," Arya said, not even bothering to look up from the new book she had picked up in the trade depot on the edge of the mountains. It was a love story about a man leaving home for a war, and it had hit too close to home for Merin, so she had asked Arya to stop reading out loud. Arya was already a good fourth of the way through it, and it had only been a couple of hours since they had been waiting for conditions to change to get the best access through the mountains.

"It gets colder?" Merin asked in disbelief.

"You really should take up some sort of distraction. It really does help," Arya said, still not looking up from her book.

Merin looked down at the things she had bought in the last town over. A journal with soft leather-bound pages sat on the top of the pile. She had thought she might fare better with writing than reading but wasn't sure what to write about yet.

She pulled the blanket closer. A cold wind tore through the wagon as the door opened.

"Should have warned ya," Pa said with a laugh at Merin's shiver. "But we're about to head into the mountains. Just thought you should know."

Arya nodded over the top of her book, but Merin sat up to see out the window. It had been one thing to be outside the gates of the city, but this was entirely different. This was somewhere that Bryce had never been, Kor had never been, nor Tiernan. This was her adventure. And she was going to write about it.

She took out her pen and set it to the paper. At first, she just described the jagged rocks that seemed to clutch the wagons as they disappeared behind bends in the path, but then she started noticing more. There was movement in the snow. Birds flying, and footprints left by what she assumed were hares. The sun reflected off of the snow forcing her to close her eyes and retreat back to below the window.

She lay there with her eyes closed looking into the black of her eyelids.

"Arya?" Merin asked, her eyes still closed.

"Hmm," she responded.

"Was your mother always blind? Was she born that way?"

"Yeah. No one was sure why."

"How did she meet your father? How does someone who is blind end up in a traveling sort of lifestyle?"

Arya put the book down and looked at Merin for a moment.

"Same way as anyone, I guess. Pa used to work for a theater troupe. They traveled around doing shows, and in one of the cities, he met my mother. He says she was beautiful beyond compare, and she came to their shows every night they were in that town for a festival. But every night, she would come and stand a little to the side, next to this stone building facing away from the performers, so after they were done with the show the last night, Pa finally approached her. Once he figured out she was blind, he thought she had just mistaken where the shows were or turned away because she was blind."

"But she hadn't," Merin said, stopping writing down the story.

"She had been listening to the sound waves bounce off the building. It had made them louder and clearer. She showed Pa. Had him stand there facing the wall like he was in trouble in school, and then she sang to him from the stage. He said he had never heard something more beautiful and clear. He asked her to join their troupe that instant. She agreed. Said she wanted to hear the music of the world."

"And they fell in love?"

"I think Pa was already in love, but yes. They decided to get into the trades when Vycky was born. The troupe split in half. It was an easier paycheck than doing shows. Especially in the East where there were lots of regulations about entertainment. But the other half that kept performing still makes sure to set up near certain stone buildings so they can be the loudest and clearest performers out there. It really draws the crowd to them. I've seen it a few times when we cross paths with them. We always stop for a show."

"Your mother was a Magic?"

"Why do you ask?" Arya asked.

"You called her music her magic."

"What else could it have been? You should have heard her. But magic? No. I guess not in the way that we think."

"I've heard someone sing with the magic of the wind. It was beautiful."

"Your friend, Aer?" Arya asked.

Merin nodded.

"I was sorry to hear that she had died. She wasn't particularly nice, but she was a force, and I didn't mind that."

"She wasn't nice," Merin said with a small laugh. "But she was kind, and I think that's what really matters. I miss her."

"You always will," Arya said. "I miss my mother, and sometimes I still expect to tell her the story I've just finished or about the treasure I've found in the market. I still expect to be sung to when I feel ill."

"I can't imagine losing my parents. We may not agree on much of anything, it seems, but at least I hope that is something that might change."

Suddenly, a strong wind shook the wagon and rattled Merin to her very bones.

"Aer had the ability to speak with the winds. They came to her from all over and brought her insights about the world. Do you think these winds could have made it all the way to Kaybrum?" Merin asked.

"Yes, I'm sure of it."

Arya picked up her book then. Merin looked down at what she had written. She gave herself a few lines of space and began to write again. This time, she wrote a story. A story about a girl who could ride the winds through the mountains.

The wind didn't startle her the next time it rushed into the wagon; it felt more like an old friend just coming to check on her. It felt like Aer. She continued to write a story about a Magic—one that Tiernan and Bryce would enjoy.

The words flowed through her as she snuggled into the blanket Arya had given her, listening to the soft pages of a love story being read so close by. Merin let her imagination soar away from her far through the mountains and off the narrow path into places unknown.

She turned the page in her notebook, closed her eyes, and began to sketch. She hadn't been an excellent art student; she had preferred things with right answers. Things that people could tell her she had succeeded at definitively, but for the first time in a long time, she didn't feel the tight clench on her heart to impress people or make people see her worth. She was simply a little snow in this monstrous pass of mountains, able to just be. Able to forget the world she left behind and the one that she was headed to. A moment not to be a hidden Magic or a political one. A moment just for herself.

Her fingers seemed to work without needing her eyes to focus, although with the snow, they were moving slower; she still didn't trust herself to focus on the small details. She drew sketchy lines allowing herself to go over the same piece a few times with imperfections and crisscrossed pen marks.

"What are you drawing?" Arya asked after a while. "You've been sitting there smiling for about thirty minutes."

"Did you finish your book?"

"No, I've just gotten to the point where the two people who are clearly in love and should be together find some reason that is only ever obvious to them to force each other away. I get so frustrated. I always have to put it down for a while," she said. "You seem to be having a grand ol' time over there."

"It's nothing," Merin said, looking for the first time at the drawing in front of her as a mostly finished piece. It was rough, and she would have never submitted it to her art teacher, but she liked it. It reminded her of Aer, the way that she could have been. Free.

"If you say so, but when we get to the East, you should get some ink. They have the best ink over there. Some of it comes from this shell thing they find in the ocean. It's this beautiful purple color, so deep it's almost black until you put it in the sunlight." Arya chattered on about the different things she was looking for in Sepsrym.

"More books?" Merin asked.

"The East rarely has any good love stories. An adventure or two, but mostly overly grandiose histories and science. The West is truly the best at love stories. They've condensed it down to perfection. For a really good adventure, the North."

"And the South?"

Kor had never mentioned any books from Hadran. He so rarely talked about his childhood with her, so she wasn't sure what kind of stories he had heard as a child.

"Magic."

"Magic? Really? But Hadran is so harsh on people with magic."

"They weren't always, and magic is built into their history. The current opinion is not always the permanent opinion. I think someday Hadran will be the center of magic."

"How many times have you been to Hadran?"

"We don't go much now. Vycky liked the plants, and my mother loved the sun. I think it was easier for Pa to let those trade routes go when they stopped coming with us."

"That makes sense. Bryce is always avoiding things that have hurt him in the past. And I understand it, or, at least, I try to, but it feels like it just limits him."

"It took Pa years to go back to Hadran after my mother passed. He said it felt like the sun was hollow there. But we did go back. Some things just need time. Bryce is strong."

"He is."

"You aren't really visiting family, are you?" Arya asked suddenly.

"No," Merin said finally. "Korvo's been in the East, and he sent us a note that he needed me. Well, he needed a healer, so something is wrong."

"I figured it must have been something else."

"Why do you say that?"

"Because you haven't talked about your family in the East, and you've barely mentioned the ones in Kaybrum. Everything you seem to be looking forward to is back in the city. This is the longest conversation we've had where you haven't asked me how long until we get to Sepsrym like you want this to be over."

Merin started to argue, but Arya put out a hand.

"I don't mind. I just want to make sure I can cover for you."

"I didn't tell you because I didn't want you to have to lie for me."

"Is it lying? Korvo sounds like he is family to you and Bryce. And a connoisseur of love novels is never going to miss a little ring around a right finger. Bryce is family. As far as I'm concerned, your lie is intact."

"I . . . I . . . uhh." She faltered. "Thank you."

"I'll help you if we get stopped and questioned at the border, but you look like most of the citizens of the East. I doubt anyone will question your story. Now, I'm going to go to sleep. When we wake up, we should be close to the border."

"Right. Of course."

Sleep eluded Merin. Outside, she heard the soft crunch as the wheels rolled over fresh snow, and she listened for the soft calls of the owls hidden in the night.

CHAPTER THIRTY-ONE
KORVO

KOR LOOKED AROUND HIM. THEY HAD MORE SICK MAGICS than he wanted to count. The cough left trickles of blood on the edges of their mouths that seemed to darken with the fear that was coming from their eyes. Merin had to be on her way.

Jaxson came and sat down next to him.

"I hate to ask," Jaxson said. "I think we need help in seeing what is coming next."

"You want me to use the collar."

Jaxson nodded. If Jaxson was asking, then there must be no other option. Dacia was spent. They couldn't make a move without her, and the sick were taking their supplies faster than they could replenish them. And they still hadn't been able to get back to Tiernan.

He gathered the collar from the little carvings he had made while he was on the ship and headed up as high as he could. He held it in his hand. The metal caught the light—the break from where they had cut it off Aer.

Aer came to him immediately.

"Long time no see," she said casually. "I don't blame you. Jaxson is pretty good-looking. A little too poetically mysterious for my taste, but hey, I get it."

How badly he wanted to hear those words from her. Normally she was just a floating ghost—a voice, something not so solid. But here on the boat, with the winds ruffling through his clothes, she was here. Present.

Kor looked around. He saw Jaxson on the deck below. Kor waited until he disappeared into the captain's quarters to check on Dacia.

"You're a figment of my imagination."

"Well, that's rude," Aer said.

"You're not real. And these people, their suffering, is real. I need to help them, Aer."

"That's what I've been trying to do."

"No, you just make me want to go home. I know I was wrong to leave them. I can't do this. I have no plan. I have no way to save anyone. Not you. And now, instead of seeing the future or the past, all I see is you. I see you in the cards. I see you every time I touch this collar. I see you in my dreams."

"Yeah, I've noticed."

"Aer, you are gone. You *died*. I watched you die. I buried you. I watched as they cut this from your neck. Aer—"

"As always, you are the one doing all the talking. You think you're the only one who has answers. The only one who can see memories. I've had a lot of time to think."

"Convince me you are real."

"How can I do that? Anything only you and I would know are things you remember about me. You see the future, Kor. Just believe in something for a few minutes."

"If it's you, then are you alive?" A tiny seed of hope fluttered in him that, somehow, he hadn't failed.

"No. I'm dead. Part of my connection to the elements is still connected to the Earth. As you used the collar, it connected you to me. But also, I think the collar changes magic. It shifts it. More than the General knew. He thought it just bypassed our control systems. Which it did. Oh, believe me, that was a *lot* of lightning. It felt like I was being torn apart." She glanced up.

Kor shuddered at the thought of her feeling that.

"But it changed the way the weather felt. I was part of the clouds, the rain, the lightning. I was everywhere it was. I was freedom and wind. I was alive in the most thorough way possible. There is more to magic than we knew. And I think the more you use the collar, the more it changes your magic. You've started being able to see me. You've started getting visions from other things besides the cards."

Kor looked away.

"Am I wrong, Kor?"

He shook his head.

"I think you're seeing beyond the cards. You are seeing into the very fabric of time on Earth."

"The fabric of the Earth?"

"Time. It's, like, umm . . . It's like the cards. There are millions of destinies in the deck, but the exact one that will pop up comes because of your magic, right?"

"I guess." His magic had always been harder to pin down than Bryce's, Aer's, Merin's, or Tiernan's. They were all connected to the elements, but the past, future, and time itself seemed to weave through everything on Earth.

"You're connected to time. You see it in the cards, and now that past and future are extending. You are becoming part of the fabric of time. Which is why you can still see me. You can still communicate with me because I am somewhere in the fabric of time."

"But why can't I talk to Merin or Bryce or—"

"Because they don't know they're in the fabric of time. I do. I can see it all clearly."

"So you're saying I can talk to dead people."

"That I am not sure about."

"You're saying you're real and dead. And I can talk to you."

"That might be because of the collar. And traces of my connection to the earth. Look, you were the one that did all the thinking and planning stuff, okay? I'm just here to give the report, like always."

"Aer, I miss you."

"I know. But now, let's sort through the cards, shall we? Like old times. Tell me what you see and feel. Be open, Kor."

He felt for the deck. Collar in his hand, he picked up the first card. The card he had always thought represented Aer. He hadn't drawn that card since she had died. It didn't matter how many times he had shuffled or how badly he had wanted to see it, it had eluded him. And now, here it was, staring back at him. She was real. She smirked.

"Okay, now let's figure out how to stop these bastards."

Kor drew the next card. Images flooded him. Darkness, dampness, an echoing cough. A flicker of light.

"Take control, Kor. You're not a vessel for the future anymore. You can see more."

He hoped she was right. He moved toward the light. It was a flicker of a flame in the palm of a hand. Tiernan's hand. He still had magic, but his face looked contorted, rough. He was only a child. Kor reached for him, calling his name. Tiernan sat upright as if he was looking for something. Kor stepped back. Could he really interact with the visions?

"Where are you?" he thought.

The vision changed; he was on a sandy tower, looking out at the sea. There was their ship far down below. The sand whipped him as the wind at the top of the tower hurled itself at him. He looked down on the beach. Dacia. She was losing control.

"Next card, Kor," Aer whispered into his ear. He felt his hand touching the cards, but he still felt as if he was standing on the tallest sand tower in Sepsrym. Immediately after he stopped touching, the beach disappeared and he was back to the rocking of the ship in the waves.

He touched the next card. It felt like cool water. Fresh water. An ash-streaked Raven flew across the sky. It landed on the mast. A band wrapped around its leg. A single tear dropped from its eye.

Merin was close. He could feel that now. He could sense her moving toward him at that very moment. *Hurry,* he urged the presence that was Merin. *Hurry.*

"What I don't get," Aer said, making Kor come back once more to the ship, "is why they are taking our magic. We're useful. Look at your poor captain. And beyond that, with Magics to hate and despise, they always have a common enemy. Why fight amongst yourselves when you have a built-in scapegoat?"

Aer was right. Taking their magic had seemed cruel and undignified punishment to Kor, but how did it help them? There were whole industries that relied on Magics. And more Magics would always be born.

He could feel his energy waning. This deeper connection, it felt like being able to breathe when you first burst to the top of the water. Where the air goes in rapidly and too fast. It burned. His fingers twitched, and he felt the strength leaving him quickly. The collar. He had forgotten about the downside. How could he do that?

"One more card, Kor. Then you need to rest."

He nodded. With some effort, he flipped the next card over. There were two rulers. From afar, they looked like they were dressed the same. They were drenched with jewels. Their clothes were pressed and embroidered with gold. The vision zoomed in behind the rulers. One was holding a baton that went directly into the back of the other ruler. While the one with the baton pressed into his back opened and closed his mouth, the other took a large sip of water from a golden cup.

"The General. He's just a puppet."

"Serves him right," Aer laughed. "But why? What is the end game here?"

Kor reached for one more card, but it was getting too hard to move. It felt like he was drunk, and his movements were hard to control. His vision started going black.

"Kor, no one will hate you if you choose to be with Jaxson," Aer said before the vision went totally black. He saw the winds pick up and tear at the flags on the top of the mast but leave the sails completely alone. Then everything went black.

He floated in that blackness for a while. It was a peaceful darkness. Like floating in the salt lakes, where the salt kept you afloat without trying.

He thought he heard someone saying his name, but he wasn't sure he cared. It was so nice to float in the darkness. There was nothing that needed his attention. Everything seemed so far away or so long ago.

"Kor. Korvo. Korvo, open your eyes."

He wanted to say no, but the voice seemed so worried. It was disrupting the peaceful feeling. Slowly, he opened his eyes.

His other senses came back to him. The feeling of wind pulling on his clothes, the rough calluses of a hand on his face. Then he saw the gray sky and, finally, Jaxson's face. Kor blinked. He reached up his hand to touch Jaxson.

The larger boy smiled. Kor tried to stand, but Jaxson didn't let him do anything more than sit up.

"I think I asked too much of you," Jaxson said. "But it looks like your friend's winds were still looking out for you."

The winds were settling now. No longer ripping at him but slightly moving his clothes back and forth, making sure he was okay.

Kor saw that the collar was in Jaxson's hand. He had pried it from his grip. That was what brought him back. For the first time, Kor felt afraid. Afraid that if he used the collar again, he wouldn't want to come back.

"I wouldn't have," a voice whispered to him in the wind so very faintly. Kor wasn't one hundred percent certain he had really heard it. But what had Aer called it? Freedom. The thing she wanted more than anything. Crappy way to get it.

"I think it's going to be a while before you are good enough to climb down the mast by yourself," Jaxson said.

"I'll be all right," Kor said, sitting up. Everything ached. It was like he had run a hundred miles and then swam from the East back to Hadran. Even the little muscles in between his toes protested as he tried to get on his knees in an effort to stand up.

"I'll go down first," Jaxson said. "Just in case you slip," he added as Kor, unsteady on his feet, grabbed for the edge of the platform. Kor just nodded.

It took them longer than he expected. Torn between moving fast so his strength didn't give out and the protesting of any and all movement by his entire body, Kor slowly made his way down the mast. His foot slipped from its hold only once.

Down on the deck, Jaxson looked him over. Kor could only imagine what he was seeing. He hoped he didn't look as bad as he felt.

"We should get you to your hammock. Nothing a good night's sleep can't do for a sailor," he said. His tone was upbeat, but his eyes betrayed that he was nervous. He was still clutching the collar in his hands. Kor wasn't sure if he should ask for it back.

"I need to get to shore," Kor said.

"Shore? I don't think so. You look worse than Captain."

"Merin's coming. We can't waste time."

Kor had to lean on Jaxson to get back to the shore. Everything in him felt like lying down.

"You shouldn't use it again. What if it gets worse each time? If the winds hadn't acted up."

Kor nodded along. Aer. Aer had sent the winds to alert Jaxson. To keep him from staying in the black.

"What are we looking for?" Jaxson finally asked when Kor made it clear he wasn't going to elaborate on magic for a while.

"Girl, a few years younger than us. Bright blue eyes."

"That's all you got? So she looks like almost every girl that lives in the East?"

"Well, it's a good thing I know her so well."

"And if you fall back asleep? Seas take us, I'll be the one interviewing little girls."

"She's not little. I just don't know how she decided she'd dress."

They sat for a minute. Kor tried to slowly stretch out the little muscles that burned, starting with his toes. Jaxson hummed and pulled a carving out of his pocket. The dock was busy. There were people trying to get on ships, trying to get off ships, loading cargo, unloading cargo, selling cargo; there were a hundred things happening at once.

Kor should have taken Dacia. Jaxson didn't like crowds. That was becoming apparent very quickly on the ship. Being around that many people seemed to make him jumpy. Even now, his small knife wasn't softly scaling back the wood like normal—it jumped and twitched with every noise. Jaxson belonged on the sea.

Kor was starting to feel a little better. But the large sand-colored tower that loomed over the dock area haunted him. It wasn't the first time that he had seen it in one of his visions. Sometimes towers meant change, but he had a feeling the tower in his vision just meant that tower.

Kor's thoughts wandered around in the conversations of the people. Most of it was strictly business. Haggling for a price or for better contracts. He tried filtering those out. He tried listening for Merin.

"Do you know she is supposed to come today?" Jaxson murmured after an hour or so sitting on the dock.

"She's coming," Kor said, but he had to admit he was getting less and less sure. If he could only use the collar again. Jaxson must have seen him looking at the pocket he was holding it in, because he shifted so his back was to Kor.

"I'm not losing you to this awful science. I'm worried enough about Captain. I don't need you needing support too. Ships don't need freeloaders." But the concern was still in his voice, even if Kor couldn't see his face.

"She's coming," Kor said with a little more confidence than he actually had.

Another hour passed listening to conversations until a sound that perked up his ears wafted toward him.

"I'm meeting family," Merin said as a couple of sailors cornered her. Kor's heart lit up at the sight of her. She was fine. A little travel-worn, but good.

"Ahh, Ms. Merin," Kor said, rushing as best he could to meet her. "Your family sent me ahead to gather you."

"Do you know this Hadranian?" One of the sailors sneered at Kor.

"Of course, Mr. Segal was a private tutor of sorts. Thank you so much for your help, gentlemen."

"Mr. Segal?" Kor whispered as they walked away.

"I panicked."

"Lost your knack for lying on your feet after a week apart from Bryce?"

"He would be so disappointed." She laughed. It sounded like music to his ears.

"Merin, I'd like you to meet Jaxson. Jaxson, this is Merin, the answer to our problems."

"It's nice to meet you, Ms. Merin." He took her hand and held it to his lips. "Ahh, excuse me. Mrs. Merin."

"Mrs.?" Kor asked.

"I'll tell you later. It sounds like we have something much bigger to attend to."

"Come, there is a lot to do."

He led her to the boat. He felt her wobble as they got onto the deck. Had he really gained his sea legs in such a short amount of time? It had felt like it was just a day or two since he was last in Kaybrum, but just a glance at Merin told him it had been a lot longer.

She seemed older. Not in a bad way, but mature. She looked confident in the way that she hadn't when he had left.

When they went below deck, Merin gasped. She tried to cover it, but it was clear to Kor.

"These people," Merin said as she knelt down to a young woman who was curled into a ball. Her knees pulled into her chest every time the cough ripped through her body.

"The lovely East decided to strip them of their magic. And there were repercussions," Kor said finally. There wasn't a more delicate way to put it. They were all dying.

Merin closed her eyes. Her thumb pressed to the forehead of the woman, her other hand holding the woman's shoulder still.

Merin's collapsed, and her body straightened.

"I . . . I can stop the cough," Merin said. She hadn't even opened her eyes. Kor could see the sweat collecting on her brow. This was going to take all of her strength.

The woman relaxed. Her knees unclenched, and her eyes fluttered. Merin motioned for water. Jaxson brought her a cup. Merin held it to the woman's lips. Her lips parted just enough for Merin to get the water in.

"Are they all," she paused, standing and handing the empty cup back to Jaxson, "like this?"

"Some more, some less," Jaxson said, looking around the room.

"Do you know how they took away the magic?" she asked. Kor shook his head.

"None of them seem to remember," Kor said. "Do you get a sense of what happened?"

"No, but back in Kaybrum, they were experimenting on the kids in the Refuge."

"They were what?" Kor's voice cracked.

"What's the Refuge?" Jaxson asked.

"How do you know? What did you find?"

Merin hesitated. Her hands wrung on the fabric around her waist.

"Merin, if you know something—"

"I read Bryce's file. I . . . I told him I did it, but not until after I shared what was in it with Hayden."

"I bet he wasn't happy about that." Kor shook his head. "Why would you share it with Hayden of all people?"

"I was trying to show him what he didn't understand. I was trying to explain why Bryce snapped at him. Why the Refuge was such a big deal. I did it for Bryce. But that's not the worst part. Hayden figured out what they were doing. They were trying to figure out what the connections were for Magics. They wanted to be able to take magic at will."

She went to the next patient. An older man who was darker than Jaxson. White hairs were sticking out in uneven lengths in his beard. Kor wondered how long he had been captured. Hadran men didn't often grow beards, and they sure wouldn't have let them grow scraggly. The man barely moved when Merin laid her hands on his forehead. She spent a few moments with him. Then, his breathing increased.

For the first time since they had found the Magics, Kor let himself feel the slightest bit of hope.

CHAPTER THIRTY-TWO

BRYCE

There wasn't much to do about the school the first few days. Everything was running like clockwork. And Merin had schedules in place way before she had left. The court still hadn't set a date for Thomas's trial, so when he wasn't working with the older Magics, Bryce was spending a lot of time in the garden.

"I can't tell if I'm not half bad at this," he said to the plants, the Magics in the ground, the air—it didn't really matter, "or if everyone only trusted me because they already did the hard stuff." He found himself talking out his lectures for the older kids to the plants. Talking about jobs, control of magic, the law. He practiced in the garden so that the words sounded sure and professional long before he said them to the kids.

"Twelve Gods," he said after yet again losing his train of thought on Magic pride. He had been putting it off because he just couldn't get it right. Everything sounded generic, like it was coming from a book about the gods written for children. Something like "everyone is special" just felt flat, hollow.

He twiddled with some of the leaves of a bright green vine. Even though he could have filled in the garden within a matter of minutes, he had let the plants grow naturally. He had gained his control back, and that made it more important to listen to the plants themselves instead of just asking them to do his bidding. Now that he could almost communicate with them, he had to actually listen.

"Working on something?" Hayden asked. He was leaning on the outside fence. His hair was swept easily to the side, and it hung there like it couldn't be jostled out of place. Bryce grimaced. Even though Hayden had been instrumental after Kor and then Merin had left, it still didn't mean he liked the boy.

"Still working on the talk I'm supposed to give to the older boys."

"Aren't some of them still waiting for trial dates?"

"Exactly. I want to do this soon. Before the trial. Which could happen any day at this point."

"What's it about?" He let himself through the gate and sat down on a bench at the edge of the circle Bryce had made.

Bryce sat in the dirt. He had put the bench there for Merin so she wouldn't have to get dirty but could still be near him while he worked.

"Pride in being Magic."

"Ahh, like the special talents that you have? Magics are extraordinary. Gifts like that really should open doors. Magics *should* value themselves. Take pride in their abilities."

Bryce laid down. He watched the clouds as he sighed. "It's so much more than that, though. Being special has made us hated. Some Magics hate their magic. Many wish they had been born without it. Even when they publicly support the rights of Magics, they just wish they were normal. That they didn't have to fight. Wishing sometimes that they were somewhere else. Someone else."

"Doesn't everyone wish they were someone else on occasion?" Hayden asked.

"Who else would you want to be? An emperor?" Bryce scoffed.

Hayden didn't respond. He put his hands in his lap. Bryce took that as a sign to continue. "As soon as others knew about my magic, it felt like a death sentence. My family hated me. My father ignored me. My mother cried every time she saw me, like I was some sort of ghost. It didn't seem like a good thing."

"You could have had your own farm. Someone would have taken you in. It feels like a bad bet not to."

Bryce got to his feet. "Maybe. But coming here, Kor taught me that I had to be proud of the struggle too. That it was part of what made me—for a serious lack of a better term—special. Without the struggle that we've faced, we aren't anything really. The struggle is currently part of the package. It's not that it's a good thing, but it's made us strong. It made us a better community because we had to rely on each other." The words felt heavy in his mouth. "We made it through the shit they put us through. The things we were punished for that were not our fault. Ugh."

He stopped suddenly.

"What?" Hayden asked. "Seemed like you were getting somewhere."

"That's the thing. I don't know where I'm going. The struggle has gotten me into more fights than I can count."

"I can account for some of those." Hayden rubbed at his jaw. Bryce smiled just a little.

"But I don't want these kids to feel like suffering is something that is necessary. Like Merin shouldn't feel like she's less of a Magic just because she was spared the Refuge and the tattoo. I don't want it to become a competition of who had it worse. I just can't get the words right. They're there in my head, but it's like they're swirling around, and I can't get them out in the right order. I just get frustrated." He paced back and forth, leaving dusty divots where he stepped.

"It's a complicated topic. Could you start with the 'be the best *you* you can be' speech and work up to this one?"

Bryce sat again. Maybe it would be better to wait for Kor to come back. He had the right words for things—or Merin. She might be able to work out what he was going to say with him. But this non-Magic, his foreignness, just made the words swirl away faster.

"Do you know why I couldn't grow this garden for so long?" Bryce asked suddenly.

"Soil was bad? That's the excuse the farmers always seem to give me when yield is sub-par."

"Yes, but *why* was the soil bad? Most of Kaybrum has great soil. There used to be a river that came through this way. At least, that's what Aer used to say. It left good nutrients. I could grow anything anywhere in this city, but not here."

"My knowledge of plants generally stops at the price tag," Hayden said.

"Right below us, there are bodies. Young Magics who were killed in the Refuge. Their bodies were dumped here. There was so much hatred and anger, Kor had me purify the place. Nothing would grow before that."

"Bodies? How many?"

"I don't know. More than one, less than a million. Does it matter?"

"I guess not," Hayden said.

"I don't know how they died. A run-in with the guards, the torture and experiments, starvation, neglect—we have no idea how they met their deaths."

"It seems a shame," Hayden said. He paused to consider his next sentence. "Bryce, would you be willing to show me where they did some of these experiments?"

"Why would I do that?"

"I want to understand. I want to honor the people below us."

Bryce's mouth opened, and he took a breath, but no words came out. He let out his breath.

"Okay, but on one condition."

The rooms were mostly cleaned up. There wasn't much to indicate what they used to be. He had Tiernan burn most of the old furniture after he had broken it into pieces, but there were still some places that would be enough. There was the room. The room that he had tried so hard to forget about and even had for a short time. Until Merin had admitted to reading his file. It had all come rushing back, and he hadn't gone back in since.

"Sure," Hayden agreed. "What is it?"

"I get to choose which questions I answer."

"Sounds fair enough. Lead the way."

Bryce's thoughts moved like quicksand as he led Hayden to the room. What questions would Hayden have? What answers did Bryce have? Would he have the same reaction when he saw the room again? Would this really help Hayden understand? Had he done the wrong thing trying to keep Merin away from all of the dangerous stuff that would hurt her?

Did people really need to know more about their suffering? They had changed their minds about the Refuge after seeing Tiernan and Aer struggling to survive. But at the same time, why should people get to feel good for seeing their trauma? By recognizing it and offering their sympathies for it, was it letting them off the hook for it happening at all? Would they feel absolved by knowing? Each thought thumped in his head with every footstep he took.

They twisted down the path to the last room. He opened the door.

It looked the same. Yet, now that he was expecting it, it looked like any other room. It probably looked like nothing in Hayden's eyes.

"What was this room for?" Hayden asked.

Bryce pointed out the spots for the gas to come in.

"What do you remember about this room?"

Bryce told him of the bare memories he had. The feeling of terror crept into his belly.

"Do the other kids know about this room?"

"I haven't asked."

"What do you plan on doing with the room?" Hayden asked.

"I don't know."

His answers weren't much, and they probably weren't doing justice to the inhumane treatments suffered here, but they were honest. He felt the pressure in his throat forming into a knot. Now was not the time for long-winded explanations.

"Next room." He walked him to the chamber where the General had held him. There were still remnants of the plants that burned on the floor, their ashes smeared from when Kor and Aer had dragged him out. Bryce let himself touch them. The feeling of burning had been excruciating.

Hayden's questions were brief. Bryce answered all of them. After all, this room became public knowledge when Kor rallied to get everyone on their side after Aer's death. Kor had left the fabric up that the General had created. He said it was too dangerous to leave it somewhere where anyone could find it. Where it could come back. There was no way for it to come back if it never left the school.

"The last rooms, they won't look like much," Bryce said. "Merin was thorough."

"What happened here?" Hayden asked.

"Merin already told me you read my file. I don't know what happened to the others. No one likes to talk about it. They don't need to hear about it from someone else."

"Do you think the kids on trial . . . ?"

"Were they in here? My guess is most of them, yes. We burned all the files we found. No one should have to read about themselves referred to as a number."

"Have you read yours?"

"I lived it. I'm still trying not to relive it every night. I don't need a reminder on any of the details I've managed to forget."

Bryce glanced around him. For the first time, he looked at the room as Hayden had probably been seeing it before. A clean room with desks and books. They were just walls. Just floors. There were no ghosts or leather straps to hold him down. There were no men poking or prodding him. It was just a school building. And while Hayden's face showed he was imagining the things that had been done here for the first time, Bryce realized he didn't feel them anymore.

He didn't feel like he couldn't breathe or that he wanted to run but was glued to the ground. Everything hadn't gone fuzzy. He had shown each of these places to Hayden and answered all his questions. Not always thoroughly, but he had answered them.

"Anything else?" Hayden asked. Bryce shrugged. The dirt was gone, and the grime had been scrubbed away. The Watchers had long been reassigned somewhere else in the city or on the outskirts of the city.

"It's just a school now," Bryce said, and he meant it. He felt the weight of something lift from his shoulders. He had been trying to hide all of the pain. Stuffing it under the carpet like it would somehow go away, but now that he had faced it, shared it, it finally felt like it was lifting. Like he could let it go.

"Bryce," one of the older boys called from the landing below where they stood.

"Yeah?" Bryce asked.

"Some man is here to talk to you. Some important guy. At least, he looks rich enough to be important."

"I'll be right there," Bryce said.

Hayden was still looking around the room.

"You staying up here?" Bryce asked. "There isn't much to see. Better to talk to the dead outside."

Hayden held up his hand in a salute to say go on without him, and Bryce did just that. He even jogged a little as he went downstairs. Maybe Councilman Jaqui had come by; he had come a few times to the school to see how it was going. He had stopped asking about Kor, and he had been coming less frequently of late.

He made it to the bottom of the staircase, trying to come up with a generic lie if asked about where Kor and Merin were. He was so wrapped up in fabricating a story that he hardly noticed the man who was shuffled in next to the hearth.

When he finally looked up, Bryce recognized him immediately. Those same blue eyes had stared at him enough times through Merin's face.

"Mr. Pomry, to what do I owe this pleasure?"

"They set a trial date." He stepped closer. Bryce could see the wear on the man's face. His wrinkles looked deep with worry.

"When?" Bryce asked. He knew it had been coming, but it still felt like a shot to the gut. Everything else had been a warm-up to this. And for everything else, he had Merin to lead the way. He had been hoping she would be back before they set the date. Maybe it was still a ways off.

"The thirteenth," Mr. Pomry said.

"That's three days from now," Bryce said. He heard a tiny little squeak break through his voice. It made him feel more insignificant than he already did.

"They agreed to this trial, but that doesn't mean they're going to make it fair," Mr. Pomry said.

"Says the man who was on that side not too long ago," Bryce said. He regretted it immediately. Merin had wanted him to be nice. "I apologize. I didn't need to say that." He still meant it, but he knew his mouth could get him into trouble.

"I appreciate the apology, but I don't think you are wrong. I was the enemy, but now I hope I might offer some assistance."

"You would help me?"

"Believe me, if there were someone else, I would love to speak with them. But there isn't. My Merin left you in charge of this, and if I want to show my daughter I've changed, then I guess we will have to work together."

"When would you like to start?" Bryce said. Three days wouldn't be much time.

"When do lessons end for today?" Mr. Pomry looked around. There were students scurrying about, but nothing directly happening.

This was the break during the day when the little ones were done, but the older kids out working hadn't come back yet.

"We have a break now until after dinner, but then I have to lead a class."

"Well, let's start now. I brought some things that might be helpful." He shifted his gaze over to a bag of books that he had left on the hearth. They were big books. Older even than the ones Merin had found. The fancy script on the spines made Bryce's head swim. Why did they have to write the letters so many different ways? It was hard enough putting them all together in the first place. "I was hoping you could show me some of the case files and your notes?"

"Yeah, sure. Just come in." Bryce led him to their makeshift office. The map they had used to figure out Kor and Merin's trips East was still up, but Bryce had started pinning other papers over it. He found that if something was in a pile, it got lost, but if he put it where he could see it, he would remember to do it. He thought Kor would approve—even if he had inadvertently put a bunch of pins through the map.

"How well-versed are you in the case of MaCavity versus Westenbrook?"

"I've never heard those words before in my life. Ma-whoosits and Westenbrook?"

"MaCavity was a Magic that had a trial before Kaybrum was the capital city. Westenbrook was the capital then."

"And?"

"Well, I think you should read it."

"Okay." It felt like this was turning more into a lesson and less like help. Westenbrook hadn't put together this trial; Kaybrum had. That's what he had to worry about.

Mr. Pomry handed Bryce the thickest and oldest book he had ever seen. And he had seen the gospel of the Twelve Gods in the temple his mother used to take him to plenty of times. But somehow the lives of all twelve gods and all of their miracles and powers still paled in comparison to this book.

"Oh, just this?" Bryce smirked.

"To start. Case files and notes?" Bryce couldn't tell if he was joking. The man had said it with a straight face, but clearly, he was mistaken about something. Bryce reached into the desk and pulled out the case files.

Under the files was Kor's note. Bryce let his fingers brush against it. Kor had said he trusted him. Merin had said she trusted him. Maybe it was time for him to trust someone else. When Merin's father was already thumbing through the files, Bryce picked up the ancient text.

Inside, the script was heavily flourished. The loops didn't even look like they belonged to letters. No letters he knew were in these shapes. He could feel his heart rate racing. He tried tracing his finger and sounding out the letters one at a time. He wasn't even sure where one started and another stopped.

He let out a long sigh.

"Something the matter?"

"I can't read this."

"Too boring? Complex?" There was a hint of mockery in his voice.

Bryce's teeth clenched together. He wanted to yell, but he took a deep breath instead.

And as calmly and coolly as he could, he explained, "Too loopy. These letters don't look like letters. I know I should recognize them, but this script is too complicated. Everything starts blending together."

"You don't know how to read cursive?"

"I barely know how to read. Merin only started to teach me right before the Refuge was taken down. Magics weren't allowed to be in school."

"Even when you were small, before people knew your . . . talent?"

"There's not much choice in schools for a poor farm boy. Especially when his parents were worried others might confirm their suspicions."

"I see," he said and put out his hand. Bryce's shoulders fell. He had already messed this up. Kor might believe in him, but that was out of love and compassion. No one besides his friends was going to believe him. Bryce reluctantly placed the book back in Mr. Pomry's hands.

Merin's father looked the book over. He flipped through the pages and put it down on the table.

"I'll transcribe the important parts while you're doing your lesson today," he said finally.

"Wait, what?"

"I think it would be good to get your perspective on the transcriptions on this trial, but it will be better if you are able to read it and go back over it multiple times. I'll write out the main parts here, and anything that you seem to think is important, we can go over later. But first, I need you to explain this part of your notes."

Bryce looked over. There was a note in Merin's tiny handwriting. The letters were all in perfect order. They were curved slightly so that it made them seem more friendly than the printed words in the books she gave him to read. His heart ached.

"Merin wrote this." He read it aloud quickly. "'Ask Hayden if this could be connected with what he mentioned at his office.'"

"What does it mean?" Mr. Pomry asked.

"Hell if I know," Bryce said. "You could ask Hayden. He's upstairs last I saw him."

"We'll come back to it," he said, shifting through the notes more. "Most of the cases first happened in the marketplace. I'm sure it has something to do with that. Could something in the marketplace have caused this to happen?"

Bryce took a deep breath. It had taken him months to tell Merin what he was about to tell her father.

"Mr. Pomry, I think you should know something. After the Hadranian General held me in a room upstairs made from the same metal collars that they forced on Tiernan and Aer outside the Refuge on that day, something changed about my magic."

His eyebrows lifted.

"At first, I thought it was about control. That I was losing control, but I think it just changed the way I interacted with the plants."

"How so?"

Bryce fumbled for the words to explain to him the inner light and the innate feeling from his feet to his nose that said things were different, more alive.

"Could these children have been affected?"

"I was the only one that they put into that room. Aer and Tiernan were the only ones in the collars. I don't think . . . wait, the jackets. The General gave all of Aer's people jackets."

"Her army?"

"Her people," Bryce said firmly. "He gave us all jackets. Gray jackets. He had claimed they were to help us, but they were just one more experiment."

"None of the kids were arrested wearing matching jackets. That would have led to the immediate assumption that they were in some sort of gang."

"I only spent time in a room with the material, and it's still affecting me. They don't need to be wearing them as long as they have worn them for some significant amount of time."

"What happened to these jackets?"

"I don't know. I haven't thought about them since that day. I suppose some of these kids could have gotten hold of them. Someone could be selling them or maybe they were just remnants from that day. I don't think they were taken away when people were brought in. Aer was still wearing hers when . . ."

"Yes. I remember."

"You were there?" Bryce asked.

"I had gotten a message that my daughter had burst into her school with an ash Raven drawn on her chest, calling for people to come see the plight of the Magics at the Refuge. I came down to make sure she stayed safe. I spent years keeping her safe. Keeping her out of danger. And then you all dragged her into the heart of it."

"No one dragged her. Merin makes her own choices. She is the most educated out of all of us, obviously, and she made her choices with all the education your money could buy."

This was the fight that he had been waiting for. Things had been going too smoothly before. For a single moment, Bryce had begun to think that things were really starting to fall into place. That he could finally glimpse a future of happiness and peace. But it was all about to unravel.

Mr. Pomry drew a deep breath like he was about to have a lot to say. But he held it and closed his eyes.

"I was there," he said finally. Bryce nodded. Was that a true statement? He wasn't sure. He just knew that the fight had been avoided for now. He stood up and paced around the room. The adrenaline from preparing for battle was still circulating through his veins and made it almost impossible to be still.

"I can find out if the jackets are on the market somewhere tomorrow morning before the afternoon classes." He had a million other things on his plate, but the twitch in his limbs wasn't letting him focus. He had to keep moving.

"Right. I think it's about time for your talk," Mr. Pomry said. Bryce sighed. He still didn't know what he was going to say.

Bryce nodded and headed out to the little room beside the old mess hall. Bryce had found it easier to meet with the kids somewhere they hadn't been while they were in the Refuge.

A few boys were already there. There were always some who didn't come. They had work or didn't think they needed to be lectured to by Bryce. He didn't think of himself as a teacher. He was an expert in only a few things and one of them was plants. There were no other Magics that had the same connection to the Earth that he did that he knew of, so that didn't help him too much. But he also knew what it was like to be in the Refuge. He knew the nightmares these kids had. And now he knew what it felt like to have control of something that was so sacred before and feel like it was slipping out of your fingers.

"What's he doing here?" Thomas snapped. Bryce turned to see that Mr. Pomry had followed him down to the room. He had brought the book with all the fancy lettering and a notebook that he said he would be working on, but Bryce hadn't expected him to come down with him.

A few of the other boys murmured their contempt. The last time they had seen the older man was when he was opposing them in court.

"He is not prosecuting anymore. He's been reviewing our cases. They've set a date for your trial," Bryce explained.

The murmurs in the room were silenced. A date. Bryce knew that they understood what that meant. This trial would decide their fates, or at least for some of their friends.

"Before we start tonight, I need to ask you all something."

"I'm not answering anything with him here. It could all be a trap."

"You're making yourself sound guilty," Bryce said. "Besides, this question is important. Were any of you involved in the standoff at the Council Building?"

A few of the boys mumbled that they wished they had been there, and some others shook their heads.

"I was there," a girl said. She only attended his talks now and then. Bryce wasn't even sure he knew her name, and he didn't remember her within the walls, but it was always dark, and there were usually a lot of people.

"What did you do with your jacket? The one Aer gave you," Bryce asked her.

"The jacket? What's that got to do with anything?" she asked.

"Just tell me, what did you do with the jacket?"

"I sold it."

"Sold it? Where?"

"New shop in the marketplace. I got a pretty good sum for it too, since it was so nicely made."

"You sold something like that?" one boy asked. Bryce had told them about the fibers in the jackets in case something ever happened again.

"I wasn't going to keep something that showed I was on the losing side of something." She turned to Bryce. "Things are all well and great for Magics now, but how long are you going to be able to keep this up?" She gestured around at the walls.

Bryce swallowed hard. It was like the voice in his head had come to life.

"As long as I can," Bryce said finally. "Look, Aer was right that we needed more than the school. We needed people to actually see us. But Kor was also right that we needed to be able to raise ourselves up. We couldn't keep waiting on other people."

"Aren't you still waiting?" the girl asked. "Without Nagely money, this wouldn't even be possible. I see you walking to the market and getting groceries and goods from him for free. What happens when the charity runs out? No one has seen Kor for weeks. Everyone is giving up on this place besides you. You were there with Aer. You used to be willing to fight."

"I *am* fighting. Don't you see that? I'm fighting in the courts for all of you. I'm fighting to keep this place afloat. We suffered, yes. But isn't the whole goal to not have that happen for the people after us?"

"So I should feel good that I made it through? *Have* we made it through? We came out of the Refuge just for the courts to start putting us in regular cages. They still hate us. They just do it quietly. They do it while supporting our 'cause' but not us. They've always liked us when we were useful, but soon they are going to realize we won't keep being useful, and they'll want to take it away."

"So what do you think the answer is? Do nothing?" Bryce asked.

"Nothing ever changes."

"And yet you fought with Aer for change."

"I fought to fight. You, of all people, should understand that."

"And I grew up," Bryce said. He could feel the adrenaline flowing again. It was making his heart beat faster, and he knew if he looked at his hands, his fingers would be trembling. "I grew up when Kor asked me to. I know they still hate us."

"It's always going to be Magics and non-Magics."

"They don't hate us because we have magic," Bryce said. It was out of his mouth before he had even processed it.

"Is this going to be some speech about how people fear things that are different from them? I've heard it before, along with every other speech just like it. But sure, go ahead and entertain me," she said.

Bryce almost laughed. Not because it was funny but because he finally figured it out. It had everything to do with non-Magics. Hatred was the only way to keep the Magics down. Everyone needed someone else to hate. Someone lower than them in the social strata.

"You know who I was treated the worst by?"

"The men who tortured you?"

"Besides them. It was my family. My magic could have made my family's farm the most successful in the country, but they hated me. Because they needed someone to hate. They needed someone lower on the stairs of life. Because if there was no one lower than them, they'd have to start looking at their own lives. Kor's family was the same."

"And what about the Council members who worked with the General?"

"They need people below them too. If people were all equal, they wouldn't get to stay in charge. Give everyone a common enemy, and the powerful don't have to justify their own corrupt actions."

Every second it was becoming clearer to him. All the talks Kor had done, the people Aer had rallied. Things weren't going to change because they persuaded people. People weren't going to be persuaded unless it was in their best interest. And people were selfish.

The other boys began speaking now. In low tones, Bryce heard them hashing out the same argument amongst themselves.

"That's enough for tonight. Take the rest of the night," Bryce said. The adrenaline was gone. His body felt heavy. He rubbed at his forehead. His hands were still shaking slightly.

The kids eyed him suspiciously like it was a test. He sighed.

"Just go and think about it," he said. The boys filtered out slowly. The girl lingered like she had something more to say, but after opening her mouth a few times, she turned and left with the rest of the kids. A few of them went upstairs to the rooms they lived in; others went out.

"Did that go the way you were expecting?" Mr. Pomry asked.

Bryce snapped. "Did it look like it?"

"It looked like something," he said, closing the book in front of him.

"Yeah, what did it look like? Me, losing my temper?"

"It looked like you were winning an argument. Maybe not in the beginning, but you got there. And that's what matters."

"It didn't feel like I was winning. It feels like all I did was convince everyone it's pointless."

"Maybe."

"And that's winning? I realize you want Merin to be done with us, but that feels like a stretch."

"Did she argue back? Not right away. And that's all that matters with a court case. If it ends and you're the only one talking, you're going to win. I'm not sure if that is the strategy you'll want to take in the courtroom, but you got the right idea."

"You lost me."

"Let me handle the law, and you just do," he gestured up and down at Bryce, "that in the courtroom, and we'll get through this."

"We?"

"I told you I would help."

Bryce sat for a second. His index finger rubbed at the furrowed forehead. Now that the adrenaline had fully worn off, everything felt impossible again. If what he had just said was true, how could they ever change anyone's mind without finding a new, lower enemy for them to hate?

"How do we do it?" Bryce asked.

"The court case? I made some notes while you were talking. I thought it would last longer, so I'm not quite—"

"How do we stop the hatred? It's never been about magic. Not really."

"Yes, well, if I knew how to fix that, I'd be a very wealthy man."

"You are a very wealthy man."

"I guess."

"Show me the notes," Bryce reached out for the first set of papers. Mr. Pomry's writing was similar to Merin's, but his letters looked like they were lined up for battle. There was no softness in them, just order.

Bryce read through them, but even with the straight lines, the words swirled around. He traced along them slowly with his finger so that everything stayed in order. Mr. Pomry didn't say anything and just kept working on his notes. When Bryce got through the first page, Mr. Pomry straightened up and rolled his shoulders back.

"What do you think?"

"Well, it was mostly about MaCavity. He was charged with being Magic. He pleaded not guilty. But he was a Magic. He even showed people in the courtroom his abilities. He didn't deny those, just that he was a Magic. It doesn't make any sense."

"How would you define a Magic?"

"A person with special connections to the different elements of the earth."

"That was what he argued. He argued he was a person, not a Magic. He argued," he said, handing Bryce the next page. Bryce scanned it quickly. "He argued that while he had the ability to do amazing things, that did not make him anything other than a person."

"And how did the court react?" Bryce leaned in.

"How do you think they reacted?"

Bryce fought the reaction to feeling like he was being talked down to.

"Not well," Bryce said, looking down at his feet. He could feel the edge of anger bubbling in the back of his neck. A slow boil.

"Correct. There are hundreds of pages here on how they tried to test him. How they thought to separate Magics out. What makes someone human?"

"Is that a real question?" Bryce looked up at him. He met Merin's father's eyes, so similar to Merin's, and held eye contact.

"For them, it was." Mr. Pomry didn't look away.

"And what did they decide?" Bryce asked finally.

"They decided he was human. A person with magical abilities."

"So he won the case? After all of that?"

"I'll leave the rest of my notes here tomorrow. That will help you get through the results."

"But he won the case. He was human."

"Bryce, you've always been human. Has the world treated you that way?"

He didn't wait for an answer. He stood slowly and walked himself out of the room.

"I'll see you tomorrow, Bryce."

Bryce went straight to the room Kor had made for them. Two empty beds stared at him, and the silence was deafening. He paced for twenty minutes or so before he worried someone might hear him moving around. The younger kids would all be asleep.

The General hadn't thought he was human. The men in this place hadn't thought he was human. He laughed. Hours ago, he was finally feeling like he had conquered the Refuge. He had conquered the fears. He had felt on top of the world, and now? Now he felt nothing but alone. Alone and hopeless.

He sat on Korvo's bed. If only he could write a letter to Kor or to Merin. Or hear Tiernan chuckle lightly about the fire in his hand. Instead he was stuck, the only help he could get from non-Magics who didn't even like him. Hell, one of them probably hated him and the ground he stepped on. He laid back on Kor's pillow, willing himself to understand what Kor would do. What would he think? What would he say? He sat staring into the dark for what felt like hours, having nothing but questions to keep him company. Eventually, he dozed off.

For the first time, he fell asleep in the building and didn't dream of the Refuge. He dreamed of the courtroom. They had him on a large scale. They were stacking things on the other side. All of his thoughts and his feelings were being weighed. He felt the slight jolts as the weights began to center. The two sides evened out.

The faceless judge in the dream called out.

"Human."

Bryce sighed.

"Guilty," the voice continued. The dream went black. He woke up in a sweat. Staring at two empty beds. And the window was open.

He didn't remember opening the window, so he went across the room to shut it. He pushed on the glass, but it didn't budge.

It wasn't that strange that something in this old place was a little busted, but it was still dark, so he grabbed a lantern to figure it out. In the opening of the window were brambles that had grown up the side of the building while he slept.

"Did I call for you?" he asked the plants. He let them slip around his finger carefully to avoid the stickers that came along with any good bramble. As it wrapped around his fingers, Bryce carefully guided them out of the window. "It was just a nightmare. I'm all right," he whispered to the plants.

He let himself think, standing with his forehead against the cool glass. He was alone. He wasn't able to read the books needed to figure out the answers. And now he was back to square one of losing control.

He wandered down to the garden, out through the back door. There on the door was a note: *I sold it to Eastern Supply and Trade.*

The jacket. He may have nothing else, but at least he had a clue. He grabbed the paper and stuffed it into his pocket. The shops might not be open this early, but at least he could scope out the store. It wouldn't be the hardest thing to do.

CHAPTER THIRTY-THREE
MERIN

THERE WAS SOMETHING THERE, JUST BEYOND HER REACH. Something was hiding amongst the folds and divots in the mind. It was moving around, and she couldn't seem to find where it was coming from or going to.

It was there in all of them. There were other symptoms too. The cough that had dried throats and the sweats that had nearly dehydrated a few of these poor people. They needed so much more than she could give them. She went from person to person, but she could only give so much before she wouldn't be able to help the next.

"Merin, are you able to give enough to one more person?" Kor asked gently in her ear. She was tired. It had been days of this.

"Can I get a drink of water?" Merin asked. Her lips were chapped.

Jaxson nodded and rushed away to get her one.

"There are more?" she asked after Jaxson had rushed off.

"Out there, yes. But you've only seen the ones we've rescued."

"Who's left?"

"The captain. Jaxson's sister."

"She's a Magic?"

He nodded.

"Is Jaxson?"

"No."

"Are you together?" she asked.

"What? How did you—"

"It was pretty obvious. Or maybe I'm just missing Bryce. Vycky's cousin was lovely, but after spending every day with Bryce, it's been hard to be apart. And the way you looked at each other, that was something."

"The way we looked . . . We didn't look any way special."

"It's not that special look. It's the everyday one."

"Why did Jaxson refer to you as Mrs.?"

"Well, umm, that's the thing. There were court cases for a few of the kids. Only guardians can present at the trials. There were too many for just Bryce." She twisted the ring on her finger."

"I see," Kor said. He sank a little into the box he was seated on.

"Kor?"

"What in the name of the Twelve Gods was I thinking? I left you in charge. You figured out a way. I forced you to become adults too quickly because I left without any real plan in place."

"It's not that big of a deal. And clearly, this is where you needed to be."

"I'm just putting a bandage on everything again. I'm not stopping anything. I can't even figure out the real cause behind all of this. Nothing seems to be making sense."

"You need to rest. You look awful. Like you've spent more energy than your body can even handle. I can try to help." She reached over to touch his hand, but he pulled it away from her.

"Save your energy for the captain."

Jaxson came back with a glass of water. She sipped it slowly. It trickled down her throat, cooling her down. It also helped the nausea from being on the boat.

"I've never been on a boat," she told Jaxson when she handed back the glass. She stood and immediately wobbled.

"Just try to—if you're going to lose your lunch—to do it over the side," Jaxson said with a smile. "Come on, the captain is in her quarters."

She was grateful when he extended an arm and walked her to the door of the captain's rooms. Kor followed behind. She just needed to let him rest, and then they could talk about things more rationally. Maybe together they could sort out what was happening in Kaybrum and the East.

It was dark, but there was a small breeze rippling through the front room.

"Hello?" Merin called into the darkness.

Jaxson stepped inside, holding the door for Merin.

"Captain, I brought a healer," Jaxson said.

A groan came from the back of the cabin.

"Dacia?" Kor asked. "When did it get this bad?"

"I'll be fine, you big worry wart. You brought a healer? Have they seen the people below?" A ragged cough echoed in the room.

"I was able to help a little," Merin said.

"And their magic?" Dacia asked.

"I'm still working on that."

"Boys, go ahead and see yourselves out," Dacia said. Kor began to argue, but Jaxson pulled him out behind him. "You are a friend of Korvo's?"

"Yes. We opened the first school for Magics in Kaybrum together. How did you and Kor meet?"

"Chance meeting at the dock. He needed to go East, and I needed information."

Merin lit a lantern on the side of the bed Dacia was lying in. The light made her face glisten from the sweat that had formed around her hairline. If Merin didn't know Dacia had a fever, she would have thought it made her look beautiful.

Dacia coughed. It jerked her body so hard she curled into a ball.

"You're worse than the others."

"I know, but don't tell the boys."

Merin placed her hands on Dacia's forehead. "I'm pretty good at keeping secrets."

Merin felt with her magic inside of Dacia. Things were ragged and confusing. Her magic kept hitting dead ends and whirlpools, and she couldn't seem to get it to go where she needed to go.

"Can you talk while you work, or would that be too much? I just hate sitting here like an invalid."

"Sure," Merin said, "but I think I'll need to hold your hands." By bypassing the most difficult part of the body, the brain, she might at least be able to try to fix the cough before she ran out of power.

Dacia extended her hands into the lantern light. Merin looked closely. There was the mark of a pirate.

"Pirate, huh?" Merin said. "Can't say this is how I pictured the pirate ships I read about."

"Probably because I'm not a pirate. Just a troublemaker for the people in charge."

"I think that makes Kor a pirate too, but he's got enough marks on his body to last a lifetime. He probably doesn't need one more."

"I see you're rather markless," Dacia pried.

"I escaped that fate."

"Escaped a lot of suffering." Dacia's eyes were far away. Merin looked away and pulled back. It was happening again. She was different; she wasn't real enough.

"We're lucky. It probably means you can sneak into a lot of places where the rest of us can't. If you get your sea legs under you, I could always use a healer on the Phoenix here." Dacia sat up.

"I'm sorry, I don't understand."

"We all suffer in our own way. Some of us get it worse, like Kor and I, but that doesn't mean all aren't useful. A ship needs people with a lot of skills. Different backgrounds means different skills. Different skills can keep you alive."

"Your skills have kept this crew alive." Merin changed her grip on Dacia's hands and started working again. She felt her magic running along the ridges of Dacia's ribs, making its way to her lungs.

"True, but they might also be killing me."

"What happened? I don't mean to pry, but it might help me figure out what is happening to everyone."

Dacia sighed. For a while, she didn't speak, and Merin worried she had overstepped. Had she not learned her lesson about asking about other's trauma? She knew Bryce, she loved Bryce, and still, he hadn't wanted to tell her. She had only met Dacia moments ago and was already asking for her story.

"I was tortured. They tried to force my magic. I was used to move ships quickly, when there was no wind for years. My brother rescued me."

"Tell me about the torture. I want to know if it was similar to what happened in Kaybrum."

"It's not very clear. I often passed out. I was using so much magic that I was exhausted all the time. I remember being pricked with needles."

"This was a few years ago?" Merin asked. "The pain feels old. It feels layered."

"What do you mean?"

"Like how a broken bone can heal incorrectly. So it heals, but the real problem isn't gone. With the people below deck, everything felt clean. Like someone took a knife to their connection to magic, but yours feels . . ."

"Like I was at the beginning of the experiment."

"I don't get it. The Hadranian General, I'm sure Kor's mentioned him, was trying to prove Magics were out of control. He said they were experimenting with this woven metal stuff to make Magics lose control. If they were doing that, why were they also trying to cut yours off? Especially since they were forcing you to work."

"Maybe it was a mistake. I was on the ships way before what happened in Kaybrum."

"So you really were the start. I'm so sorry."

"Sorry don't move a ship," Dacia said. "Can you fix it?"

"I'll need more time and some rest, and you need some rest too."

"Merin, I am serious about the position on the boat, and I usually get what I want. I am the captain, after all."

Merin laughed. She could never see herself on a ship. Granted, seeing the world outside of Kaybrum had been incredible, but she missed the city, and she missed Bryce.

"Kor," she called when she exited Dacia's room.

He turned and looked at her, a smile creeping onto his solemn face.

"How did it go?"

"All right. I'll need more time. I need to rest, though. I'll take another stab at it in a few hours. Where's Tiernan? Your letter said you got our package. I can only assume that meant—"

"I've seen him."

"He's not here?" Merin felt fear rising in her throat.

Kor looked away. The smile dropped from his face.

"He was captured. He insisted on staying behind when we rescued these people."

"He was what? That poor little boy. Kor, we have to go get him right now."

"If we move now, we risk everything we've already accomplished," Kor warned.

"Don't you feel like this is one of the times when you have to risk things?"

"Tiernan." Kor swallowed hard. "He'll be okay. He just needs to make it to the next new moon. That's three days."

"*Days?*" Merin wanted to grab her bag and run to him.

"If we wait until the new moon, Dacia will be able to move the ship without being caught. Then we can grab more than Tiernan."

"If you can help the captain and the others," Jaxson said, looking up from his wooden carving, "we'll be able to move sooner."

"So if I can't figure it out, we can't get Tiernan?"

"We'll get him. I promise," Kor said.

CHAPTER THIRTY-FOUR
TIERNAN

SINCE KOR HAD ESCAPED WITH SOME OF THE MAGICS, whoever was in charge seemed to be getting desperate. Every few hours, they would come and get a Magic. They shoved them up the stairs, and then Tiernan lost track of their footsteps. They would be gone for several hours and then escorted back. Then the cycle would repeat. Every once in a while, one of them didn't return. There were fifteen of them. Only Tiernan and a few of the other younger ones hadn't been pulled up.

"Can you still use your magic?" Tiernan asked when the latest man was brought back to his cell.

"I still feel it. The light inside me," the man said. He tried to smile, but a coughing fit crumpled him into a heap on the ground.

That meant whatever they were doing to make them lose their magic took multiple attempts. They might still have a little more time before most of them had lost their magic. The hours ticked by slowly.

Tiernan let a small ball of flame run along his hand. He thought of Kor and Bryce and Merin. He missed them. It was harder to be back in a cage when he knew there were people out there who cared about him.

The older man next to him shivered. Tiernan scooted closer and let the ball of flame grow a little. He set it in his palm and put his hand down next to the man. The man looked at the flame for a moment, before nodding and hugging his knees into his chest.

Kor would have the right words. He would tell them it was all going to be okay. Tiernan had none of those words. He had told Kor he would stay and protect these people, but he regretted that decision every second. He would still fight, just like he had burned down the last cage he had been put in, but now he was scared.

Tiernan heard footsteps on the stairs.

"We've decided it's time to fight," one of the older kids whispered to Tiernan.

"Kor will be back," Tiernan insisted.

The older kid nodded but looked down at the old man in the fetal position on the ground.

"We have to do it before we can't. No one will blame you if you're scared." He put his hand on Tiernan's shoulder.

Tiernan nodded. The other boy retreated back to where he was before. It was quiet again in the cage except for the sound of the feet moving down the stairs. That noise had become deafening. They moved faster than normal. Or . . . he closed his eyes to better focus. The fire in his palm disappeared. It wasn't that they were moving faster. There were more of them. At least two more sets of feet coming down the stairs. One was heavy, and it sounded like it was clad in a sturdy boot like the guards. Extra guards meant they expected resistance.

The other set of feet wasn't heavy. The steps were soft and leathery; they didn't make much sound other than a light flapping echo to the heavy boots. Tiernan sighed.

The extra guard was probably just a bodyguard for whatever higher-up was coming to stare at them. They had done this in Hadran too. Every once in a while, someone would want to come see the work the General was doing, and they would be paraded in front of their cages. Tiernan had always hated when they came.

Tiernan slinked into the shadows. He wanted to be able to see whoever was coming before they saw him. He had to try to avoid them for as long as possible. He gleaned over the older kids. Two girls, the boy who had talked to him, and a set of younger twins he hadn't seen let go of each other's hands. Two adults were rallying themselves up off the floor, but Tiernan wasn't sure they would even make it. They might do more harm than good in a fight.

The leathery sounding shoes stepped up first. It was a younger man, older than Kor but much younger than Bethlem. He was heavy set, and the amount of bulky clothes that were draped around him only added to his frame. On his chest, a large emerald pinned the fabric all in place. Gold ribbons lined his sleeves and collar. Heavy gold chains hung around his neck.

There was little guess that this was the emperor. Tiernan studied him. He tried to think of what Kor would do. He would look for something to connect with, something to make a plan about. Bryce would look for a weak spot. Merin would look him in the eyes. Tiernan forced himself to look at the man's eyes. They were a soft shade of blue that complemented his light features. His hair was golden and, despite being tied up, curled around the edges of his face like a frame. A gold circle crested his head.

Tiernan took a look at the others in the cage. The resolve had weakened a little on their faces. Instead there was a glimmer of hope, but Tiernan knew the truth. If the emperor was there, it did not mean good things. It did not mean he was coming to make sure they were eating well and getting fair treatment. The higher up the person was, the worse their treatment got. That was true in Hadran, and Tiernan could only believe it would be true everywhere.

"How long until all of them are ready?" The emperor turned and asked the heavy boots who had stopped off to the side of the door.

"A week," the voice echoed in the hallway. Tiernan's blood ran cold. He knew that voice. It only made it more familiar sitting in a cage. The General. The Hadranian General was here. Tiernan tried to shrink even more into the wall. If the General saw him, he would recognize him. He would make sure Tiernan was one of the ones who never came back.

Tiernan could feel the fire inside of him looking for a way to escape. Everything was hot and cold at the same time. He wanted to run, and he couldn't move. He held his breath.

The metal key scraped into the hole in the door. Tiernan couldn't look. He knew he would be visible once the man came into the room, and if the others attacked, he would follow suit, but just for a moment longer, he wanted to escape the piercing blue eyes of the General.

The General took up most of the doorway. He was dressed in a different military uniform than the one of Hadran. One that must have been for the East. Gray and emerald made him look even bigger in the shadows. Or maybe that was fear. Tiernan didn't spend a lot of time debating; he just wanted to keep his magic in check.

A flying rock smashed into the wall right next to the General's shoulder. He turned and glared. The boy who had whispered in Tiernan's ear was standing. He was breathing hard, and the whites of his eyes showed how terrified he must have been. His knees quaked, and Tiernan wondered if it was strength of will or petrification that was keeping the boy standing. Tiernan knew how it felt to have those eyes stare directly at you. To see you and yet see nothing but a waste of time and space.

The General started toward the boy. Another rock careened toward the General. He ducked. The others couldn't move. Tiernan knew what was coming. The General would destroy that boy. He wouldn't give it any more consideration than if he were killing a fly.

Tiernan stood. He let the fire out. The cage filled with bright light that surrounded the boy. The General turned. His murderous stare locked on. Realization washed over his face, and a sickening grin sent shivers down Tiernan's spine. The General advanced.

"Take him with us," the emperor said. "Alive, if you please."

"You want this boy?" the General asked.

It was clear that the emperor was not used to being questioned. His easy demeanor flickered to venom instantly.

"Bring him. Now."

Tiernan silently said his prayers. Not to the Twelve Gods that Kor and Bryce were always invoking, but to the people who had actually saved him—Kor, Aer, Bryce, Merin. Anyone who could hear him. Anyone.

But they weren't there, and metal clamped around his wrists. He didn't resist. Throwing fire around would only put the others at risk. At least he would find out what they were doing. If he made it back, he could help Kor.

The walk up the stairs was long. He had known they were underground. That had been clear, but now Tiernan could smell the sea air. It was the first time he had been happy to smell it.

They had climbed hundreds of stairs, and Tiernan's legs were starting to give out. He hadn't been doing much walking, and the stairs were endless. The General prodded him in the back with his knee, and Tiernan kept going up.

Finally, they came to a door and stopped. The door was solid wood, one piece, and locked with as heavy a lock as the one on the cage he had just left behind. The emperor, who hadn't even broken a sweat after all those stairs despite his heavier frame and even heavier clothes, produced a key from somewhere in his swaths of clothes. The lock thudded as it opened.

Inside, the colors were striking. Jewel tones were mixed into the entire sandstone room. There were emeralds hanging from the chandeliers, and deep purples and blues hung loosely as curtains on the windows. Gold trim adorned a bed frame that peeked out from another room.

He was about ready to pinch himself to make sure he wasn't dreaming when something very shiny caught his eye. A golden cage. The General pushed him to move forward. The cage was small. Enough room for Tiernan to stand and walk a half step or slightly more. If he curled up, he could lie down on the bottom. It wasn't the worst cage he had ever been inside, but he wasn't sure why he was here. No one seemed to remember what had happened to them after they had come back from wherever the guards took them, but this place would have been hard to forget.

"Why am I here?" Tiernan asked first in Hadranian and then in the common tongue. The emperor looked at him.

"I have much to ask you," he said like it was the most obvious answer he could have possibly given. "General, excuse us. I'd like to get acquainted with my new pet."

"He might look innocent, your eminence, but—"

"Goodbye, General."

The General turned and disappeared back out the same door. Tiernan heard the sound of his boots fade on the way down.

The emperor circled the cage, looking at Tiernan from every angle.

"If you come too close, I can burn you."

"Oh, that is exactly why I have chosen you."

"Chosen me for what?"

"I want to know everything there is to know about your magic. How does it work? How do you control it?"

"You want to understand magic?"

"Your magic, to be specific. Fire. I want fire."

"Someone without magic would never understand."

"I think you doubt me too much."

"I know nothing about you except you are torturing those poor people down there."

"Yes, quite unfortunate. The General has been a little harsh with some of them, I'm afraid. But it has proved useful. We are so close to understanding how magic turns on and off."

"On and off?"

"It's been a long-term project of mine. Took years. Spread it around to multiple places to better my chances. But now, it's finally time to see it come to fruition. And you will help me."

"I will not help you take magic from anyone."

"Oh, no. You will help me when I obtain it. When I can become fire."

"You hate Magics."

"I won't be a Magic, boy, I'll be a god. And no one will stop me."

CHAPTER THIRTY-FIVE

BRYCE

THE MARKETPLACE WAS QUIET WHEN HE GOT THERE FIRST thing in the morning. A few shop owners were out sweeping in front of their doors, and the stalls that sprung up along the street during the day were just starting to arrive and get settled in. It had rained a little overnight, so the sky was somewhat muted, and the roads were dark from the water. It seemed so normal that Bryce began to doubt if there was anything here that could be behind what was happening to magic. It felt like any other day in Kaybrum.

"Bryce," Vycky called. Her shop was down a few streets, but florists were already busy making calls at this time. She had a small wagon with her for delivering bouquets.

"Vycky, how are you?" Bryce jogged over to her and took the handle of the wagon from her.

"Just a typical day, you know. You think Arya has talked Merin's ear off yet?"

"Maybe. They should be in the East by now, yeah?"

"Should be, but the East's borders have been more particular about letting people in and out these days. Some people are having to wait days to get their papers checked."

"Shops in the market having any trouble getting supplies? Isn't there somewhere called Eastern Supply and Trade?"

"My dad does business with them occasionally, but they seem to be doing just fine. I think Hayden's been helping keep their supply going. He's really trying to make the market diverse. It feels like there's a few more stalls every day."

"How come you decided to stay in Kaybrum?" Bryce asked. It was a question that seemed like it had an obvious answer before, but now, with both Kor and Merin in the East, Bryce wondered for the first time if they would want to come back. What if they decided Magics needed them more there? "Your sister still travels with your dad, but you decided to stay here when you were about her age, right?"

"Lots of reasons. Mostly I got tired of not having any real relationships outside of the caravan. They are great, but they are family. And like any family, you need some space from them. On the road, it's hard to make lasting friendships, and it's also hard to grow a garden. But my dad and my sister were born for the road. I don't think either of them will ever stop. People are just built differently. You just have to figure out what it is that you want. Thinking of leaving?"

"No, I was just wondering."

"I noticed the garden over by the school this morning," Vycky said. It caught Bryce off guard." Is everything okay?"

"Why do you ask?"

"The back door was covered in thick pricker bushes. They aren't usually your style. Roses, sure, but not something that harsh. I would have expected plants that would blow in the wind and be calming, but the side of the wall looked like you were trying to keep people out."

"The plants moved while I was sleeping. I had a nightmare; that's all."

"I know you miss Merin, and I can understand why you would have nightmares, but maybe you should talk to someone. Sylvia and I are always here for you, and so is Bethlem. You aren't alone, Bryce. And Merin and Kor will come back. They don't strike me as people who would want to stay in the East."

"What is the East like?" Bryce asked. They were nearing her shop, but he was interested. It would be easy enough to snoop around the store in the marketplace when it opened.

"Sandy. Proper. It's like walking through a fancy party all of the time but without the glamor. Just the rules. People don't chat much in the streets. I didn't really know anyone, though, so maybe it's different behind closed doors, but outside, it just felt like people were walking on eggshells."

"Sandy?"

"Most of the country is close to the ocean. In the capital, some of the buildings are even made from sand. The seat of government for the emperor is this huge sand tower. It's this light brown color, like the weakest of teas. My sister finds it fascinating, but I found it boring. Everything looked the same. Sure, it's impressive when you first see it, but then it sort of just gets boring. There aren't a lot of flowers either."

"Sounds awful."

"I think people like you and me are better off on this side of the mountains. Thanks for pulling the cart, Bryce."

"No problem."

"Do you want to come in and chat some more?"

"While I help you make some more bouquets?"

"Well, I do find it helps to do something while you talk," she laughed. "Really though, do you need to talk?"

"I'll be okay. But I'll come by if I need something."

"You had better."

Bryce smiled and waved as he headed back toward the main street. Vycky had been his friend almost as long as Kor. She was always looking out for him, even if it did also help her business a little.

Without the wagon, the distance seemed to shrink, and he was back at the marketplace not too long after all of the shops were starting to open. He could smell the oil heating up in the stalls that sold food and the warmth of bread cooling in the windows of the bakeries.

The Eastern Supply and Trade had opened its doors. Bryce wished he had a better reason for wandering in. Maybe he should have talked to Hayden first. No one would question why Hayden was checking things out, but after everything that had been happening with the Magics in the city, not every business was happy to have a Magic just walk in to browse. He didn't have much money, and he wasn't even sure what they sold if they did ask him why he was there. He didn't think "I was wondering if you are helping hurt the people of this city on purpose" would be such a friendly opening line.

"Are you looking for me?" Hayden's voice said from behind him.

Bryce turned, half expecting there to be nothing there. Had his thoughts conjured Hayden?

"Since Merin left, I just wanted to know a little more about the East. I thought maybe this place could help. Figured I'd come early when I wasn't really needed at the school." The lie slipped from his mouth easily. He wasn't sure why, but he felt like he couldn't ask Hayden about the jackets now. Not out in the open.

"I'll come in with you. It's been a while since I checked in here, and I can help if you have any questions."

"Sure, yeah. That would be great."

Relief flooded Bryce.

Hayden grabbed the heavy wooden door and opened it for Bryce.

Inside, the room was bright. Light blue and coral vases and blankets were lined along the corner. There were powders and spices he had never heard of. They must have come from near the ocean.

"Most of these don't do anything, but people cling to their traditions, you know. People from the East *love* the East. See that guy," Hayden pointed. "That's the emperor. Most people in the East have a picture of him in their homes."

"Why?"

"They adore him."

"I don't even know all of the Council members' names."

"It's part of the culture. Most houses here have books about the Twelve Gods, but you hardly see anyone following the teachings. It's just part of life."

"Ahh, Young Master Hayden," an older man said from behind a large counter. He was not a tall man, but his features were striking. He had bright blue eyes, almost as icy as the General's, but his face was covered in a light gray beard that helped soften the look entirely.

"Mr. Hendricks, how have you been?"

"Good, good. I'm so glad you suggested incorporating the trade part of the store. It's really helped now that the East is being so careful about what comes and goes."

"Has it been profitable?"

"Yes, and I've even gotten some new customers. Usually, it's the same faces here. And let's be honest, how many things from the fatherland can a few Eastern families buy before they don't need anymore? Come have a look. It's growing by the day."

Bryce looked to where the man gestured. There were clothes and other goods that looked a lot more like things from Kaybrum. Jackets that children had outgrown, and blankets and quilts made from scraps.

"My wife, she's been making these quilts."

"They are beautiful," Hayden said, running his hands over them.

"They make her a lot happier than working in the store, and they still make us money."

Bryce walked over now. The quilts really were beautiful. They reminded him of something his mother would have made and spread over his bed in the wintertime because he was furthest from the fire in their house. He reached for one that was hanging a few feet from where Hayden was standing. There was something so familiar about it; he couldn't help but get lost in thoughts about the farm.

He traced the design that was stitched over the scraps of different fabrics. The stitches connected to form a tree in a circle. There was a beauty in the stitching that screamed of care and love.

He sighed.

"Something caught your eye?" Hayden asked.

"Just reminds me of home."

"You came in here to learn a little about the East, and you found the most Kaybrum thing in the place." Hayden laughed.

Bryce felt a blush ripple over his face. "I had better get back to school."

"Of course," Hayden said. His face was serious, but Bryce tried to ignore it. "I'll be by around noon for my classes."

Bryce nodded without really hearing him and headed out.

His clue had led him nowhere. Even if they had purchased the jackets Aer had given out, there weren't any there now, and it hardly seemed like that old man had done anything on purpose.

On his walk back, he tried pushing the case out of his mind, as each time he thought about it, he saw the judge from his dream.

When he got there, a package of papers was sitting for him on his desk. Notes from Mr. Pomry.

Bryce began to read.

The only way to determine if MaCavity was human was to see if he reacted like humans did. To see if he bled like humans did. If he died like humans did. He consented to these tests. And it was over his body that they had decided he was human. And that being human superseded the ability to use magic. In Westenbrook, it became law that people could only be punished for acts done rather than abilities or identities.

"He consented to die?" Bryce asked the empty room. This innocent man had died so that other Magics would be seen as human. And they still weren't. Was this some sort of cruel joke to show him it was pointless?

He threw the paper across the room. His imagination ran wild. Had they cut him open? Poked around on the inside and found nothing to tell him apart from any man? He had the same heart and the same lungs and the same, well, everything that was inside of them.

But did that mean the connection was somewhere they couldn't see or was it something everyone had?

His head pounded. All of this was like pulling at strands of spider webs floating in the air. Every time he thought he had grabbed one of them, he realized it had already floated away.

He sighed. He had some time before he had more errands to run, so he could lie down for a moment. The dreams he had the night before had not really let him rest. He walked into the room. Falling asleep on Kor's bed had left the quilt on top messy, and for a second, Bryce expected to see his mentor walk through the room. He walked over to straighten it. It looked familiar. Big bright bolts of cloth were sewn together in strips. Kor had always loved color, but there was something else that was familiar. It looked like the handiwork of the lady from Eastern Supply and Trade.

Had Kor purchased these blankets? He went over to his own. It was much more toned down in color, but the handiwork looked about the same. A little bit messier, maybe. These might have been some of the first ones she made.

His nap completely forgotten, Bryce raced back down to the common area. He wasn't quite sure where he was going, but he was sick of hitting dead ends.

"Did you get my notes?" Mr. Pomry stood up from a desk made for a child.

Bryce almost didn't recognize the stern man in such a compromising position. It was almost comical.

"I read them, but I don't know how it helps us. Unless you just wanted me to see that this whole thing is pointless."

"Pointless, how? I assure you I didn't have you read them for a laugh."

"Pointless because to prove his innocence, he died. Died to prove we were just human and that everything inside of us is the same as what is inside people like you, and yet here we are, being treated the same hundreds of years later."

"I think this is our key argument—"

"That we are the same on the inside?" Bryce snapped. "That either whatever makes us have a connection to the world around us is something invisible or that everyone has it inside?"

"I was going to say that Westenbrook law is incorporated as precedent by Statute 5256, and we could use MaCavity's sacrifice to help stop these trials completely, but I think you are on to something much better."

"Much better, how? I don't understand what you are saying. Just tell me step by step."

"What I am saying is that what you just said might save us from the trials completely, regardless of the law."

"That magic is invisible?"

"That it is already inside everyone," Hayden said from across the room. Bryce hadn't noticed him come in.

"How does that help?"

"It means everyone is a Magic." Hayden said.

"Even the idea of control. How can we judge a few Magics for some slip-ups with their magic when the rest of us can't control ours? Control is about the ability to determine the behavior of something. I have no control over magic. Am I to be tried as well?" Mr. Pomry asked.

"That's ridiculous," Bryce said. They were spouting nonsense.

"Laws are ridiculous sometimes. Technicalities rule," Hayden offered.

"What are you even doing up here? Don't you have a class?" Bryce snapped. His patience was running through fast, and Merin would never allow him to put hands on her father.

"I was bringing you a present, but I can leave if you prefer."

"A present?"

Hayden handed him a package wrapped in brown paper. Bryce untied the twine to reveal the blanket from this morning.

"I know you're missing a lot of people right now and home, wherever that is. I just wanted to help."

Bryce unfolded the blanket. He could really see the stitching of the tree now. There were little pieces that twisted perfectly to form smaller trees. It was amazing that this was from the same person who had barely stitched together the lines of fabric upstairs.

He wrapped the fabric around him. The light inside of him grew; he could feel it connect to the plants out in his garden and even the echoes of those further away. He pulled it off of him.

"You don't like it?" Hayden asked.

"It's beautiful, and I know why Magics have been losing control."

"You do? If something is causing it, then we might be able to get the damage charges reversed."

"Look." Bryce pulled a few of the small desks together and laid out the blanket.

"What am I looking for?" Hayden said as he leaned in real close.

Bryce scanned the fabric, this time not getting sucked in by its beauty but looking for one specific thing amongst all the colors.

"Here." He pointed at a scrap of the cloud pattern. "And here." He pointed at another.

"Gray fabric?" Hayden asked.

"Doesn't it look familiar?"

"It looks like gray fabric." Hayden shrugged.

"You weren't here that day. Mr. Pomry, does it look familiar to you?"

"The jackets. These are scraps of the jackets the Magics wore when they marched on the Capitol Building."

"The ones the General gave us. The ones that bypassed our abilities to control our magic."

"But Magics had to wear those jackets for the results to work," Hayden said.

"Exposure can do the same thing. Remember that room I showed you, Hayden, with this sort of fabric on the walls?"

Hayden nodded.

"And how I told you I was trapped in there for hours, and it's still affecting my magic?"

Mr. Pomry recoiled ever so slightly, but Bryce was on a roll and didn't bother to call him on it. "And last night, I was sleeping under

Kor's blankets, and my magic called out to the plants while I was having a nightmare. Kor's blanket came from the same shop as this one. It's not as nice looking, so it probably didn't cost as much. And Magics often buy anything that they can get that's cheap."

"Which means—" Mr. Pomry started, but Bryce cut him off.

"Which means Kor's been sleeping under that blanket, not knowing it was affecting him. I need to write to him now."

He scrambled for paper and something to write with, but before he had gotten two words into a letter, he realized that he had no idea where to send it, how to send it, or how to mask his message in a way that would make sense and not get Kor arrested.

He slumped over the paper.

"Please help me write a message to Korvo," Bryce said. He looked up at the two people across from him. "It needs to be coded, and I don't know how to do that."

"Of course," Mr. Pomry said. Hayden just nodded.

They played with words and phrases for the better part of twenty minutes before they came up with the right note:

Kor,

Have your dreams been seeming out of control? My new quilt has really given some power to my sleep cycle. I bought it at Eastern Exchange. It's been quite popular. Lots of my friends have gotten one. Its popularity is causing quite the commotion out here. It is so warm, it's like when I sleep with my jacket on. You know, that gray one? I really hope you take care of yourself.

-Bryce

Bryce read it over again. He wasn't sure that he would have understood it if Kor had sent it to him. But Kor had Merin and the two of them together would be able to figure it out.

He scribbled down a postscript:

Tell the doctor I said hi.

Happy with their message, he folded it up and remembered the next part of his issue.

"Where should I send it?"

"Where did his come from?" Hayden asked.

"Just a message service on the docks of Sepsrym."

"Send it to him in the care of the harbor master," Hayden suggested. "They'll send some kid messenger out to find him. It's how a lot of sailors get their mail. We use that a lot when we have to talk to cargo ships with multiple stops."

"Thank you for your help," Bryce said quietly before grabbing the letter and heading out to find the nearest messenger. It would still take days for the message to get to Kor. And even then, it would take another few days to get any sort of reply and even longer if someone was going to come back.

Bryce sighed. He was going to have to face all of this on his own.

He flagged down a messenger and slipped a small bit of coin into his pocket to ensure that it got on the first shipment out. Kor had taught him that coins often did a lot better talking than fists, and he was finally able to attempt it. The messenger smiled, pocketed the letter, and scampered down the street, headed toward the offices near the front gate of the city.

Bryce watched him for as long as he could keep his eye on him, and then he headed back toward the school.

When he stepped inside, he took a moment to appreciate how far it had come. How far he had come. If what Mr. Pomry had said was true, they might still be able to win these trials and come out ahead. If he was going to be any use to anyone, he needed to sleep. He was about to head up to his room when he remembered the blanket that Hayden had purchased for him.

He couldn't sleep under it because of the small strips of jacket in it, and he also needed to make sure none of the other kids took it by accident. While the public had been moved by poor Tiernan losing control, they weren't going to take kindly if the new magic school suddenly collapsed because a couple of kids had gotten cold overnight.

Bryce went by the great hearth and shuffled around the bits of fire. He added more wood, and he hoped it might keep them warm enough that no one would need heavy blankets until he could figure out whose blankets might need to be recovered.

Mr. Pomry and Hayden had already left, and after one last look at the roaring fire, Bryce finally headed up to his room. The spiral staircase that used to beckon to him as torture now was beckoning him to a soft bed. He was halfway up the first floor when he heard Hayden's voice coming from the office. He sounded excited. His speech was going faster and faster. Bryce walked back down. Maybe they had come up with some sort of strategy for the trial.

"I'm telling you; the theory is solid. I'm sure it will work. You just have to give me a few days to perfect it. I'm so close. So very close."

"We don't have much time. The trial is in two days, Hayden." Mr. Pomry sounded even more direct than normal.

It made Bryce hesitate at the door.

"This is so much bigger than just the trial. This would change the whole world. Anyone could have magic. Just think of the possibilities."

"Think of the consequences," Mr. Pomry huffed.

Hayden rambled on.

"I *am* thinking about the consequences. The consequences that your daughter felt her whole life. You had to hide her. You were worried for her. Her whole life would have been so much different if everyone had magic. It would be socially acceptable. Think about the possibilities for Merin."

"What are you talking about?" Bryce said, finally shaking enough of the shock from his body to be able to move into the room.

"You said it yourself, Bryce: we are all the same. So, I've been working on a way to give everyone magic. Then you won't be treated badly anymore. It will be desired. Not feared."

"That is the worst idea I have ever heard."

"Listen, Bryce. I'm trying to help. I'm trying to make things better for you and Kor and Merin and all of these kids."

"You don't know what you're talking about. Being a Magic it's, it's . . ."

"Bryce, I know what has happened to you over the years, and it wasn't fair, but suffering doesn't need to be part of being Magic anymore."

"You still don't understand. I showed you the rooms where they tortured me. I told you what this place was like. How can you just ignore all of that? How can you just decide that the one thing that made those things tolerable, the one thing that made me special, the one thing that gave me a reason to keep fighting—that one thing— you want to give to the very people who did this to me."

"The boy has a point," Mr. Pomry said. Hayden ignored him.

"Bryce, you pushed people out. I had to read your file to really try to understand. This will allow people to see that magic isn't some- thing to fear but something to embrace."

"No."

"You don't really have a choice in this, Bryce."

A thought dawned on Bryce. "You used the research."

"What research?" Mr. Pomry asked.

"The research they did as they tortured us. You used my file to figure this out. You didn't want to understand me. You didn't want to understand those dead kids in the garden. You wanted the final pieces to your puzzle. They tortured me. Gassed me. Took my blood and experimented on me. I thought you were my friend, but I'm just another way to turn a profit for you."

"I am your friend."

"I don't get how you think you can stand there and call yourself that."

"I'm trying to make the world a better place," Hayden said. His eyes were growing desperate. His voice cracked, and for the first time, a bit of his hair fell out of place and cast a shadow over one eye.

"And how will people be given this new magic?" Bryce snapped.

"My—"

"You're going to make them pay."

"Well, research is very expensive, so it's natural that—"

"This has never been about me or Merin or Kor. And to think they trusted you. I trusted you. This has always been about profit. I wish you had never come here. I would rather the school had closed and I was sent to a labor camp than—"

"That is a little harsh, don't you think?" Mr. Pomry said.

Bryce felt a growl building from the bottom of his chest.

"I would rather I died in the Refuge or that Tiernan had burned us all up when the General tortured him so that you would have never seen those records."

"I'm not the only one who is trying this, Bryce. In the East—"

"Leave." Bryce's voice was cold. Decisive.

"Bryce," Mr. Pomry tried.

"Leave. Both of you. Hayden, I swear on the Twelve Gods, if I see your face again, I will unleash such wrath on you that your face will never look the same."

There was a crash as one of the windows on the door broke. Long, thick brambles wound their way through the frame of glass shards toward them.

"Hayden, I think you should go," Mr. Pomry said.

"Bryce, I just want you to see." He took a step toward Bryce.

Bryce hit him square in the eye.

The contact felt good. It felt real.

Hayden's hand flew to his face. There was some blood, and it was obvious that the eye was going to swell.

"Fine," Hayden said finally. He opened the door. Waiting for him with thorns inches long scratching at his arms, vines blocked his way. "Call off your plants, Bryce."

Bryce waved his hand, and the plants moved to open a path for Hayden, but not before they had ripped his clothes and broken skin in multiple places.

"Never come back, Hayden. You are a traitor."

Hayden walked into the night. Bryce fought the urge to let the plants swallow him. He heard them calling to him. They wanted to answer his anger. They wanted to bring him justice. Bryce took a deep breath and told them no. *Let him go. Just don't ever let him back.*

"You could have gone without hitting him," Mr. Pomry said.

Bryce had forgotten he was even there. He sagged into the nearest chair. The magic that had flooded his veins was receding along with the adrenaline, making him feel weak and empty.

"Maybe he won't figure out the last few steps," Mr. Pomry suggested.

Bryce sighed. "It's Hayden. He'll find a way."

"Come on, we have a trial to plan for."

CHAPTER THIRTY-SIX
KORVO

KOR TOSSED IN HIS SLEEP. AER KEPT CALLING HIS NAME, but she wouldn't appear. He called back, but then she fell silent completely. He woke, her name still hanging from his lips.

He hoped reading the cards might soothe the feeling from his dream. He rubbed at the knots at the base of his neck. He could have let Merin deal with them, but she needed her strength for much more pressing issues.

He tried to quiet his mind, find his inner light, and then he took out the cards. He shuffled them three times. Each time, cutting them at random. When he felt sure he didn't know which cards were where he drew the first card.

Aer's card. Of course. He pressed his hand fully onto the card. He pictured her. At first, he could just hear her voice calling his name, then came her laugh, and from there, he reconstructed her voice. "Aer?" he asked the blackness of the card.

She appeared then in his mind.

"I've been waiting for you," she said. Her arms were crossed, and it was such a familiar stance of mild annoyance that Kor almost laughed.

"I'm new to this whole talking to people outside the realm of time thing," he said.

She sighed. "You'd better get good fast. Tiernan's in trouble."

"We're going back in a day, and if Merin keeps making progress, we might even be able to go sooner than that. But Dacia can't move the ship."

"Screw the ship, Kor. Tiernan is in danger."

"He's been in danger. Why is it so important now?"

"The emperor has him. The General is there. The winds are screaming his prayers."

"Tiernan doesn't pray to the Twelve Gods," Kor said.

"He still doesn't. He's praying to us. To you. That you will come get him. You have to get him, Kor. You need to move now."

"I don't have the power. Merin hasn't finished—"

"I know. But something is wrong. I can feel it in the winds all the way from Kaybrum. Something bad is coming."

"What is coming?"

"You're the one with the cards. I just feel the wind. Draw another card."

"Will you disappear?"

"I don't know. Eventually? I'm not there anymore, Kor. Eventually, I may not be here either. I don't know how it works."

Kor nodded.

He put his fingers on the deck and pulled a card, hoping that Aer would stay with him.

The card flipped over. The Fool.

He focused on the card. Images, though not as strong as when he used the collar, began to form. A puppet. This time, a marionette that looked exactly like the General, down to his stoic and aggressive features, was being spun around by a giant blonde child. The child grabbed other puppets. He made them dance. They blurred together to form emerald streaks that looked like flames. Green and blue flames that became the whole world.

"Aer?" Kor asked. "Can you see what I see?"

"Not this time. What are you seeing?"

"Emerald flames. The whole world becoming emerald flames. And there were more puppets."

"Anything about what the emperor is trying to achieve?"

"Nothing I could define. Maybe I . . ."

"Don't use the collar. Too much power and you'll be gone. Please, Kor." Her voice was desperate. The voice she used when he asked her to stay the night the first time.

"I won't."

"Get to Tiernan before he becomes one of those puppets."

"Right. Goodbye, Aer."

"Go. I'll be here. And Kor? Ask for help. Don't try to do this alone."

He didn't promise, but he nodded and put the cards away, then slowly opened his eyes to see the night. He woke Jaxson, who was soundly sleeping beside him in his own hammock.

Kor shook him lightly.

"Jaxson," Kor whispered. "Jaxson. We need to talk to the captain and Merin."

"It's the middle of the night. I think they need to sleep."

"This can't wait."

"Okay." He rolled out of the hammock, shrugged on a jacket, and followed Korvo to where Merin was sleeping.

Kor tapped her lightly on the shoulder, and her eyes flung open.

"We need to talk."

She followed him wordlessly up to the captain's quarters. Jaxson knocked and then let himself in. Kor could hear their brief conversation being carried out in whispers, but Jaxson came and opened the door. Kor and Merin followed him in.

Dacia was sitting up in bed, looking a lot stronger than she had the last time he had seen her. Whatever Merin had figured out must be getting somewhere.

"What is so important, Kor? Did you see something in the cards?" Dacia asked.

"Yes and no. I know the full-scale attack isn't ready." Merin still hadn't cracked whatever was keeping their magic at bay. "But, Tiernan is in trouble. I'm not asking for us to take everyone. I just know I need to go. And if anyone wants to come with me, I would take their help."

"I want to go," Merin said.

"You're needed here," Kor said, putting a hand on her arm.

"What if he's hurt? What if I can't find the cure after all?"

"You might need this." He handed over the collar. She recognized it immediately. Her lips pushed together.

"Have you been using this?"

"Yes, but only when needed. It seems to—"

"Make you lose control," she said sharply.

"Change your magic in a way that feels like you are losing control. And maybe you are. But we need to get these people better. It might be the only way to save Tiernan," Kor said.

"You had this sort of power, and you were hiding it from me?" Dacia snapped. There was a fire and a hurt competing for space in her eyes.

"I told him not to tell you," Jaxson answered. "You would have asked for it, and I wasn't sure it wouldn't tear you apart at the seams."

"Shouldn't I get to be the judge of that?" Dacia asked.

"Not when I know what decision you would make. You'd risk everything, but I can't lose you. This ship can't lose you. You are everything to these people. You are everything to me. Don't make me lose the rest of my family," Jaxson pleaded.

"Fine."

"I'll go with you, Kor. We'll go in, get Tiernan, and return for the others when we're at full strength," Jaxson said.

"Right."

"I could order you not to go," Dacia said. She exhaled, and her chest collapsed with it. "But I won't."

Jaxson helped Kor pack some supplies, but they hardly spoke.

"I wouldn't have given it to her," Kor said. "And I haven't been using it."

"I know. I wish I could throw that thing into the deepest part of the ocean, but I can't bring myself to do it," Jaxson admitted.

"Because it's come in handy. I know. I could have thrown it away. I could have let them bury it with Aer. I could have left it in Kaybrum, but I didn't. I couldn't. And now Merin will feel its effects. I can't say they aren't completely unpleasant, but such risks."

"Captain won't let her push too far. She might be one to push herself to the brink of destruction, but she would never let a crew member do something so reckless."

"I hope you're right. We need to focus on saving Tiernan. I'm fairly certain that they are still holding them in the large tower, but I don't think he's underground anymore."

"And how do you suppose we get into the most guarded building in the capital? We barely got into the basement with the keys. I highly doubt they gave some lowly guard the keys to the upper floors," Jaxson asked.

"We walk in."

"We walk in? You know, you've talked a lot about your great plans and all of the work you did in Kaybrum, but I am starting to wonder if those claims weren't highly over-exaggerated."

"Sometimes, the best way to avoid suspicion is to just follow the rules."

"And what rules are we going to be following?" Jaxson asked incredulously.

"We're a supply ship. We've been in and out of the harbor a few times, and people know we've been here. We bring some supplies to them."

"What supplies? All we have is a hull full of sick Magics and some leftover food."

"Do we have crates?" Kor asked.

"Yes? Empty ones."

"Let's take a few with us. Big ones. We might be able to sneak out Tiernan in one."

"That's not the worst plan I have ever heard."

They wrangled two empty crates and started toward the harbor. The crew had pulled them in quickly, and once they were off the ship, they slipped back out into the deeper waters to hide.

Jaxson's eyes lingered as the ship disappeared.

"We'll be fast," Kor said. He leaned over and put his hand on Jaxson's hand that was holding up the crate.

Jaxson looked down at Kor's hand, and while he was tempted, Kor did not pull away. Jaxson smiled.

"In and out."

On the short walk to the tower, they discussed what they should say was in their crates, and what they would do if they were inspected. As they got closer to the tower, Jaxson slowed.

"I liked it better when we were headed for the dungeon."

"And why is that?"

"Heights."

"You can't be afraid of heights. I've seen you climb the mast without once looking down. You're completely calm up there."

"On the ocean. Where Captain and the sea are ready to catch me, but here?" He shook his head. "Here, there is only death waiting for you if you fall."

"Well, I doubt they're being held somewhere too high. We will probably get to see the first floor and nothing more."

"I hope you're right."

"Thank you for coming, Jaxson." He squeezed his hand.

"Of course."

"What's in the boxes?" a guard asked at the back entrance of the tower.

"Fabrics for some celebration," Kor said. "We're just the delivery boys. They don't tell us specifics. Is there a party or something happening?" In places of power there were always events going on. It was safe and vague.

"Every day it feels like. Come on in, they'll be able to help you in the servants' area. Take the first door on your left."

"Thanks," Jaxson mumbled.

And they were in.

CHAPTER THIRTY-SEVEN
BRYCE

BRYCE FELT STRANGE IN THE OUTFIT MR. POMRY HAD purchased for him. It was too stiff and clean. Merin had brought him clothes before, but they were usually old clothes that her dad hadn't wanted, and he was not the same size as Bryce. This time, Mr. Pomry had taken him to a tailor, where they had poked and prodded him. They tried insisting on keeping the pant legs long to make sure they hide the Raven's head tattoo, but Bryce refused. Surprisingly, Merin's father had agreed with him.

The whole time, he had been quizzing Bryce on questions the prosecution might ask or things they would bring up. Sometimes they were benign: words to define or types of objections they could raise. Other times they were more personal about the kids on trial. And sometimes, they were even about himself. Where did he learn these things? How had he been educated? Why should they trust someone who had been sent to the Refuge so many times and had a record with the courts?

The first time he asked something personal, Bryce had felt his adrenaline spike, just a little. It must have shown on his face because Mr. Pomry said, "You can't let them get to you. I will ask you a hundred times so this becomes as easy as telling me your name and age. You need to stay calm and just tell the truth. Don't apologize for the truth. Just tell it."

"Right," Bryce said, but the questions still made him feel

uncomfortable every time they were asked. He learned to push down the feeling of anger and replace it with confidence and disinterest.

"I'll be sitting in the gallery," Mr. Pomry said. "But don't look back. Look straight ahead."

Bryce nodded.

At the front staircase of the courthouse, Mr. Pomry turned right to find his seat up in the gallery, but Bryce stayed outside the courtroom doors. He had done this before for the smaller trials in the beginning, but this one meant more than any of them. He took a deep breath, counted to seven, and opened the door to the courtroom.

Everything was the same as he remembered. The wooden boxes for the prosecution and defense stood facing each other. The judge's platform was in between, rising above the top of both of them. Bryce took his seat.

The prosecution came in—a man Bryce had never seen before, but it didn't make him unfamiliar. He gave Bryce the same familiar side eye he received often, especially in the richer parts of the city. He knew this man had no empathy for the kids on trial. He didn't care that they were being influenced by the work of the Hadranian General that was designed to destroy them. He wouldn't care that they were innocent. He knew that look too well.

Bryce stood as the judge came in and took his seat. He looked ridiculous in his oversized robes and tall square hat, for which Merin's father had no explanation for other than tradition. The judge's face was bored. His eyes looked down at the papers in front of him, but they weren't focused. He was going through the motions. Bryce fought the urge to look back at Mr. Pomry and instead took his advice and looked ahead.

They had decided, without Bryce, that the kids on trial were not allowed to be present, but that was all right. Having more Magics in the room wasn't going to get them any more sympathy. It would make the trial about one kid instead of all of them. He needed real change, not a bet on whether they would like the look of one of the kids.

"You may be seated," the judge called, and Bryce found his seat. He stared ahead looking at the prosecution. Looking at the man who would argue against their humanity.

"The case against Thomas Melnieve versus the City of Kaybrum will now commence. It is this court's understanding that Mr. Melnieve was released into his guardian's custody through the first of these hearings but will not be present today in the courtroom. The prosecution may call their first expert witness."

They called the shopkeeper who had accused Thomas of causing damage to his merchandise. He spoke of facts and figures, things that made Bryce think of Hayden. He tried to force him from his mind. This was no time to get distracted.

"The defense may approach," the judge said.

"Do you believe the boy intended to inflict damage in your store?" Bryce asked.

"I doubt it. He seemed pretty scared."

"Scared because he was out of control, or scared because he believed he was going to be in trouble?"

"Both, I would guess," the shopkeeper answered.

"Have other potential customers ever broken anything in your store?"

"Once or twice. A few months ago a mother of three little boys broke a vase."

"Was the mother scared?"

"No, embarrassed, maybe. It was pretty loud, but she didn't seem scared."

"Where is this going?" the judge asked.

"I'm coming to the point," Bryce said. "Did the mother get in trouble?"

"She wasn't out of control. Sometimes people just trip. Chasing after three little boys isn't the easiest task. It was an accident," the shopkeeper stated.

"The mother is not on trial, but the Magic is. Does that seem like discrimination to you?" Bryce asked.

"There isn't a law against tripping, young man." The shopkeeper looked at him. Bryce could feel his eyes weighing and measuring him. He tried not to show that he noticed.

"I have no further questions for this witness," Bryce said.

"Defense may call their first witness," the judge declared.

"I call Councilman Jaqui," Bryce said.

The judge looked up for the first time. He met Bryce's eyes. Bryce smiled politely.

Councilman Jaqui was wearing all of his councilman robes. He looked as ridiculous as the judge, but Bryce was glad for it.

"Councilman, if you could, would you explain the Council's decisions on Westenbrook laws?"

"Sure, although I'm sure this court is aware," the councilman said.

"Just for the record, then," Bryce said.

"Of course." Jaqui cleared his throat. "Westenbrook was the predecessor of our great nation, and the city of that name was the original capital city. It lay just north of where Kaybrum is now. Westenbrook laws put into place our current council and chose rulers for the first iteration of the city's leadership, so the Council declared that Westenbrook laws could be used to establish precedent since they played an active part in forming our current legal system."

"Thank you. Now, do you know what precedent was set with the case of MaCavity vs. Westenbrook?"

"I am not familiar with that case," Jaqui admitted.

"Could you read this part of the decision?" Bryce asked.

"Based on internal review, nothing separates those with magic from those without. In conclusion, all are found to be human by law." Councilman Jaqui looked up from the reading. He smiled briefly at Bryce. He knew what was coming.

"Is there a law, by Westenbrook or Kaybrum, about control humans must comply with?"

"Not to my knowledge. Just one for Magics."

"Put precedent, by law, is that all Magics are humans. In your expert opinion, as one trusted to govern the people of Kaybrum, should they, those who are able to use their magic, have certain limitations based on their level of control?"

"No, in my opinion, based on the law presented, they should not. But I am curious Mr. Segal, you mentioned those who are able to *use* magic? What do you mean by that?"

"It has become clear, through the illegal torture of children with the ability to access their connection to the elements—sponsored by the Council at the Refuge, which is now a public school—that research was being conducted to find a way to manipulate the pathways within all humans in regard to magic."

"What are you saying, boy?" the judge asked. He sat fully up in his seat. The paperwork had been pushed aside.

"I believe what Mr. Segal is trying to say," Jaqui cut in, "is that Kaybrum, albeit behind the backs of the people, was conducting research on the children in the Refuge."

"What proof of this do you possibly have?" The prosecution finally stumbled out. Bryce calmly walked to the witness table and pulled out a thick file. One that he was now glad Merin had not burned.

"I present a file taken from the Refuge after it was abandoned from city control. I offer it here to Councilman Jaqui to assess its authenticity."

"This is your file, Bryce," the councilman said in a whisper.

Bryce nodded.

"I'll need some time to review the file," the councilman stated.

"We shall reconvene in the afternoon," the judge said. "Councilman, I will join you in reading this so-called file."

Bryce turned slowly around, catching just a glimpse of Mr. Pomry's smiling face. They weren't done, and the case wasn't won, but Bryce felt like a winner.

"You know," Mr. Pomry said when Bryce met him outside. The smile was gone, and a furrow had deepened in his soft wrinkles. "I've been thinking. This not only sets a precedent for Magics, but we may have inadvertently set it up that we can't stop Hayden from selling magic to anyone with a large enough coin purse."

"Or taking it away from anyone they deem disruptive." Bryce sank to the ground. How had he made things worse? If this had been the law of the land before, his family would have probably forced him to get his magic shut off the first time it was revealed, or the Council would have taken it away after he was thrown in the Refuge or when they didn't find him useful anymore. He couldn't think of a worse fate.

He breathed deeply. Yes, yes he could. Those poor children in the garden of the Refuge. No names, no records, no families, and all for the same reasons.

"We still did the right thing, that is, if they allow it. They still might find some reason to deny it," Bryce said.

"We will know in a few hours. Either way, I am proud of the work you have done," Mr. Pomry said.

The hours passed quickly. There were so many things buzzing

around in Bryce's brain that he barely felt the time go by. When they called him back into the courtroom, he could hardly believe it.

"Before we begin, as this new evidence changes the circumstances of the original proceedings, we will need to question you, Mr. Segal, before the court."

"Why me, sir?" Bryce asked, but he knew. He just wanted to make sure it was on record.

"Because it is your file you submitted for evidence."

"Who will do the questioning?" Bryce asked.

"I will," the judge answered.

"All right." Bryce moved to stand where the witnesses stood to take their oath and did so. Now that he was a witness, he could see the people sitting high above the courtroom looking down on them. There were a few people he didn't recognize, but the most important people he did recognize. He saw Mr. Pomry, and Bethlem sat a few rows behind him. He must have arrived right before the session had resumed because Bryce had not seen him in the halls during the recess. But there was one face that he had no joy in seeing. Hayden Nagely was sitting a few seats over from Mr. Pomry. He chatted briefly with the person next to him like they were out for a night at the theater. Bryce could have strangled him. Mr. Pomry's eyes caught what he was looking at, and he gave Bryce a look that told him to drop it. He remembered that look from his own father. He dropped it. His insides might be boiling, but there were bigger issues in front of him. Hayden might be there to see if the verdict would allow him to make a profit from magic, but in no way did that mean Bryce was going to let him win.

"This is an accurate description of what you faced in the Refuge?" the judge asked.

"Yes, to the best of my knowledge."

"To the best of your knowledge?"

"As you read, I was often knocked out with gas so they could perform experiments and take blood samples. Those parts I only vaguely recall, as one can understand."

"Right, and the rest?"

"The descriptions in the file are accurate, although I think they fail to really capture how it feels to be almost drowned or whipped constantly in the feet. It also leaves out the significant portion regarding a room in the Refuge that was created by the Hadranian General that would make it more difficult for a Magic to regulate their ability to connect with the elements."

"You mean that they would lose control?"

"I do not. I mean temporarily misinterpret how their magic was being used. Like a small child figuring out where their hands and feet will go as they grow. It is a moment of learning, but this was done in an attempt to make us seem out of control and make people fear us."

"What have you done with this information so far?"

"My file was kept by accident. My friends hid it because they thought it might be troubling for me. I still have nightmares about the way I was treated in the Refuge, and they didn't want those to get worse."

"Was this the typical treatment of people put in the Refuge?"

"Yes, I was one of thousands of files in the Refuge."

"And what happened to those files?"

"We burned them out of respect for the people who survived the torture. They did not need a reminder, and we did not think the information contained in them would be helpful to anyone unless they were trying to further the bastardized work of messing with the connections in humans to the elements." He looked straight at Hayden. Let the court record reflect what Bryce thought of his work.

"I see," the judge said. "The councilman has confirmed that these have all the appropriate signatures and stamps to make them official Kaybrum government records. And you came by them within legal means. They will become records of the court for any and all to see."

"I know. I'm ready for people to see what happened to me. They should know what we went through due to fear and greed," Bryce said.

"You may resume your questioning of the councilman."

"Thank you." Bryce stood and walked slowly back to his box.

Jaqui stopped him as they passed.

"I'm sorry. I didn't know."

"Then let's make it worth something."

The older man nodded.

"Councilman, is it your understanding that these experiments were conducted to discover how to turn magic on and off in people?

They were, in essence, trying to figure out the intangible connection between the elements and Magics?"

"Yes, that seems to be my understanding."

"We know that the Hadranian government was helping with these experiments through the involvement of the General, who had dealings with some previous members of the Council. And we know that these experiments were at least somewhat successful in altering a person's connection to magic."

"Yes, that is correct."

"Would you say that, in turn, if everyone has this intangible connection, that the rules of control should apply to all people?"

"Yes."

"Control is about the ability to determine the behavior of something. You have no control over magic; are you to be tried as well?"

"Well, I should hope not," Jaqui said, looking a little surprised.

"If the government was working toward a future where magic could be manipulated at will, should it not then mean that they believed, as they had been working on this for years, that all people were capable of magic?"

"I would hate to put words in the mouths of my predecessors, but it does seem like they thought it might be possible."

"If Kaybrum was responsible for altering these children's magic in any way, should it not be the city of Kaybrum that is on trial?" Bryce asked.

"Objection," the prosecutor called, but Bryce could see the look on the judge's face. He was a man who wanted to be in the history books, and this would be a place for him. Bryce just hoped he came down on the right side of history.

"Let's see where he is trying to go with this," the judge said.

"Thank you, sir," Bryce said.

"Councilman, you may answer the question."

"It does seem that there may be evidence to suggest that the young people who have been recently affected may have been influenced by actions made by the Council."

"Whether this court believes that people who are capable of connecting to the elements—which the previous city council of Kaybrum seemed to believe is *all* people—should be held accountable to the law, or if the city of Kaybrum is to take responsibility for these fluctuations in Magics, it is clear to me that one thing is obvious. The current law is outdated and should not hold value in the courts until it is examined with the full extent of Kaybrum's knowledge."

"I . . ." Jaqui was stunned. "I guess I would have to agree. The law seems outdated."

"Objection, just because a law is outdated doesn't mean someone hasn't still broken it," the prosecutor yelled from his booth.

"In this very courtroom, women were given the right to own property one hundred years ago," Bryce said. His voice was calm and steady. "This was after women were arrested for not giving up their land to another male family member when their husbands died in war. Those women were found not guilty as the law was deemed unjust and in need of changing."

"That's different. There was no damage," argued the prosecutor.

"It sets a precedent," Bryce said with a smirk. He had thought of that this morning. His mother used to tell him about his grandmother who had chased all of her younger brothers off her land when his great-grandfather had died. His mother had always used funny voices for all of the brothers. It was one of his favorite bedtime stories, and it was about the only law he knew before meeting Korvo.

"Kaybrum law follows precedent," the judge said clearly. "Based on the councilman's expert opinion and what I have heard today, I find," he had to look down to remind himself of the name in question, "Thomas Melnieve not guilty by reason of faulty law. And more, I find that this law needs to be reexamined, and while the prosecution may wish to re-try in the future, I will have to say all current and ongoing trials of this nature will be dropped. However, all parties will still be financially responsible for any property damage."

"Thank you, sir."

Bryce's mind went blank as the judge dismissed them from the courtroom. He had done it. Was he dreaming? No.

It was done. He felt so elated he thought he might throw up from the amount of energy forming in his body. He didn't hear anyone or anything until he got outside to Bethlem. The old man's arms folded around him in a giant hug. Tears were streaming down his face. Bryce realized there were tears on his face too. Bethlem didn't say anything. Bryce didn't either. There was nothing to say.

Mr. Pomry just smiled and stood to the side. He placed a hand on

Bryce's shoulder. Then he walked away. Bryce wanted to call out to him and thank him, but a crowd had begun to surround him. There was a reporter, Councilman Jaqui, and a few other people he vaguely recognized.

"You've made history, young man," Councilman Jaqui said, shaking Bryce's hand once Bethlem had let go. "You and Korvo have really changed things for the Magics of this city. I'm just glad I've been able to help."

"I need one more thing. Do you have any way to get a message to the East faster than by messenger post?"

"To the East?" Jaqui raised an eyebrow.

"It's important or I wouldn't ask."

"Right. Come with me."

Councilor Jaqui walked quickly toward the Council Building. Bryce almost had to jog to keep up.

"Birds?" Bryce asked when they got there. "That's it?"

"They are the fastest at carrying notes, and they can get through the mountains before most caravans."

"It would still take days?" Bryce asked. He didn't have days to get in contact with Kor and get a response. Even if the bird could get there in a few days, what were they going to do? It would take them the better part of a week to get back. And even then, how could they stop Hayden? He might have figured it out by then.

"I'm afraid there is nothing faster. What is so important, Bryce?"

"Hayden Nagely carried on with the research." Bryce's breath was beginning to come in raspy bursts. "He's close to being able to turn a person's connection on or off."

"He is doing what?"

Bryce didn't need to look at Jaqui's face to know that fear was pooling between his eyes.

"Why?"

"Hayden will control everything. The Nagelys will have ten times the power of the Council or the Eastern emperor or whoever runs Hadran and more money than any of them as well."

"When did you learn this information?"

"Last night."

"Why didn't you mention it before?"

"I had to win the trial. Even if it meant opening up the law for Hayden to come out publicly with his research. I had to win."

The tears from before started again. This time, they weren't joyful tears of relief but sorrow from the bottom of his heart. Jaqui brought him over to a chair, and at first, Bryce resisted sitting down before finally collapsing into jerking, percussive sobs.

He covered his face with his hands, but the sounds of his sobs only seemed to echo.

"Bryce, how can I help?"

He just shook his head and cried even more. Cried for the children buried in the garden, for what had happened to him, that he was alone and his friends were far away, that he had won and still had lost, for the future where Magics could have their magic taken away at any time.

"We go to work," Mr. Pomry said from the doorway.

"Mr. Pomry," Jaqui said. Bryce wiped the tears from his eyes, but his breath was still ragged.

"We go to work making laws against what he can do. We start today. We work continuously. I've done my fair share of wrongdoing for the Council. It's time to start doing the right thing."

"What sort of laws?" Jaqui asked.

"I thought Bryce might be able to help us with that. And when they return, Korvo and my daughter, Merin."

"Bryce?"

"First law, make it illegal to take away someone's magic." He wanted to end it there, but he knew there might be some who wanted to live a normal life. "Without their consent."

"We need to move quickly before people really start considering what it would be like for this to be possible. Easier to get it on the books now when it's just a thought than later when it's an actual possibility."

"I'll get the paperwork started, gentlemen, if you'll join me," Mr. Pomry offered.

"I need to send that message," Bryce said.

"I'll take it from here." Mr. Pomry put his hand on Bryce's shoulder, which almost started the tears again. He needed to get himself pulled together before he told the others what had happened at court.

Bryce stared at the message he had written. He hoped the birds would fly their fastest.

Dear Korvo and Merin,

You'll be happy to hear that little Thomas and friends will be home for the foreseeable holidays. Our new teacher, the merchant, isn't going to work out. He's been tied up with too much experimenting, so I have had to fire him. His ability to turn things into profit based on his research is stunning. I can't imagine he won't be bringing this to the East soon. The research belongs to me, though, so if you see him, tell him I won't let him get away with it.

Best,
Bryce

He rolled up the message and placed it in the container on the foot of the bird he hoped would be the fastest.

"Find a wind going East," he whispered to the bird, "and fly like our lives depend on it." He opened the window, and the bird flew out into the sky. He watched it head East until he couldn't see it anymore.

CHAPTER THIRTY-EIGHT

MERIN

MERIN SPENT THE MORNING TENDING TO THE PEOPLE, AND when she was satisfied that everyone was more than stable, she headed up to see Dacia.

She knocked. "Captain, I'm coming in." She didn't wait for a response.

Dacia was very much in the same position she had been in when Merin last saw her. She was sitting up, but the strain of it was written across her face and in the tension of every muscle in her body.

"I'd like to try and figure out what is going on with you," Merin said, sitting down.

"Do you think the boys are all right?" Dacia asked.

"Kor's the person I trust most in any situation. I'm sure they will be back soon."

"They had better hope so," Dacia huffed.

"Are all people who connect to the winds this stubborn or just the ones I've known?" Merin asked.

"You knew Kor's Aer?"

"I did. I was there when she died. She sacrificed everything for the little boy Kor and Jaxson are trying to save right now."

"Lucky boy to have more than one person willing to risk everything for him."

"He deserves some good luck."

"Are you going to use that collar?" Dacia asked.

"Not if I can help it. It makes people feel like they are out of control at first, and I don't have time for that. Now, if you don't mind." She held out her hands, and Dacia put hers in Merin's palms. Merin closed her eyes.

She searched all the places where it felt like her magic hit a brick wall. It was like scar tissue, but not solid. There was no mass to it.

"Wouldn't it be easier to work with them down below, where everything is clean-cut?" Dacia asked after a while.

"But you still have your magic, at least a little. If I can figure out how it is getting through—"

"You might be able to figure out how it got blocked in the first place. I see. Kor sure knows how to pick his crew."

There was a knock at the door.

"Yes?" Dacia said.

"Message for Korvo or the doctor," a sailor said.

Dacia nodded, and Merin got up to grab the leather-wrapped message. She opened it. A smile spread across her face.

"I take it it's good news?" Dacia inquired.

"Not exactly. But speaking of Kor's crew, Bryce has figured out why the Magics in Kaybrum were losing control. They were being exposed to the same thing as that collar. I knew he would be able to do it."

"They were losing control? Does Kor know?"

"He left before it started. A lot has happened. This is much bigger than I thought. If the same thing happened to you as what happened in Kaybrum, it must have started in the East and gone down Hadran and into Kaybrum. And whatever it was, I think we are near the end game. I should concentrate."

"Excuse me," the same sailor from before came in. "Another letter for you, doctor."

"Another one?" She doubted Bryce would have been reckless enough to send another just to say hi. This one wasn't wrapped in leather. It was just rolled up and tied with string. The date on the outside was stamped just the day before. How could he have gotten something here that fast?

"Better news?" Dacia asked.

"Worse. I let a monster into our lives, and now the whole world is going to pay for it."

"Now you sound like my brother telling sailor tales. What do you mean?"

Merin slowly explained what Hayden had done and how she had been the reason it had happened. She had shared Bryce's information, and now Magics would feel the brunt of her mistake.

Her body slumped. Dacia squeezed her hands.

"No one would blame you for holding the collar."

"I can do this," Merin said. She closed her eyes again. It took a moment to calm herself and picture her inner light. She breathed in and out. Then, she let her magic go. With every breath, she sent more out. It filled Dacia. For a moment, Merin could picture Dacia's inner light. It was a deep purple. Her magic searched it. Prodded it. It sparked around her. Merin remembered the child in school who had said it felt electric when they were out of control. This was how it felt now.

Her magic encircled Dacia's, smoothing it down. The sparks seemed to fall back in line. Merin felt Dacia shift, but she couldn't worry about that now. Merin adjusted her breathing pattern again, this time changing it to match Dacia's. The purple light brightened. It strengthened. It pushed at something, pooling up into more than just a line. Merin pushed her magic to follow Dacia's. Together, the magic swirled. It began to move steadily.

"I can feel it," Dacia said, taking a deep breath.

"I'm not sure I can totally fix it," Merin said, opening her eyes. "But it should be stronger now, and I think I can help the others. Rest for a minute, and then I'll be back."

"Good, because we need a plan."

Merin went from patient to patient. Flooding them with magic until she was able to imagine their inner light. Then she was able to find the spot where the line had been cut. The place felt metallic to Merin. They had probably injected small fragments of metal into the poor Magics. Small enough that the body could pass them but not small enough that they didn't do damage on their way through.

Each of them had their magic back now. She could see the relief in their faces. She would be able to do more later, and Kor would be able to teach them more about their inner lights, and that would help, but if nothing else, they had regained their connection to the elements, and now she could help Kor get Tiernan back.

"Merin," Dacia called. "Come quick!"

"What is it?"

"I can hear them again. The winds. I can hear them."

"Good."

"They tell me Jaxson and Kor are on their way back."

"That's good, but then why do you look more stressed?"

"Because the winds say they smell like blood," Dacia said. They both turned and looked out over the harbor.

CHAPTER THIRTY-NINE
TIERNAN

KOR HAD TAUGHT TIERNAN THAT PEOPLE WERE LESS dangerous when you could keep them talking, so he tried to keep the emperor talking.

"A god?" Tiernan asked when the emperor came back after a few hours. "They don't seem that powerful to me. My friends pray to them all the time, and the gods haven't done anything. My friends, however, they've done plenty."

"You think too small. I will have *your* magic. I will have fire, and I will have the ability to take it away. I already have. You've seen it with your own eyes. I'll have all the power."

"Will your people follow you? You've filled them with hatred for Magics. Your general hates them more than anything. Do you really think he'll follow you?"

"I gave them an enemy. I will have defeated that enemy. They, especially the General, will follow me to the gates of hell. He told me about you. You've spent most of your short little life in a cage. I know more about the world than you ever will. I have outthought you and your little friends. There is nothing you can do to stop me."

"You don't understand magic. You said you wanted me to help."

"Little children have magic. I'm sure it won't be difficult for me to figure it out if you get too annoying. Now be a good little pet and sit quietly."

The emperor turned his back to him. Tiernan strained to see what the emperor was looking at but gave up after a moment.

"Your eminence," the General said. "Everyone is getting impatient for an announcement. What should I tell them?"

"Tell them to wait. I'm changing the world here."

"Yes, your eminence. A letter came for you."

"Set it down."

The General moved to set down the leather-bound letter. He made sure to smirk at Tiernan as he moved. Tiernan wanted to shoot him with fire, but he knew he had to behave. Kor would come, and it would be helpful if he heard any important information that might come through. He sat down in his cage.

"Great news," the emperor stood. Tiernan tried not to react. He just stayed seated being a good little pet.

"Should I gather the representatives?" the General asked.

"Not yet, but I finally have an answer. And as soon as I can get them here, we will have our new world."

A bell sounded outside the door. The General snapped to attention.

"Seems some of our little Magics have escaped," the emperor said. "Deal with them. I don't need them alive."

Tiernan swallowed. The General pulled his gun from its holster. Flashes of the fight where he had seen Aer be captured came to him. He wished whoever was in the tower would run away.

He didn't watch as the General left, but he could hear the heft of his boots running down the stairs. Tiernan listened long after he could hear the boots. Then he heard two shots ring out and the sound of broken glass. He took a deep breath. At least those Magics hadn't died in a cage.

CHAPTER FORTY

BRYCE

THE SCHOOL WAS RUNNING FINE, AND THAT WAS THE ONLY
relief that Bryce could find. Mr. Pomry had spent the entire day
working out of the office on the new laws. It was slow going, but Mr.
Pomry said they had to be specific. It took hours for him to write all
of the subsections for each new law. A single sentence could easily
turn into fifteen after considering the implications of each law from
every angle.

The sun shone through the windows, and Bryce caught himself
more than once looking out to see if there was a messenger bird. *I
only sent it yesterday,* he thought to himself, but he couldn't help it.
Kor's office was now covered with legal texts, and drafts of laws were
stuck up on the walls all around. Bryce walked over to where the map
was and looked underneath the many drafts pinned on top of it. The
East was so far away.

"You have to stop worrying," Mr. Pomry said.

"That's like asking the sun to stop shining," Bryce scoffed.

The room darkened.

"Did you do that?" Mr. Pomry asked.

"No," Bryce said.

"I didn't see any clouds this morning," Mr. Pomry said.

"I'll look." Bryce walked over to the window. The glass was still
hot from the sun, but all above the windows, the plants had grown
long thorns, and the thorns were shading the windows.

"It's plants?" Mr. Pomry asked, looking up.

"It's trouble is what it is. Hayden is here."

"How do you know? You can't see the front door from here. Are you sure they aren't just—"

"I told them to never let him back in."

"You told the plants?"

"Not in so many words, but yes. And if they are protecting the doors and windows like this, it means he's here. Why would he come here?"

"One can hope he has seen the error of his ways," Mr. Pomry said.

"Somehow, I don't think that is possible."

They heard a scream from below.

"Bryce, call off the plants," Mr. Pomry warned.

"Why?"

"Because we finally have the law on our side, and the last thing we need to do is hurt the wealthiest man in the city."

"Fine," Bryce said. He reached out to the plants and told them to let Hayden pass. They protested, but then he felt them pull back into themselves. *Don't go far,* he thought.

Mr. Pomry was already on his way down the stairs to the front door. Bryce followed quickly behind.

When Mr. Pomry opened the door, Bryce saw cracks along the road before he saw Hayden. His plants must have moved quickly if they had created craters that big in front of the door.

Hayden staggered in. His clothes were ripped, and a fresh cut on his cheek was dripping onto his white jacket.

"I told you never to come back," Bryce said.

"You don't understand, Bryce. It's finally my chance to say the same thing to you. You don't understand. This is the future."

"You are playing with fire, son," Mr. Pomry said.

The ground shook beneath them.

"He's not playing," Bryce said. "He's done it. Those cracks aren't from my plants. There from him. He's using magic."

"Merin always said you were smart."

"Smart enough to know you don't know what you are doing. Hayden, what have you done?"

"I've changed the world, my friend."

"I am not your friend."

"I did this for you. For Merin."

"You did this for yourself." Bryce spat on the ground.

"No." Hayden reached out his hands. The earth shook below them again. "Listen to me. I did this for you. I am just like you now. I understand everything. I am one of you. You and I are the same."

"We could not be more different. Mr. Pomry, you should leave."

"I'll stay."

"Please go. He's going to lose control, and my plants will protect me, but I can't guarantee they will protect you. Please, Merin will never forgive me if something happens to you. I will never forgive myself if something happens to you."

Mr. Pomry nodded and slipped out the door.

"It's just us now, Hayden. We can settle this however you want, but I am not letting you do this to anyone else."

"I'm not afraid of you punching me, Bryce."

Bryce could still see the angry bruise under his eye from their last encounter. Chunks of stone lifted from the floor. Bryce braced himself. Hayden yelled. It was guttural and strange. He was losing it.

"Go home to your family, Hayden. Let this go."

"I wanted to be part of *your* family. Didn't you ever see that? I worked at this school. I bit into my profits for you to survive, and every step of the way, you have fought me, hated me the whole time."

"I appreciated your help," Bryce said. He tried to look at Hayden's eyes, but the rumbling rocks kept taking his attention.

"It was never enough. Not for you or Merin. My fathers are disappointed in me. They're going to send me to Langburn. To an island, Bryce. They'll ruin everything. The marketplace will go back to normal without me. All you have to do is believe me that this is the right thing. This is the only way. I am doing this for you. Why can't you see that?"

"Hayden, this is nonsense. Stop. Take a deep breath. Like we taught the kids. Count to seven."

"Why can't I be enough?" the older boy sobbed. The rocks flew across the room. Bryce barely dodged the first few, but the last one struck him in the back of the head. He fell to his knees. Another struck his knee. He felt the plants rush over him.

He heard more rocks clatter to the floor, the building groaned, and then nothing. Everything went black.

"Bryce?" a voice cut into the void. "Bryce?"

"Vycky?" Bryce called out. It was still dark. He realized the plants were still covering him. Slowly, he told them to move. They did, taking the largest pieces of rubble with them. When he rubbed the dust out of his eyes, the sun was still out. He guessed it had only been an hour or so since Hayden had been here.

"What happened?" Vycky asked, looking around. Bryce followed her eyes. He sat in a pile of what used to be the walls. The first floor was ruined. Holes dotted the floors, and debris was scattered everywhere. Cracks ran up every wall that hadn't come down on top of him.

"Hayden Nagely happened. How did you know to come?"

"The plants were going crazy. All at the same time, they pulled toward the school. I figured something had to have happened."

"Is Hayden gone?"

"Yes, he left the city. It was big news in the marketplace. I heard the rumors buzzing on my way over. They said he left on some sort of flying machine. Leave it to the Nagelys to have some sort of technology the rest of us could only dream of."

"Bryce!" It was Mr. Pomry. Suddenly the man's arms were around him. "Bryce, I was so worried. I brought Bethlem."

"Hayden's left for the East," Bryce stated flatly.

"The East? Wouldn't he go north?" Mr. Pomry asked.

"I have a feeling he'll go to the highest bidder, and that would be the East."

"What about Hadran?" Bethlem asked.

"They don't have as much money as the East." Bryce felt fear beginning to overtake him. His eyes jumped around the room like he could find the answer somewhere around him, but it was useless. His eyes could barely focus as they were. All at once, his headache became too much and he doubled over in agony.

"We'd better get you to a healer," Bethlem said. He reached out a hand. Bryce tried to take it, but his legs wouldn't support his weight.

"I'm not sure I can move?" Bryce said.

"I'll bring one here."

"I'll stay with him," Mr. Pomry said.

"Me too," Vycky chimed in. "You just relax, Bryce. We're here."

CHAPTER FORTY-ONE
KORVO

AFTER FREEING SOME MORE OF THE MAGICS OUT AS A diversion, it didn't take long to figure out the emperor had Tiernan at the top of the tower. They ran up the steps as quickly as they could. At least one guard saw them. Korvo heard the bells ringing. They ran faster.

Despite their quick rise, Jaxson kept time with Kor.

"How much further?" Jaxson asked. His unease was easy to read on his face.

"I think we must be close now," Kor said, taking a second to catch his breath.

"Ahh, Korvo. We meet again," a familiar voice called from behind them.

Kor spun. His eyes locked onto the General. He froze.

Jaxson put his hand on Kor's back. It was enough to pull him out of his shock.

"Too bad this will be the last time." The General raised his gun. "I so wished you would get to see this new world. I would have loved to see magic taken from all of your little friends, one by one."

Kor stared at the barrel of the gun. It shone with the light from the window. Kor hated to think how high they were, but there was no time. The first shot rang out. It ripped through his right shoulder. He stumbled back. Jaxson grabbed his hand to keep him steady on the staircase.

"Kor," Jaxson whispered. The rest of his words were lost as the second shot rang out. It skimmed his right deltoid.

Kor, trust me. Trust me, Aer's voice filtered into his head. He wasn't sure if it was real or not, but there wasn't much else to do.

"Trust me," Kor said, grabbing Jaxson's hand tightly, and he pulled him toward the window. He hit it with as much force as he could, and they tumbled out of the window. The ground was further away than he could have even imagined.

Please, Aer, he thought. Suddenly, a wind surrounded them. The sand below was no longer racing to meet them. They weren't flying. They just weren't falling as fast.

They landed softly on the sand. Jaxson's eyes were filled with terror. He was shaken.

That's all I had, Aer whispered. *I have to move on now.*

"I know. Thank you for saving us. Thank you for saving me," Kor said aloud to the invisible winds. His breath was ragged. The pain in his shoulder had spread. He felt himself losing consciousness.

I'll see you on the other side. Keep fighting. I love you. I always have.

"I love you too, Aer." The wind cupped his face for just a moment and then disappeared.

"We have to go," Jaxson said, wrapping his arms around Kor's waist. He pulled Kor onto his shoulders. "I'll get you to Merin. Just hold on." Then everything went black for Kor.

In the blackness, Kor could feel Aer's loss. For a moment, he wished to follow her into the after. He wanted to be with her. She wasn't going to be in his dreams anymore, and that was reason enough to follow the darkness.

A bright blue light invaded the darkness. He tried to push it away. *Let me go,* he thought. But the light only got brighter. It filled the darkness.

"Kor," Merin's voice came in. He surrendered to her light. He let her pull him out of the darkness.

"Jaxson, give him some space," Dacia called.

"You had better not die. You made me jump out of a tower, and you can't get away with that," Jaxson said.

Kor felt a smile creep onto his face.

"There he is," Merin said.

Kor opened his eyes. The three of them were surrounding him. He tried to sit up.

"Rest. I've fixed the major damage, but I can't do much else right now. I used too much energy this morning."

"If I had known you were going to be jumping out of windows, I would have helped," Dacia said.

"If I had known we'd be jumping out of windows, I would not have gone," Jaxson said. "I thought it was you helping," he said, looking at his sister. "The winds slowed us down."

"It was Aer," Kor said, finally struggling up enough to a seated position.

"Aer?" Merin asked.

"I can explain later. But I need to go back. They'll assume we're dead. I can sneak back in."

"You will do nothing of the kind," Merin said.

"I can move. I have to get Tiernan," Kor said. His eyes pleaded with her.

"Kor, we have a plan," Merin said. Dacia echoed her grin.

"And we have magic," Dacia said, flexing her fingers.

The plan was simple. The Magics would create a huge distraction on the beach outside the tower, and then they would send in a team to get Tiernan. Kor insisted on being on the team.

"This time we won't bother with the stairs." Dacia said. "Your friend Aer gave me an even better idea."

After a deep breath looking at the tower, Jaxson was on board to go back in. He put one hand on Kor's shoulder and another on his sister's. "Let's go save Tiernan and the others."

The other Magics were easy to convince. They would have followed Merin anywhere after she had given them back their magic. The Black Phoenix made its way quickly into the harbor. The crew and Magics swarmed the docks. Kor ran in the middle of them. He had the collar in his pocket. It might not help him, but someone else might need the boost.

They stormed the beaches in front of the tower. Dacia began whipping the winds into a frenzy. Soon she had a tornado on the beach. Sand was flying everywhere. The sharp sting of the sands would keep most people from getting close. Jaxson took Kor's hand, and together, they plunged into the center of the tornado.

In the eye of the storm, they could see the other Magics fanning out. Swirls of water, beams of light, and bolts of electricity were visible all around them, and there were vibrations running in circles under the sand and sonic waves moving through the air, surrounding and protecting the Magics on the beach. Jaxson leaned over.

"I know this is not the right time, but just in case—" He kissed Kor. Kor let himself melt under the feeling. When Jaxson pulled away, Kor's lips still tingled.

"Into the wind," Jaxson said. And still holding hands, they let the winds bring them up.

Up and up and up. They passed the broken window. Kor looked down. Guards had swarmed the beach, but none were attempting to get close to any of them. He could see Dacia, but he couldn't find Merin. He shook himself. Merin was capable on her own. Hadn't Merin and Bryce shown him that they were no longer the children he needed to protect? They could handle themselves. Kor looked back up. They were approaching the last window. He squeezed Jaxson's hand, who had shut his eyes tight.

"It's time," Kor said above the whipping of the winds.

Jaxson kicked at the window. It shattered with the second kick. Glass shards fell on silk curtains and pillows. The sharp pieces sliced into the delicate fabrics.

There was Tiernan, alone in a golden cage. The little boy's eyes lit up when he saw them.

"Kor! I knew you would come."

"Sorry it took me so long," Kor said, coming to stand next to the bars. "Any idea where he keeps the key?" Kor said.

"He keeps it around his neck."

"Great," Jaxson said. "I'll look for something we can use to pry the bars apart and get out of here."

Kor reluctantly left the side of the cage to help Jaxson look.

"Why did they put you up here?" Jaxson asked as he pulled the curtain rod from the wall above the broken window. He wedged it between the gold filigree bars and started bending the metal. The thin metal began to move. Kor leaned on the rod with his whole weight, wincing as his shoulder screamed in protest. A hole large enough for Tiernan to squeeze through opened. The boy dove through, wrapping his arms around Korvo.

Kor hugged him tight.

"The emperor wants to be a Magic. He seems to think he can do that."

"He might be able to," Kor explained. "They've been experimenting for years all over the world on a theory about how magic works and how to turn it on and off."

"It's not a theory," Hayden said. Kor whipped around. "I cracked the code."

"Hayden?" Kor asked. It was Hayden for sure, standing next to who could only be the emperor, but something about Hayden seemed off. His hair was messy and hung over his eyes. There were scratches all over his face and hands. "What are you doing?"

"Business is business." He said it coldly. It hardly sounded like him.

The tower around them rumbled.

"Knock it off," the emperor snapped at Hayden. Hayden's eyes seemed to retreat into themselves. The emperor held out his hand in front of Hayden. "Give me the solution. I will be a god."

Hayden dutifully pulled a large syringe out of the bag hanging across his shoulders.

"No, you don't," Jaxson said. He ran at Hayden.

The two of them fought for the syringe.

"General!" Hayden yelled. The room started shaking.

Kor ran for the door. He had to stop the General before anything else. The General came running up the steps, his boots slamming against the sand.

"You!" he said when he came into the room.

"Me."

"How are your little cards going to help you now? Are you going to *see* your way out of this?" The General laughed.

"This is who you chose to align yourself with, Hayden," Kor said, still staring at the General, though his attention was on frantically trying to come up with a plan. He saw Hayden wince out of the corner of his eye. Jaxson pinned Hayden against the wall. Hayden struggled to free himself. The tower rumbled even more.

Was Dacia doing that, Kor wondered. He didn't have time to ponder for long because the General lunged at him. Kor stepped aside, barely avoiding a flurry of punches.

"Tiernan, stay by the window," Kor called as he fought to keep his feet underneath him.

Jaxson slammed Hayden's wrist into the wall. He yelped, and the syringe fell to the floor.

The General advanced again on Kor. A fist collided with his cheek. Kor staggered back.

"Forget him. Get the vial," Hayden yelled. The General grimaced but picked up the vial and left. Hayden sagged to the floor.

"Do we follow?" Jaxson asked.

"You get Tiernan out of here," Kor said, staring down the corridor.

"What about that kid?" Jaxson asked.

"Leave him. He's not worth it," Kor said, acid in his voice.

"Korvo, let me explain," Hayden pleaded, but Kor had already grabbed Tiernan.

"Wait, what do you mean 'you'? What about you? Aren't you coming?" Jaxson asked.

Kor shook his head and handed over Tiernan. Jaxson held him close.

"Hold on tight," Kor explained. Tiernan nodded. Kor knocked the last few fragments of the window from its pane.

Jaxson stood behind him. His eyes were shut tight.

"I can't believe I am about to do this for a second time," Jaxson moaned, but he stepped up to the window frame.

"Jump. Now," Kor said.

For a moment, they were falling. And then the winds picked them up. This time it wasn't a gentle fall, but a turbulent spin down through the winds of the tornado. The sand beat at their skin and clothes. Tiernan buried his face in Jaxson's chest. Kor lost sight of them as they fell.

Dacia wouldn't let them fall, and Kor couldn't run away again. This had to be the end.

CHAPTER FORTY-TWO
MERIN

SHE SAW JAXSON JUMP. THE BEACH HAD DESCENDED INTO chaos. She wondered if this was how Aer had felt. How Bryce had felt when they had protested in the streets and the Watchers had fought back. Magic was everywhere, but so now were the bullets. Dacia was powerful. She was keeping the worst of it at bay. She had powers that Merin could only wonder at. But power could only hold for so long.

She waited, but Kor never jumped. Merin kept her eye on the window. Nothing. He had stayed. Or he was dead. She shook the last thought; he had stayed. He had placed the entirety of Magic life on his shoulders, but she wasn't going to let him.

She glanced to make sure that Tiernan had made it to the ground safely, and then she sprinted for the door of the tower. It was swung wide open where the crew had gone down for the other prisoners. She saw them now straining to stay on their feet but still fighting. She sprinted up the stairs.

Her calves were burning, but she kept going. Higher and higher until she finally had to stop for breath. There was blood on the ground. She reached down to touch it; it was dry. A broken window a few steps above her told her this was where Kor had gotten shot. She took a deep breath.

A thundering sounded above her, and Merin jerked to attention. She waited for the thundering sound to become footsteps, but they never did.

"Probably just noise from the beach," she said to herself. She pulled herself up and kept going. It was only a dozen or so more steps before a door off to the side of the staircase was ajar. She heard a familiar voice. The General.

"I know you are there," the General called. "I can see your shadow."

His chair scraped against the sandy floor, and Merin felt her heart jump.

"Do us both a favor and don't run. I've had enough of these foul stairs for a lifetime." He had reached the door now. Merin was frozen in place.

"Another Kaybrum brat," he said, looking her up and down. Merin couldn't move. "What's a nice girl like you doing with the likes of them?"

"How do you know I'm a nice girl?" she managed to ask.

"You run around with that little plant bastard, don't ya? I heard the Council wondering about you. Seems a shame to bring such rumors on your family name."

"I am a Magic."

"That's even more of a shame, but I will feel a lot less guilt throwing you out a window now." He reached out and grabbed her shoulder.

"You'll regret that," Merin said. She had worked on relaxing people to the point of sleep before. She focused her inner light, but a slap across the face kept her from concentrating.

"I highly doubt that. It's hard to regret something that brings a person so much joy." He held her now by the chin. Merin could feel where his hand had made contact burn. She tried to jerk away, but he held her fast. "Maybe I'll break a few fingers before I throw you out, just to get some stress out."

Merin felt for her inner light. She could use her magic as long as he was touching her. She searched for the places where the light connected, just like she had in Dacia and the others. She pictured it in her mind, and she let go. Let go of the dam that held the stream steadily in place. The light flooded her, pushing her fear and anger to the side.

She could feel him now—not as the coarse hand that grabbed her but his heartbeat, the blood moving through his body, and then, she found the inner ticking of his mind.

Her magic flowed into him. It filled the nooks and crannies, looking for something. It slowed his breathing by spreading over his lungs and twisting around his heart, but there had to be a better way. She continued to search.

There were no protections keeping her at bay like with Bryce. She saw right into it. His memories became mixed with her magic. She saw them flash by: his childhood, the army, Hadran. She saw flashes of Korvo and Tiernan. Pieces of the war. She could feel tears sliding down her cheeks. Then she saw Bryce through his eyes. She saw the fear as he lit the match. Watched him crumple as the vines burned.

"Turn it off," she screamed. They had sunk to the floor. She was on her knees; he was slumped to one side. He didn't respond, but a grin was plastered on his face.

"Turn it off," she said again to herself, squeezing her eyes tight. She concentrated until her magic was no longer a raging river but a scalpel ready to be used. Then she cut away at the memories, cut the ties that held them. One by one, they disappeared like the lights had been turned off. She kept going. When she opened her eyes, the General was still there. His hand was still touching her face, but he was no longer conscious. He was alive; she could see his chest moving, but he no longer posed a threat.

Merin charged out of the door and flew up the staircase. She wasn't even tired. Something like that would have caused her to be weak in the knees before, but she hadn't felt it at all. She felt unstoppable.

Another open door appeared at the end of a hallway at the top of the stairs. This time, she didn't hesitate and ran for the door. She heard voices, familiar voices. Korvo.

"I had hope for you Hayden," Kor's voice was thick with poison. She had never heard him speak like that before. "I let you into my family. I asked them to trust you."

"You don't understand. I didn't think—"

"You did. You thought about it a lot," Merin said, stepping into the room. There were three shapes in the darkness. Korvo's outline she recognized immediately. Hayden's took a moment. She wasn't used to his slumped posture, his ticking hands, and his messy hair.

"I thought I was doing something good," Hayden said, looking at her. As she got closer, she could see his eyes pleading with her.

"If you thought that, you wouldn't be here."

The tower trembled.

"Knock that off, boy, before you get us all killed."

Merin forced herself to look at the third person in the room. He wasn't someone she recognized until he turned on the lantern next to him. Then he was unmistakable: the emperor.

It clicked.

"You did it, didn't you?" Merin said, turning her eyes back to Hayden. "You gave yourself magic."

He nodded. "You kept telling me I didn't understand. I just wanted . . . I just . . . but . . ."

"You don't have control, do you? You're going to bring this tower down around us."

The whites of the emperor's eyes shone in the dim light, filled with terror.

Hayden cried, clutching his knees to his chest.

"It won't stop. I can't stop it."

"It takes time, Hayden. Isn't that something you needed to know before you did this?" Kor said. His voice was back to being, at most, that of a disappointed parent. "And you," he turned toward the emperor, the venom back in his voice. "You want fire magic? You want to be a god? You made it your life's mission to turn people against us so that you could come in and be a god. You used us. I'll make you pay for what you've cost my friends. What you've cost me." His calm demeanor made the hair on the back of her neck stand straight up.

"General," the emperor commanded.

"He won't be coming. He doesn't even know who you are," Merin said. "I've taken his memories from him, every last one."

Kor looked at her. "Merin, did you—"

"I didn't use the collar. I figured it out on my own." Merin turned to the emperor. "I did what it took you years to attempt to do. I have complete control over magic." She said it with a confidence that made the emperor shrink back.

Kor nodded.

He slowly turned back to the emperor. "Now you will know how my friends felt all those years."

"Korvo," Merin said calmly. "You can't hurt him. He's the emperor. People have his picture in their houses."

"So?" Kor asked.

"So," Merin said, coming to rest her hand on his shoulder. "Not even Aer would think that was a good idea. You'd become a monster."

"He made me into a monster. All the things I've lived through. The people I've lost. He's going to keep doing it. If I don't stop him—"

"That's where you are wrong, Kor. You don't have to do anything. Let someone else carry the burden this time."

Kor looked at her for a long time, then he nodded. "What do you need?"

"Hold him."

Kor advanced on the emperor. The man moved quickly for a large person, and the first time, Kor only caught the layers of fabric. The second time he lunged, Kor was able to grab the man's wrist.

The emperor fought back.

"Help, you idiot. I'm paying you enough," the emperor yelled at Hayden. Hayden barely picked his head off of his knees. "Throw a rock at them, punch them. I don't care. Just be useful, or you can kiss any sort of reward goodbye."

Hayden stood.

"Haven't you done enough, Hayden?" Merin said. Hayden didn't answer. He just moved toward the emperor.

Kor struggled. She could tell he was still hurting where he had been shot. He wasn't going to be able to hold the emperor long enough for her to access his mind. What she was going to do when she got there, she still wasn't sure, but she couldn't let Korvo kill him.

Hayden reached out, and Merin's heart sank. Then he grabbed onto the emperor's arm. He wrapped his arms around it and closed his eyes. The tower trembled. Pieces of the ceiling came tumbling toward them. Hayden was lost from view, and the emperor was buried on one side. Kor sunk against the wall.

"Merin," Hayden whispered under the rocks. "Do what you need to do."

She stepped forward and put her hands to the emperor's forehead. The connection was strong. She released the current, and it swelled inside him. It rooted for something she could use. She couldn't very well erase his memory. Everyone knew who he was. It would only take him a little time to regain his hatred for the people around him. Change needed to come from within. But how?

Her magic dug deeper and deeper. One thing kept coming up. The Twelve Gods. There was fear there, respect, reverence. The emperor was chosen by the gods; that was where he got his power. That she could work with.

She concentrated, and she began reworking the memories of the last few days. She wove a story around them. Tiernan, Korvo, and herself. They were messengers from the gods. They had come to punish him for his sins and lead him back down the right path. It wasn't perfect. She was sure she had left things out, but his mind seemed to take to it. She felt his guilt and fear bubble to the surface.

She left a message for him loud and clear: *You need to make amends. You need to change.* She repeated this until she felt his mind echo it back to her, and then she let go.

"It's done."

"What did you do?" Kor asked.

"He'll remember what he's done, but he should feel very different about it now." She said. She was too tired to try to explain it all. She wasn't even sure she really could.

"Thank you," Hayden said from under the ceiling pieces.

"You're not dying here. You don't get off that easy," Kor said, pulling him from the rubble.

"I understand if you want to erase my memory. Erase the formula I created. Erase me."

"No," Merin said. "You need to live with what you did. Formula and all."

"But I . . ."

"You have a lot to atone for," Kor said.

"There's more. There's something you need to know," Hayden said. Tears were streaking the dirt and sand on his face. "When I left Kaybrum, I think . . . I think I hurt Bryce badly."

"What?" Merin's heart skipped. Her stomach plummeted. She had thought Bryce was safe. She hadn't thought to worry about his safety. Kor leaned against the wall, his eyes closed.

"I couldn't control it," Hayden cried. "That's not an excuse. I hurt him, and I ran."

"He's alive," Korvo said. "I can feel him. He's hurt, but he's alive."

Merin let out the air that was trapped in her lungs. Hayden looked like a huge weight had been lifted from him.

"Do you still want to let me—"

Merin put her hand up. "Even more of a reason to make you live with what you have done. Now, help me get Korvo down those stairs. There's still a fight on the beach."

Shouldering Kor between them, they made their way down the stairs. At each window, they stopped to check on what was happening below.

The Magics were starting to fade, and the soldiers and guards were readying for an approach.

They reached the final door. The salt air felt fresh on Merin's face.

"We will need to fight," Merin said.

"Maybe not," Korvo groaned. "Look."

The soldiers were retreating. They were laying down their arms and turning toward the tower.

"They were winning," Merin said.

"They're following orders," Hayden said. He pointed to the men shouting on the rock wall at the top of the beach. "Whatever you did to the emperor must have worked."

"Let's hope so, but just in case they are going for reinforcements, let's get back to the boat," Kor said.

CHAPTER FORTY-THREE

KORVO

TIERNAN LOOKED A LITTLE WORSE FOR WEAR, BUT THAT seemed to be more about being on the water than any injury. He smiled as Kor came toward him. Kor stopped for a second. He had seen this before when he first got on the ship. When he had touched the railing, he had seen Tiernan on the ship smiling at him. And now, the vision was real.

For a second, he doubted what he was about to do next. The collar was safely stored in his pocket. And Dacia had gotten them exactly where he had asked her. The deepest, most vacant part of the ocean between the East and Hadran. It was time now.

He made his way to the mast. Jaxson stood at its base, a worried look in his eye.

"You could keep it," Jaxson said. Kor knew he didn't really mean it, but still part of him wanted to give into his words, but Aer was gone, and she wouldn't have wanted him to hold on to something that had made her anything less than free.

Kor laid a hand on Jaxson's shoulder and gave him a half smile before climbing up the mast himself. He could have flung the collar from the side of the ship, but there was something poetic about this.

The winds nudged him and curled around him as he climbed. They were still searching for Aer. He let them grab at his clothes without stopping. At the top of the mast, he said a silent prayer to the Twelve Gods for the people they had rescued. Some had dispersed amongst the other ships in the harbor, heading back to where they had come from, but some had stayed. Kor wasn't sure if they were heading to Kaybrum or the North or if they too had fallen in love with the boat full of pirates.

At least, one of the pirates. Kor glanced down at Jaxson. His hair freshly braided and his face recovered from the fight. Jaxson had said they could go north together. Dacia had said they could stay on the ship. He wasn't sure what he was going to do. His mental list clicked on. Throw away the collar, apologize to Bryce, and then—then there was nothing. There was no plan, no revenge, nothing. It was terrifying, and freeing.

He lifted the collar from his pocket. Thousands of futures and destinies rippled through him. He fought the urge to find his future in the echoes of time, and then he tossed the collar from the mast.

Its smooth silver shimmered in the light as it plummeted toward the water. Kor could still see it even after it hit the water. He watched it until the last traces of it had disappeared beneath the surface.

The people who had gathered below were silent. Kor hadn't expected a cheer, but the silence also felt deafening. Each of them lost in their own thoughts of what would happen once the boat touched down in Hadran.

Kor's feet lingered on the last rung on the mast until Jaxson put his hand on his back. Kor took a deep breath and let himself down onto the deck. Jaxson's hand guided him through the gathered crowd to Dacia's quarters.

"Captain thought you might want some time alone," Jaxson said as he opened the door.

"Do I have to be alone?" Kor asked.

Jaxson smiled. "Of course not, but you might need to specify who you want. I could go get Tiernan and Merin."

"You know I am asking you to stay."

"I know. I just wanted to hear you say it."

Kor reached over and grabbed Jaxson's hand. A moment turned into two. They sat on the bed in silence.

"What do I do with Hayden?"

"I never thought you would see yourself as a jailor."

"You think I should just let him go?"

Jaxson took a deep breath and sighed. "You are not responsible for

EMILY K. BRAY

him. He comes from a wealthy family. It's not like he can be charged. Why not just let him live? Let yourself live."

"I don't know what living is." Kor stared down at his knees.

Jaxson brushed Kor's cheek with his hand. "It's about time you found out."

"I don't know if I can leave Kaybrum, and I can't ask you to leave the sea."

"We both need a change. Let's go to Kaybrum, and then we figure it out from there. I've got to meet this Bryce that I've heard so much about."

"Poor Bryce. He's going to want to murder Hayden."

"Maybe it's time you let Bryce worry about what Bryce does."

Kor gave Jaxson a look.

"Obviously, we won't let him murder anyone," Jaxson laughed. "Now, you should rest."

Kor nodded and let his head relax against the pillow. Jaxson sat on the edge of the bed and pulled a small knife out of his pocket. He picked up a block of wood from a basket and started to whittle. Kor could hear him humming as he closed his eyes and took a well-deserved nap.

330

CHAPTER FORTY-FOUR

BRYCE

Vycky burst into his office completely out of breath.

"What's wrong?" Bryce asked. Vycky held up a finger and took a few deep breaths.

"They are back . . . Arya said she saw them . . . in the town outside the city. Arya is waiting at the gates for you."

Bryce hardly heard a word she said after "they are back." Kor, Tiernan, and Merin. It hadn't been that long since they had all been together, but it felt like years. Bryce looked down, wondering if they would notice the changes he felt in himself.

"Why outside the city?" he asked, but Vycky shook her head.

"Arya didn't know," she said, her breath now steady. "Merin didn't say."

"Thanks, Vycky."

"You'd better go now," Vycky said. "I can stay at the school."

Bryce started to speak.

"I already filled my orders for today. I know you're feeling mostly better, but you can still accept help."

Bryce nodded.

His leg was still sore from his run-in with Hayden, but walking helped stretch his knee. Bethlem and Vycky had helped him keep the school running while he was healing. A few students had dropped out, but he could fix that. If Kor and Merin were coming back, they would be able to make it better. Things were finally going to work out.

At the edge of the gates, Bryce took in the green of the outside world. He felt calm amongst all the green. He reached out and brushed the base of the plants with his magic, and a slow wave went through the open field.

"Bryce Segal?" a Watcher asked.

Bryce jumped. "Yes?" Bryce braced himself.

"Arya said to send you to her. She's over there." He tilted his head toward a group of wagons. Bryce nodded.

"Th-Thanks," Bryce said.

Arya talked non-stop during the ride. It gave Bryce a chance to think. All of the reasons they hadn't come into Kaybrum streamed through his mind: they didn't want to come back, they were hurt, they had been branded criminals.

"Are you even listening?" Arya asked.

"I hate to admit it, but no. I'm sorry."

"That's okay." Arya blushed.

"Vycky said you had talked to Merin?"

"They got to town right as we were about to leave. Merin is good. She's actually so good. You'll see. I know you'll notice immediately. And that boy Korvo brought home, he's a looker."

"Kor brought home a boy?"

"Jax, or Jaxson, something like that. He's funny. We'll be there soon. You can see all of them. Umm, but there is one thing you should probably know." She looked down and trailed off.

"Is everyone okay? Is Tiernan okay?"

"Everyone is fine," she said. "Vycky said you weren't going to like this part."

"Arya, just tell me before my imagination can think of something much, much worse."

"They brought Hayden with them."

"I'm going to punch that pretty little face of his so hard," Bryce snarled.

"I know he hurt you and did something bad. Vycky wasn't super clear, but—"

"But what? What if Korvo and Merin don't know what he did?"

"Just maybe focus on seeing your friends more than seeing Hayden."

"Yeah?"

"I've read a thousand books, Bryce. And ignoring people is always more punishing than anything else."

"Don't you read love stories?" Bryce laughed.

"Isn't everything a love story? Isn't that what we are all looking for?"

"Maybe," Bryce said.

The buildings of the town had started to come into view, and Arya was uncharacteristically quiet.

"I haven't been here since I ran away from home," Bryce offered. "It looks smaller."

"Maybe you've just grown."

"Yeah . . ."

They rode the rest of the way with Arya quietly singing off-key to herself.

❦

"Bryce!"

Bryce heard Tiernan before he saw him. He looked bigger, older.

"Hey, Tiernan," Bryce said, scooping him into a hug.

"Bryce," Kor said, slapping him on the shoulder.

"You look a little rough, buddy," Bryce said.

"Right back at you. Don't worry. Merin will fix that right up."

"Where is she?" Bryce asked, looking over Kor's shoulder. He saw a tall, dark man standing a few feet away. That must be Jaxson. Hayden stuck his head out from behind him. Bryce let his eyes just glance away, not without seeing the hurt in Hayden's eyes first. Maybe Arya was right.

"She's out getting some food in the marketplace. We weren't sure when you were going to get here."

Bryce didn't need to hear any more. He let his feet move down a path pulled from deep within his memories. He didn't need to look up to know where the different places were along the path. Familiar voices drifted in and out around him. No one here would recognize him. It had been years, and he was sure his parents had told people he had died in some tragic accident.

He took a deep breath. The most familiar smell filled his nose. His mouth began to water. He looked up, and there was his mother. She had her head down, but he could tell it was her, and there was no mistaking the smell of her pastries. He watched her deft hands fold the dough. He started toward her, and then he saw it. The iron bracelet. The one that said she had lost a child. Him. She had lost him and told people he was dead. He stopped.

"Bryce," Merin said.

Bryce had to force himself to look away from his mother, but he couldn't resist Merin. Arya was right. He could tell right away that something had changed. She was still as beautiful as she had ever been. Her eyes were still as kind, but there was something else behind them now. Confidence. She wore it so well.

He closed the distance between them in two steps folding her into his arms. Her forehead rested against his sternum.

"I've missed you," they said at the same time. The grass around them changed to a dark green.

He released her enough to kiss her on the forehead. "I've been so worried about you."

"I wasn't worried about you. I knew you could run the school."

Bryce noticed that she had a bag in her hands, crumpled from their embrace.

"You bought pastries from my family, didn't you?"

"So she *is* your mother. I thought as much. You should talk to her."

"She's wearing an iron bracelet. She tells people I'm dead. I might as well stay dead. You're my family." He turned to go, but Merin held his hand tight.

"Then, I'd like to formally meet my mother-in-law," Merin said.

Bryce opened his mouth to argue, but he let Merin guide him toward the booth. He squeezed her hand tight.

"Hello again, dearie." His mother smiled at Merin. "Nothing was wrong with the pastries, I should hope."

"No, ma'am. They're delicious. I just thought there was someone you might want to talk to."

Bryce's mother glanced at him. He felt her eyes move over him.

"Bryce?" she asked, her voice a whisper.

"Hi, Mom." He didn't know what else to say. "I see you have met Merin."

Her eyes dropped to their clasped hands. She smiled.

"I have, and some of your other friends."

"You brought Kor here?" he asked Merin.

She shrugged. "I wanted to know what he thought about me bringing you here, and Tiernan loves the food."

"And what did Kor say?"

"He said I was married to you, so I should be the one to decide."

"He knows?"

"He knows."

"Bryce?" his mother asked. She reached up to touch his face. Bryce closed his eyes. If she had just acted this way before, he would have never run away. Never met Korvo or Merin. He'd never have helped the kids in the courts.

"I'm sorry," his mother whispered.

Bryce gently lifted her hand from his face and put it down. "I'm happy. It took a while, but I am happy."

"Still," his mother said.

"I'm going to go," Bryce said, "but I'll come back."

"You will?"

"Sounds like my friends have gotten used to the food." He smiled.

He walked with Merin, hand in hand, back to where he had left Kor and Tiernan.

They swapped stories for an hour while they stuffed themselves with pastries. Hayden sat awkwardly at the edge of the group. Bryce made sure to never look at him directly.

"So what's next?" Bryce asked.

Korvo's face dropped in contemplation. "I don't know, but we'll figure it out together."

THANK YOU!

Thank you for reading! If you enjoyed this book, please leave a review on Amazon, Goodreads, BookBub, The Story Graph, or anywhere else you like to track your recent reads. Alternatively, you could post online or tell a friend about it. This helps our authors more than you may know.

- The Team at Torchflame Books

ACKNOWLEDGMENTS

Getting to come back to the world of Kaybrum and spend more time with the characters I had created felt like coming home to old friends, and in that spirit, I want to thank all the friends and family that have supported my writing journey and all the other crazy things I put into the world. It truly takes a village, and I have found my village to be the most supportive and understanding there is. That includes my readers. I wouldn't be here without you or the hard-working people who put my book together. Thank you for your support and for coming back to join us in book 2.

I hope you will continue to join me along for the ride in Kaybrum and beyond. Follow along at Emilykbraywrites.com or on Tik Tok and Instagram @emily.k.bray.

ABOUT THE AUTHOR

Emily K. Bray is a high school Creative Writing and Drama teacher in Washington State. She has taught hundreds of students to share her love of writing, stories, and words since 2013. Now she hopes to share this joy with others with the continuation of the Kaybrum Chronicles. She lives with her husband, daughter, and dog. Besides her love of writing and teaching, she also enjoys musicals, crafting, and spending the day under a large blanket.

Connect with her on Instagram (@emily.k.bray), TikTok (@emily.k.bray), or on her website at emilykbraywrites.com

THE KAYBRUM CHRONICLES

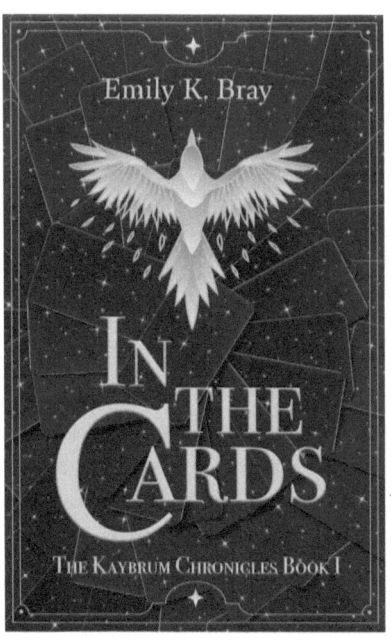

IN THE CARDS

In Kaybrum, magic isn't outlawed, but it's far from accepted. At seventeen years old, Korvo has spent his life learning all society will teach him and campaigning for the freedom of his fellow Magics. When a young fire magic arrives in the city, tensions rise among his adopted family. Change can't come fast enough, and soon Korvo is wrapped in a war eerily similar to the one that defined his childhood. But this time, he's determined to make the war end in his favor.

OUT OF FIRE

Following the battle that bought their rights to education, Korvo and his friends must work together to rebuild the Refuge into a school rather than a correctional facility. But the deeper they dig into the Refuge's past, the darker the secrets become. Spread across the continent in search of the true root of the prejudice against magics, Korvo, Bryce, Merin, and Tiernan must learn how powerful they truly are.